What Reviewers Say About Bold Strokes Books

"With its expected unexpected twists, vivid characters and healthy dose of humor, **Blind Curves** is a very fun read that will keep you guessing." – *Bay Windows*

"In a succinct film style narrative, with scenes that move, a character-driven plot, and crisp dialogue worthy of a screenplay, …*the Richfield and Rivers* novels are…an engaging Hollywood mystery…series." – *Midwest Book Review*

Force of Nature "…is filled with nonstop, fast paced action. Tornadoes, raging fire blazes, heroic and daring rescues…Baldwin does a fine job of describing the fast-paced scenes and inspiring the reader to keep on turning the pages." – *L-word.comLiterature*

In the **Jude Devine mystery series** the "…characters seem fully capable of walking away from the particulars of whodunit and engaging the reader in other aspects of their lives." – *Lambda Book Report*

Mine "…weaves a tale of yearning, love, lust, and conflict resolution …a believable plot, with strong characters in a charming setting." – *JustAboutWrite*

"While these two women struggle with their issues, there is some very, very hot sex. If you enjoy complex characters and passionate sex scenes, you'll love **Wild Abandon**." – *MegaScene*

"**Course of Action** is a romance…populated with a host of captivating and amiable characters. The glimpses into the lifestyles of the rich and beautiful people are rather like guilty pleasures... a most satisfying and entertaining reading experience." – *Midwest Book Review*

The Clinic is "…a spellbinding no

"**Unexpected Sparks** lived up to . enjoyable…Dartt did a lovely job at building the relationship between Kate and Nikki." – *Lambda Book Report*

Sword of the Guardian is "…a terrific adventure, coming of age story, a romance, and tale of courtly intrigue, attempted assassination, and gender confusion…a rollicking fun book and a must-read for those who enjoy courtly light fantasy in a medieval-seeming time."
– *Midwest Book Review*

"Of Drag Kings and the Wheel of Fate's lush rush of a romance incorporates reincarnation, a grounded transman and his peppy daughter, and the dark moods of a troubled witch—wonderful homage to Leslie Feinberg's classic gender-bending novel, *Stone Butch Blues*." – *Q-Syndicate*

In *Running with the Wind* "…the discussions of the nature of sex, love, power, and sexuality are insightful and represent a welcome voice from the view of late-20-something characters today."
– *Midwest Book Review*

"Rich in character portrayal, *The Devil Inside* is an unusual, unpredictable, and thought-provoking love story that will have the reader questioning the definition of right and wrong long after she finishes the book." – *JustAboutWrite*

Wall of Silence "…is perfectly plotted and has a very real voice and consistently accurate tone, which is not always the case with lesbian mysteries." – *Midwest Book Review*

Visit us at www.boldstrokesbooks.com

LOVE ON LOCATION

by
Lisa Girolami

2008

ISBN10: 1-60282-016-3
ISBN13: 978-1-60282-016-6

THIS TRADE PAPERBACK IS PUBLISHED BY
BOLD STROKES BOOKS, INC.
NEW YORK, USA

FIRST EDITION, MAY, 2008

CREDITS
EDITORS: CINDY CRESAP AND J. B. GREYSTONE
PRODUCTION DESIGN: J. B. GREYSTONE
COVER GRAPHIC: SHERI (graphicartist2020@hotmail.com)

Acknowledgments

To Len Barot for giving me the chance of a lifetime.

To Cindy Cresap and Julia Greystone, my incredible editors, who taught me so very much, made me sound better than I am, and who were absolute joys to work with (Julia, were there too many commas in there?)

To Lee, Herbert and Pam, three wonderful beta readers who took their valuable time and energy to help me make sense of the manuscript and challenged me in productive ways.

To Sabrina who pushed me to be a better person and to connect with my feelings.

To the entire BSB family for their consistent and generous support.

To the BSB readers who are a most amazing group of magnificent people.

To my mother and father who, through their passionate love of reading, brought the gift of books into my life.

And to Pam P., who was the inspiration for this story. Those rainy days in Florida and the project we built together forever live warmly in my heart.

DEDICATION

This, my first novel, is dedicated Lauren
who always believes in me.

CHAPTER ONE

"Those evil scumbags." Hannah clutched Kate Nyland's arm as they made their way past the camera flashes and constant shouts of "Hannah! Look this way!"

"And you love them," Kate said.

"You bet your ass."

As she usually did, Hannah Corrant stopped halfway down the red carpet and turned to the left side of the crush of people, pulling Kate even closer.

"Over here, Hannah!"

"Hey, Hannah!"

More flashes erupted as the paparazzi zeroed in on the couple. Hannah smiled seductively and Kate tried not to squint into all the lights.

When they turned to the right side of the throng, Mitch Sibell from Channel Two News pushed a microphone toward them. "Hannah, it was rumored that you weren't going to be here due to exhaustion."

"It's just that doing films back-to-back can take its toll." Hannah beamed. "But I'm feeling better now."

"Kate," Mitch said, "I take it you've been taking care of Hannah?"

The flashes and shouts seemed to get more intense. "Sure have," Kate said as Hannah pulled her away. "Thank you, we're late."

Kate opened the door to the Kodak Theater and they stepped in. A sea of Hollywood's "industry people" filled the elegant lobby. Trusses with massive lights lit the space with moody colors, and the grand staircase created an atmosphere of magnificent opulence.

"Let me guess, your agent set that exhaustion thing up." Kate had to speak up over the crowd.

"Yup."

"You know I hate to get pulled into that crap."

"It's harmless. And it keeps me in the spotlight, which means you get some airtime, too, Kate."

"Let's go home after this, okay? No after-parties."

"What's with you lately?" Hannah frowned. "Do you want to put on fuzzy slippers and sit on our asses watching reruns of *M*A*S*H*?"

"Actually, after being out every night for the last eight nights that sounds pretty good."

"Shit, Kate, we're at the peak of our careers. Hollywood is lying there at our feet. You can produce any movie you want and I can get any lead role now. Lately you've been a stick-in-the-mud."

The mud Kate actually felt stuck in was right there in the middle of the Kodak Theater. Millions of dollars, actors and actresses, studio executives, and more diamonds than Liz Taylor could ever wish for, and Kate knew that Hannah was right. This was the place to be. What was she so unhappy about?

"You can be so frustrating," Hannah went on, "It's no fun anymore going out with you. These are your people, too, you know. It wouldn't hurt to mingle and find the next great director for your films."

Just then, Cliff Forman, the lead in the latest blockbuster superhero movie, walked past with his entourage. He stopped to peck Hannah and Kate on the cheek before moving on to others.

"I think we need a little 'us' time, Han."

"This is 'us' time. Christ, are you PMS-ing or what?"

"I don't want to fight again, but all we do is go to function after function. I don't think the press will miss you for one night."

Hannah glared at her. "Don't ruin this for me."

Typical, Kate thought. She just wasn't up to taking a stand that would turn into another fight. She took Hannah's hand, "Tell me why we're here for a play?"

"Grant Howser directed it in between films. He's going to Russia next fall to shoot *Catherine the Great,* and I'm on the short list to star. He needs to see me here."

"Isn't that what your agent's for?"

"Hannah." A voice cut through the noise and they turned to greet Bettina Constable with *Hollywood Voice* magazine.

As Hannah schmoozed with Bettina, Kate wandered off to get them drinks before curtain call.

CHAPTER TWO

The plane on which Kate had managed to appropriate the very last first-class seat peacefully made its way toward Orlando's International airport. The gentle clinking of ice cubes against the inside of her glass of ginger ale lulled her as she gazed at the flat terrain that rolled along outside the window. As she turned to swish the cubes around in her drink, a slender hand came into her peripheral vision. The flight attendant had leaned down to remove the glass. Kate smiled up at her and the woman smiled back. As the attendant straightened herself, the dainty point of her airline-issue scarf fell back gently against the base of her neck. This, Kate noticed, was a far cry from the bedraggled scarf of the Los Angeles attendant Kate had seen only five hours before.

The overcrowded gate back at the airport in Los Angeles had been a disorderly mass of yelling, arm waving, and mass chaos. One broken airplane and a severe storm somewhere over Missouri had caused a crowd of at least one hundred people to mob the already taxed gate agent. The travelers swarmed around her, clutching their carry-on luggage and laptops with the death grips of exhausted cliffhangers, and all of them chattered at once. Kate fixed her gaze on the ragged scarf of the agent in front of her as she stood there waiting for the determination of her fate. It looked like a noose that she kept in reserve just in case she found herself at the end of her wits.

The agent's head was down, scanning the flight monitor with a frown that would scare off Mussolini. "Ticket, please," she said, not looking at Kate.

It was only when Kate handed over her platinum frequent flyer card along with her e-ticket that the agent looked up.

"Oh," she said taking the platinum card, "You're one of our elite frequent flyers, Ms…" she glanced at the card, "Ms. Nyland."

Kate smiled politely even though a large, rather smelly businessman was pushed up against her, along with many others, clamoring for a seat on the flight.

Kate stretched her five-foot-nine frame, already feeling the restriction of her surroundings. She shifted the weight from her right leg to her left. The agent smiled at her. "Kate Nyland. The movie producer, right?"

"Yes." *Please say there's a seat left.* Kate was praying inwardly.

"I saw *Last Night in Rome*. It was really great."

"Thank you. Really."

"I saw you in *US Magazine* last week." She paused, then quickly offered, "At the opening of *Last Night in Rome*." She smiled again. "Must be exciting."

Kate wasn't sure whether the agent was referring to the Hollywood life or the thrill of work well-done. Either way, Kate thought her very sweet. A simple, "Yes," seemed the most proper response.

Flicking Kate's platinum frequent flyer card with her finger, the agent said, "You're one of the very few lucky ones today, Ms. Nyland." With the swiftness of an experienced professional, the agent stamped a boarding pass and handed it to Kate. "First class, seat 3A." She then returned her card and added, "Five hundred and eighty-seven thousand miles means a lot to us at National Skyways. Have a great flight."

Normally, the notion of a few hundred thousand miles accumulated in her frequent flyer account did little more than ruefully remind her that work seemed to rule her life. But on such a trying afternoon, that little flash of platinum made the fortunate difference between the last first class seat remaining and sitting some countless hours longer in the City of Angels and smog.

Kate sipped on her ginger ale as the airplane made its way toward the southeast. The takeoff had been flawless and she put her head back to relax into her thoughts. She went through her mental notes about her latest film, *The Glass Cross*. They were four weeks from the commencement of principal photography, and the production crew was working diligently and efficiently. Most of the locations had been secured by the location manager; the casting was complete, except for a few bit parts, and the actors were in daily rehearsals. Everything was going fairly well, except for the one part of preproduction that necessitated the trip she was currently making. She then thought of Hannah, the woman she had been dating for almost a year. She felt secretly guilty at the comfort she enjoyed being away from her. Kate sighed. What a mixed bag of emotions she felt when it came to that woman.

Hannah Corrant, pronounced Kor-ONT, as the press liked to remind their readers, was a stunning actress with golden blond hair and the kind of shapely legs that one of her previous co-stars had described as "the kind that could wrap around you twice." A string of wildly successful movies had raised her to "it-girl" status, and she quickly moved over to the top entertainment agency in Los Angeles. Hannah was on the hot ticket chart with a bullet.

She had started her career as an out-lesbian, and the press ate up all the audacious photo opportunities, as well as some of the best sound-bites Hollywood was offering up recently.

The night that Kate and Hannah first met, they had attended a fund-raiser for the Los Angeles Gay and Lesbian Center. Dubbed "Women's Fantasy Night", the luxuriously decorated party was held at the Luxe Hotel on Rodeo Drive in Beverly Hills. Its primary purpose was to raise money for the Center's community outreach programs. Its secondary purpose was to give the well-established women of Los Angeles a playground to meet, socialize, and be seen. All for a good cause, a few hundred women would enjoy a spectacular evening of cocktails, entertainment, dinner, and a silent auction.

The Beverly Hills Luxe Hotel was no newcomer to swank parties. Its opulent ballrooms and elegant décor set the stage for the evening. The theme changed each year. That year's theme was "Fantasy." The women could expect that the silent auction items had a suggestive imagination behind them, if not a blatantly wild bent.

Kate had gone solo, meeting up with five of her closest friends who were also from the entertainment industry. She had been the one to sponsor a table. With a last minute option to purchase the rights to a very interesting novel, she was almost a no-show that night. The table was paid for, and lord knew, her friends were not wall flowers, but they nevertheless showed up at her office and dragged her away from the script. The work was left unfinished, and Kate was enjoying an Amaretto sour and perusing the silent auction items.

Each auction item had the night's fantasy theme in mind. Some were trips to exotic places, some were baskets of sexy goodies, while others were services like spa packages and limo rides—all with a sensual, whimsical, or adventurous fantasy built in. There were tables upon tables of auction items. Each was elaborately decorated, and a description sheet was placed next to the auction bid sheet. Each auction item started with an opening bid and a posted incremental bid amount. In order to start the bidding, all one had to do was sign their name on the first line and enter their bid amount. The next person would come along and raise the bid by signing their name on the line below the first bid and entering an amount that was at least as high as the incremental bid amount, and so on. Of course, the fun was in checking back on a bid sheet after signing it to see if someone had come along and outbid you. If they had, you were free to bid again. At the end of the evening, time would run out, the bid sheets would be collected, and the last name on the sheet, the one with the highest bid, would be announced.

"This one's for a trip to the Bermuda Triangle. No lie." Carrie, a film editor and one of Kate's friends, had called the group over to see.

The bid was for six nights in Bermuda, plus a private jet to the approximate location where throughout history, a total of eight planes had vanished. It was called "The Bermuda Triangle Fantasy Challenge" package that dared the winner to "Take a chance on making history again!"

Kate and the other five women studied the offering.

"Sounds kind of romantic," said Beth Samuels, Kate's best friend, and owner of a motor home rental business. They'd known each other many years, both of them having cut their teeth in the film industry when they were barely out of their teens.

"Romantic?" Melanie, an independent producer, countered. "I guess, but I wonder who'd be liable if you actually disappeared?"

Sarah, Beth's lover, was deadpan, "Not the giver, Mel, which is the reason this would be the perfect present for your ex-lover."

Melanie nodded with interest.

Kate began laughing, not so much at Sarah's crack, but at Melanie's ardent consideration, and was unexpectedly bumped from behind. She turned around to find Hannah Corrant reaching out to her.

"I am so sorry. I didn't mean to bump you," she said as she placed a steadying hand on Kate's arm.

"It's quite all right," Kate said.

Hannah's hand remained on Kate's arm for a moment. "The crowd is getting pretty tight in here." She smiled a devilish smile and then wandered off.

"Hannah Corrant. Wow."

Beth nodded in Hannah's direction. "Eagle Scout Productions rented five motor homes from me and one was for her. They were shooting *Call It Down* in Oxnard for six long weeks."

Sarah nodded. "Hannah played a vice cop in that one. You should have seen the flimsy dress she wore."

"Pretty incredible body," Carrie added.

"I saw it," Angie, a motion picture animal trainer, finally piped in. "So vice cops wear revealing clothes nowadays?"

With a shake of her head, Carrie grinned. "No, but vice cops have to unwind after work, now don't they?"

Angie snorted. "I don't know whether I should be thankful or not that I work more with animals than people like Hannah."

Sarah, Beth, and Carrie said simultaneously, "Thankful."

Melanie admonished her friends. "Come on, she can't be that bad."

"I believe they were talking about actresses in general," Kate said.

"Mostly true." Carrie sipped on her drink. "Though I have heard that Hannah's quite a pill."

"A pill?" Angie said.

Sarah nodded. "Hard to take."

A slow grin spread across Melanie's face as she looked in the general direction of where Hannah had gone. "Sometimes, it just might be worth it."

The fund-raiser guests began to make their way into the banquet room to find their assigned dinner tables. The master of ceremonies, a well-known lesbian comedienne, took the stage and welcomed everyone. Kate and her friends settled in at their table just as the lights dimmed.

"We have a great evening planned," the comedienne began as the crowd quieted, "and I would like to point out that it's been a long time since I witnessed this many lesbians shut up at once."

The crowd of about three hundred laughed and clapped as she

went on. "And your being here tonight is most important. We're here to raise money for the Los Angeles GLBTQ Mental Health Services community outreach program. Wow, what a worthy cause. There are thousands of men and women living in our area who can not afford their own medical care, mental health care, and so many of the other services the center offers. And you have so graciously given of your pocketbooks to keep these programs going."

The crowd clapped again, and she took that opportunity to add, "And who knows, if the Republicans ever worm their way into Hollywood, then all of you out there may need these services as well."

"Isn't that the truth." Melanie nodded grimly.

"Sadly, yes," Sarah said.

"And let's see, we'd add services like classes in, 'The-world-doesn't-revolve-around-me'…'The-get-a-real-job-for-a-living' class… and of course the most widely attended class will be the 'Get-used-to-not-having-your-own-private-dressing-room.'"

Beth groaned. "My motor home business would be sunk."

Just as dessert was being served, the evening's entertainment of singers and other acts was finishing up. The comedienne returned. "Thank you, everyone. You've been a great audience. I wanted to remind you that you have exactly twenty minutes to get your bids in at the silent auction. We've got over one hundred great items back there in the Governor's Salon, and we want you to reach deep down into your hearts and purses and find more money to give. If that doesn't work, then reach deep down into your girlfriend's purse and find money *there*. Thank you."

Carrie folded her napkin and placed it on the table. "Come on, you all, I want to see how much the bid for the Bermuda Triangle Fantasy Challenge package is up to."

Sarah chuckled. "Carrie, why don't you bid on it?"

"I just might."

"There's a one night package for two to New York for dinner that I think I'll bid on," Kate said as she got up from the table.

Beth, Sarah, and Melanie got up as well.

"Just one night?" Sarah asked.

Kate nodded. "One night. It includes round trip air, a mystery dinner and drinks, and one night's accommodations at the Essex."

"That sounds great." Mel said excitedly.

As they all walked toward the Governor's Salon, Beth asked, "Kate, who would you go with?"

"Don't know. I just thought it'd be a great getaway."

Melanie nudged Kate's arm. "Kate, you can pick any of a number of dates."

Beth corroborated Mel's comment. "True. Kate's never had any problem in the dating department."

Kate shrugged. "Just making one stick is the hard part."

Mel added, "Be careful who might stick. Your one night in New York could turn out to feel like an eternity in the Bermuda Triangle."

Carrie leaned close to Kate and said, "You just go on and bid your heart out. And then go have fun…with whomever."

Beth went off to bid on the Virgin Islands Fantasy Escape package for Sarah and herself, while Carrie decided to check out the Bermuda Triangle Challenge. Melanie and Sarah headed for the bar while Angie went in search of the African Safari that she'd overheard someone talking about.

Kate made her way through the crowd of women and back to the "One Unforgettable Night in New York Fantasy" package. The package described the trip as a private chartered jet for two from Los Angeles to New York. A limo would pick up the passengers and whisk them away to a specially arranged dinner at a mystery location. After dinner, the two fantasy travelers would be driven to another mystery location for their choice of champagne or wine, and then the last stop would be a VIP room at the Essex House overlooking Central Park. A morning breakfast would be served just before the limo ride back to the chartered jet bound for Los Angeles.

The bidding was already well underway, and with less than twenty minutes left in the bidding, Kate wrote her name down and filled in the next bid increment, which was an increase of $300 over the previous. She stepped back and heard a voice right behind her. "I see I have some competition."

Kate turned and found herself face to face with Hannah Corrant again. Arguably the hottest actress in Hollywood, Kate had never met her, but there was no mistaking who she was.

"You're bidding on the New York trip?" Kate asked.

"Yes. Sounds great, doesn't it?" She stepped around Kate and wrote a higher bid down, canceling Kate's bid.

Kate was going to let it go, but when Hannah turned to face her again she said to Kate, "Any other trips that you'll bid on instead?" She had a smug look on her face.

Kate smiled and picked the pen back up, and wrote down another bid for New York.

Hannah smiled back. "I want this trip."

The sense of entitlement in her tone made Kate cringe. She had dealt with more than a few of the "my-shit-doesn't-stink" type of people in her life, and Hannah was an apt fit. Kate flipped the pen back and forth in her fingers. "I'm sure you do."

"You see." Hannah stepped so close to Kate that she could feel her peppermint-tinged breath tickling her nose. "I've been working non-stop for months now, and I need to get away. *Really.*" Hannah then glanced down at the bid sheet, making it obvious that she knew who Kate Nyland was. "*You,* Miss Nyland, of all people, would know that. You do understand what I mean, don't you?"

Kate *did* know what Hannah meant. But it had nothing to do with needing a holiday. Winning the trip had just become the prize in a game Hannah had been playing with Kate. She no more needed this particular trip than she needed a tummy tuck. Hannah could call any number of people, her personal assistant, her manager, the president of the studio filming her most recent movie, and they would hastily drop everything to arrange a trip to New York via her choice of private jet, to her choice of hotels, and for her choice of days.

Kate took the pen from Hannah and again wrote in a higher bid. Turning to Hannah she said, "It's all for a good cause, isn't it?"

Hannah sighed heavily and held out her hand. Kate hesitated before finally offering the pen to her. Hannah delicately took it from Kate's hand. With a bit of drama, she wrote on the bid sheet, turned back to Kate to smile at her, and walked away. With the pen.

Kate chuckled to herself, shaking her head. What a piece of work. Very gorgeous, but a piece of work nevertheless. She looked down at the bid sheet. Hannah had not only increased the bid by the incremental amount, she'd added ten thousand dollars to it.

"Congratulations on your win," Kate said to no one.

❖

"Another drink?"

Kate retreated out of her thoughts to face the flight attendant. "Yes, please."

The last of Texas passed beneath her, and Kate drew a deep breath, relaxing into her seat. It suddenly amused her how disproportionate the energy was between the two seating areas in the plane. Those in the coach section were happy and energetic, most on their way to Walt Disney World and Universal Studios. They bubbled with visions of Mickey Mouse, the Terminator, and the anticipation of a week of theme park food. Conversely, those that sat just five feet farther forward in the plane were more serious. They crunched last minute numbers for their stockholders meeting, scratched out notes on legal pads, and poured over spreadsheets on their laptops.

And there she sat in Levi's, a white button-down Fred Segal top, and deep brown Cole Haan mules, looking ready for neither a sales presentation nor a roller coaster ride.

She was flying into Orlando for a simple one hour meeting with a company that was building sets and props for her next film, *The Glass Cross*. Her motion picture production company, StormRunner Productions, would be shooting part of the movie in Orlando, and the company she was visiting was the best choice for the construction of cost effective sets and props that would be used right there on an Orlando soundstage. Based in California, StormRunner would save money by building those particular sets and props in Orlando rather than manufacturing and shipping them from California. So, in those few hours between her arrival and her departure, she needed to kick the ass of that vendor, one who was threatening to drift harmfully behind schedule. Then she would turn around and fly back to Los Angeles later that afternoon for a script meeting and two budget reviews.

To most people, she imagined, a one day cross-country turnaround was an utterly insane notion. To Kate, it was normal. Movie-making was both exhilarating and nerve-racking and demanded a lot from a person. She reminded herself often that she had willingly signed up for this fanatical life. She had been smack dab in the middle of the hectic madness for longer than she could remember.

When the flight attendant returned with another ginger ale, Kate took the stir stick and began swirling the ice around in the drink. Thoughts of Hannah drifted lazily back.

About two weeks after the fund-raiser, Kate's assistant Laney Smith called out from the outer office, "Kate, there's a…call for you."

"Thank you," Kate began to say, but Laney was already standing at Kate's office door. "Okay, what's up?"

"Why do you ask?" Laney was smiling.

"Because your hesitation always means that someone unexpected is on the line. Plus, you never come to my door to tell me that I have a call."

"I had to see the look on your face." Laney grinned.

"So, who is it?"

"Hannah Corrant."

"Hannah…" Kate paused. When she saw that Laney was still smiling, she blurted out, "What, already?"

Laney's head bobbed from left to right. "You're a successful lesbian…she's a successful lesbian…"

"Oh, for the love of Pete, Laney. You're always matchmaking."

Laney's grin could put the Cheshire Cat out of business. "Could be fun. But I hear she's a bitch."

"Yeah, well, I can only imagine."

"She's on line two." Laney turned to go back to her desk.

Kate picked up the blinking telephone line. "It's Kate."

"I'm glad I found you," the voice floated, warm and dreamy, across the line.

"It's not hard to find me. I'm listed." *What was she calling for?*

"Your work number, yes. Your private number, no."

Private number? "So I take it this is not a business call."

Hannah chuckled slowly. "No. It's about the auction."

The auction. The one you so brazenly commandeered? "The auction, yes."

"It's for two. Two to New York."

"Yes, I remember."

"I'd like you to come with me."

You've gotta be kidding. She chuckled. "Why me?"

"I find you attractive. I've wanted to get to know you for some time."

And…? "And…?"

"That's the only way I knew to get you to go with me. Outbidding you. I'm certain if you had won, you would have taken someone else."

"True."

"Well, I feel badly for stealing it away from you."

Stealing it away from me? You were showing off. Throwing money around is bigheaded and conceited. "As I remember, it didn't look like you were that upset about stealing it."

"Buyer's remorse. So will you go with me?"

"Well, I'm sorry for any guilt you're feeling, Hannah, but I'm sure there are a lot of other women out there who would love to witness your repentance. Have a nice flight." And Kate gently dropped the receiver into its cradle.

Laney flew into Kate's office. "You just blew off Hannah Corrant. Wow! That's great. They don't cover these kinds of things in the trade magazines, now do they?"

"You were listening in?"

"No. I could only hear your side of the conversation, but I could tell. Whammo! Dropped like a hot potato." Laney was bulging with questions. "What was that all about? When did you meet her? What is this about a flight?"

It wasn't until another two weeks had passed that Hannah tried again. This time, she sent the original auction package to Kate—the vouchers for the jet, dinner, hotel, everything. Along with the envelope was a note that read:

> *Kate. I suppose we got off on the wrong foot. I am sorry*
> *to have rubbed you the wrong way, both at the fund-*
> *raiser and on the phone. Please accept these vouchers*
> *as an apology. And take whomever you like.*
> *- Hannah*

The envelope sat on Kate's desk for another week, mostly because she was in production on a film in Chicago.

Five weeks to the day after the fund-raiser, Kate called Hannah and asked her out to dinner. She thought she'd at least give her a chance. Certainly she knew the talk about town. Hannah was conceited, self-centered and arrogant. Three very strong strikes against her. But she was also a fine actress, a hard worker, and very, very confident.

Dinner had gone well. Hannah seemed different that night. She had been charming, attentive, and funny. Kate accepted another few dates with Hannah, and on the fourth date, opening night at the Los Angeles Gay and Lesbian Film Festival where Kate had sponsor tickets, Hannah asked whether she'd yet gone to New York.

Kate had to admit that the dates had been fun and that they'd really enjoyed themselves. So she weighed the option of asking Hannah, deciding that one night in New York couldn't be that bad.

The travel agency that had donated the "One Unforgettable Night in New York Fantasy" provided wonderful service. A private chartered jet took off from Los Angeles and put down in New York just after seven p.m.

Kate had really enjoyed the flight. Hannah had been delightful and sexy, and they had talked about Hollywood, sharing "oh shit" stories of haughty conduct and wealthy excess. The limo was waiting for them on the tarmac and took them to the very popular Hangawi restaurant.

They were led to a private table in the back of the restaurant where they talked over a spectacular dinner. Later, they were taken to Cru for an after dinner drink. Kate had really relaxed by then and could tell that Hannah was enjoying herself as much as she was.

They sipped the exquisite wine and talked until well past midnight. The paparazzi finally caught up with them as they left Cru. Kate had wondered at some point during the night whether they'd be followed and photographed. Hannah had expected it.

"It's always just a matter of time," Hannah had said with a bored nod.

The last stop of their Fantasy night was the Essex Hotel overlooking Central Park. As Hannah and Kate's limo arrived, the bell captain moved strategically between the couple and the cameras, though Hannah turned to wave, causing an explosion of flashes. While the bell captain shooed away the paparazzi, the concierge took them to the elevator. Their VIP Suite was quintessential Manhattan with its refined elegance and art-deco sophistication.

The concierge had just thanked them for the tip and closed their door with a quiet click when Hannah took Kate in her arms and kissed her.

They'd kissed after the last couple of dates in LA, but not like this. The kisses were deep and soulful. Hannah enveloped Kate in her arms, her lips hot and luscious against Kate's. Moving to the bed, they fell onto it and were almost swallowed up by its rich, pillowy softness. The amount of wine they'd consumed was enough to have them peel their clothes off a bit faster than normal, and Kate just let it happen. Now down to just their undergarments, Hannah's body felt fantastic on top of Kate as she lightly grazed Hannah's thighs and back with her nails. Hannah sucked in a breath before grinding into Kate in slow circles. At Kate's first moan, Hannah reached underneath Kate, unsnapping her black lace bra.

Kate was struck by how passionate Hannah was, speeding up and slowing down at just the right times. The first few hours were a blur of fingers, mouths, and orgasms, and then, sometime after three a.m., they ended up in the bathtub.

Big enough for four more people, the tub gave them room to splash about in a few more wet positions before Hannah hoisted Kate up onto the edge of the tub and went down on her again. Kate held on to the Roman faucet, feeling as if she would tumble out of the tub at any moment.

Another bottle of wine was brought to their room at five thirty in the morning, where they paused for half an hour to sit on the windowsill of their hotel room. In luxuriously thick bathrobes, they had opened the windows to the early morning dawn over Central Park, and then toasted the city, the film industry back in Hollywood, and the beginning of their relationship, before Hannah dragged Kate back to bed.

They barely had time for their morning breakfast before the limo arrived to drive them back to their chartered jet bound for Los Angeles. The flight attendant pretty much left them alone since they spent most of the flight making out.

"So it's official?" Hannah asked in between kisses.

"What's official?" Kate asked.

"We're seeing each other."

Kate laughed. "I suppose so."

"That's great. Really great." Hannah smiled. "And worth the donation to…whatever it was."

❖

On the commercial flight to Orlando, Kate eased the air phone out of its cradle and slid her credit card through. She dialed her office and the receptionist answered right away.

"StormRunner Productions, good afternoon."

"Hi, Francis, how are things?"

"Great. Laney's been waiting for you." She swiftly connected Kate to her office.

"You have two messages from the Art Department and a call from Riley." Laney filled her in quickly. Riley was the stunt coordinator.

"Okay, who else?"

"Jane Stark called to tell you she's sending over tickets to the Director's Guild screening of her latest film. Charlie Gunner found a new location for the office scenes, though he says it's about fifteen minutes farther away. And Leo Buckley called about a completion bond."

Leo was one of the production executives at World Film Studios and was assigned to represent the studio's financing of *The Glass Cross*. Located on World Film's lot, StormRunner Productions was an independent entity. The two companies had a contract between them for StormRunner to produce motion pictures for World Film. The studio had a degree of control since the financing was theirs, but with Kate's formidable and respected reputation, she swung a fairly heavy bat when it came to the movies she wanted to make. However, being subject to the studio's financial concerns, the studio sometimes requested a completion bond for a film, which technically was an insurance policy that paid if the production's completion came into jeopardy. Completion bonds were expensive, and the cost would come right out of StormRunner's budget.

"Would you please address a thank you card to Jane for me? I'll fill it in when I get back. Tell Charlie if it's the offices in Highland Park, I'm not crazy about it. If it's the one in Culver City, it'll work just fine. And could you connect me to Leo, please?"

"Sure. Do you want me to stay on the line to transfer you to other calls?"

"Yes, please."

Presently, Leo came on the line. "Kate?"

"Yes, Leo. What's this I hear about a completion bond?"

"It's for Ralph Markowitz." Ralph was one of the actors who had been cast for the film.

"Ralph?"

"Seems he has a history of heart problems."

"Heart? He's thirty-eight years old, Leo."

"Well, the studio physician called with files from a doctor who saw him four years ago."

"You're not serious about this."

Leo lowered his voice. He was obviously still in his office at the studio. "Seems Ralph has a pretty big problem with cocaine and alcohol. He's been hospitalized three times for overdosing."

"Shit," Kate said evenly. She knew he had a history of drug use, but she hadn't heard all the details.

"He's supposedly been clean for over a year, though. Doing well from what I hear."

"Still…" Kate said, drawing out what she knew must be more bad news.

"Well, he tried to cover it, but you know how quickly the paper trails get picked up on in this town."

"I need to discuss this with Amy." Kate knew that she had to get with the director fairly quickly and decide whether to keep Ralph Markowitz on the movie or not.

"Okay." After a pause, Leo added, "So you'll get back to me on this?"

"Yes. I'll call you back, Leo."

"Do you want me to get Riley next?" Laney was right back on the line.

"No. I need you to connect me to Hannah."

"Oh, brother." Laney hadn't liked the actress from the day she had first started dating Kate.

"Laney Smith, when are you going to warm up to Hannah?"

"When I set her on fire for being such a bitch to you at times."

Kate laughed despite the need to scold Laney for her insolence.

Kate had never dated any of her films' stars, and she had never let someone she was dating be considered for a role in her films. It's not that it was unethical. Producers and directors did it all the time, but Kate knew how messy an affair like that could become. And she knew all too well how quickly things could turn from lovey-dovey to very bad. Originally, another actress had been cast as the lead in *The Glass Cross*, and Kate keenly remembered the day that changed.

Two months earlier, Sage Siegel, the original lead actress, was found by the Hollywood police in a seedy motel. She'd been found in the middle of an impromptu party given by drug addicts. Unconscious, on a filthy, condom-strewn bed. Next to a suitcase full of china white heroin. With a needle in her arm.

Kate had been the one to post bail for Sage and then to call her once Sage had arrived home. She'd known that Sage was a heavy drug user, but the heroin had surprised her. She wanted to have a candid talk with her about the seriousness of the situation and to explore any possible chance of redemption. Whether it was Sage's embarrassment and shame at falling back into the habit or her inability to make sense of anything through her drugged haze, it was crystal clear that Sage no more wanted to discuss cleaning up than she wanted to negotiate a compromise.

"Sage, it's Kate."

"Fuck you."

"Are you okay?"

"Fuck you."

"Sage, come on, we need to work this out." Then the line went dead.

Sage was again chasing the dragon.

As difficult as it would be for StormRunner, especially in the final weeks of preproduction, Sage was fired and off the picture for good.

StormRunner Productions usually had three motion pictures in the works at any given time, one usually in preproduction, one in production, and one in postproduction. As executive producer, Kate shuffled between each film, leaving it to the producers she hired to manage the details of each production. They reported the status of their productions on a daily basis, and it was up to her to decide where her experience and influence needed to be directed. But as it happened to work out this time, Kate currently had only *The Glass Cross* in preproduction and no other projects in the works. She could spend more time concentrating on it. This had been a deliberate decision on her part, as the budget was high enough to merit more of her direct attention. Other than a few scripts in the initial stages of development, Kate was looking forward to following this movie rather closely.

And, as executive producer and owner of StormRunner Productions, it was Kate, along with her director, Amy Parsons, who would ultimately decide who to recast in the lead role. So moving quickly was something they most assuredly had to do. As it would turn out, Hollywood would move quickly for them.

Within ninety minutes of the firing of Sage Siegel, Hannah Corrant's agent had called Kate to pitch his client to her.

Currently one of the most up and coming actresses in Hollywood, Hannah was on the A-list of every studio in Hollywood and was a martini's breath away from her next multi-million-dollar paycheck. Hannah's last two films, combined with the early press on the film that she was currently shooting, would most certainly catapult her to the next plateau of stardom. Add to that mix, Hannah and her handler's ability to choose the right parts at the right time, and it was that lightning strike that every actor prays for. Movie studios and production companies liked to be within close range of those lightning strikes.

The slight wrinkle was that Hannah was now sharing Kate's bed, which made it hard for Kate to remain impartial. She called her producer, Frank Collins, into her office to bounce the idea off him. Frank's opinion was worth quite a lot, and she hoped that he'd warn her off of the notion.

"Well," Frank had said after a long silence, "Hannah would be perfect for this role."

A bit reluctantly, Kate nodded. "She's the right age and has the right look."

"And she's hot right now. I saw her on at least five covers today."

Making the cover of a magazine was tantamount to replacing Ben on the almighty bill of legal tender, green ink and all. "I don't even have to run any numbers. Hannah Corrant and our script, that's an appetizing equation."

"I'm not sure we can afford her." Kate brought up the financial spoke of the logic wheel.

"You and I both know that we can make it work."

Still, something told her not to go down this road. "I don't know, Frank…"

"But listen to how the Hollywood press buzz would sound." Frank dramatically lowered is voice. "'Hannah Corrant, star of *The Glass Cross*.' That's powerful, Kate."

"I suppose I can't argue with that."

"Your decision, Kate. And as always, you'll be in charge over Hannah, if that's of any assurance."

"Only slightly."

Frank scrunched his brows together, "Could Hannah use your relationship to try to get things her way?"

Kate stared at him. "Does the Pope wear a hat?"

"Well, the production lasts only thirty-four days," he reminded her. "And we *are* on location in Florida and Austria for most of it."

Admittedly, it was easier to shoot on location. The studios would leave the production alone, for the most part. And it would be easier to deal one-on-one with any of Hannah's industry-known tirades or power plays without the studio getting involved.

Frank smiled at her. "You're going to the desert with her this weekend, why don't you talk about it?"

"I suppose I could…" Kate wavered.

"And one more thing," Frank added. "She's money in the bank."

True, the movie-going audiences were interested enough in Hannah, good script or not. And Kate knew she had a good script. Add together star power and a strong story and that equation could produce a box office smash.

The next call was to Amy who hadn't even asked any questions. "Hell, yes. Hannah would be perfect for this as well," she had said, the Sage saga beginning to fade from memory. "I didn't think we could ever afford her nowadays, but I'd kill to have her come aboard."

In the end, Kate wasn't quite sure what finally made her consent. Maybe it was the fact that the simple equation added up and that Frank's observations had made sense. Maybe it was that Amy had creatively pushed for the decision knowing Hannah could deliver a great performance.

Or maybe Kate had decided to make the deal with Hannah's agent because she knew very well that motion picture studios fought long and hard over star appeal, and StormRunner Productions was positioned to deliver that force right into the hands of World Film, the studio that housed her company.

But then again, maybe it was that Hannah had finally convinced her of that very same notion during a very erotic celestial shower treatment under the desert stars at the La Quinta Spa and Resort one sweltering night that very weekend.

Hannah could be most persuasive.

❖

Laney came back on the air phone, "She's on the set at Paramount. They're getting her now. Shall I stay on the line with you and the meat hook?"

"Laney, be nice."

"Don't like the girl, Kate. She's arrogant and doesn't care for anyone but herself. And I don't want to see that cute little sirloin tender of yours get skewered."

"Do I pay you to be brutally honest? I thought the job description said *marginally* honest."

"What can I say? I exceed even your expectations."

Hannah came on the line, and Kate heard the slight clicking sound of Laney disconnecting.

"Kate, what's up?" Hannah sounded curt. She was shooting *Legions Gone*, a motion picture that would wrap just before she could join Kate's crew.

"I just wanted to say hello."

"Bad timing. They've just finished lighting for me. I'll see you tonight." The line went dead.

Kate shook her head, sighed, and dialed Amy Parsons. She told her what Leo had said about Ralph Markowitz.

"I can't believe it," Amy said. "But since it's been over a year, why is the completion bond required?"

"They think his heart has been compromised enough to warrant it."

"Damn," Amy said. "What do you think?"

"First, I don't want to risk his health. Second, the completion bond is too expensive."

"I agree. He's great for the part, but it's not worth hurting himself over."

"Are you thinking what I'm thinking?" Kate asked.

"Yes. I think we should recast."

"Okay. I'll tell Jeffery."

After calling the studio and being told Jeffery Salzenberg, the head of the studio, was out of the office, Kate left a voicemail telling him that they would be dismissing Ralph from his contract and recasting the role.

CHAPTER THREE

The plane had begun its descent into the Orlando area. Kate stretched and began to think ahead to the business meeting she had traveled across the country to attend.

Her producer, Frank Collins, had been overseeing the construction of the sets and props for the movie. StormRunner had awarded the contract to a company called Florida Design and Fabrication for the production of many of the sets and props. At a value of two point five million dollars, the contract was an expensive one. StormRunner Productions could not afford to have any slip ups, so when FDF notified Frank that they had a scheduling problem, Frank called Kate. Though Hal Rosen had been hired as the production designer and was the one who normally would have been making all the decisions and keeping the design and fabrication schedule on track, he was not available to travel. Kate had agreed to let Hal finish his last film, one that overlapped with hers. Hal had worked with FDF early on designing all the sets and props and finishing the initial set drawings.

Because Frank was sick with the flu and Hal wasn't available, Kate had to make the trip herself. She would catch this early morning flight to Florida, solve the current problem, and take an afternoon flight home.

She had a complete comprehension of Hal's designs. They were among the details she always kept on top of for each of her films. She put her head back and closed her eyes, listening to the screeching of wheels touching down in alligator territory.

Certainly, the last thing she had anticipated was the untimely and inconvenient detour to Florida. And as brief a task as it was, a one-hour meeting would suck up the whole day. Even a simple accident on the already dreadfully congested LA freeway system was enough to snarl Kate's hectic agenda. But there was no way around a face-to-face meeting. The sets and props that had to be built by FDF were long lead-time items, and any delays in their delivery jeopardized the already very tight preproduction schedule. Kate couldn't afford to trust that FDF would solve the problem based on the company's word alone. A physical presence would send a strong message to FDF's management that schedules would not be slipped. Period.

She had skipped the meal on the plane since thunderstorms had rolled through most of Texas, tossing the plane and food trays about. The possibility of dumping the beef Wellington into her lap hardly seemed worth the risk. But with the plane now safely down on the ground and taxiing to the gate, she realized how hungry she was. She checked her watch to see whether there was time to eat on the way to the meeting. No such luck. They were expecting her within the hour.

Well, they weren't exactly expecting *her*. She'd never been to FDF. They were expecting Frank, and they dutifully complied when they got word to expect a next-day visit in response to FDF's admission to some schedule delays. She did find solace in the probability that an unfamiliar face would get FDF's attention. But chances were, after they realized Frank wasn't the one waiting out in their reception area, they'd more than likely reach the conclusion that Kate was his assistant, not the executive producer and owner of StormRunner Productions. She doubted they would remember she was the one who finalized their contract. The dealings had taken place over the phone, after Frank had returned from Florida on a pre-bid trip. Aside from the contract with her inked signature being couriered back to Florida, Frank's presence was all they knew.

Kate speculated that even after they realized she was the executive producer, they would have no clue of her knowledge of every detail of FDF's contract with them. Even though Frank had handled all the dealings since contract signature and was the one who took the regular trips to FDF's shop every two or three weeks, Kate had followed all the details of the contract and the work to date.

As the jet way was being pulled up to the airplane door, she thought of Frank. He was the best producer with whom she'd ever had the pleasure of working. The success of her production company stemmed from two things: her extremely capable employees, and the depth of her involvement in her company. She often mused that she couldn't own a company and *not* know everything that was going on, down to the material selections of any number of set pieces and props, as well as the change orders incurred upon every job that had come through StormRunner Productions.

A wet blanket of Florida humidity wrapped around her as she exited the airport. Feeling as if she were breathing underwater, she went in search of the rental car agency. Her assistant Laney always arranged a Lincoln Continental. This amused Kate to no end because a Lincoln Continental was the last car she would pick for herself. Laney had decided that the owner of StormRunner Productions should drive in something that said "successful and unflappable." How that translated to a Lincoln Continental, Kate would never know.

As she drove toward FDF, Kate became increasingly entertained at the possibility that FDF just might mistake her for Frank's underling. If she played along for a while, it could give her a chance to see how they would react to her. If they mistook her for a subordinate but still treated her with respect, she would be duly impressed. If they figured out that she was the owner but still treated her with respect, *without* kissing her ass, well, that would be a good thing as well.

She pulled into the parking lot at Florida Design and Fabrication. The lot was full of SUVs and pickup trucks and she took one of the spaces marked Visitor, parking next to a blue Jaguar XJK with a license plate that read FDF-1. The rolling door of the main shop's large loading dock was open, and people marched about wielding various tools, while others worked on set pieces and props that she knew were part of her film. She had seen the progress photographs that had been e-mailed in between Frank's trips, but now she beheld the set work in person. She walked up the steps to the front door and stopped. From there she could see more of the inside of the FDF shop. With a smile, she recognized the large entrance to the salt mine and a few of the interior mine walls, complete with wall torches and rail car tracks. Those sets dominated a great portion of the shop, and they were magnificent.

The receptionist made a phone call to announce her arrival.

Promptly, a gentleman approached, obviously looking for Frank. He glanced at the receptionist who motioned toward Kate.

"I'm Brett Desmond, Sr. Everyone calls me Brett, Sr." He extended his hand to her. "Frank couldn't make it?"

She took it, nodding. "Yes, that's correct. I'm Kate Nyland."

She looked for a seed of recognition or even a blink indicating that he had placed her name. No such seed or blink.

"Yes, well, welcome," he said releasing her hand. "Let's go into the conference room, shall we?" He smiled graciously, though it was way too early to conclude whether the gesture was sincere.

Though the reception area and offices of FDF were modest and functional, the conference room was a study in client comfort. The entrance sported wide, floor-to-ceiling glass doors. Thick, dark maroon carpet traveled across the floor. Adorning the walls were luxurious oil paintings. On one of the side walls hung a huge wipe-board that tracked all of FDF's jobs. Close to the entrance, an antique sideboard offered hot coffee and tea and a platter of fruit and pastries. The centerpiece of the room was a mahogany conference table. And in expensive black leather executive chairs, four people sat smiling.

As Brett, Sr. and Kate walked toward the table, he introduced her to the smiling people.

"Everyone, this is Kate Nyland from StormRunner Productions." He then gestured to a man in beige pants and green golf shirt emblazoned with the FDF logo. "This is Jeff, our estimator and financial analyst." Jeff quickly stood, shaking Kate's hand.

Brett, Sr. turned to the man next to Jeff. "This is Kurt Grossman, who is the project manager on your job." Kurt had a shock of red hair and his eyebrows were so blond, they were practically invisible. He wore a pale gold FDF-embroidered golf shirt with beige pants as well.

As they shook hands, Brett, Sr. pointed to a tall brunette woman wearing a blue and white checkered summer jumper with a white shirt underneath. "This is Tanya, my secretary, and this," he nodded to the last person at the table, "is Brett, Jr. He handles sales."

Brett, Sr. and Brett, Jr. shared strong genes. They were both dark skinned and dapper. Their hands were the same, rugged yet manicured. But the similarity of their laugh lines and round cheeks most gave away their relation. They wore more expensive slacks than the others, but their shirts were the same golf shirts bearing the company logo, obviously requisite apparel for FDF. Brett, Sr. did well for himself, and she supposed that Jr. was following those footsteps closely.

Kate shook Tanya's hand and then Brett, Jr.'s.

"Well, hello." It was as if Brett, Jr. had just seen his first woman. Kate only smiled wanly to the smarmy response.

The FDF employees settled back into their chairs, and Kate circled around to one of three empty chairs that were situated along the back wall facing the glass-paned entrance. If anyone intended on referring to the schedule, she'd have to turn around in her chair to see the whiteboard, but that was fine. She felt much more comfortable facing the door. She always did. From where she sat, she could see the activitiy of the people out in the reception area as they crisscrossed, holding papers, carrying models, and talking on cell phones.

"Would you like some coffee, Kate?" Tanya asked.

"Please," Kate responded, happy to be getting something in her stomach.

As Tanya rose from her chair, Brett, Sr. held up a hand to her. "I'm already up. And Tanya, just sugar for you," he said as he fetched two cups. His lack of chauvinism toward his secretary was duly noted.

Jeff took advantage of the pause and got up from his chair to get himself a cup of coffee. Brett, Sr. offered Kate some fruit and a muffin, and though she could have jumped the whole platter, she politely declined. She would be less successful in putting pressure on the company with kiwi seeds in her teeth.

Brett, Sr. handed Kate and Tanya FDF-emblazoned cups of coffee and settled down into a chair. "Where's Dawn?" Brett asked the room.

"She's sorting out the paint shop problems I told you about," Kurt, said as he helped himself to the sideboard platter and sat back down. He had a cup of coffee and some scrumptious-looking orange slices. "She said she'll be here in a few minutes."

"That's all right. We can get started." Brett, Sr. turned to Kate. "As Frank must have informed you, we experienced some setbacks recently and we're a little behind schedule." He chuckled. "Well, I'm sure you're aware of it. Frank wasn't due out here until next week."

Kate nodded as Brett, Sr. opened the meeting.

"I'm sure you've seen the memo we sent StormRunner Productions requesting an extension in delivery."

"I have," Kate replied.

Brett, Sr. went on. "Please let Frank know that we're still on schedule with the first group of props and show action pieces. That scope of work will be delivered by..." he turned to study the whiteboard over Kate's shoulder "...December ninth. That's the day after tomorrow."

Before Kate could turn to look at the whiteboard, she caught sight of a woman through the glass-paned wall by the conference room door.

The woman had been stopped by another co-worker and was being queried about something. The door was open, but Kate couldn't hear what they were saying. She was suddenly transfixed at the sight.

Though dressed much more casually than the ones in the conference room, the woman was absolutely stunning. Kate took in her strong, tanned legs that stretched between cut-off denim shorts and black, ankle-high work boots. She was roughly Kate's height, around five foot nine, maybe slightly shorter. And she was obviously not a stranger to exercise. Since the woman was in profile, Kate could only see a little bit of her face. A loose T-shirt disguised any further detail, but glowed like snow against arms as golden as her legs.

Kate knew she was staring but couldn't help herself. Suddenly the woman turned, looking right at her. Kate jolted, wondering if her own staring had somehow dispatched some super-sensory vibe that the woman had picked up on. Their eyes were suddenly connected, burning intensely, and the magnetic pull was tremendous. Kate felt weak and vulnerable. A swallow caught in her throat, and the thrumming of her pulse filled her ears.

Then the muffled echo of Brett, Sr.'s voice swam in her ears.

"...sure you'll be pleased with."

"Excuse me?" Kate blinked as she turned toward Brett, Sr.

"The props that will be completed day after tomorrow...I was saying that we're finishing up some great props that I'm sure that you'll be pleased with."

"I see." Kate managed to get a hold of herself. "I'm looking forward to seeing them." She glanced toward the door again. The woman nodded good-bye to her co-worker and entered the conference room. Kate quickly diverted her gaze but knew she'd been caught.

Oh my God was all Kate could think.

"Ah! There you are." Brett, Sr. raised an open palm toward Kate. "Kate, I'd like you to meet Dawn Brock. She's our lead art director, and now foreman on your project."

Kate stood to shake Dawn's hand. For a long moment, they looked directly into each other's eyes. "It's nice to meet you."

Dawn furrowed her brow so imperceptibly that unless one was staring straight at her it would have been undetectable. Kate, however, had been staring.

"Pleased to meet you, as well," Dawn said and lowered herself into a chair across from Kate. The room seemed to suddenly vibrate. Like a cauldron of liquid ebony, Dawn's curly jet-black hair percolated about her shoulders. Her eyes were a dazzling light sable color. They glowed against her tan face and so strangely seemed to be pulling Kate toward her that Kate found herself gripping the arm of the conference room chair to make sure she wasn't floating out of it. Her first thought was, *She's absolutely beautiful.* Her second thought was, *Kate, you have a girlfriend.*

She quickly snapped back to the meeting as Brett, Sr. continued. "I just put Dawn in charge of your project because I felt we needed to give StormRunner Productions special attention."

Kate took a sip of her coffee, gulping down the hot liquid, hoping it would keep her focused. Brett, Sr. turned back to the whiteboard and pointed to some dates. "Now, as I was saying, the first group will be delivered day after tomorrow. That is correct, isn't it, Dawn?"

Against her better judgment, Kate took the chance to look at Dawn again. She seemed to be in her mid-thirties and Kate guessed that she was of Native American descent. And she was exquisite. She was ample where Kate was lean. Her shoulders were broader, her arms more muscular, and her T-shirt gracefully rested over full breasts. Her hands looked strong and capable and bore two rings, a simple band on each ring finger. One was gold, the other silver.

"Yes, it will. When Frank was last here, he bought off all of group one except for final paint on the sinking boat and five other props." She paused and tilted her head toward the chart on the wall. "AP 43-16 – the animated cave bat."

What's gotten into me? Kate wondered. *I've never acted this way...maybe I'm coming down with the flu.* Kate took a deep breath to assist the return of her brain to the discussion at hand.

Brett, Sr. turned to Kate. "The second group is what we'd like to discuss with you."

Okay, Kate thought, they were finally getting to the point. Before she left LA, Kate and Frank discussed the possibility that FDF could be trying to pull something over on StormRunner Productions, which was why she had flown out rather than wait for Frank to recover from his flu. And though Kate had a plethora of questions and directives, she held off. Brett, Sr. still hadn't played his hand, and Kate needed more facts.

"We knew Frank would be unhappy. We are unhappy, too," Brett, Sr. said. "And I think he'd be satisfied to see that Dawn's now in place."

Frank had mentioned Dawn Brock. He described her as "the only one who really understands what StormRunner Productions is trying to accomplish."

"Now we can get past the difficulties of late and satisfy StormRunner Productions." Brett, Sr. smiled at Kate.

Kate nodded then said, "Let's talk about the recent 'difficulties.'"

"We have had a lot of work go through the shop recently. We can't always project what parts of the fabrication process will hit each department when. Our most impacted department has been sculpting. That, and the fact that some of our other clients have given us unrealistic due dates. Believe me, StormRunner Productions has not. But they can't all be as competent as your company." Brett, Sr. had ended the sentence sounding as sincere as he could while Kurt nodded in cheery agreement. Kate could care less about the sincerity of his compliment. What he had just done was reveal the reason FDF was pushing to change StormRunner Production's delivery dates, which obviously had nothing to do with StormRunner Productions. And more than likely, Brett, Sr. and Kurt had rehearsed this meeting in hopes that they could wheedle their way around the issue and get Frank to acquiesce. She knew that certainly would not have been the case. Frank was very strong-minded. And it amused her that having someone other than Frank appear in their offices had obviously surprised them.

Brett, Sr. gestured back to the whiteboard. "What we'd now like to discuss is shifting the schedule in a way that would best serve the project's needs. Kurt has analyzed group two and has some suggestions that I think will forward this effort."

Boy, were they laying it on, Kate thought. For their own shortcomings, and most assuredly not for the benefit of StormRunner Productions, they were trying to slip her scheduled delivery dates. Worse yet, they were trying to make it sound like it was for StormRunner's own good.

Kurt stepped in. "Now, I think the most appropriate final delivery date for group two would be January 5. This allows us to produce, for StormRunner Productions, a product that most accurately represents the first-rate work that FDF is used to generating. By shifting the work, as you can see here on the schedule that we've worked very diligently on, we found the best way to utilize our resources. Your project is very important to us, and because of that I'd like to go over the new dates line by line. I normally don't do that, since Frank is here every other week and pretty much knows how we function, but the difficulties we encountered with group two have become apparent in the time since he was last here. So, I was prepared to go line by line with him as well." He hesitated and then asked, "Is Frank in the office? Do you think we could include him via conference call?"

Kurt was now trying to go around her, or mistakenly go over her head.

"No. He's unavailable," she said calmly.

"I only ask because we feel, as I'm sure you do, very serious about continuity in our client relationships. Frank has a very good grasp on the contract."

"Like I said, Mr. Grossman, Frank is unavailable," she replied. "Please continue."

"Pardon my asking, but Frank is authorized by StormRunner Productions to make," he paused for effect, "very expensive and important decisions. While I appreciate your trip out here, are you authorized? And more importantly, are you qualified? Because any decision made here today is final. Frank won't be able to make any changes down the road without a huge impact."

Kate wondered if Kurt was tripping over his own machismo or just plain obtuse. She responded evenly, "I'm very aware of the ramifications of this meeting."

Kurt hesitated. "Ms. Nyland, I'm sure Frank wouldn't have sent you without good cause, but the details of this project are very hard to keep up with."

Kate stifled a grin. She was mildly surprised that Kurt wasn't letting go of this. Didn't he know that in their quest to sell this lame subterfuge, someone new to the game would be a godsend, someone to baffle with bullshit, and would not be the hindrance he acted like she was? Kate drew out a dramatic sigh, which came off as she intended, to let Kurt know she was tiring of his banter. "Let's continue, shall we?"

The slight tightening of Kurt's lips spoke volumes. "Of course. Tanya, please hand out the schedule to everyone."

Kate was so amused at the theatrics, that there was no room for annoyance at Kurt's assumption that she was Frank's subordinate.

Brett, Sr. spoke up. "Kurt, let's now go over the individual line items on the new schedule."

While Kurt droned on, Kate surveyed the room. She studied Brett, Jr., Jeff, and Tanya. Their body language indicated that this conference room was a second home to them. They all made notes on their own notepads, sipped at mugs of coffee, and had that characteristic blank expression on their faces. They obviously spent many an hour in client meetings just like this one. She glanced at Dawn, and her body language suggested quite the opposite. She had that slight restlessness that said, "Okay, let's get on with this because I hate meetings," but interestingly enough, behind that mild tension seemed an ardently sedate demeanor. Then again, Kate had known many Dawns. They lived most comfortably in the fabrication shops, the art studios, and on movie sets quite a far distance from the "suites and offices." She was sure that Dawn spent little mental energy on the politics of the profession and all her heart on the quality of the craft. And though there were truly many Dawns, none had ever jangled Kate's insides. Reluctantly, she turned back to Kurt who had been going on for quite a few minutes.

"And after we fiberglass the bludgeoning stick prop, we'll start cleanup of the glasswork the first week of January…"

Okay, that's enough of the babbling, Kate decided. "Pardon my interruption, Kurt, but I think I can save some time here." She glanced around the room. Suddenly she had everyone's attention. "I presume you all would rather not be sitting in here talking about the work when you could actually be out there doing the work."

Her words spoke most directly to Dawn, who was listening as intently as the rest, but with slightly more amusement.

"Well, of course, Ms. Nyland." Kurt smiled a little too severely at Kate. "That is our intent. Now if I may," he said as he turned back to the whiteboard.

Kate held up a finger. "Pardon me again, Kurt, but before you continue going over this new schedule, I'd like to clear up a few things."

Kurt looked to Brett, Sr. who nodded slowly. Kurt's jaw tightened. "Please."

Kate turned to address Brett, Sr. "While I am empathetic to your business difficulties, with all due respect, Mr. Desmond, the setback you have encountered is not the responsibility of StormRunner Productions. Though I appreciate the comment that StormRunner is a competent business, I find that insufficient reason to assume that StormRunner would compromise its work schedule to make up for those difficulties."

Brett, Sr. straightened in his chair. "Ms. Nyland, we are not saying that we're looking for a scapegoat for another client's problems, but the fact remains that these new delivery dates are much better suited for the type of product your company is requesting."

"And how is that?"

Brett, Sr. hesitated. "Kurt?"

Kurt responded, speaking slowly and enunciating each word as if Kate were five years old. "The new schedule will allow FDF to focus on these set pieces and props and put the best manpower and technical know-how to it."

Kate drew a breath and then let him have it with a level tone, deadly enough to mean serious business. "Mr. Grossman, I certainly hope you're not insinuating that, for the *delayed* delivery date, you will give StormRunner Productions first rate work, because that implies that you would have delivered, for the *originally* agreed upon timeframe, something substandard. I trust that what StormRunner Productions originally paid for was FDF's first rate work. And what StormRunner also paid for was a timely completion of all three phases of that first rate work, based on a schedule that your company acknowledged was reasonable. May I remind you that the principals of each company agreed to this contractually? What that intimates is that the scope of work, the price for that scope of work, and the timeframe in which to complete that scope of work were all agreed to. In writing. The signing of that contract, of course, implied that each side realized that they would benefit from the transaction. But delaying the schedule does not benefit StormRunner Productions."

She continued through the thick silence that pervaded the room. "Now, I do expect the original dates to be met. They were doable dates when they were agreed upon. StormRunner, as you know, has to soon commence principal photography on the motion picture that FDF is building the sets and props for. Everything you're fabricating needs to get to the Orlando studio where it will have to be set in place and ready in three weeks. The director of photography needs one week to light the sets and props. Then principal photography starts. There is absolutely no room for a slip in schedule."

Kurt stood there fuming. He then clapped his hands together. "Well, that means then that we will have to accelerate the schedule. We'll need to analyze the financial impacts. It'll take us a day, and we'll get back to you." He nodded as if to dismiss Kate.

Kate cocked her head slightly. "Mr. Grossman, let's not get our nomenclature confused. An accelerated schedule presumes that you have been asked to deliver work sooner than requested. This is not the case. I believe that you meant to say a *recovery* schedule. And just in case you aren't clear about what that is, a recovery schedule gets the work back *on* schedule." Kate then nodded toward Dawn. "I assume that Dawn's recent promotion to foreman was done as part of that recovery effort. I trust it's a good beginning."

Dawn seemed to be quite entertained. She was sitting back as relaxed as a cat reclined in a late afternoon patch of sun while the rest of the group held on to their chairs or paperwork like passengers feeling the first hit of the *Titanic* against the iceberg.

Kurt's voice had dropped an octave and slowed to an ominous crawl. "Ms. Nyland, with all due respect, are you qualified to be debating the legalities of the contract?"

Kate had the urge to peek under the table to get a gander at the size of Kurt's foot. He'd soon be shoving it in his mouth. "I am, Mr. Grossman."

Ignoring Kate's response, Kurt reached into a binder on the table and retrieved the contract. "Frank worked diligently with us to come to this agreement, Ms. Nyland, and I really don't believe we should go any further with this discussion until we consult him."

Without a trace of emotion, she turned to Brett, Sr. "Mr. Desmond, would you please check the signatures on the last page of the contract?"

Brett, Sr. stared at Kate a moment and then took the contract out of Kurt's hand. Kate watched as Brett, Jr., Tanya, and Jeff leaned forward in their chairs. She looked at Kurt. He remained rigid. She looked at

Dawn who had had been watching her with thinly veiled amusement. In any other instance, Kate would have smiled at Dawn. It would have been a warm, cheery smile, but now was not the time, so her face remained flat and indifferent.

She turned back to Brett, Sr. just in time to see his eyes widen and then blink back to normal. He swallowed. "Ms. Nyland. I'm sorry. I didn't recognize your name when we were introduced. It's been a while since you and I signed this contract and, of course, until today, we had only spoken once on the phone." He turned to Kurt whose eyebrows were melded together in a puzzled frown. "Kurt, Ms. Nyland owns StormRunner Productions. She knows this contract as well as anyone. And, as Frank has attested to me many times, she follows the work here as closely as if she were doing it herself." He turned back to Kate. "I'm sorry. It's very nice to finally meet you."

"My pleasure, Mr. Desmond."

Before she could continue, Brett, Sr. shot Kurt a perturbed glance.

Through clenched teeth, Kurt said, "Please accept my apologies, Ms. Nyland. I didn't know…"

"Quite all right." She'd just ascertained that those with political clout at FDF were more cunning than sincere. Not insurmountable, but noteworthy. She would have to watch them more closely.

"Now," she went on, "I expect group two's recovery effort to remain contained within group two and group three with three. I am saying this now because I don't want to receive a phone call telling me that these problems snowballed and caused a delay in the fabrication of group three. I would never tell you how to manage your resources. We wouldn't have chosen FDF if we weren't sure that your track record was respectable and solid. I have all the confidence in the world that you will remedy this snarl, get back on track, and hit the dates lined out in the contract.

"While I remain firm on my delivery needs, I am also here to help you, not hinder you. I am open to whatever suggestions you all may have in this recovery effort that will help expedite the process. That may mean rethinking a fabrication method, for instance. Or you might suggest a change in materials if some of the ones we originally specified have a longer lead-time to procure. I will review any proposals. Of course, I expect the creative intent to be maintained, but I'll be open to compromises. If we find a fair trade-off, I will sign a change order accordingly." She then turned to Brett, Sr. and addressed him specifically. "You have three weeks, Mr. Desmond."

Brett, Sr. nodded. "That sounds very equitable. We will review the remaining work and let you know what recommendations we come up with. How long are you with us?"

"I have a flight out later this afternoon."

"My word, that's a quick turnaround." He stood up, gesturing that the meeting was over. "Well, since you don't have much time, I imagine you'd like to tour our facility now. I'm sure you'd like to status your pieces out in the shop."

"I would, thank you."

"Dawn, would you please show Ms. Nyland around?"

Dawn guided Kate toward the shop. Attached to the main offices, the shop was nevertheless a world apart. The khaki pants and golf shirt dress code stopped dead at the door. In the shop realm, workers of every shape and size bustled about, all in their own choice of clothing. The only uniformity was that the balmy Florida weather had compelled most of them to don shorts and light T-shirts or tank tops.

The shop was departmentalized by process. The sculpting area dominated the middle of the shop's floor. Off in one corner, a fiberglass area housed many of StormRunner's props. And only the elaborately outfitted carpenter's mill surpassed the impressive metal shop in its array of tools and equipment.

"We can start in the paint shop since the last of group one is being finished there." Dawn pointed to the loading dock before turning to Kate. A faint twinkle in her eyes matched the sudden smile. "It's outside and around back. If we get your approval today, we'll get those ready for shipment to the studio."

A ripple of elation coursed through Kate, even though she wasn't exactly sure of the cause of Dawn's smile. "That'd be great."

The paint shop was housed in a single building approximately sixty-feet-by-sixty-feet. Workbenches lined three walls, and the fourth wall housed a paint booth. A ten-foot square table sat in the middle of the room and currently housed StormRunner's props. The walls of the paint shop were starch white with occasional test spray areas of just about every imaginable color. A tall table with some stools was where the more intricate brushwork was performed. Two women were busy painting a large canvas backdrop that looked like it would be used for another client's commercial or still photo shoot. Kate and Dawn spent half an hour reviewing the props from group one. Kate signed off on them all.

Dawn brought Kate back to the main shop. On a workbench, many of the group-two drawings lay in a pile, along with the beginnings of a clay sculpt of prop 12-7, the salt mine torch. That prop, like many others, would be sculpted and then a mold would be made of the original. Using that mold, multiple torches would be produced. Dawn and Kate were discussing the design of the torch when Kurt came out of the offices and into the shop. He searched the shop a moment, clutching a thin stack of stapled papers.

"Ms. Nyland." He approached the women holding up the papers. His jaw was firmly set, and any southern hospitality had long since disappeared. "We've spent the last hour going over the rest of this schedule, ah, the original schedule, as well as the prop lists. We found a way to streamline the process for a large portion of work. As you must know, in group two we had proposed that all of the props be sculpted in clay and then molded."

Kate nodded. "Yes, especially prop 19209-1212–the Maiden of Salt statue, prop 1215-225–the lantern, and animated prop 2515-21–the cavern door hatch, which you are sculpting as one-offs." She didn't have to look at the chart Kurt held for reference. She knew it forward and backward.

Kurt hesitated. Kate couldn't tell whether he was impressed or pissed off at her attention to detail. "Yes, well, ah..." he stammered awkwardly.

Already a step ahead of him, Kate knew exactly what he was going to say next. She'd decided he just hadn't been able to get past the well-deserved scolding he'd received. Indeed, Kurt's face seemed just a bit redder.

"Yes, ah, well as I was saying, we propose taking those four props and carving them out of heavy foam, not clay, and then use the direct fiberglass process. That way, we can not only...*recover*," he snapped rather forcefully, "but we can probably credit back a few thousand dollars."

Kate didn't even take the courtesy to pretend that she was mulling it over. But she did slip out a sigh that was quite obvious. "I thought you'd say that. As you must know, the problem with direct fiberglass is that, whenever you don't mold a piece from clay but rather lay fiberglass over a foam carving, detail is lost. Direct fiberglass never retains the individual characteristics, especially if it's done quickly."

"I understand," Kurt said, his grip making the paperwork shake, "but we'll spend extra time with the glassing and keep as much of that detail in as possible. But…" Kurt paused, "I must tell you that the extra time, especially if the crew works Saturday and Sunday, will cut into the savings we can credit back."

Kate smiled inwardly and decided to let Kurt run a little longer with his cockamamie story. "How so?"

"Well, extra work for the crew on Saturday and Sunday. You see, we'll need to pull them off other jobs to do this, not to mention the cost to open up the shop. Electricity and wages will have to be passed along."

Kate almost laughed. Kurt was either an asshole who endeavored to be cunning or just a stupid bastard. Either way, if he constantly found it necessary to try to one-up her, Kate could take the time to constantly put him back in his place.

"Are you familiar with the delay clause in the contract we have with you?"

"Ms. Nyland, I don't make it a habit to memorize every single contract we have, but I do know this business, thank you."

"Let me help you with that one, then. The delay clause states that any vendor costs related to schedule slippage on the part of the vendor is not a billable." This was a standard clause that was in StormRunner's fabrication contracts, and she had experience exercising it with other vendors. "Please make sure you review the contract, Mr. Grossman, and don't hesitate to call me if you have any questions."

Bored with Kurt's diatribe, Kate turned to Dawn. "How much direct fiberglass work have you done?"

Caught in an expansive grin, Dawn quickly recovered, "Quite a bit. It's trickier with detailed pieces, though we've pulled off some victories."

Kate then studied the work. "If you can be the one who oversees the direct process, we'll be fine."

"That's the plan."

"Very well," Kate said. After all, she was here to get results. She turned to Kurt. "Before I can agree to the direct fiber process, I'll need to review the recovery schedule."

"Give me an hour." Still angry, Kurt turned and was gone.

"I have to admit, direct fiberglass still makes me a little nervous," Kate confided in Dawn when Kurt was out of earshot.

"I understand. But in the script, it seems that the props from group two never get close to the camera. They are in the background, right? At least that's how I read it."

Kate smiled. Dawn Brock was not only stunning, she was sharp and an astute problem solver. "You read the script?"

Dawn nodded. "I always do. I don't believe we can do justice to the work if we don't understand what the client understands."

"Wow," Kate murmured, surprising herself that it slipped out. "Yes, the script reads that way. The props are in the background. But there's always the chance that the director will want to move things around, maybe pull one or more of the props into the foreground to frame a shot or start on a relatively benign, static object and then pull the camera back, things like that."

Kate picked up a drawing of Prop 19209-1212, the Maiden of Salt Statue. The prop was written into the story as a figure that would serve as a locater in the salt mines scenes. The Maiden of Salt was the entrance piece to the mine. Located about fifty feet in, the figure stood at the point where the first set of wooden slides, the method of decent for the workers, marked the beginning of the seemingly bottomless drop into the mines. The Maiden of Salt was the stoic and poised sentinel that salt miners of past centuries would touch to bring them luck as they began their descent into the bowels of the earth. Her arms were slightly outstretched, as if welcoming them in and also beckoning them home. She was just as beautiful and mysterious as the busty female figures carved on many a ship's prow. As long as she stood sentry, the miners would be reassured, day after day, that they would return safely from their salty tunnels.

"This is a good example to illustrate my concern," Kate said. "The delicate curls that make up the hair around the maiden's face, as well as the facial detail, would more than likely be lost in the direct fiberglass process."

"Yes." Dawn studied it contemplatively. "But we could carve the body out of foam, up to the neck, and then sculpt the head out of clay.

The head is the most important feature on this piece. So we could mold just the head, retaining the detail, and save the time and cost of molding the whole thing."

"So, for instance on the maiden's bustier, you'd cut in the folds after fiberglassing it?"

"Exactly."

They were speaking the same language, and Kate was grateful that Dawn understood her concerns. "I suppose it could work…" When she looked up, Dawn was smiling again.

"Okay," Kate said, "That's three times. Now you have to tell me."

"Tell you what?"

"Either my zipper is down or there's something else that is amusing you so."

Dawn laughed, shaking her head, "No, no. I'm not laughing at you. It's just that we don't get a lot of…strong women around here."

"And?"

"It's refreshing. Not a whole lot brings Kurt's mouth to a standstill."

"Being bossy is not my favorite thing to do."

"Well, I enjoyed the heck out of it." After a moment she said, "Come with me," and picked up the drawing, turning to leave that area of the shop. Kate followed her to a workbench in the far corner. A woman was laying out a design drawing that Kate recognized as they approached. It was prop 12-9191, dinosaur bones.

"Kate, this is one of our best sculptors, Krissy Donaldson. Krissy, meet Kate Nyland from StormRunner Productions."

Kate held out her hand and took Krissy's. It was calloused and tanned from many hours of work and sun. "It's very nice to meet you," she said warmly.

Krissy smiled. "Nice to meet you, too."

"Krissy's the lead sculptor on the group two props," Dawn said and then turned to Krissy. "We're talking about a combination foam and clay sculpt."

Krissy nodded. "Done that before."

"I think the dinosaur bones shouldn't cause us much of a problem." Dawn indicated Krissy's drawing, her slow southern drawl piquing Kate's interest. "They can all be directly fiberglassed."

Kate sensed an accent from a state other than Florida. Maybe Kentucky or the Carolinas.

"Okay," Kate agreed to the production method for the bones.

Dawn pointed to the drawing she held. "With the Maiden of Salt, I wanted to explain to you what Krissy and I have done in the past when using the combination method with pieces like this." Dawn moved in to point to different parts of the Maiden of Salt drawing, and as she did, Kate watched Dawn's strong, exquisite jaw line and the slight, almost imperceptible turn of her nose. Dawn tilted her head toward the drawing, and Kate watched her as she spoke about the creative process, pointing out her fabrication plan. She watched Dawn's lips move languidly, and she was surprised at the realization that came to her, those were the sexiest lips she'd ever seen. Though in the outer recesses of her brain, Kate was conscious of the folly of her thoughts. She felt like a sailor too drunk to duck a wave as she stood there taking in all of Dawn. And then from her lips, Kate's eyes lifted to Dawn's. She was captivated by those eyes, a heart-stopping, extraordinary mix of sleepy and sexy.

There was something unique about this woman that Kate tried to pinpoint. She sure didn't act like the women she was used to dating in LA. She was certainly not like Hannah, who was a little too wrapped up in what she was doing to care about much else. Dawn was sincere and capable without caring who noticed. It wasn't about who would react to her accomplishments or who would praise her to the press. Dawn seemed the type of person to stand alone in her competence and talent without accolades and awards. Even in the short time since she'd met Dawn, there was a complete connection in their conversations.

And we're having a two-way dialogue, Kate thought. *What a concept.* She hadn't had that with Hannah since, well, she couldn't really remember.

Kate saw those eyes suddenly turn to look at her and saw Dawn's mouth, which was no longer talking but closed in a slight grin.

"Pardon?" she said.

"If we over-sculpt the folds in the bustier," Dawn said, "leaving at least an extra quarter inch, we'll be able to cut more detail into it after the fiberglass is applied. I think it will work."

Kate mulled over the Maiden of Salt drawing. "If it was done very carefully."

"We could do a mockup and show you," Dawn said. "I'll have Krissy work on this and apply direct fiberglass to the body and let you decide. If you don't like it, I'll have another one sculpted in clay and we'll be back to the original plan."

Kate hesitated.

Dawn added, "Without going over schedule."

Kate studied Dawn's face. At first she thought the comment was a mild taunt to her recent admonishment of FDF's schedule problems, but instead she found a face awash in playful teasing. She could have stared longer, and certainly Dawn wasn't breaking the gaze. And in that moment, everything was perfect. They stood face to face, equals in business, working out the details of a project that they both understood in the same way. And it was refreshing.

Then Dawn opened her hands, palms up. "I control the shop, and I only promise things I can deliver. Competently."

Easing into a smile, Kate asked, "When could you do the mock up?"

Dawn looked at Krissy, who was also smiling. "Tomorrow. About noon."

Kate glanced at her watch.

"Your plane," Dawn said.

"Yes. I've got an hour before I have to leave for the airport, less actually, because I have to return the rental car."

"Let's at least see whether Kurt is finished with the proposal." Dawn led Kate back to the conventional confines of FDF's offices. Kurt was still elbow deep in papers, diligently trying to rectify the schedule problems. He looked up to see Kate and Dawn in the doorway.

"I'm not quite finished," he said.

Kate had to make a prompt decision, either leave without seeing the recovery proposal and Dawn's mockup or stay until the next day. She knew that leaving now, in the midst of a flurry of activity to rectify Kurt and Brett, Sr.'s mismanagement of late would not be advantageous. She couldn't afford to let FDF lose their newly found momentum.

She had commandeered the meeting earlier, interrupting Kurt's diatribe, to stress the seriousness of the terms of the contract between StormRunner and FDF.

Receiving the recovery schedule via e-mail the next day wouldn't suffice. She was there to get results, and she needed to make sure things were under control before she left, which included seeing the mockup in person. And after all, she had offered to partner with them to find a resolution to their scheduling dilemma.

Kate would have to extend her stay.

Brett, Sr. had accepted the news of the extra day's stay with a warm smile, and when she informed him that she would be changing her flight, Brett, Sr. gracefully offered the use of his personal phone in his rather regal office. The charge in Kate's cell phone was fading so she was grateful for the land line.

Kate called Laney who swiftly and expertly filled her in on a day's worth of messages, including the plea from Jeffery's office to call him as soon as she landed in Orlando. Laney connected Kate to Jeffery.

"Kate," he said, "nice flight?"

The sound of shuffling papers and the perfunctory distance in his voice convinced Kate that she could have told him the plane had almost crashed and it wouldn't have necessarily registered. "Fine, Jeffery. What can I do for you?"

"Keep Ralph on board."

That was surprising. Up to that point, Jeffery hadn't acknowledged Ralph one way or the other. Per usual, the head of the studio had an interest in who was being cast in the top billed positions and gave his nod to Sage Siegel, and later, Hannah Corrant, but his interest in Ralph didn't make sense. Ralph's medical condition, due to his drug use, had become a liability to the production. Jeffery's studio had been the one to demand the completion bond on Ralph, which meant they thought he posed a risk to the movie. And now Jeffery wanted to keep Ralph on the film.

"Ralph? Why?"

She heard Jeffery sigh, "It's political, Kate. Let's just leave it at that."

"Jeffery, I can't just leave it at that. This is my picture, and Ralph is now a wild card."

"He won't be a wild card. He says he's off the stuff now."

"That doesn't mean a whole hell of a lot, Jeffery," Kate argued.

"Look, just do me this favor, huh?"

"I need to know what you know on this one." Kate would go toe-to-toe in order to preserve her upper-hand as a producer. She was not going to blindly take a risk on Ralph.

Jeffery paused, obviously weighing his options. "We're in negotiations with Ralph right now."

"Negotiations for what?"

"For a script he owns the rights to. It's a good one—"

Kate finished his sentence, "—and he really wants the part in my movie, too."

"Yeah. He does. Granted, he's an arrogant bastard, but you know he's a great actor, Kate."

"Yes, I know that, but it's too risky."

"It'll be fine." He punctuated the last word as if trying to finish the conversation.

"Jeffery, cut the shit." Kate knew she should cool it with someone who was not only the head of the studio, but one of the most powerful men in Hollywood, however, this was her picture. "It's your studio that wants the completion bond on him. You obviously think he's a risk."

"Okay, okay." Jeffery sighed again. "I'll pick up the cost of the completion bond. The studio will cover it, so it won't go against your budget. Are you happy?"

"I don't want to put his health at risk."

"So go easy on him." Jeffery tried to make a joke and sniggered. Then just as quickly, he collected himself by clearing his throat. A foreboding seriousness found its way into his voice, "Kate, I want the script from Ralph. He wants your picture. I'll pay the bond. I'm adamant about this."

Kate was silent long enough that Jeffery added, "I'll have him checked out by our physician again right before he leaves for Orlando. And then I'm done with this conversation."

Kate had to decide whether this was worth pressing. Though it went against every fiber in her, she decided that this was not a hill she'd die fighting on.

She called Amy and relayed the story to her. Amy was just as unsure as Kate about keeping him on board. It was difficult for both of them because they knew that Ralph would execute the role as the principal Austrian villain perfectly. He was a great actor. But he had a drug problem and the risks were high. Working long, grueling hours on the set could cause him great harm if his body was compromised. He could also cause the set problems if he began to exhibit signs of drug use, sloppy work, and late or absent days.

"We'll make it work, Kate. I'll stand behind your decision."

"As much as it was my decision, which it wasn't. But thanks, Amy."

"I'll rearrange your meetings tomorrow morning since you'll be flying home then, correct?" Laney was on the line again.

Kate laughed. "How did you know I had to stay?"

"Easy. It's past four o'clock Florida time, and you haven't called the office once. You always call me when you're off to your next appointment or to the airport. So I knew that you were wrapped up in business. I could always cancel the reservations. Anyway, I figured that you had more business at FDF, so you're booked on the same flight tomorrow afternoon. This time, I got you in seat 2A, your favorite. No racing to the airport to beg for a seat again."

"You are brilliant."

"And you are staying at the Peabody on International Drive. It's halfway between FDF and the airport. You're on the concierge floor, of course."

Kate laughed once more. "Have I given you a raise this year?"

"Twice. But the second one didn't count."

"Remind me why…"

"You said I couldn't tell anyone because no one else got a second raise."

"I did say that."

"Now all that's left is to cancel your dinner date with Hannah tonight."

"Dinner…" Kate suddenly remembered that Hannah would be expecting her on the set to pick her up that evening. "Oh, boy," she murmured, "Hannah's not going to like this."

"Shall I call her?"

"No, I will. But thanks."

CHAPTER FOUR

After work, Dawn sat at Faces, the local lesbian bar. Krissy sat next to her as they nursed wet, cold beer and watched the comings and goings of the bar patrons.

"Who died and made you queen for a day?" Krissy nudged Dawn's elbow.

"What?" Dawn had been daydreaming.

"I saw," Krissy said.

"You saw what?"

"Hell, girl. I've been working for you too many years. I don't miss much. I saw the way you were looking at her."

"Who?" Dawn asked, but it was a ridiculous question.

"Kate Nyland." Krissy smiled mischievously. "She's not only dazzling, she's the owner of StormRunner Productions. She's that big producer, you know?"

"And she is here to kick our butts because we're behind schedule."

"Where do I line up?"

Dawn flicked a finger, wet with beer bottle condensation, at Krissy. "She's as professional as they come. And she's not here to find a date, so all the looks in the world won't do much."

"I'm just saying, I haven't seen that look from you in years. Maybe never."

"It'll be short-lived, I assure you. Kate Nyland is a celebrity."

"Speaking of celebrities, can you believe that Hannah Corrant is in the movie as well?" Dawn shrugged. "You know that Hannah Corrant is a lesbian."

Dawn nodded. She'd read the magazines. Hannah had been out from the start of her career. It had been timed right, whether calculated or accidental, when Hollywood studios were not only warming up to lesbians, they were taking advantage of the extra press.

"Tell me she's gay," Krissy pleaded, gaping at Dawn with interest.

"You just said she was."

"Not Hannah, Kate."

"How am I supposed to know?" However, Dawn did know that there was a certain way that Kate's eyes bore into hers when she had been out in the hall by the conference room. Dawn had been instantly captivated. Her mind swirled and she felt that something extraordinary had just caught up to her. It was as if some strange day of romantic reckoning, one she'd never even imagined, was suddenly upon her. Like a convergence of something. Paths? Fate? Whatever it was, it had suddenly smacked right into her that afternoon when she had first seen Kate watching her from inside the conference room. Her chest had tightened and the air suddenly felt dangerously thin. Had Brett, Sr. not called her into the meeting, Dawn would have bolted outside, into the shop's parking lot, toward some desperately needed oxygen.

"Hey." Krissy looked concerned. "You okay?"

Dawn struggled to come back from some dizzy dream. She gripped the bottle to register that the beer was actually in her hand and shifted to make sure that the barstool was firmly underneath her. "Yeah. I'm fine." She took a breath.

"So?"

"So?"

"Do you think that she's gay?"

"I believe she is."

"Of course, you didn't find out for sure."

"Was that a statement?"

Krissy nodded.

"What do you mean by that?"

Feigning a sigh, Krissy replied. "You aren't the kind to chase after the babes."

"I've pursued my share."

Krissy scrutinized her. "Dawn darlin', you're the empress of reserved."

"I hold my own." Dawn looked away, toward the pool table. "Besides, *that* woman is out of my league."

"Bullshit. You are a pretty bright star yourself. You could easily be the owner of your own company if you ever decided to leave FDF.

Geez, Dawn, the only reason the shop doesn't spin out of control is because of you."

Dawn took a swig of her beer. "Hardly, Krissy."

"None of those *boys* in the front office could manage the shop like you can. And the shop is where the real work gets done. Plus, do you think you would have ever pulled a stunt like the one Brett, Sr. and Kurt tried to pull on Kate?" Krissy harrumphed. "They got in over their heads and then tried to make StormRunner Productions pay for it."

Dawn shook her head, taking a deep swallow from the bottle.

Krissy nudged her again. "Management sits out there in their nice offices and sweet talks companies into giving them work. Shit, anyone with a business account and directions to a fancy restaurant could do that, Dawn. And they know damn well that what they sell, they have to deliver. But see, they can't deliver it. You can. And they know it. They really need you."

"You're being very kind."

"Kind, nothing. Dawn, you are definitely in the upper league."

"But Kate…" Dawn shook her head.

"Well, I must say that you weren't the only one looking interested."

"Cut the shit, Krissy."

"She looked at you like she'd just seen the Holy Grail."

"No way." Dawn's body suddenly reacted to the thought. Her chest felt hot and her stomach fluttered strangely. "Not her. She's so…so…" *Could Krissy be right?* It was too scary a notion to trust.

"Don't let that swanky LA manner fool you. Besides, I'm bettin' she's a lesbian and that means she undresses women one zipper at a time." Krissy elbowed Dawn for effect. "Same as you and me."

Dawn turned back to Krissy. "No doubt with a loving wife at home."

"Maybe."

Chapter Five

You're still in *Florida*?"

"I'm sorry, Hannah. I had every intention of zipping in and zipping out." Kate checked her watch. It was six thirty eastern time, three thirty Pacific time. She had checked into the hotel and realized that she had one half hour in which to call Hannah and then make it back downstairs to the hotel's boutique in order to pick up something to wear on this unexpected stay in Florida. That is, if Hannah didn't start a small-scale tirade.

The audible sigh she heard on the other end didn't sound promising. "Kate, honey, I had a feeling you wouldn't be able to just fly across the country and get back here in time for dinner. You know how important dinner is for me."

Hannah had asked Kate to accompany her to the Robert Hafton dinner party that evening. Hafton's dinner parties were notorious. Two parts decadence, one part self-indulgence, and a whole bushel of Hafton ego trip, his dinner parties were one of the hottest tickets in Hollywood. This was the place to be seen. The paparazzi were practically given linen invitations and custom chalked vantage points on the street outside his Bel Air mansion.

And Hannah would be there, no matter what. The press ate up the ample photo opportunities she willingly provided as an out-lesbian. Hannah had always been straightforward in her career advancement plans, and when she and Kate met, the public came with the deal. Certainly Kate had dealt with the press and paparazzi as the head of StormRunner Productions, as well as a stint as the vice president of Epic Studios, the largest producer of action adventure pictures, but the amount of press attention Hannah was currently receiving was staggering.

And Hannah wanted Kate by her side. Hannah was a striking, successful, driven actress, and Kate was a beautiful, successful, driven producer. Linked arm in arm, Kate and Hannah turned heads. That fierce combination, however, would not be walking into the dinner party that night.

"Of course I know how important dinner is to you, Han. If I didn't have to travel, you know I wouldn't have."

"I suppose." But she didn't sound convinced.

Kate tried a different tact. "You know how this production is going, Han. You, of all people, should understand that my schedule is as demanding as yours."

After another inflated sigh, Hannah suddenly blurted out, "Fuck!"

Wearily, Kate fell silent.

Hannah huffed. "This is going to look so bad. Me going alone. Fuck, Kate. Going alone, what does *that* say? Hannah isn't in demand. Hannah is desperate."

"What? That doesn't make any sense, Han."

"It doesn't? And what? Flying off to alligator alley the night of the Hafton party *does* make sense, Kate? Do you know how important it is for me to be seen correctly? This is a shitty time to do this to me."

"I'm very aware of that fact, Hannah. All I can say is that I need to stay." There was only one way to appease Hannah. "This is your movie, Han. These sets and props are in jeopardy, and you know we start shooting in a few weeks. I need to make sure everything's ready for you, and right now, they're not."

There was a pause and then Hannah blew out her breath, which formed the very elongated and exaggerated, "*Fuck.* I suppose I'll tell them that my movie is in jeopardy and you just had to take care of things. For me. I told you to go."

Kate didn't have the energy to contain the weariness in her voice, "Whatever works."

"That's the best I can do, goddamn it."

Kate sighed. "You'll do great tonight, Han. I'll be back tomorrow."

"Tomorrow's the cast and crew screening of Clement's new film."

"Yes." Kate had twenty-four minutes to get a change of clothes.

"Take me to dinner and then to Zephyr Lounge after? *Hollywood Lives* magazine is doing a piece on underground Hollywood clubs and I want to make the issue."

"Should I ask how you found that out?"

"Easy. The ten friggin' percent my agent gets doesn't just go for reservations at Cecil's, which, by the way, we already have for nine thirty."

Kate laughed at the locomotive manner in which Hannah scheduled her life.

Hannah ignored the laugh. "Is that slinky black Vera Wang of yours dry cleaned? You look hot in it. Wear it tomorrow night."

Hannah knew what she wanted and when she wanted it.

CHAPTER SIX

Frank, Kate's producer, had said that most everyone at FDF arrived for work by seven a.m. Not the most pleasant fact, as Kate's body was still convinced that it was the very early California hour of four a.m. She nevertheless pulled the Lincoln Continental into the parking lot just before seven. Since this was her only business while in Florida, there was no use in sitting around the hotel. Plus she knew her early arrival would reinforce the seriousness she had tried to emphasize in making the intended schedule. The receptionist was not at her desk, but Kate surmised that she probably did not arrive until eight or so. Many of the management offices were still dark as well. She made her way out to the shop. The loading doors were wide open to attract whatever cool morning air would come before the onslaught of afternoon humidity. The din of machinery met her as she stepped through the shop's door. Table saws, drills, sanders, and hammers beat out a cadence that flowed smoothly, each shop worker concentrating on their task.

Kate surveyed the shop, looking for the StormRunner pieces. As she scanned the worktables and equipment, she soon spotted Dawn.

Her back was to Kate, and she was sculpting something. Kate stood there a moment and took advantage of her position to watch her. Though Dawn wore the same ankle-high work boots, today she had on a pair of faded denim shorts and a red baseball cap. The baseball cap contained a practical ponytail, which spilled magnificently from the cap. And it was obvious that, despite the attempts of a thin white T-shirt to conceal it, her tanned back was graceful, yet strong. Kate swallowed past a fierce catch in her chest.

Kate had known her share of dynamic women. The studio executives, actresses, and lawyers she interacted with were strong women, forging their careers in a tough industry. But watching Dawn, she sensed that there was much more substance to her than all the power lunches had ever demonstrated. A different kind of attraction coursed through Kate. It was a longing to be around Dawn to share thoughts, philosophies, and ideas together.

❖

The red clay had long ago surrendered its hardened state as a result of hours of manipulation and kneading and was now soft and pliable. And the clay felt great in her hands. Dawn concentrated on the addition and subtraction of just the right amounts of maroon-colored earth as she formed the cheeks and nose bridge of the maiden's head. She'd been engrossed in sculpting since four a.m., having been unable to sleep. Getting up hours before first light, she'd driven to the shop to exorcize the image from her mind's eye and into clay form. She now worked ardently to realize the picture that was in her head, and had been in her head all night as she lay in bed. The brow and forehead were shaped precisely as she'd memorized, and the cheeks and chin were just right. The maiden's hair fell in graceful cascade, framing an elegant face and a gaze both observant and kind.

She concentrated on the last touches of lips that curved slightly up in the corners. She was attempting a mouth that suggested a silent but lucid wisdom and had leaned back to study her work when a voice very close to her ear murmured, "Good morning."

She jolted, yelping "Oh," and turned to see Kate, closer than she could have ever wished for.

"I'm sorry. Did I startle you?" Kate's smile was warm but apologetic.

"Yes. I mean, no…"

They both stared at each other for a few uncomfortable seconds and then Kate laughed. "I believe I'm to blame for that death grip."

Dawn looked down and realized that the lump of clay she'd been holding was now oozing between her fingers. She quickly deposited the mess onto the workbench. "I wasn't expecting you this early." She thought Kate looked exquisite. She wore a pair of black dress slacks and an untucked designer blouse, in a shade of lilac that brought out the blue in her eyes.

Kate stepped closer, regarding the sculpture. "You're working on the Maiden of Salt statue?"

"Yes. I got here before Krissy so I started on this right away. I imagine you don't have much time here before you leave, and I wanted to get as far along with this as I could."

"I appreciate that." She took another step closer.

Dawn's breath caught in her chest, and all she could do was grab a trimming tool and return to the sculpture.

Kate watched Dawn work in silence. For as many years as Dawn had been sculpting, she was suddenly aware of how intimate the process was. She watched her hands skillfully smooth over the rough spots with doting care, as if massaging the muscles of a tired body.

She looked up at Kate wondering if it was obvious to her as well. Kate smiled at her. "You've been working hard."

"I wasn't sure when your plane was leaving."

"At four this afternoon." Kate was watching Dawn's hands intently.

Dawn followed Kate's gaze to her hands and self-consciously lowered them from the sculpture. "I was trying to get some more detail on the face of the Maiden of Salt statue before showing you what it would look like. That way you could see it before it went to mold."

Kate took in the whole sculpture. "It's amazing how much you've gotten done. The details are well rendered."

Dawn nodded. "It goes pretty quickly once you've got a picture of it in your mind."

Kate took another step closer, leaning left and then right.

Dawn grinned as Kate suddenly said, "Is that...me?"

The corner of Dawn's mouth turned up into a smile. "Yes."

"Wow. How did you do that?" She scrutinized the clay sculpture. "We only met yesterday."

What Dawn wanted to tell her was that all she could think of since the day before had been Kate's lovely face, and that all the time she'd been creating the sculpture, it had felt like Kate had been right there with her. Instead she offered up, "You just get a picture in your mind."

"Well, it's amazing, but I think you've been too kind to my likeness." Kate shook her head adding, "You've carved off about ten years and forgiven the crow's feet." This made Dawn laugh full-heartedly and Kate joined in.

As the laughter subsided, Dawn began to form a ball out of the clay that she'd been holding. With fluid hands, the ball rolled into an egg shape and then back to a perfect ball.

Without looking up, Dawn said, "I was thinking about the script."

"*The Glass Cross?*"

Dawn nodded slowly, considering her next words as earnestly as she considered the clay forming in her hands. "I liked how the main character goes from being scared, initially, to brave and self-assured. How she finds the strength of character to keep going."

"Especially when everything is telling her to turn and run," Kate said.

"That's very compelling."

"Sounds like you say that from experience?"

"Yes, I suppose." She looked up from her clay. "There have been some horrific projects I've worked on in the past. Sometimes I go out for the installation phase on some of the work FDF has done. Once in Tallahassee, we had a thirty foot diameter replica of the Earth that we were lowering from a crane onto the roof of a restaurant. The weather forecasted a storm, but that's pretty typical in Florida. What they hadn't predicted were tornadoes."

"Oh, no"

"Oh, yes. We were all up on the roof in the critical thirty minutes between lowering the Earth replica and welding it to its truss system, and the clouds turned black and dove toward the ground faster than you could ever imagine." She took in Kate's fretful expression and continued. "Winds started whipping around us, and we knew there was a tornado close by. The crane operator couldn't just release the Earth replica and get the hell out of there because it would have crushed us. But the Earth was swinging around, and we were certain one of us would get hit or thrown off the roof."

"I can't imagine what that would be like."

"Well, it was either turn and run or stick with it and finish securing the Earth. Plus, the winds were getting stronger by the minute, and the crane might have toppled over from the inertia from the swinging Earth. So we hunkered down and fought like hell to secure and weld it in place. One person got hurt from flying debris, and it took forty long minutes, but we finally got out of there and sought shelter for the rest of the evening across the street in the fire station.

"That took a lot of courage and commitment."

"Not something I want to commit to ever again," Dawn said and laughed when Kate did. She thought she'd be more intimidated by this successful woman. After all, Kate lived in a world that was full of glitz and glamour, not power tools and fiberglass dust. But Kate had been transfixed when Dawn had told her the story. And now, Dawn found it hard to disengage from Kate's gaze, feeling her breath threatening to escape her as she looked into those cerulean blue eyes.

Suddenly Dawn looked back down, pressing the ball of clay in her hands again. The whine of a wood saw and the whirring of a sander filled the gap in their conversation. People shouted clipped words in construction shorthand, and the shop phone rang off in the distance. Dawn formed another shape from the clay. Her hands worked the fist-sized portion of red, damp earth with ease and reverence. She began changing its form in each stroke, a pulling motion, then short strokes of her thumb, and the form turned, and she kneaded and pulled again. As pieces were pulled off one end and added to the other, and as the reddened earth was rubbed and contoured, an angel began to take form. Divine and ethereal, her wings were not at her sides nor stretched out in flight, but half unfurled as if ready to envelop someone in a protective embrace.

Dawn looked up. "Do the salt mines really exist? I mean the way they're described in the script, traveling miles underground?"

"Yes. Most of our table salt comes from Austria." Kate laughed. "Those little granules of salt travel farther than most Americans do in their entire lifetime."

Dawn had busied herself with the clay angel, unable to calm the growing excitement at being so close to Kate. She finally looked back up at her and handed Kate a smaller piece of clay, one she'd pulled off the initial formation of the angel. "Have you been there?"

Kate took the clay. "Twice."

"So Tracy goes to find *The Glass Cross* down there in the mine. The one her aunt wants her to find."

"That is," Kate added, "if those mysterious and sinister strangers that know why she's now in Salzburg don't beat her to it."

Dawn nodded. "And who have, in fact, been waiting for her because she's the only one who could know exactly where it is."

Kate nodded back. "This clay feels strangely therapeutic."

Dawn smiled at her but then retreated to the safety of the angel in creation. Still nervous, she took a deep breath. "I really like the script."

"I'm glad you do. Otherwise it might be a bummer to make all these props for it."

"Oh, I get enough of the kinds of jobs that I'd rather not work on, but we take all comers here."

Kate laughed. "I know what you mean. There are some scripts that I'm sent that I can't even get through."

Dawn finished working on the angel and gently laid it in on the workbench as Kate continued rolling her clay into a half-ball, half-egg shape.

"I really enjoy talking to you," Kate said. Dawn looked up and smiled.

"You must talk to a lot of people in your business."

"I suppose. But most are difficult at best."

"You get those, too?"

Smiling directly at Dawn, Kate nodded. "They're not as genuine as you. I mean, you're really such a fun person to talk to. I hope we can talk more as this movie goes along."

"I'd like that. And you're wonderful to talk to as well." Dawn hesitated before adding, "I suppose I shouldn't say that I've always heard that Hollywood types are full of themselves."

This time, Kate laughed heartily. "Well, you wouldn't be far off the mark. It's a pretty crazy community."

"No offense, I hope."

"None taken. But you're right. There are a lot of stuck up people with a grand sense of entitlement."

"But not you. I don't get that sense at all."

"I'm not sure Kurt feels that way."

Dawn chuckled, "Well, Kurt is also full of himself."

Kate smiled and turned her attention to the Maiden of Salt statue. "I suppose it's a guess as to who will be the first on the film crew to figure out that it's me."

"I can change it if you think it looks too much like you, if that's not acceptable for the film…I mean I know the rendering you sent us is different, but there were some similarities so I just went with it…"

"No, it's great. Now that the body will have the direct fiberglass applied to it, I hope that it will look as good as this sculpt, that it will all look like the one piece. That's what I'm most concerned about."

"Let's take this head over to the body and see how it matches."

"The foam body sculpt is ready?"

"Already done."

"Really? We just agreed to do the mockup of the direct fiberglass body right before I left the shop last night. It's already done?"

Dawn nodded. "I stayed last night to do it. Then came in this morning."

Kate smiled. "You didn't have to do that."

"I knew it was important. And your plane *does* leave today." Dawn smiled back.

"That it does. Shall we take a look?"

When Dawn placed the head on top of the foam sculpt of the body, Kate took about ten steps back and stood there, squinting. "You really captured the look of the maiden's bodice."

"I was trying to imagine where the camera would be and trying to determine whether the two pieces looked like they would match after being fiberglassed." Dawn saw Krissy over Kate's shoulder as she walked across the shop's floor. She started to smile back and almost lost her grip on the maiden's, or Kate's, head.

Kate pointed to the sculpt."You said that you'd be cutting in more detail on the body, after the fiberglass is applied, right?"

Dawn nodded. "Yes, it'll be quite easy, actually."

Kate stepped closer to Dawn. "Well, it looks great, even up close." She stopped next to Dawn's uplifted shoulder and reached up to help her take the clay head down.

When their hands touched, they looked at each other and chuckled, but the token gesture belied the intensity that swept through Dawn. The sudden closeness of their bodies made her throat tighten, and all she could manage to do was focus on getting the statue's head back to its safe resting place on the workbench.

Krissy provided much needed rescue when she suddenly appeared. She had about twenty pieces of matte board in her hands, each exhibiting different colors. These were the paint samples that they'd prepared for the props. The order of business was that the props would be molded, then sanded and, after a base coat of paint was applied, the laborious task of scenic painting would commence.

Because the props were supposed to be of ancient origin, each color swatch showed different patinas and aged finishes. Kate inspected each of them and indicated to Krissy and Dawn that they looked good, but that she would like them sent to Hal Rosen to consider which one would look best under the lighting he was planning.

❖

Kate spent the rest of the morning going over the schedule with Kurt and Brett, Sr. She told them that she'd approved of the new fabrication method and requested progress photos to be e-mailed to her. At close to eleven thirty, Brett, Sr. insisted that he take her out to lunch before she left for the airport. She consented to the gesture, and as Kate pulled out of the shop's parking lot to follow Brett to the restaurant, she caught a glimpse of Dawn and Krissy just outside the shop doors. They were working at a sunny table, sanding down the torches from the salt mine entrance set.

She stopped the car and jumped out. Brett, Sr.'s car lurched to a stop as well. As she made her way toward Dawn and Krissy, the women stopped sanding and pulled down their masks.

"I didn't get a chance to say good-bye." Kate trotted up to a stop.

"We wondered where you ran off to." Krissy squinted into the sun, smiling cheerfully.

"Well, I can tell you that being in the shop is much more fun than the front offices."

"I'll second that," Krissy grinned.

"You're off to the airport?" Dawn asked.

Kate nodded. "Yes. But I didn't want to leave without thanking you for your hard work. You and your team have really made this trip a success."

Dawn smiled. "It's our job."

"It's your talent, too," Kate added.

"I liked our talk."

"More soon?"

"Yes. Absolutely."

A silent but connected moment passed between them.

"Well," Kate said, "I'd better go."

Dawn took Kate's extended hand. "It was nice meeting you."

"It was certainly nice meeting you, Dawn." Reluctantly, she eased out of Dawn's grasp and reached out to take Krissy's hand. "Krissy, thank you for the paint samples."

"Will we see you again?" Krissy called out as Kate turned to leave.

"Yes. You will," Kate answered, and Krissy turned to look at Dawn.

Kate got behind the wheel of her rental car and started the engine. With four weeks until the start of principal photography, Kate knew she needed to concentrate on the film's production in Los Angeles. There were still deals to negotiate, a budget that was still slightly over the Studio's authorization, some product placement deals to be made, a press campaign strategy to mount, and a litany of other issues that demanded her attention. But all of that seemed oddly insignificant as she brought her hands up to her face to take in the thick and earthy fragrance that the damp clay had conferred upon her hands.

As they watched Kate drive off, Krissy placed her hand on Dawn's shoulder. "What a creature, that woman."

"Yes, she is," Dawn replied, a weighty pit settling in her stomach.

"She'll be back, you know."

"Of course she'll be back. The movie is shooting in a few weeks, and she's the executive producer."

"She'll be back for you, my friend."

Dawn stood there looking out toward the now empty road down which Kate had just departed, long after Krissy lovingly patted her on the shoulder and had walked away. And even for a few minutes longer than that.

CHAPTER SEVEN

Dawn got home just after seven o'clock and lay down on her bed. Staring at the ceiling, she ran the day through her mind. Spending time with Kate had been fantastic. More than anything, she had wanted to work at double speed because she knew it was important to Kate. Working toward a challenging deadline made her feel enlivened. Dawn had a burst of energy and had gotten a lot of work done that evening. It had been easy, though tiring, but working that hard, for Kate, compelled her even more. Dawn thought about the first time they'd touched, when Kate took her hand to shake it when they first met. The image, however, kept changing backgrounds. Dawn pictured Kate taking her hand as they hiked up a mountain. She pictured Kate taking her hand as they went to dance on the dance floor at Faces. Then she pictured Kate taking her hand as they walked into their new home together.

She rubbed the tiredness from her face and got up to change. She was glad she'd remembered to wash her softball clothes the day before since she'd worked so late. The game was at eight, and she looked forward to it. She knew as soon as she warmed up and jogged the bases once or twice, she'd feel less exhausted.

She wondered if Kate would ever want to come watch her play ball. She'd love the opportunity to spend more time with her after the game, going out for pizza and beer.

But who am I fooling? Dawn grabbed the bag and went back inside the house. *What would a famous producer care about a hick Florida softball game? She was used to glitzy Hollywood parties and hanging out with celebrities.*

Dawn's blue collar work and mundane living only proved that they lived in different worlds.

Kate's a princess visiting the village, and I will never rise to royalty.

CHAPTER EIGHT

The Zephyr Lounge was a kaleidoscope of motion, lights, and sound. As one of a handful of exclusive underground clubs, the Zephyr Lounge was housed in a long ago closed down shoe store. It was hidden behind a very decrepit storefront in the seedy part of Hollywood. From the street, the building had not changed much from the days, some forty years back, when women would take their atomic age children into Sal's Family Shoes and outfit the whole brood with Buster Browns. The gold lettered shoe sign was still readable on the plate glass window. However, there were plywood boards just behind the glass making a burglary attempt by method of a thrown rock or brick fairly futile. In the true LA underground vocabulary, the exterior held no indication of what lay on the other side of the plywood boards. There were no signs, no shiny doorknobs, and no valet parking attendants, and it looked no different from the rest of the dilapidated and forgotten storefronts that lined this forsaken old street of an era gone by. The crumbling sidewalks and litter strewn doorways caused the passerby scarcely a second look. And that was exactly the intent of the underground promoters.

The old shoe store, with the window glass grayed with age and the weather-worn door, hid a remarkable secret as desirable as the home addresses of movie stars. For what lay beyond Sal's Family Shoes was a magnificently designed restaurant and bar, decorated in the style of the fashionable and prosperous forties with rich, dark carpet, elegant mahogany woodwork, and tuck-and-roll leather booths. The Zephyr Lounge did no advertising, had no telephone number, and no outside sign. And it was packed to the rafters every night.

The lounge was divided into two bars and restaurant seating areas. The front room was for non-celebrities. The back room was reserved exclusively for the Hollywood crème de la crème. In the back room, agents entertained actors, producers closed deals, and studio executives pumped screenwriters for the next big idea. Whatever your mission, you could only do it in the back room if you were part of the in-set.

Earlier that evening, after the screening of Jacque Clement's film, Kate and Hannah had dinner at Cecil's, a sixty-year-old Hollywood landmark restaurant. Hannah's agent had gotten her the coveted reservation, and she and Kate dined at one of the more desirable tables. The paparazzi had photographed them going in and were still there when they left.

More paparazzi were present when they arrived, just after eleven p.m., at the Zephyr Lounge. Uncharacteristically, Hannah had rushed by them, denying them any good photo opportunities, but Kate realized as they got through the door that the only photographer that really mattered was the one that would be inside the Zephyr Lounge, the one from *Hollywood Lives* magazine.

Once inside, Kate was finally beginning to relax. It seemed unlikely, in this hectic underground club amid a large, tight crowd of industry people, most of whom she knew, that she could actually unwind. Maybe it was the surreal feeling that the club provided. Maybe being smashed together in the middle of a mass of actors and studio people helped her feel just a little less exposed. In the lion-plagued Serengeti, a gazelle in the middle of a pack of gazelles is able to feel just a little more protected than the ones exposed at the outer edges.

Through the smash of people, Kate glimpsed the fluidity with which the cocktail waitpersons maneuvered around with the same polished coolness the bartenders had. The Zephyr Lounge was one of *the* places to be seen in the birthplace of the Oscar.

Kate had been dating Hannah for a little over ten months and had accompanied her on her recent rocket ride toward fame. With the release of her second feature film, Hannah had become a household name, and the media attention was only starting. Add to that the buzz from the movie she was soon to wrap, and reality, as she had known it, was definitely changing.

Overall, Kate couldn't say that she necessarily liked life according to Hannah. But it was understandably part of the package: specifically Hannah's demanding schedule, Hannah's popularity, Hannah's star-demands, and Hannah's attitude, which seemed to expand in haughty leaps and bounds. And of all the star aspects, the attitude was the most problematic.

Kate thought about Dawn and the life she had made for herself in Florida. In comparison, Dawn's world was so much more exciting. Just being around her had felt so real. Dawn was an excellent artist but didn't brag about it. She was lovely without trying hard. For a moment, a pang of sadness thumped in Kate's chest. She looked over at Hannah, who was on her cell phone to her agent demanding a limo pickup to an interview that weekend.

Kate wouldn't have cared about a limo. And Dawn wouldn't have cared about one either.

She stopped suddenly and studied Hannah and herself. Like a scene from a movie, their life came instantly into focus. Hannah had picked Kate up in her stealthy silver Mercedes SL55 AMG. Priced at $135,000, it was a supercharged two seat ride of sumptuousness. Hannah was wearing a beautiful vintage ivory Valentino dress. It was very sophisticated with elegant beads that sparkled around a rather low neckline, which seemed to effortlessly trap the diamond pendant that hung teasingly close to the top of her exposed cleavage. Her Prada high heels matched perfectly, as did her Prada bag, which had been casually tossed on the floor of the SL55. Diamond pendant earrings sparkled ferociously.

Kate was dressed in the "slinky black Vera Wang" that Hannah had asked her to wear that night. And while Kate wasn't used to anyone telling her what to wear, the Vera Wang dress was one of her favorites, so she had let it pass. Her satin charcoal-colored Jimmy Choo high heeled pumps were her most comfortable evening shoes, and she wore the black pearl necklace she'd been given as a thank you from World Film Studios when she signed her development and production contract four years before. The charcoal color of her necklace matched her shoes, and both complemented the black dress. She grabbed her small Donna Karan clutch which held not much more than her money, ID, one credit card, lipstick, and her keys.

The screening of Clement's film had been a blur. They'd arrived late, not because of Kate—certainly her plane from Orlando had landed in quite enough time—but because Hannah had chosen to arrive late. Making an appropriate appearance was alive and well-done in Hollywood. So they'd almost missed the start of the film, which was just as well because by the time they reached the Director's Guild for the screening, they were embroiled in quite a quarrel.

In the last few minutes before arriving at the Director's Guild, Hannah had told Kate that she would need two motor homes for their upcoming film production. Kate was not in the habit of granting that request to an actor, especially when the request was stated in the form of a notification rather than a question. Quite frankly, she couldn't even remember ever getting that specific request. Normally, every lead actor got a motor home when filming required a production company to shoot on location or at a soundstage that did not have adequate facilities. It was a standard part of their contract. The lead talent also got the best rooms at the best hotels while away from Hollywood, but during the day the motor home would serve as their lair of creature comfort. It provided a comfortable place for each actor to change, relax, go over lines, do business, and for the more antisocial or conceited of Hollywood's talent, take their meals away from the crew. The motor homes that Kate used were the best and largest available, with amenities that rivaled any posh hotel suite. One was enough, and Kate told Hannah so.

Hannah shot her a fuming glare. "I really want *two*."

"Hannah, no one gets two motor homes. There's no reason for it."

"I'm not going to have the makeup and hair people in the same motor home as the one I'm trying to relax and dress in. I need my privacy."

Kate sighed. "Hannah, you know damn well that your makeup and hair will be done in the makeup and hair trailer with everyone else."

"Not with Kiley Warner."

"Kiley Warner?" Kate asked, "Why not with Kiley Warner?"

"She's an unholy bitch, and I can't stand her. I can't believe you cast her."

This was the first Kate had heard of this. "You'll have to fill me in, Han."

"Kiley Warner is a snake. She will fuck you twice. The first time will be in bed and the second time will be behind your back."

Kate tried to stifle a laugh, but it snuck out anyway. "You've just described about half of Hollywood."

Hannah's tone grew angrier. "Kiley has already told a lot of people that I was everyone's last choice for the film. She also said that she would be the one getting the rave reviews on *The Glass Cross*."

"Since when do you care about what she says?"

"Since she fucking knows most of the directors in town, Kate, Jesus, don't you read the goddamn trade rags?"

"Hannah, I wouldn't worry about Kiley. She has a minor role, and you've got the lead."

"I want two motor homes, Kate. Two motor homes will make a statement. It's not just Kiley, I think I deserve it."

"No second motor home, Han."

Hannah was just reaching a red light at the intersection of Sunset Boulevard and Doheny and screamed, "Fuck!" as she slammed on the brakes, skidding to an abrupt halt that threw Kate violently forward.

"Hannah, shit. What the hell are you doing?"

"With *you*? I wonder," she spat.

Kate fumed. "What's that supposed to mean?"

Hannah shook her head, snorting through her nose. "Your big fucking production company and your big fucking budgets…" She was seething. "…what a controlling bitch you are."

It was Kate's turn to flare, "You'd better watch yourself, Hannah."

"Or what? You'll fire me off the picture?" Hannah was livid, bordering on going out of control. "Impossible. My contract's iron clad. You should know, you signed it."

Her contract was far from being iron clad, but Kate was not going to even broach that subject. She took a breath and kept her voice as even as possible. "What the hell are you doing?"

"The question is, what the hell are you doing? You leave me to go by myself to Halfton's last night, and I was the only one standing there looking like a goddamn lonely asshole because I didn't have a frickin' date."

"That's what this is all about?"

"You made me look like a freak." Hannah was now screaming at her. The light turned green, and Hannah roared through the intersection, barreling down Sunset Boulevard. She swerved to avoid a car that was pulling out of a parking space and laid on the horn, still screaming at Kate. "I can't believe I'm gonna be working for you. I'm the one who gets all the press, Kate. I'm the one people will be paying to see, not you. Do you think that all the poor schmucks in Pocatello, Idaho, know who the fuck you are?"

Kate finally blew. "That's enough. You're acting like a five-year-old. And slow the goddamn car down."

Hannah slowed the car, slightly. Neither spoke another word until they arrived at the Director's Guild.

Just before the two valet attendants opened Hannah's and Kate's car doors, Hannah leaned over and kissed Kate. The kiss was short but intense. Kate broke the kiss abruptly. Hannah leaned close to Kate's ear, "I'm sorry, baby. I'm under a lot of stress. I'm really sorry."

Kate was seething.

They got out of the car and Hannah stopped her again before the doorman opened the door for them.

Amid the paparazzi calling out Hannah's name, she said into Kate's ear, "I really need to get better at handling my stress. I'm really, really sorry, babe."

Kate replied with a weary, "Okay."

Hannah smoothed out the side of Kate's black dress. "Kate, you're certainly pretty, but when you dress up like this, you go from pretty to gorgeous." Hannah leaned closer adding, "And gorgeous photographs better."

❖

Kate had grown less furious with Hannah after they'd navigated their way through the paparazzi's flashing strobes, all the way in to the theater, and after she had had a chance to calm down in the lobby before the screening. Kate had seen some old industry friends, and Hannah had respectfully stayed with her rather than strike off on her own, as she usually did, to find someone who would venerate her. Hannah had been on her best behavior, holding Kate's hand or gently placing her palm on the small of Kate's back. When they entered the theater and took their seats toward the back of the theater, Kate had decided to try to enjoy the rest of the night.

During the film, Hannah remained attentive to Kate. She had reached over a few times to stroke her hair and had held her hand, squeezing it a few times, smiling warmly at her. About an hour into the screening, Hannah had leaned over during a particularly dramatic moment involving a murder sequence to murmur that she was bored and horny.

The rest of the film was lost on Kate because Hannah had managed to worm her hand up Kate's dress, and it was all Kate could do to stay still. When Hannah's hand found the part in Kate's legs, Kate had only half a mind to refuse the advance. Granted, she didn't want to share any of their intimacy with thirty or forty of their closest theater neighbors, but she had to admit that it had been erotic. As Hannah's hand massaged her, Kate, who was quite constrained to her seat and certainly wary that any strange movement from her would make their tryst quite obvious, was compelled to remain as still as possible. The slow advance of Hannah's hand made it easy to take her time to decide whether she'd let Hannah continue. But the motionlessness that was manageable at first, proved to be quite challenging. Hannah's hand, which was more than incredibly practiced, competently encouraged her on, and Kate was soon scarcely able to remain still. She grew increasingly wet and a flush raced across her cheeks and ears. She focused on her breathing as it was the one thing she could control, given that the rest of her body had already succumbed to Hannah's efforts. But that smooth and even breathing soon betrayed her as well, as she began to gulp back ragged and heavy breaths. She refused to glance over at Hannah because her peripheral vision could already discern the colossal smile plastered on her face. Kate knew that she only had a minute or less to either remove Hannah's hand as inconspicuously as possible, or just let it happen.

So she just let it happen. And at once, the explosive feeling inside her, forced inward rather than outward, was like an incendiary device detonating white hot surges with nowhere to go. She felt a blistering heat in her ears and legs and arms as she came in Hannah's hand, a furious throbbing whose forced containment had gone disrespectfully against nature. The body was not physically designed to be completely still during an orgasm.

She bit her lips to keep from screaming out, clutching the seat to hold herself down, and squeezed her eyes closed to keep them from popping out of her head.

It had felt wickedly fantastic.

As they ordered aperitifs at the post-film party at the Zephyr lounge, Kate caught Hannah staring at her with a rather roguish grin.

"What?" Kate asked.

"I can't get that picture out of my mind." Hannah said.

"Which are you referring to? The one that was up on the screen or the one in our seats?"

"There was a screen?" And then she was interrupted by another

A-list actor. They exchanged air kisses and chatted for a moment while Kate flagged down a passing cocktail waitress.

The craziness of the evening, starting with the fight and ending with the sexual tryst in the darkened seats of the theater, had rendered Kate quite exasperated. The argument about the motor home was not yet over, and Kate knew they would butt heads about it again. Hannah would not win that argument, but for now, it was easier for Kate to stave off another tantrum for as long as possible. Hannah made her so mad at times, but she had to admit, she was certainly passionate and driven.

Kate was a jumble of emotions. With as much anger as she felt toward Hannah over the argument, she had strangely felt as much attraction for her when she'd come in her hand.

"Kate? You know Chad Montgomery…" Hannah turned to her.

Kate had cast Chad in a film she produced a year before and liked him very well. He was charming and polite and always arrived to the set on time and with lines memorized. Chad reached over and kissed Kate's cheek affectionately.

"Of course. Chad, it's good to see you." Kate smiled when Chad withdrew from his genteel greeting. Kate also caught the slight puzzlement that quickly washed over Hannah's face, obviously deciphering the difference between the detached air kiss she had received versus the loving peck that Chad had given Kate. Hannah stared at Kate for a moment.

"We met last year on *Meeting You Twice*."

"Oh, yes," Hannah jumped in, "the film you did with Kate."

"Yes." Chad smiled warmly then grinned at Kate. "The very one I'm anxious about because of its delayed release date."

"Believe me, Chad," Kate said, "it wouldn't be prudent to go up against the release of Brad Kramer's film this Christmas. A spring release next year will be much smarter. Plus, we needed those reshoots."

"I'm glad we got the reshoots done." Chad smiled at both Kate and Hannah. "And I know the film needed it. It's just always hard waiting for a release when you know you've been a part of a great project. Isn't that right, Kate?"

"True. And remember, Christmas was going to be a challenge for us. Globe Studios has already committed most of their Christmas release budget toward pushing their film."

Hannah nodded. "Their Santa and the North Pole extravaganza is going to pull a huge theater audience."

Kate knew that her studio would still be in the running. World Film was going up against Globe Studios with another film that they had in their stable.

"World Film is going to release Screaming Eagle Production's action adventure against Globe's film." She placed a hand on Chad's shoulder and squeezed. "Let them battle it out this Christmas. We'll take Spring Break, okay?"

Chad's voice almost bubbled. "Okay. But it's just such a good film."

"Don't fret, Chad," Kate added, "*Meeting You Twice* will release before you know it. But now you'll have the added benefit of not having to miss Christmas to go on the press junket."

"That's the truth," Chad laughed in relief. He was a pleasant man, one of those Hollywood dream actors who were not only great to work with, but didn't demand ridiculous perks and who always endeavored to please their cast and crew.

Chad turned to Hannah. "Kate's a great producer, Hannah. You're gonna love working with her."

Kate got pulled away from Hannah and Chad by a World Film executive. The severely uptight female executive, sporting a hair-sprayed bob, wanted to introduce Kate to "the next fifty million dollar box office" though Kate wondered oddly what had happened to the current Orlando Bloom. When she returned, Chad had left and Hannah quickly wrapped her arms around Kate.

"Chad invited us to his place in Beverly Hills for a swanky party," said Hannah as she leaned slightly into Kate, "so we'll head over there."

Kate sighed inwardly. One more activity on the already full agenda. "Han, let's just go back to my place or yours and relax."

"Relax? This is *important.* I need to be out there, being seen."

Kate had heard that line a thousand times. "Missing one more party won't kill you."

"I know it seems like all play to you. Going to social functions to network is part of my job, Kate."

For most of the time that they'd been together, it had seemed to Kate that they were less a dating couple and more an occupational couple. Most nights were arranged around an industry function.

Their romance had been short-lived. Certainly, their trip to New York had seemed the only time they'd spent really getting to know each other as they talked and shared their pasts. A romance had flared that trip, but when they had gotten back to Hollywood, the call of business was upon them.

Now Hannah and Kate rushed from function to function: galas, openings, parties, and screenings, with scarcely a free night. And the only nights Kate could remember not going to Hollywood functions with Hannah were the nights Hannah was on a film shoot that required exterior night shots. Indeed, Kate had her own functions to go to, many of them being the same functions as Hannah's. Notably though, prior to their meeting, Kate would attend the obligatory screening, dinner meeting, or charitable event, but forgo most of the parties and cocktail lounges. By then most of the business had been tended to. Networking had occurred, ideas had been generated, alliances forged, and deals had been struck. The parties and cocktail lounges served mainly in the celebration of purchased scripts and cemented movie deals—the ultimate forty million dollar nightcap whose drunken exploits managed to become grist for the rumor mill the next day.

Kate would often skip the after hours revelry, get home by the more normal hour of midnight, and send champagne the next day. And besides, Kate knew that many actors and producers avoided the night owl scene and their phones still rang. But there would be no convincing Hannah of that.

With the new dating schedule set in place after her trip to New York with Hannah, Kate would spend each day at the office from seven until six and then head straight to Hannah's nightly events. She saw either Hannah's or her own pillow each night from approximately two a.m. to six a.m.

She felt utterly and wholly exhausted. And lonely.

Hannah broke into her thoughts with a seductive squeeze to her rear. "I've got Chad's address. Let's get the valet to get the car."

CHAPTER NINE

K ate and Frank were in the middle of one of their last preproduction meetings before relocating to Orlando. There with them were Amy Parsons, the director; Nathan Firth, the line producer; Sandra Batnow, the director of photography; Jamie Riggs, the production manager; Riley Campbell, the stunt coordinator; and Charlie Gunner, the location manager.

If Kate were the captain of the ship, Frank and Nathan were the first and second officers. They ran most of the meeting just as they ran most of the day-to-day activities around the movie production.

Kate remained involved in all production aspects, advising more than executing. But if something went awry, it was Kate who pulled out the big guns and made the requisite phone call or personal visit. When an overbearing studio executive or a smug actor stepped on too many of the production crew's toes, Kate would handle the call personally, usually snuffing out the problem by the end of the call.

Frank would remain in LA to keep them in touch with the home office while they were away on location.

Nathan Firth was not a full time member of the StormRunner Productions staff, but had worked on the last two movies with Kate and Frank. Nathan would supervise the physical aspects of the making of a motion picture, like scheduling the order in which the film would be shot and negotiating deals with subcontractors.

They'd gotten to the part of the production meeting where Frank asked Amy how the rehearsals were going.

"Well," the director said, "everyone seems to be getting along. Peter is working well with Hannah. The chemistry is great. They looked enchanting on the film test we ran."

Peter Carson was cast as the male lead to Hannah Corrant's female lead. He would play the blind Englishman that Tracey, Hannah's character, would befriend in Austria and who would come to her aid

LISA GIROLAMI

in the film. He was absolutely dazzling, the kind of handsome that a seasoned makeup artist could roughen up into a perfect blend of eye-catching good looks.

"And Hannah. Is she behaving herself?" Frank had glanced at Kate when he'd spoken, but it was done so imperceptibly that only Kate caught it.

"She did ask me for a second motor home," Amy said.

"No second motor home." Kate said and then turned her attention to Jaime. "Is everything ready in Orlando?"

"Everything's ready," Jamie said, "with the exception of the hiring of a few of the local crew members and finalizing the hotel deal. We have the rooms, but since we've booked more than 2,000 room-nights with the eighty-four cast and crew members we're flying from LA for the three week shoot in Orlando, I'm now negotiating a much better rate."

"That's a good thing," Frank acknowledged, "and did they get us adjoining floors?"

"Yes. And we've secured the rooms and suites."

Frank moved on to the schedule. "We're on a Monday through Sunday shooting schedule for three weeks in Orlando. Then a skeleton crew and the actors will travel to Salzburg, Austria, for one week. Kate and Nathan will be flying out early. Actually, they'll be leaving the day after we wrap the shoot in Orlando, to get things in place for the crew's arrival. So after a week of shooting in Salzburg, we pick up the crew again for the exterior scenes in Los Angeles for two quick days back here."

He looked around the room. Everyone was studying the schedule they had in front of them and were nodding their heads.

"I'm a little nervous about going to Orlando to shoot on soundstages first," Sandra Batnow, the director of photography, said to the group. "Shooting most of our cover sets at the beginning of the schedule is nerve wracking."

"You mean the salt mine interiors," Jamie said.

"Yes, that's exactly what I mean. And since they're called cover sets because they're scenes that can be moved up in the schedule in the event that it rains on the days we're trying to shoot any of our exterior sets, that doesn't give us any margin for error with the rest of the schedule. There's so much that can go wrong outside the studio gates. Our last two days in LA should be okay, but the week in Austria might be pretty unpredictable as well."

Kate agreed, "It's not ideal. All of us would have rather saved the salt mine sets in Orlando as cover sets. That way we'd have somewhere to shoot and not lose time and money having the crew wait around. But two things forced this shooting order: the deal we struck with the studio in Orlando to shoot in the beginning of January, plus the unavailability of some of the exterior sets in LA until the end of our schedule. I can't tell you how much I wish we could save the interior salt mine scenes in Orlando for our cover sets."

"Kate and I talked about the exterior scenes in LA," Amy said. "Since we'll need to establish the main character's residence as being in LA, we'll get those shots however we need. What I mean is, if it's raining on one or more of the days that we're shooting in LA, we can write some dialogue into the scene to make it all make sense, because getting some LA icons established in those shots, the Capitol Records Building, the Hollywood sign, can happen whether it's raining or not."

Frank chuckled as he said, "As long as there isn't an earthquake with a magnitude greater than 6.0 and rioting doesn't break out again, I think we'll be okay."

"I can shoot around crumbled freeway overpasses and rioting, no problem." Sandy deadpanned.

"And even though most of our cover sets are in Orlando at the beginning of the schedule," Jaime Riggs said, "the interior of Tracy's house, as well as her office, can serve as cover sets. I mean, truly, counting all the mine scenes, virtually seventy-five percent of this film are interior scenes."

"Austria will be another story, however," Nathan added. "I'm glad the parts of the script that take place in the Austrian salt mine scenes are going to be shot on soundstages in Orlando. There are still many major exterior scenes that need to be shot in Austria. The exterior establishing shots of the actual Austrian salt mine, and the Salzburg restaurant, hotel, and streets."

"That's our most challenging part of the schedule, all right." Kate said, "But again, if we expect rain, we can be ready for it and shoot with it."

Amy nodded. "We chose Salzburg for two reasons. First, I think the charm of the city is unparalleled. You'll see that it's situated on both banks of the Salzach River and framed by two steep hills, the Kapuzinerberg on the left bank of the river and the Mönchsberg on the right." She smiled widely. "It's perfect. And it's in close proximity to the Bad Dürrnberg Salt Mine in the nearby town of Hallein. That's the actual salt mine that was the inspiration for the script."

Kate turned to Nathan. "Have you finalized the travel list for Austria?"

Nathan counted on his fingers. "Our two lead actors, Peter Carson, Hannah Corrant." Nathan nodded around the room indicating those present who were on the list and continued, "Amy, of course, and Jean, Jamie, and Sandra. I'm checking with the Director's Guild, but I think we're only going to need to travel Jennifer Billington, the first assistant director, and Kyle Penny, the second AD. Then, let's see, Toochee, who has agreed to handle both hair and makeup, and you and me."

"We've written Ralph Markowitz out of the exterior scenes for now, so he won't be traveling to Austria," Kate said to the group. "There is a problem with the completion bond and we're going to avoid any further complications until we can get it cleared up."

"Ralph? A problem? It's got to be a health problem," Jennifer guessed. "Those are usually the only problems that crop up with a completion bond."

"That's correct." Kate said, "They say there might be a heart problem."

"Heart? He's younger than I am," Toochee exclaimed.

"That's why we're going to try to get this cleared up quickly. In the meantime, he's not traveling to Austria, and we need to keep tight-lipped about it. We don't want any bad publicity."

"We'll keep tight-lipped, Kate," Nathan assured her. "And we'll also keep tight-lipped about the extremely expensive shipment of Long Beach baseball caps that are being sent to Orlando for the location shoot." Nathan reached over and tickled her ribs as the rest had a laugh.

"Ah, hah, very funny," Kate said. She was famous for wearing baseball caps on film sets. They came in many colors and varieties, but each one was emblazoned with her home town, Long Beach, California, on them. She always found it easier to pull her hair back into a pony-tail and pull it through a cap for the long and tedious film shoots. On location, the Prada outfits and the Jimmy Choo shoes would get put away, and the baseball caps would travel when film mode was deployed.

"Just make sure they get there unscathed," she said. "The cameras can fall off the trucks, but lose one of my caps, and I'm shutting the production down."

Frank called out, "Jamie, make sure you name the baseball caps as additional insured on the insurance policy, will you?"

As everyone laughed, Jamie pretended to write it down.

They spent another two hours going over the day-by-day details of the shooting schedule, and then Kate ended the meeting at three that afternoon.

She had just enough time to get home, shower, and dress for a date with Hannah. They would be attending the *Hollywood Film and Television Fashion Awards Show* which was to go live at five p.m. in Hollywood for an eight p.m. airing in the eastern time zone. Hannah had been nominated for an award and had asked Kate to be ready for their limo to pick her up at four p.m.

CHAPTER TEN

Dawn and Krissy had ordered their first beer of the evening at Faces. It was just after eight thirty p.m. and the bar was fairly crowded for a Monday night. They'd appropriated two stools in the middle of the bar and chatted amiably with Sandy, the bartender. It wasn't until Dawn took a good look around the bar that she realized it looked different. The big screen TV, which usually broadcast only sports or music videos, was decorated with balloons and streamers, and some glitzy show was on. Hanging from the ceiling just above the TV was a banner that read Fashion Victims Celebrate! Along with the two couches that were always there were ten rows of folding chairs full of women in front of the TV.

"What's going on tonight?" Dawn asked Sandy.

"The Hollywood Film and TV Fashion Awards Show started a half an hour ago."

"Since when does the best lesbian bar in Orlando care about a fashion awards show?" Dawn said.

"Since all the Hollywood babes are prancing around in sexy outfits. They're showing the best fashions in this year's films and TV shows. I'm imagining that the actresses will get more airtime than the actors."

Krissy whooped. "That's my kinda show."

Dawn laughed. "Slow sports night, huh, Sandy?"

"Yup, but look at the crowd we're getting."

Dawn had to admit that the bar was unusually packed, and most of them were gathering around the TV.

"We have two-for-one Cosmopolitans tonight since it's a Hollywood cool drink," Sandy said. "Want one?"

Holding up her bottle, Dawn said, "No, thank you. Beer's just fine."

Just then a voice came from behind Dawn, "Can I buy you another, then?"

She turned to see Bridget, a woman she'd met over the summer while running in an AIDS benefit 10K race. A grinning Krissy nudged Dawn, who ignored the bump.

"Bridget. It's good to see you." Dawn offered her the empty barstool next to her.

Bridget took the seat. "Good to see you, as well."

"I don't think I've seen you since the 10K run. What have you been up to?"

"I was working in Miami for about four months."

"You're in building construction," Dawn offered. "Construction estimating, correct?"

"That's correct," Bridget said. "Good memory."

Dawn held up her bottle. "It's the hops. Good for the brain."

"I see." Bridget chuckled. "I'm glad I ran into you tonight."

Krissy nudged Dawn again, peering around her to smile at Bridget. "And I'm Krissy, Dawn's best friend, and my job, as best friend of course, is to make sure my friend here gets the beer you just offered her."

"Krissy," Dawn admonished.

Bridget laughed. "She's right, I did offer you a beer." She turned to Sandy. "May I please have another round of Amstels for Dawn and Krissy?"

Dawn held her hand up. "Krissy displayed bad first-meeting manners and doesn't deserve a beer."

"Hey," Krissy exclaimed, "I'm just hurrying things along."

Bridget laughed, telling Sandy, "And I'll take an Amstel, as well." She turned to Krissy reaching out a hand. "I'm Bridget. It's very nice to meet you."

Bridget bought the round of drinks and they chatted amid the growing clamor of women who were gathered around the TV.

Krissy got off the barstool. "Come on, y'all. Let's go watch the babes."

"Go ahead," Dawn called after her. "But we need to leave in a few, remember? We've got to go back to the shop."

Krissy waved her acknowledgment and joined the rest of the women in front of the TV.

"You're going back to work?" Bridget asked when Dawn turned back to her.

Dawn nodded. "We have a pretty big contract that we're behind schedule on."

"Let me see if my memory is as good as yours." Bridget deliberated briefly and then said, "It has to do with construction as well...but it's more creative, right?"

"Yes. Florida Design and Fabrication."

"Themed restaurants and amusement parks."

"Right again."

"So are you currently working on a restaurant this time or an amusement park?"

"Neither, actually. I'm in the middle of building sets and props for a motion picture."

"Is it going to be shot here in Orlando?" Bridget asked.

Dawn nodded. "Starting in January."

"That sounds exciting."

"It is, I suppose." Dawn's thoughts of Kate began to get in the way. Every time Kate would look at her, she'd feel caressed, causing an intense spark that would ignite in her chest and flush her skin. Kate absolutely took her breath away. And there wasn't a goddamned thing she could do about it.

Furthermore, here was an available woman, right in front of her, but all she really wanted was for the very unavailable Kate to be there instead.

"I just love movie stars," Bridget gushed. Dawn only nodded as Bridget continued, "I came to watch the show, but then I noticed you over here."

"From all the commotion over there, it sounds like it's a good show," Dawn said, suddenly feeling exhausted.

Bridget finished her beer. "Can I buy you one more?"

Dawn smiled warmly. "No, thank you. Another beer would put me to sleep."

"So, you're actually going to miss the Hollywood Fashion Awards." Bridget mocked disappointment.

"As much as I hate to admit it, yes," Dawn said. "I'd really better get going."

Bridget pursed her lips in a half-smile, genuine disappointment forming.

Admittedly, it felt good to have a cute woman paying attention to her. But she couldn't feel even a little excited about Bridget. It was as if Kate had gotten under her skin. And the one woman she'd gladly run after was not available.

But Dawn had been incapable of changing that fact. *Geez, shouldn't only available women have this effect on me? It's so unfair.* Kate had been relentlessly on her mind, filling her days with images of their time together in the shop and haunting her nights with a troublesome longing.

And even if she were available, she couldn't be interested in me. Not for a serious relationship, anyway. Don't go letting yourself get all wrapped up in this one, Brock. She'll go back to her life in Hollywood, and you'll be the only one who remembered these past weeks. Dawn got off the barstool and placed a hand on Bridget's arm. "Come on, I'll escort you over to the festivities around the TV and then fetch Krissy."

Krissy offered her seat to Bridget and she and Dawn started to say their good-byes. The show came back from a commercial break. Suddenly, the bar patrons hooped and hollered as the category for Sexiest Dress in a Motion Picture was being announced.

The roar of the Faces bar crowd crescendoed and the place went nuts.

Dawn tugged on Krissy's arm. "Come on, let's go. We gotta get back to work."

CHAPTER ELEVEN

A nd the nominees in the category for Sexiest Dress in a Motion Picture…Hannah Corrant, for her role as Celeste in *Roll By*."

As the audience applauded the nomination, Hannah leaned over and snuggled excitedly against Kate.

The Kodak Theater in Hollywood was standing room only, and the audience applauded loudly as the on-stage presenter read from her TelePrompTer, "Hannah's role as Celeste, the murderous seductress, posed a challenge for her…"

The film clip began to play showing Hannah in an extremely sexy mid-thigh dress, gliding elegantly down the hall of a hospital corridor. The narration began with the announcer's voice describing the scene, "Hannah's character, Celeste, exudes an air of sophistication and trustworthiness, all the while plotting the murder of her sick husband. She is on the way to her husband's hospital room with a pistol hidden in her bra, which was difficult to conceal given the extremely sleek and plunging lines of the Stella McCartney dress."

The announcer continued as Hannah's film clip faded to black and a live audience shot of Hannah sitting with Kate appeared on the theater's screen. "Hannah Corrant in *Roll By*."

The audience again applauded, and as the last clip began to play, the presenter announced the last nominee of the four in the category.

Hannah turned to Kate. "Do you think the other nominees' film clips look good?"

Kate could side-step quicksand when she had to. "Yours was incredible, Hannah."

As the last film clip ended and the male voice said, "Maggie Stollweather in *Bring Me Three Pieces*." Hannah applauded along with Kate. The four nominees were now on a split screen and the presenter was opening the envelope.

At that moment, both knew that they were on camera, and while Kate concentrated on managing the natural nervousness she was feeling, Hannah worked the lens.

In the brief pause before the announcement, Hannah grabbed Kate's hand and squashed it in her own.

"And the Hollywood Film and Television Fashion Award for Sexiest Dress in a Motion Picture goes to…" The presenter paused for effect, which only caused Kate's left hand further pain.

All Kate heard next was, "Hannah Corrant, for…" because suddenly Hannah grabbed Kate's neck and pulled her into a very on-screen and nationally televised kiss. The audience cheered, and in a flash, Hannah leapt up to make her way to the stage.

Carrie Monahan, Kate's friend and her film editor, who had been sitting behind her, leaned forward and patted Kate's shoulder. "She'll be a handful tonight."

Fairly sure the camera was now off her, Kate nevertheless held her hand up to cover her words. "You said a mouthful."

CHAPTER TWELVE

"Dawn, get your ass over here," Krissy hollered across the FDF's shop floor. Dawn looked over to see her frantic friend looking strangely similar to the way she looked that night at Faces when Krissy had had three too many beers and was sixth in line for the bathroom.

Krissy was excitedly shaking a *Hollywood Live* magazine in her direction and, for the life of her, Dawn couldn't imagine what had wound her up so. She shoved the magazine at Dawn, "Look at this."

A double-page spread on the Hollywood Film and TV Fashion Awards illustrated what looked to have been an elegant night. And on the right side of the spread was a photograph of Hannah Corrant, beaming from a podium on a stage. The caption read, "Hannah Corrant accepts the award for Sexiest Dress in a Motion Picture."

Krissy turned the pages that Dawn was now holding. "But that's not the craziest part. Look."

Ten pages later, Krissy stopped turning and jabbed her finger at the magazine. The article was titled "Hollywood's Underground Clubs," and staring back at her was yet another picture of Hannah Corrant. With Kate Nyland. They were arm in arm, dressed exquisitely, and looking very happy. The caption read, "Actress Hannah Corrant arrives at the Zephyr Lounge with date, executive producer Kate Nyland, following the screening of Jacque Clement's new film, *Winsome Warrior.*"

"Ain't that the shit," Krissy exclaimed. "They're dating each other. Kate Nyland is dating Hannah Corrant. Damn. I thought Kate might be seeing a woman, but I was wrong. She's seeing a *superstar.*"

Dawn read the first paragraph of the article out loud, "With no signs, no advertising, and no phone number, the underground clubs of Hollywood are the most desirable places, if you can find them. And the only way you can find them is to be an upper echelon player. Or be lucky enough to know one."

Krissy pointed to the middle of the article's text. "Lookit…read that part."

Dawn continued to read, "'At the Zephyr Lounge, considered to be the most underground of the underground clubs, executive producer Kate Nyland and actress Hannah Corrant, who is cast in *The Glass Cross*, an upcoming film produced by Nyland's company, StormRunner Productions, can be seen chatting amiably with Chad Montgomery, star of another Nyland production, *Meeting You Twice*, set for Spring release. Nyland and Corrant have been a staple of Hollywood's after-midnight club scene for the past ten months. If there were an actual VIP list, which there isn't, since underground clubs don't play by traditional rules, Hannah, Kate, and Chad would certainly be at the top. But these clubs are too cool for a list. And a top actress on the arm of one of Hollywood's most profitable execs can put an underground club on the map. In the secretive and exclusive world of underground clubs, the stars make the club, because the club's existence is reliant almost entirely on the attendance of Hollywood's *haut monde*.'"

"Ain't that the shit," Krissy said again.

"Yup," Dawn remarked flatly. She handed the magazine back to Krissy and walked away.

Krissy found her a few minutes later inside the paint shop, banging cans around. "You okay?"

"I told you she was out of my league." She threw two empty cans toward the trash bin.

Krissy leaned back against the paint booth wall and laughed.

"You don't have to rub it in, Krissy."

"Rub it in?"

"Yeah," Dawn grumbled as another paint can slammed against the rest. "I like her, okay? I'll admit it."

Krissy flicked her hand as if casting aside the thought. "Hell, I knew you liked her. I'm laughing, my friend, because you're wrong."

Dawn's throat tightened roughly. "She's in *Hollywood Live* magazine for shit's sake."

"Looks can be deceiving."

"She's with Hannah Corrant, Krissy. End of story."

"Not end of story."

Dawn finally stopped banging the paint cans and turned to face Krissy. "What the hell are you talking about?"

Then Krissy nodded knowingly. "It's just starting."

Dawn had no idea what Krissy was acting so cocksure about. "Krissy, if this is a game, I am just not able to play right now."

"No game. She likes you."

"Kate…" She considered skeptically and then said, "Not hardly."

"Well, I guess we're going to find out for sure, aren't we?"

"How so?"

"Kate's on her way out here."

"When?"

"Tomorrow."

❖

Kurt was just turning out the lights in his office when Dawn met him at the door. "Dawn. I was just leaving for a golf game with a client. What's up?"

"StormRunner Productions," was all she needed to say.

"Be here tomorrow." He nodded.

"And you were going to tell me…when?"

"I didn't tell you? Geez, Dawn, I'm sorry."

"A really important client is showing up tomorrow, on an account that Bill Sr. put me personally in charge of, and you didn't tell me?"

"Hey. What's all the anxiety about? We're caught up in the schedule," he said casually, then threw in a sarcastic adjunct, "Excuse me, the *recovery* schedule."

"That's not the point," Dawn fumed. "You need to tell me when a client's coming to the shop. Especially on a Saturday when we're only in for a half day because the shop has to be cleared out for the Christmas party tomorrow night."

"Okay, okay. Sorry." Kurt closed his door and stepped around Dawn. "Geez, Dawn, it shouldn't be a big deal for you. I'm sure you can move *The Glass Cross* props and stuff to the back warehouse along with the work we're doing for our other clients. Just take her back there and show her your art director talents and impress her for us. Brett, Jr.

or I will take her to lunch on the FDF credit card afterward. She'll be as happy as a kitten with a big roll of yarn." As he turned to walk away he added over his shoulder, "And we'll get her bossy little ass pointed toward the airport long before our party begins."

Irritated, Dawn shook her head. "Fuck," she said, but Kurt was more than halfway down the hall and out of earshot.

CHAPTER THIRTEEN

The first four hours Dawn had been at the shop Saturday morning were spent moving all the current work to the back warehouse, which was a ten-thousand-square-foot building behind the shop. It was used for storage and large scale construction projects. Normally, projects that were too large for the shop were situated in the outdoor yard in front of the shop, but for those large scale projects that could not be exposed to the frequent afternoon rain, outbursts that were notorious during Florida's muggy summers, the warehouse became their home.

With its Paul Bunyanesque thirty-foot ceilings, it seemed as cavernous as an aircraft hanger, which was exactly what it was. In the decades long before FDF claimed these buildings as their home, the hanger was the active headquarters of the Starway Airplane Company and sat industriously next to a fifty-acre field which sported a long, bumpy dirt runway.

Almost everything had been cleared out of the shop, thanks to Dawn's team of workers, and all that remained were some props that were ready for Kate's approval and ensuing relocation.

Most equipment and tools were moved there as well. Only those large and too-heavy-to-move pieces of wood-working or metal-smithing equipment stayed in the shop, otherwise, the floor was void of any props, wood scraps, and soldering rods. The workbenches were tidy, and the lockers and storage bins were semi-clean and orderly. Workers were busy sweeping the floor and wheeling away oil cans on a dolly, while others had started decorating for the night's Christmas party.

At just before nine in the morning, Kurt was with Dawn in the back of the shop when they heard Krissy call out, "We have a visitor." The sight of Kate walking with Krissy sent a buzz of excitement through Dawn.

"Good morning, Dawn. Morning, Kurt." Kate said as she stopped in front of them.

The women exchanged casual greetings.

"What's all the commotion about?" Kate indicated the activity in the shop with a tilt of her head.

"Our Christmas party. It's tonight," Krissy said with a wide-toothed grin.

"Back to work, Krissy. Dawn and Kate have work to do," Kurt said and walked off.

Krissy wandered away saying, "Put a stick up his ass and he could masquerade as a frosty popsicle."

After they'd gone over some of the props, Dawn offered Kate something to drink. The hot, humid air had been relentless, and they both were fairly parched. When Dawn brought back two bottles of water, Kate was sitting on one of the shop stools.

"Here you go," Dawn said as she sat down on the stool next to Kate.

"Thanks." Kate took the bottle. After a long draw, she looked around the shop. "You sure are busy."

"Yes, it stays pretty steady."

"Is it stressful most of the time?"

"I wouldn't say stressful. Just busy."

"I'm sure you have impossible deadlines," Kate said. "Not the least of which has been the StormRunner recovery schedule. And you can't be sleeping that much."

Dawn laughed easily. "It's about balancing."

"Balancing?"

Dawn nodded. "Work with life."

Kate considered Dawn's answer. "What if work *is* life?" Immediately she regretted the vulnerability she felt at voicing such a revealing question.

"It then depends on whether work, for you, is drudgery or happiness."

"Hmmm." Kate mulled it over. "I love my work, but it consumes me most of the time."

"How does it consume you?" Dawn's soft accent was full of genuine interest.

"Long hours, nightly business events." Kate gazed into the water bottle she was holding. "Weekends surrounded by work while on the phone nonstop and rushing off to more events."

"I imagine that Hollywood life is pretty exciting."

"I suppose. I mean I'm grateful that I can get paid to do what I love…"

Kate could tell Dawn was waiting patiently for her to finish her sentence. "Work consumes me, sometimes."

"But it seems like it's always new and pretty thrilling."

Kate pursed her lips. "I suppose every job can have those moments, but…"

"But even an astronaut gets bored with the view?"

Kate laughed. "Something like that. I feel as if I can't take a deep breath sometimes. I can't just…sit. You know?"

"Literally or metaphorically?"

"Both." Kate grinned.

Dawn nodded. "To just sit would make you happy?"

Kate imagined spending hours in a steamy bathtub, with no scripts or budgets to read, no phone calls to make, and no extensive to-do list tapping on her shoulder. "Really happy."

"Balance," Dawn said. "Find the time. Your soul needs to know the difference between work and life. Your body needs to know the difference. And your mind. If your mind is running at warp speed, your soul and body will not be happy no matter how serene the place. And making phone calls or doing other work-related tasks, no matter where, will not feed your soul either."

"Balance…" Kate pondered.

"Yes. Shut down the mind and work tasks. You don't even need a serene place if you truly free your mind and body. One could stand in the middle of Grand Central Station and find peace."

"You mean I don't need a tropical waterfall?"

Dawn retuned the smile. "No. But it helps."

"What do you do for serenity?"

"I walk out of here and find some nature. Trees and fresh air. When I drive to work, I make sure to notice one thing that this earth is offering. A sunrise. A beautiful cloud formation. I take time to notice all the little flowers that grow along the side of the highway. If I'm in a place that's not necessarily serene, I just change my place, my mental place, and really connect to it."

"I was just thinking," Kate said quietly, "about my drive to work every day. I can't remember whether there even are flowers along the side of the highway."

After reviewing the props, Dawn returned to her work while Kate spent the rest of the morning on her cell phone in the empty conference room that the receptionist had directed her to. She had a conference call with Amy Parsons and a music composer who lived in New York. They talked for a long time about the feel of the film, crucial scenes that would change the direction and emotion of the film, and the opening score. The composer had promised to work up some sample music and send it to them by the end of the week.

Kate spent the East Coast lunch hour talking to Frank Collins. She'd asked if the contract was in place for Jennifer Billington, the first assistant director. Kate knew that more than likely Jennifer was bringing on Kyle Penny, the Second AD that she always worked with, as well as Kimber Davidson, the third AD. All three had been on Hannah's last motion picture, which had just wrapped a week earlier. Hannah had requested them, and Kate had agreed to ask Amy, less because of Hannah's request, and more because she agreed that they were very good. They would have a week's turnaround between the last film that they were on with Hannah and starting on her film. Frank confirmed that they were all officially onboard.

Kate also called Beth to arrange the motor homes for the shoot.

"Nathan can find acceptable motor homes in Orlando," Kate had told Beth, "but their rates are more than the going rate in LA."

Beth chuckled. "I suppose they're making a killing on the snowbirds that come down from the cold-weather states. How many do you need?"

"Five motor homes and one honey wagon."

"No problem."

"Will the driver/operators rates and the travel cost me dearly?"

Beth hummed as she calculated. "Standard Teamster rates. I think I'll be able to talk to the posse. We all might be able to schedule in some vacation time so that we won't have to drive straight through. The union rates on that would kill you."

Beth's posse consisted of her girlfriend, Sarah, and some lesbian Teamster friends who worked together and always helped each other out. When one got a film or TV gig, they all worked. Being the owner of the rigs, Beth worked hard to keep a constant flow of business for the posse.

"You'll just have to pay the travel day rates for each motor home and each Teamster for the seven or so days to get each rig there. Then I'll charge you the standard motor home rental rates while in Orlando. Of course, I'll give you a four-day weekly rate on those. Then let's see…gas, expendables, you know, toilet paper, soap, the usual. And a few tickets to Walt Disney World."

"Walt Disney World?"

"Never been. Neither has Sarah. She'll be one of the driver/operators."

Kate laughed. "Okay, my friend, Disney World it is. I'm really glad you'll be making the trip. It'll be great to have you on the set."

"Very much like old times, huh?"

"Very."

"How are things at home?"

Kate meted out a hmmm. "Is that the place where people say they spend weekends doing hobbies and stuff?"

Laughing, Beth replied, "Yeah. It's where you actually cook your own dinners and make your own drinks."

"Weird concept."

"So you haven't been home much lately?"

"With Hannah as a girlfriend?"

"She must be hard to keep up with."

"Yeah, well, I knew that going in. And it's not all her fault. My life is far from normal. This business doesn't breed normalcy, but…" Kate paused.

"But?"

"Before Hannah, I could at least get home before midnight most nights. And I actually had weekends to read at home."

"Are we talking frivolous trashy novels or scripts for work?"

"Scripts," she said sheepishly. "But still, I could curl up on my couch with a hot tea and listen to the birds in the back yard."

"So you need to find the balance again."

"Funny, that's the second time I've been told that today. And it's true. It seems like I've worked twenty-four-seven for the past year. I mean, God forbid I get the flu or something."

"Well, if you get the flu, Hannah will just have to forgo her celebrity functions and take care of you."

Kate couldn't help a guffaw that escaped her mouth. "That'd be the day."

"And another thing, buddy," Beth said. "You don't have to wait to get the flu to find some balance. Start making it happen now."

"You're right." Kate sighed. "I really need to. It's just difficult to attain."

"Most things worth their weight are."

After saying good-bye to Beth, she got back on the phone and checked in with Hal Rosen and Charlie Gunner.

It was two in the afternoon when Krissy poked her head into the office. "We're ready for you in the back warehouse."

With just a few minutes discussion, Kate informed Krissy that she approved the completion of the mythological god prop. Krissy took them over to see one of the mechanical prop pieces that they were working on. Kate shimmied underneath the inscribed door of the salt mine to inspect the mechanics. Now lying on the shop floor, she was happy to find that they'd spared no expense to install a top of the line motor for the opening and closing of the huge door. Kate liked that.

As she lay on her back, finishing her inspection, it took her a moment to notice that a pair of Doc Marten work boots had appeared at her shoulder. All she could see were the tanned legs of the owner of the boots.

"You're getting all dirty down there."

Kate crawled out and Dawn held out a hand to help her up.

"Looks good under there." The feel of Dawn's hand in hers sent warmth coursing through her.

Brett, Jr. ambled over. "How's it going?"

Dawn smiled. "The bosslady is checking under the hood."

Kate nodded. "Can this be powered up yet?" Approving the movement of the salt mine door was the last thing she had to authorize. Everything else was completed enough that there were no more buy offs. And if she could buy off on the salt mine door movement, she would not have to make another trip to Orlando until the film crew returned to start shooting in January.

Brett, Jr. looked to Dawn who replied, "Give us an hour."

With all of the work completed, she might be able to get to the airport by four or four thirty and make the five thirty flight. "Great. I'll call my office, then."

The boss's son walked with Kate back into the front offices. When they got to his office door, he motioned her in. "Please, Ms. Nyland, use my office phone. I just need to get my Blackberry and I'll be gone."

Kate stepped toward the desk and stopped. "Brett, I can use my cell phone in the hall."

"No, I wouldn't think of it. Please make yourself at home," he said, stepping toward his desk to retrieve his Blackberry.

Kate moved toward the desk, thanking him, but he made no move to leave. Pausing, she wondered what else he wanted.

Brett, Jr. leaned in, closing the gap between them he said, "Our Christmas party is tonight, and seeing as we kept you here longer than you'd wanted, I'm extending a personal invitation to you. It starts at eight."

Kate leaned back slightly. "I appreciate the invitation, Brett, but I have a lot of work to do."

"We'd sure love to have such an important client as you attend. You could be my special guest. I have a bottle of champagne with your and my name written all over it."

Kate stifled a laugh as the word "smarmy" popped into her head. Brett, Jr. was oozing buckets of it at that moment.

"Well, I'll try. Thank you, again." However, even if she did attend, it certainly wouldn't be as his special guest.

❖

"I booked you on the Sunday morning flight."

Kate marveled at how efficient Laney was. She always answered her cell phone in one ring. And even though it was Saturday, she still always answered when her caller ID indicated Kate calling.

"Tomorrow morning? No, Laney, I need to get out of here tonight."

"What's an extra twelve hours? Stay and relax a little, because you certainly won't if you haul ass back here tonight."

Having a quiet evening with no plans and no interruptions did sound pretty tempting. Still, Kate found herself shaking her head. "I've got a pile of paperwork on my desk a mile high. Isn't the seven p.m. Delta flight open?"

"You're gonna give yourself a heart attack working so hard. Go find a Jacuzzi…with cocktail service."

"Why stay here when I can be back there at the office?"

"I checked with the airline. You have two choices. Do you want a coach seat tonight or first class tomorrow morning?"

"No fair. You're playing the butt-comfort trump card on me."

"Listen, the Sunday flight leaves at seven a.m. eastern time. That means you're in LA by nine in the morning. You'll be home and back to work in no time. The only difference is that you'll be more rested in first class and there won't be as much traffic on the 405 freeway Sunday morning."

"You've got this all figured out, don't you?"

"Yes."

"Do you know how much work is waiting for me back there?"

"Yes, tons. But for Heaven's sake, go have some fun in O-town for a change. You're thirty-eight. You deserve a meaningless diversion at least once more before you leave your thirties."

Kate mumbled a reply, "I'm really getting the 'balance' lecture a lot lately."

"What?"

"I said, how am I supposed to have fun when I have such a tedious schedule?" Kate sparred with Laney on this very topic much too often.

"Just say the word and I'll book the Saturday flight."

"Laney, you've been working for me for six years. How many afternoons have I taken off?"

"Maybe one a year. That makes six."

"Among other things, I correlate that to the business's success."

"Yes. But what about *your* success?"

Kate opened her mouth to form a retort when Laney added, "Your *personal* success?"

"My personal success?"

"I'm talking about your happiness, but I thought I'd use a business-type term so you'd understand."

"You sure you still need that second raise?"

Laney laughed. "Already spent. And you would never. You need to come up with better scare tactics. You're losing control over me."

"The bosses don't have the control. The secretaries do."

Laney deadpanned, "Tell me something I don't know."

"When you get back to your hotel room, grab a bottle of booze from the minibar, get schnockered and go see who looks cute down at the restaurant. It might be fun."

"Right. And Hannah would just love to hear that."

"The Meat Hook won't know."

"You're incorrigible."

"Anyway, she's busy right now on that *Access Hollywood* interview."

"Well, either way, the Project Angel Food fund-raiser is tonight. I can't miss that."

"You're not really missing it. You bought a $10,000 table, remember? Your name will be in the program, and they'll announce you at the opening address, so you're covered."

"I'm supposed to go with Hannah. And if I don't show, eight of my friends will be sitting there dealing with one pissed off actress."

"If Hannah goes."

"Why wouldn't she?"

"Without you to show off, why should she? She could care less that it was an AIDS charity event. You know, I bet she doesn't even know that it's a charity event. She probably thinks that Project Angel Food is some kind of cake baking competition."

Kate began to disagree, but in all honesty, couldn't exactly do so.

"I'll call Beth. She can tell the rest of your friends. They'll understand, Kate. They're friends. That's what they do…understand. And I'll call Hannah for you."

"She'll be pissed that this is my second cancellation in as many weeks."

"She'll get over it…eventually."

"Eventually could be a long time. But then again," Kate said, "Maria Castillas will be one of my eight friends there tonight."

"I see." Laney put it together quickly. "One of the most powerful agents in Hollywood."

"Exactly. Hannah hasn't met her yet, but she's sure wanted to. That way, maybe she won't notice I'm not there."

Laney harrumphed. "The only time she notices anything is when it's standing between her and a mirror."

"Laney, don't be nasty."

"You mean don't be brutally honest." Then Laney's voice softened. "She's going to hurt you, Kate. I don't want to see that happen. You're too nice."

❖

Kate made a few more phone calls and then Dawn retrieved Kate for the buy off of the salt mine door. Kurt was there as well, along with his pompous attitude. He had never warmed up to Kate and actually seemed to despise her. Kate, of course, ignored his demeanor, speaking with him as if she didn't notice his resentment.

What she did notice, however, was the closeness of Dawn's body next to hers. The back warehouse was particularly loud with the last of the forklifts and other machinery being moved for the upcoming party in the shop, so they had to stand shoulder-to-shoulder discussing the finer points of gears and artistic theming.

Kate felt completely captivated every time Dawn smiled. And Kate could feel Dawn's focus shift as well. When the look of business on her face dissolved into pleasure and then back again, Kate reacted in tandem. One minute they'd be discussing the rate of the thrust bearing and the next they'd be smiling at each other.

Having Dawn so close enthralled Kate, who had to keep blinking away the impulse to forget that she was there to do a job.

Consequently, the buy off took twenty-five minutes, but it was done. There needn't be any more trips to Orlando until principal photography commenced in early January. Kate said good-bye to Dawn and reluctantly left the shop. It was still early enough to race to the airport and grab a coach class seat on the last flight to LA.

But did she really want to hurry home?

CHAPTER FOURTEEN

"Y ou sure you'll be able to drive me back here tonight?" Krissy asked Dawn. They were at Dawn's house. Since Krissy lived in Mt. Dora, much too far to drive home after an open bar party like the ones FDF threw, she'd parked at Dawn's and would spend the night there afterward.

"Sure. You go ahead and tie one on." With two bottles of beer in her hand, Dawn walked from the kitchen to the den where Krissy was parked on the couch, feet up on the coffee table.

"I do appreciate it. But I'll tell you, if things work out tonight with Saundra, I might not need the ride."

Dawn flopped down on the couch. "I can't believe you have a thing for Saundra from accounting. She's straight, if you hadn't noticed."

"Well, she's been flirting with me, if you haven't noticed."

"I haven't. But then again, I haven't been looking."

"Maybe that's the problem."

"What? Not watching you pick up on women?"

"No, silly. Not looking for yourself. You're not out there much in the dating world." Krissy took a long draw from her beer before adding, "Me, well I may be crazy for flirting with Saundra from accounting, but I think she's pretty, and who knows? Maybe tonight I'll be having my own 'Twas the night before Christmas.' I'll be dashin' and dancin' and prancin' with the Vixen."

Dawn guffawed. "Well, I sure hope so. You deserve it."

"And you don't?"

"Sure, I do."

"So why don't you get out there?"

Dawn didn't answer.

"I just don't get it," Krissy said. "You are an incredible woman. If you weren't my best friend, I'd be in love with you, too."

"Come on, Krissy, knock it off."

"I mean it, damn it. Well, not the part about me falling in love with you, but the part about you being incredible."

"Yeah, well maybe she's out there somewhere just waiting for me."

The conversation then fell into silence as Dawn's last statement hung in the air, the declaration floating between them, growing more and more obvious.

Dawn knew she hadn't been out there looking much. A long ago broken heart had sealed her fate. She dated sometimes, but there never seemed to be a spark.

"Is Bridget coming to the party?" Krissy and Dawn were both staring at a car chase on TV.

"She's my date. See? I'm out there."

"You sound about as excited as my Uncle Jack did the day he went to get his vasectomy."

"Well, I do date, you know. You said I don't. I do."

Krissy got up and patted Dawn on the shoulder. "Good for you."

"What does that mean?"

"That means good for you." Krissy retrieved another beer from the refrigerator. "You like her?"

"Sure, I like her."

"How come you haven't mentioned her since we saw her at Faces?" Krissy sat back down as Dawn shrugged. After studying Dawn for a few moments, she gave words to the shrug. "Because she isn't Kate."

A silence ensued before Dawn formed the words slowly. "No one's Kate."

Krissy grinned. "But Kate."

This time Dawn got to her feet. "Why are we talking about Kate again? Geez, Krissy. She's taken. She's on a plane back to LA. Back to her girlfriend. Let it go."

She stomped off to her bedroom, but she wasn't too far away to hear Krissy say, "I won't let it go if you can't, my friend."

❖

Kate smiled as she pulled into FDF's parking lot. The decision to stay in Orlando came as she was getting into her rental car earlier that afternoon. And the decision had come easily.

There had been no logical reason to stay. The business had been finished, and she had a million things to do in LA, but all the reasons to leave flew out the window when she knew where Dawn would be that night. It was crazy to even think a single thought past that, but none of that mattered. And for the first time in forever, she was doing something that made no sense, had no rationale. She wanted to see Dawn again. A woman she hardly knew, had no idea about whether she was single or not, had no business wondering anyhow. But wanted to see again. Plain and simple.

She called Laney who informed her that not only had she already booked the Sunday flight, she'd also gotten a room at the Peabody Hotel.

In the hours since she'd been at FDF, a grand transformation had taken place. A huge sign hung from the loading doors announcing "A Christmas Paradise," and the decorating and props certainly delivered a cheery feeling. Scattered around the parking lot were wreathes and garlands hung from palm trees. Signs that read "FDF This Way" were crossed out to read "Christmas This Way." On the front of the building, tipping over the roofline toward guests below, a gigantic, fifteen foot margarita glass was pouring out its contents, which were not a tropical drink, but cascading snowflakes. Parking attendants in Santa costumes parked cars, and fake snowdrifts were scattered about. Christmas music played loudly, and quite a lot of people milled about outside. Two limos were parked out front, the drivers standing sentry next to a sign that extolled "Paradise Is A Designated Driver."

Slightly nervous, Kate got out of her car. "Nyland," she said. "What the hell are you doing? You have no idea what you're going to find. This might be a really bad idea."

Just two hours earlier, she'd convinced Hannah that she should go to the Project Angel Food fund-raiser without her. Hannah had been pissed at her for not coming back to LA but had predictably calmed down when Kate told her that uber-agent Maria Castillas would be there. It saddened Kate that neither of them was too disappointed about her missing the fund-raiser. Hannah was more interested in what Maria could do for her career, and Kate wanted to see Dawn more than she wanted to be with Hannah.

Kate realized with a loathing tug in her stomach that her relationship with Hannah had grown stale. They both were in it for the wrong reasons.

Kate looked toward the entrance to the party. "You've come this far. The least you can do is make a complete fool of yourself and then skedaddle." She took a deep breath. "What the hell?"

The Christmas in Paradise theme extended well inside the building. As Kate approached the loading dock doorway, she could see that a dance floor had been placed in the middle of the shop floor, and a lively band was playing contemporary dance music. Kate estimated that at least two hundred people were already there, dancing, drinking, hugging, and laughing. Christmas lights twinkled from every overhead beam, each of which was also decorated with mini surfboards. A twenty-foot Christmas tree hovered over piles of presents wrapped with tropical-themed gift paper. More costumed Santas in Hawaiian shirts and Bermuda shorts served hors d'oeuvres, and two open bars, themed as sleighs, were tended by elves and packed with thirsty people.

Kate made her way over to one of the bars and finally managed to order a glass of red wine. No sooner had she tipped the elf bartender when she felt a tap on the shoulder.

Brett, Jr., smashed to the gills, was smiling a big-toothed grin. "You maydit. Thass great." He took her arm. "Less go find Dad. He'll wanna say hi."

She let herself be escorted through a swarm of people, wondering if coming had been a bad decision after all. When Brett, Jr. staggered to a halt next to Brett, Sr., it became very apparent that the son had gotten only a slight head start on his dad's imbibing. Their slurring matched word for word.

When Brett, Jr. had again taken her arm, burbling, "Les' dance," Kate eased away from him. "Thanks, Brett, but I'm going to say hello to a few more people."

"So'kay by me. But I'll fine you later."

Of course, she had virtually no idea who anyone was, but it was decidedly much better to stand by herself than be dragged around by someone who would eventually throw up on her shoes.

❖

Dawn was standing with Bridget, her date. They were huddled in a foursome with Krissy and Saundra from accounting. Off to the side and close to the door that led to the main offices, they were away from the nucleus of the party. Only a few minutes earlier, Krissy had commandeered Saundra from her office. Saundra had originally elected to skip the party and catch up on the end-of-the-quarter financial reports, but Krissy had told the woman that there would be no bean counting while the Christmas party was in full swing. Saundra had happily acquiesced.

Dawn and Krissy listened politely as Saundra and Bridget talked to each other about their respective jobs. Dawn had asked Bridget to meet her at the party since Dawn had to be there three hours earlier to help set up. Bridget had arrived at the party already quite tipsy and had gone to the open bar three times in the first hour she was there.

At one point, Bridget leaned a little too far to the side, and Dawn had to wrap her arm around her to keep her from losing her balance.

"Oopsy daisy," Bridget said in apology.

"Are you all right?" Dawn asked gently.

"Just a little nervous to be with you," Bridget's alcohol confided. "I think you're really cute."

"Thank you," Dawn said. "But I think you should slow down on the Christmas cheer. Brett, Jr. makes a pretty potent punch."

"That's probably a good bit of advice," Bridget concurred.

"Well, I am really glad Krissy stole me away from my paperwork. This is a great party," Saundra said to Bridget.

As Saundra and Bridget returned to their chatting, Dawn glanced at Krissy who stood facing her. Strangely, Krissy's eyes were looking straight ahead, and she had a stupid grin on her face. Dawn furrowed her brow and then leaned toward Krissy. "Saundra's going to think you've gone mad, grinning like that. You're going to scare her away."

"It's not Saundra I'm grinning about."

"Then what…"

Wide-eyed, Krissy shook her head in a shut-your-pie-hole look. Dawn was just about to turn around to see what Krissy was staring at when she heard that alluringly familiar voice right behind her left ear say, "Hello."

Krissy reached around Dawn, her hand out. "Miss Nyland. I mean Kate. It's great to see you. I thought you were on your way back to LA."

"Good evening, everyone." Kate stepped closer to the group. "I decided to fly out first thing in the morning."

Dawn stood there light-headed, surprised at the magnificent shock and excited beyond reason. She thought Kate was long gone.

All Dawn could do was smile at Kate who smiled back at her.

Krissy jumped in with introductions, "Everyone, this is Kate Nyland. Kate, this is Bridget Wright and Saundra Schafer. Of course, you know Dawn."

"I do," Kate said. "Hello."

Bridget, however, perked up at the introductions. "Kate Nyland… the Producer."

Dawn stared at Krissy, perplexed. Bridget continued, "I saw you on the Hollywood Fashion Awards Show."

"Oh…yes," Kate said and then smiled modestly.

"You looked so great with Hannah Corrant," Bridget gushed.

Dawn, who was still staring at Krissy, clenched her hands into tight balls.

Krissy jumped in. "We're working on the sets and props for Kate's new movie, aren't we, Dawn?" She reached over, rubbing Dawn's arm in comfort disguised as a nudge.

Dawn could only nod politely and for the life of her, couldn't look at Kate. She thought she heard Bridget ask Kate, "So your movie will shoot here soon?" and then heard Kate reply something in the affirmative, but all she wanted to do was run. The picture of Kate and Hannah in the gossip magazine kept flashing in her head, and the air in the room was suddenly thick and stagnant.

Dawn looked to Krissy for support, and Krissy smiled warmly before leaning toward her. "She came here to see you, my friend. Don't think that that isn't true."

"You must have just gotten here," Bridget was saying to Kate. "You're bare-handed."

"Well, I've already had one…" was all Kate could manage before Bridget said, "I'll go get another round of drinks. Come with me, Saundra." And the two briskly walked off toward the open bar.

Krissy suddenly said, "Brett, Jr.'s on his way over here, and I don't think it's to hand out paychecks."

"I'm afraid I've been cornered for a dance," Kate said.

"Would you rather not?" Dawn ventured.

"I'd rather not."

Krissy stepped around them and toward Brett, Jr. "I'll stall him. Get her out of here."

Kate followed Dawn outside, and they walked past the limos and Santa-valets. "Where are you taking me?" She laughed. Not that she cared. What she cared about was being with Dawn.

"Two places," was all Dawn said.

Kate followed her around the side of the shop building. A small field sat next to the shop. There was a clearing of ankle-high grass surrounded by a grove of trees. In the glow from the moonlight, Kate could tell that the field was deserted.

"This was an old airstrip, many years ago." Dawn told her as they began walking. "When that housing tract was built over there, people just forgot about what was left here. The backs of the houses face the field, and I guess they don't like seeing the FDF buildings off in the distance, so no one really comes back here." Dawn led her to the far side, to a large rock that nestled between a stand of old-growth trees.

Dawn directed Kate to sit on the rock. There was enough room for Dawn to join her.

After a moment of silence, Dawn said, "Take a deep breath."

Kate filled her lungs, held it for a few beats, and then exhaled slowly through her mouth.

"Two more times." Dawn instructed and Kate did. "Listen to the crickets. Think about the stars. Feel the humidity on your skin."

Kate remembered her conversations with Dawn and Beth about balance. She indeed was getting the intent of the exercise. "So don't think about work."

"More than that. To say 'don't think about work' makes it impossible not to think about work."

"How do you mean?"

"Okay" Dawn leaned to one side and nudged Kate's shoulder with her own, "Think about anything…but don't think about an elephant."

Determined, Kate looked out across the field for a few moments and then laughed. "Now that you gave me the elephant notion, that's all I can picture."

"Exactly. So saying 'don't think about work' causes the same effect."

"And working on a movie budget while at the beach," Kate added, "still keeps me in work mode. And not moving toward balance."

Dawn nodded and smiled.

They sat there, both silent and reflective. Kate tried the exercise again, this time telling herself to think about the crickets and stars and the humidity. Without being conscious of it, she began to take deep, slow breaths. The world began to slow down. The night was balmy and the crickets chirped out a cadence that could have lulled her to sleep. Her shoulders relaxed, dropping a good two inches, and the small of her back loosened up. After a while, she felt the light touch of fingers on her thigh.

"Looks like it's working."

"Incredibly so."

"Brain dump?"

"Accomplished."

"That's what balance feels like."

When Kate turned toward Dawn, she was overwhelmed at the depth of Dawn and the amazing way she viewed life and all its wonderful possibilities.

Kate smiled happily. "Thank you for this."

"My pleasure, really."

"Don't be surprised if you wander back here some day and see me sitting on this rock."

"The rock and I would be delighted."

Kate moved her shoulder into Dawn's, nudging her back. "You said there were two places you were taking me."

She followed Dawn back across the field to a modest wooden-planked building behind the paint shop. Dawn unlocked the door and motioned Kate in. "This is my studio."

Standing in the doorway, Kate took it all in. The studio was about eight hundred square feet. Filled with artwork and paintings, it felt comfortable and inspiring. Two side-by-side workbenches lined the back wall, and brushes and hand tools hung from pegs around the room. An easel held a painting in progress, while a few smaller hand crafts were in the works on another smaller table.

"I spend a lot of time in here." Dawn flicked the light on. "Brett, Sr. gave me this space so that I could work on my own projects. He knows how much time I put in for him, so he tries to make it up to me."

Dawn turned to step farther into the studio just as Kate reached out and lightly touched her arm. Dawn felt a surge through her body.

Kate smiled at her. "It's good to see you."

Dawn let out a happy breath. "I'm glad you came."

"So am I."

"I just didn't know you were…"

"You mean my last minute decision that I'd been considering all day?" Kate grinned broadly.

Dawn smiled back. "You look good, Kate."

Kate looked down at her top. "Peabody Hotel special." And then said, "Thank you. So do you." With a deep intake of breath, Kate managed, "What kind of things are 'your own projects'?"

"American Indian works," Dawn replied. "I'm Cherokee."

"That's quite a hop and a skip from themed caverns and maidens of salt."

Dawn smiled. "Themed caverns, museum exhibits, architectural cladding, that's my bread-and-butter work."

"And what does your personal work look like?"

"Come here," Dawn said, and Kate followed her to the back workbenches.

A wooden carving of a wolf watching an eagle overhead sat in mid-realization. Jewelry and silver pieces lay on the work table.

"Here." Dawn picked up a bracelet and handed it to Kate. It was magnificent, beaded in three colors of blue so that it appeared to blend. Interspersed into the beadwork were brown seeds the size of snow peas.

"What are these?" Kate asked.

"Acorn seeds. The acorn has always had significant meaning to the Cherokee. It represents survival, strength, and intent. Like those little acorns, we all face many things on our spiritual path. We endeavor to mature, and through determination, we can grow and get stronger and stronger. The Cherokee use the acorn as a symbol of the journey of survival. It's honored as the example of how the people of our tribes, like the oak trees, survive for the betterment of the circle as a whole."

Kate studied the acorn seeds on the bracelet. "They're strong little guys, huh?"

"Like you."

LISA GIROLAMI

Kate looked up again and smiled. "It's a beautiful bracelet."

"It's yours."

"I couldn't…"

"Please." Dawn put the acorn bracelet on Kate's left wrist. "There. Remember the path of growth. It starts small and grows as big as it can."

"Thank you." Kate briefly caught Dawn's gaze, but Dawn turned away just as quickly.

Kate regarded her. She seemed so sure and yet so shy. "You hate meetings like the one we had in the conference room the day we met."

Dawn smiled. "That'd be true. It's all corporate stuff. And I'm usually not dressed for them. I'm generally covered in fiberglass dust or speckled with paint." She picked up a paint brush and moved it to a grouping of others. "I have the disposition of an hourly worker. That's where I feel most comfortable. No politics for me."

"But you're not hourly."

Dawn laughed. "Okay, you got me. I sold out. I'm salaried."

"Ah, so you went over to the dark side."

"The price I paid for taking that position."

"Foreman and lead art director." Kate considered it, nodding. "That's very impressive."

Again Dawn laughed. "Sure, and that coming from big Hollywood producer."

"Truly, that's remarkable, especially in what appears to be a good ol' boys club. And your work is incredible. I wouldn't have had those sets and props finished without you." So firm was she in her assertion that Dawn didn't even try to debate.

"Thank you," she said gently.

Any words that either of them might have been considering dropped to the workshop floor like trivial wood chips or drips of turpentine.

This time Dawn dared to look into Kate's eyes. What she found there were the same unspoken words that Dawn was also feeling. *I want this, here, with you.* It seemed that Kate was feeling the same way. And it wasn't alcohol-infused. It wasn't the party atmosphere. It wasn't even the Christmas spirit.

It burned inside of Dawn. And she thought that Kate felt it too.

And, as if Kate had read her mind, Dawn watched her expression grow more concentrated. She was aware that their breathing had escalated, growing more intense, as if the air was slowly being sucked from the room.

Kate's lips parted a little. They were sexy lips, full and inviting.

And then Kate leaned ever so slightly toward Dawn, maybe an inch closer, not enough to reach Dawn's lips, but enough to reveal intent.

Dawn's chest felt swirly and her breathing became more labored. She'd never wanted anything more than this, never believing it would ever be possible.

And then Kate leaned a little closer. Dawn watched the intensity in her face and saw her eyes flutter, closing for a moment. And in that moment, Dawn saw ecstasy in Kate's expression.

She knew that Kate could already feel the kiss that was about to come. She could, too. She wanted Kate's lips on hers, wanted to feel her body against her own, wanted time to freeze.

A shout erupted from just outside the studio. Some partygoers were walking by on their way to the back warehouse.

Kate blinked and Dawn inhaled sharply. Time couldn't stop and the kiss never came.

Kate spoke softly. "I suppose we'll be missed right about now."

Dawn blew out a pent up breath of sexually charged energy. "I suppose."

When Dawn and Kate returned to the party, Krissy found them right away. "Bridget can't hold her punch."

"Where is she?"

"Saundra has her in the reception bathroom."

Dawn turned to Kate. "Will you excuse me?"

Kate smiled. "Of course. Would you like any help?"

"No," Dawn said. "But thanks."

As Dawn walked off, Krissy took Kate's arm. "Now it's time I showed you the dance floor."

"The dance floor?"

"It's either you and me out there cuttin' the rug, or it'll be you and Brett, Jr. who's just found you again." He was indeed staggering their way.

"Brett, Jr. or no Brett, Jr., I pick you. Let's go."

❖

Dawn found Bridget and Saundra just coming out of the bathroom. Dawn put her arm around Bridget as she gingerly stepped into the hall.

"Bridget, are you okay?"

"Ugghh. I should have listened to you about the punch."

"I'll take you home now," Dawn said.

"My car's here." Bridget groaned weakly.

Saundra waved her off. "It's okay, honey. It'll be here in the morning, along with about fifty others."

Dawn reached into her pocket for her keys. "Could you please give these to Krissy? That's my house key. Could you please have her ask one of the limo drivers to take her to my house?"

Saundra took the keys. "I sure will."

❖

"How's Bridget?" Kate asked Saundra who had walked up to where they stood on the dance floor.

"Dawn's taking her home," Saundra said. "She'll be sporting a full-size headache in the morning."

As a slow song began, Krissy and Saundra embraced and began to sway together. Kate disengaged from the knot of dancers. "You two keep dancing. I'm thirsty." She walked off the dance floor.

As she stood in line at the open bar, Kate thought of Dawn taking Bridget home and a pang of jealously hit her. She was still trying to catch her breath from being with her in the studio. The excitement at being so close to Dawn had left her winded. And not once had thoughts of Hannah crossed her mind.

The queue of people at the bar stretched quite a ways, and Kate wasn't really that thirsty, so she slipped out the loading dock door and to her car.

CHAPTER FIFTEEN

Friday, January 6, was the first day of principal photography. Kate's production company had relocated to Florida over a one week period just after the New Year. Charlie Gunner, Jamie Riggs, and Nathan Firth had arrived just after Christmas to complete securing of locations and opening of the production office. Charlie was busy making sure everywhere the crew would be shooting was ready.

Nathan Firth was making sure the living arrangements and creature comforts would be ready on time. He was also in daily contact with Beth Samuels who was on her way with five motor homes and the honey wagon, which held the crew toilets. The other trucks were on the way as well, full of the cast's wardrobe, the props, the lighting equipment, the camera equipment, and other supplies and tools.

Kate and Nathan had talked over Christmas. They both were in LA getting ready for the move.

"How was Santa to you?" Kate asked the day after the holiday.

Nathan laughed. "No coal, so I can't complain. Hey, I arranged for the production company to take over two floors in the Peabody Hotel in Orlando. Floors twenty and twenty-one are reserved for us. Everyone will have their own room."

"Did they have a shuttle?"

"Not one they could dedicate to us, so I rented one for the trips to and from each location. And I was able to reserve the two Presidential Suites for Hannah and Peter Carson."

"I got you your own room, like you asked," Nathan continued. Kate had requested it mostly out of formality since this was a business trip, but also because she needed a place to work, and her suite, on the nights she and Hannah might not sleep together, would serve that purpose.

"Thanks, Nathan."

"Hey, what are you doing for New Year's?"

"Trying to get up to Big Bear."

"Trying?"

"We never seem to be able to take advantage of our investment."

"Hannah's not the woodsy type?"

Kate chuckled, "As long as the woods are outside a big picture window." She thought of Dawn and knew that she would love Big Bear. She'd love the trees and the hiking trails. And she wondered what Dawn would be doing for New Year's.

By Wednesday, everyone had arrived in Orlando. Kate made the rounds, checking in on each department. The wardrobe department was picking up last minute items. The art department was busily readying the sets and purchasing expendable items such as gaffers' tape, digital film, and more brushes and rags. The trucks for the electrical department had just arrived from LA, and their equipment was being thoroughly checked.

They'd set the call time on Friday morning for five a.m. for the crew and seven a.m. for the two lead actors. The actors with smaller roles and extras had an eight thirty call time. The first shot was scheduled for nine.

The location was Universal Studios, Orlando, on Soundstages Two, Three, and Four, and that would do nicely for Kate's crew. The salt mine set had been constructed in the past two weeks and looked great. She knew that Dawn and her team from Florida Design and Fabrication had come in during those weeks and worked with StormRunner's Set Construction and Art Departments who had arrived even earlier than Nathan. Working side by side with the film's production designer, art director, and lead construction foreman, FDF assembled the mine entrance, all of its individual passageways, and salt mine sets.

The Maiden of Salt statue had been mounted at the entrance to the mine, and Kate chuckled every time she walked by it. A little after six in the morning, Kate ran into Jennifer and Beth by Beth's motor homes, which were lined up next to each other, and they were magnificent. Each beast of a vehicle was luxurious; outfitted in all the latest creature comforts and technology and ready for service. The motor home closest to the side soundstage door served as the production office. The next one was for wardrobe, which would serve a dual purpose as a fitting room and the wardrobe department office. The next was for hair and makeup and would serve as their salon and office. Beth had then positioned Hannah's motor home and then Peter's. Beyond that was the honey wagon, and the other department trucks that held equipment, props, supplies, articles, and gadgets, as well as a few others that would serve as offices for other departments: art, lighting, props, camera, sound, electrical, grip, etc. Inside the soundstage, there were small offices that Jennifer assigned to those smaller departments like first aid, transportation, and craft service.

"Good morning, Kate," Jennifer chirped.

"Jennifer, Beth. What a great day for a movie." Kate felt happy and excited to finally start shooting.

"It certainly is," Beth said.

"How's Sarah?"

"She's great. She's on her way over from the hotel with Alissa, Sally, Robin, and Kaye."

Jennifer chuckled. "You've got the whole posse here, huh?"

"Wouldn't go anywhere without 'em."

Kate patted Beth's shoulder. "Well, I'm glad you're here. Things always go so well when you're on the set."

Jennifer then tapped her radio with her finger as she turned to leave. "Kimber will be along shortly," she told them both. "She'll give you your radios and call numbers."

Beth nodded. "Sounds good."

"Thanks, Jennifer."

At ten minutes before nine o'clock, everyone was finally in place. Hannah and Peter were done with hair and makeup and were on the set. Amy Parsons rehearsed the actors through the scene a few times, even though they'd rehearsed each scene many times back in LA.

Kate was especially fortunate to have hired Amy, who, as director, would be creating and controlling the artistic and dramatic aspects of the film. She would define the artistic vision, the emotional look, the performance, and emotional ranges of the actors. Side by side with Kate, Amy would work out creative and technical issues that posed challenges to the budget or schedule.

Through weeks of rehearsals, Kate was confident that they both had a firm grasp of the artistic vision. Kate would go to bat with the studio for Amy, asking for more time or money when necessary. Kate would rework the budget and schedule, finding inventive short cuts or compromises that would allow Amy the extra things that she felt she needed to make a particular scene or sequence of scenes work.

Months before, during the scheduling of the film production, Kate and Amy had decided that the first shot of the shoot would take place at the entrance to the salt mine. It was a short and easy scene that would set a good pace.

At nine forty, Jennifer announced to everyone on set that the first shot was in the can. Kate smiled as a cheer went up, as was tradition with film crews, and Kimber got on the radio to the motor home that served as the production trailer to give those back in command central the news.

It was important for Kate to be both on the soundstage and in the production office each day of shooting, but she'd made sure that she was on the set for the first shot of the first day, something that had been a habit since her first motion picture. Her presence, overseeing the crew and helping them form into one functioning unit, was important to establish from the start.

Jamie and Nathan were in the production office and got word of the first shot. Kate imagined them high-fiving each other and looking forward to the martini shot, which in film lingo, was the last shot of the day.

Hannah walked off the set as soon as Amy called for the first cut. She made it a point to walk up to Kate, who stood just a few paces off the set, and pull her into a spicy congratulatory kiss.

Normally this might have been reasonable, but Kate just happened to be talking with the Mayor of Orlando and the head of the Orlando Film Commission. They had stopped by to welcome StormRunner Productions to their city and were a little stunned to see the famous movie star mash lips with the big Hollywood executive producer.

Not the best move, Kate thought, however an obvious, premeditated decision by Hannah. Certainly, it wasn't that Kate hid her sexuality, but she preferred a little more decorum when it made political sense to do so.

Still, Hannah sashayed away and either the Mayor or the Film Commissioner, Kate wasn't exactly sure which one, cleared his throat and went on to gush at Kate over her great choice of cities.

CHAPTER SIXTEEN

The rest of the morning of the sixth day went rather uneventfully, which was fine with everyone on the set. During their first week of shooting, they had all pretty much gotten used to eastern standard time. And the skeleton crew, the small group of them that would then pack up and move the shoot to Austria soon, prayed for smooth sailing overseas, as well. There was nothing worse than a difficult shoot far, far away from home.

Around ten a.m., Kate was in the production office when she got called to the set for a "slight emergency at the mine entrance set" as Hal had said to her over the radio. She had been head-down in some paperwork and as she took the radio call, she looked up to realize that she was alone in the motor home. Usually, at the very least, a production assistant was always there to take land line calls. She made a mental note to let Jamie know that there should always be coverage.

Concerned but not anxious, Kate made her way to Soundstage Two, which was where the salt mine entrance set was located. When she entered the soundstage, all was strangely quiet. She had expected the usual cacophony of crew member activity, given that the red light outside the soundstage, the one that indicated that the camera was rolling and warned everyone not to enter when it was flashing, wasn't flashing. A non-flashing light meant that the cast and crew were in between shots and that it was safe to enter without the risk of ruining a shot.

She called out through the strange silence to Amy and then heard a noise coming from the mine's entrance. When she approached, she didn't see it right away. Then her eyes focused in the low light of the dramatic day-for-night lighting, and she stopped in her tracks, putting her hands on her hips.

The Maiden of Salt statue, mounted at the entrance to the salt mine, had been dressed up with one of Kate's famous Long Beach baseball caps. A wig placed on the statue's head had been pulled back

into a ponytail that was sticking out of the back of the cap. The Maiden
sported a cell phone, complete with headset and microphone wrapped
around her head. In her open hands were thousands of dollars worth of
monopoly money. A sign around her neck read, "Kate, our hero! Happy
Birthday!"

Kate blinked and then burst out laughing. The crew, who had
been hiding just inside the salt mine entrance, piled out hooting and
hollering. They all hugged Kate and kissed her cheeks. Toochee, the
make up stylist, came out last holding a large birthday cake ablaze with
thirty-eight candles. And while they celebrated and ate cake before
taking their places back on the set for the next shot, Kate realized that
even though Hannah should have known it was her birthday, she wasn't
there.

❖

After wrap, Kate had taken Hannah out to dinner at Emeril
Lagasse's signature restaurant, which was located in Universal's
CityWalk, a short stroll from the soundstages. It was Kate who had
asked Hannah to dinner. Hannah hadn't remembered Kate's birthday,
and Kate had neither the energy nor desire to bring it up.

The restaurant was loud and packed to the brim. The bar's lounge
was standing room only. Servers glided narrowly past each other while
navigating the crowd, and the clanging of silverware and the occasional
outburst of wine-loving clusters of diners bounced mercilessly off the
interior walls.

Amid the restaurant chaos, Kate was actually able to unwind. Like
the general of a battle, she looked back on the day and was content that
the film crew adapted to the first week's challenges, changes, problems,
and conflicts with the professionalism and organization of the best of
any troop.

Granted, anything could go wrong at any moment. She could get
a call that a previous day's film had scratches on it, one of the actors
could come down with measles or hives, a pipe could rupture in one
of the soundstages, flooding the very expensive sets. A litany of things
could go wrong. But for this moment nothing had, and she was going
to relax and enjoy it.

She had her hand on Hannah's knee, underneath the crisp white tablecloth, and Hannah was, for the most part, paying attention to her.

Hannah had signed at least ten autographs in the short span of time between hors d'oeuvres and the main course, but they were able to have a few quick conversations. As long as Hannah didn't bring up the second motor home request again, Kate thought, things would go nicely.

Hannah took in a deep breath, then let out a long, bored, but agitated sigh. "I see that Beth only brought enough motor homes for everyone. Meaning only one for me."

Oh shit. Kate must have jinxed it by thinking about it.

"Yes, that's correct."

Hannah's voice was controlled but full of admonishment. "I can't believe you."

So much for a relaxed evening. "Hannah, I told you. No second motor home."

"Have you seen the one I got?"

"Yes, as a matter of fact I have. It's exactly like Peter's—"

Hannah cut her off. "Beth's motor craps are pieces of shit."

"You have the latest model Allegro, Hannah. That's a four hundred thousand dollar motor home."

"It's a piece of shit."

Kate was getting fed up with the tantrum. "I don't want to get into this again."

"Well, we're into it," Hannah snapped.

At once, Kate saw absolute hatred in Hannah's eyes and it shocked her. Had she always had that look when they fought?

Hannah took an angry swig of her wine. "You see how people are to me." She hissed, "I'm a fucking *star*, Kate. Treat me like one."

The sheer ugliness of Hannah's mind-set suddenly flipped a switch inside Kate. "From where I sit, Hannah, you're a fucking three-year-old." And Kate got up from the table. She placed her napkin by her half-eaten food. "I'll call for a Teamster to pick you up here and drive you back to the hotel."

"What do you think you're doing?" Hannah yelled.

"This conversation's over." Kate walked out of Emeril's and used her cell phone to call for a Teamster to hurry over to the restaurant before the fans realized that Hannah was alone and fair game. Kate asked for another one to pick her up at the production office and take her back to the hotel.

The balmy Florida night air felt good in her lungs as she walked back to the soundstages. She stopped at the apex of a bridge that crossed over a lake leading to the studio gates. Alone at that hour of the night, she leaned against the railing and sighed heavily.

So this was her birthday dinner. How pathetic it felt to her. How could she have gotten to this place with Hannah? She supposed she first had to analyze what "this place" actually was. And the sad truth was that "this place" was being in a relationship with a narcissist. It was being dragged around by a movie star, day and night. It was being a fashionable accessory. And it was, many times, getting the wrath of a self-centered brat.

Off in the distance, she heard the trilled tempo of crickets. They chirped busily somewhere out in the muggy night air. The memory of the exercise that Dawn had taught her on the rock behind the FDF shop came back to her. She closed her eyes and took three deep breaths.

CHAPTER SEVENTEEN

Shooting through the weekend, the crew had successfully wrapped up their week. Thursday was the cast and crew's day off, but Kate spent it at the motor home/production office making calls back to LA and going over paperwork. With blue jeans, a white T-shirt, and her requisite Long Beach baseball cap on, Kate struck a casual figure with her feet up on her desk and the script, a few production reports, and a pen balanced in her lap.

Amy Parsons showed up around noon to re-block a few scenes, and after Amy made her notes, they went out for a quick lunch.

When Kate returned, she saw Beth duck into Peter's motor home. She was more than likely restocking each one.

A little while later, Beth poked her head in the production office door. "Coffee?"

"Would love some." Kate rubbed her eyes and stretched.

Beth climbed up into the motor home and pulled out a bag from her backpack.

"Coffee from our hangout in LA," Kate yelped. "I thought I'd have to go without until we got back home."

"Life's too short for bad coffee."

"I'm usually grateful for any coffee."

Beth turned to her. "That's what worries me about you, Kate. You're so often grateful for whatever just slides your way. You don't let yourself ask for more."

"Beggars can't be choosers," she joked, watching Beth fill the coffee maker.

"With food, that's okay. With girlfriends…"

"You heard about the fight at Emeril's."

"Yes."

"Who told you?"

Beth tapped her chest. "I'm a Teamster, Kate."

"Word travels fast."

"Among the union members, fast maybe, but far, not too much."

"So not a whole lot of people know about my fight with Hannah?"

"Well, lucky for you, when you called for the rides home last night, Alissa picked up the call and sent Sally and herself to come get you two. They're very good observers of people. Of course, it takes a lesbian who's been in a fight to recognize a lesbian who's just been in a fight."

Kate nodded in agreement.

Beth turned the coffee pot on. "I'm just sorry I didn't get a chance to come find you sooner."

Kate waved off the apology. "You had your hands full with getting through the first week. How's the posse?"

"Posse's all good." Beth gathered up two empty coffee mugs. "But we weren't talking about the posse. We were talking about you and Hannah."

"Shit." Kate's head dropped. "It's crappy right now."

"Regular crappy or newly crappy?"

"Regular crappy."

When the coffee was ready, Beth poured the steaming black brew. Beth sat down next to Kate and squeezed her shoulder. "Please don't get hurt by her."

"You're starting to sound like Laney."

Beth smiled. "Perhaps."

❖

"Have you heard from her?" Krissy and Dawn were going over fabrication drawings for a themed restaurant that was under construction close to the Peabody Hotel. FDF had the contract to theme the entrance, which entailed building out a grotto area complete with a waterfall and buried treasure.

Dawn was marking up an incorrect water line placement, one that would have been, as originally drawn, in the line of sight of the restaurant patrons. While no one under six would ever believe the grotto was real, hiding the water source was still obviously important to the overall look. "Who?"

"Who? Kate, that's who," Krissy made her own notes on another drawing asking the client to clarify the rate of animation of the treasure chest's lid, which was designed to open and close. "We both know I wasn't talking about Bridget, seeing as you haven't seen her since she got bombed at the Christmas party."

"You could have been talking about Bridget."

"Why would I ask about her if the only person that's been on your mind is Kate?"

Dawn harrumphed. Krissy was right. And since their almost-kiss the night of the Christmas party, they hadn't spoken. Kate would soon be back in LA with her LA life and Dawn was here, wishing she'd never, ever invited Bridget to the party.

"I suppose that's a no."

"Krissy, why would I pursue a woman who is a big shot in LA, one who already has a girlfriend, and one who will be gone before you know it?"

Krissy put her pencil down and turned to face Dawn. "Because love is blind."

"I'm not in love with her. I hardly even know her." Dawn's last words dropped in volume because she realized she'd responded with a much louder voice than was comfortable.

Out of the silence Krissy giggled. "That's okay, because lust is blinder."

"Nothing's going to happen either way."

"Yeah, well, that's what you thought about me and Saundra, but—"

"I was wrong. I know," Dawn finished. "But I'm not wrong with Kate."

Krissy shook her head and returned to marking up the drawing. "Have it your way, then."

"It's not my way," Dawn responded dismally. "It's Kate's and Hannah's."

"I wonder if the air around Kate and Hannah is as thick with desire as it is around Kate and you."

Dawn dropped her head into her hand and she furiously rubbed her forehead. This wanting, this ache for Kate was killing her.

"Are you going with Brett, Sr. to the set of *The Glass Cross* Monday?"

"No." Dawn returned to the drawing.

"Why not?"

"I don't want to go."

"Why?"

"Just because."

Krissy pressed, "But why?"

"Because I don't want to see them together," Dawn said.

"It *is* love, then."

"How can it be love? I don't even know her. I haven't spent more than an hour with her at any given time."

"It doesn't take any longer than a heartbeat, my friend."

"This is flippin' useless, this conversation."

Krissy reached over and held Dawn's shoulder. "I've never seen you like this."

"I've never been this way."

"Just go see her."

Dawn just shook her head. "She's really out of my league."

"I wish you'd stop saying that. No one's out of anyone's league. When it all boils down to it, people are just people, my friend. Shit, girl, get your head out of your ass."

She drew in a big sigh, finally yielding. "I do like her, Krissy. Damn it. It just hurts to know that she…" Dawn's shoulders fell as she let out a pained breath.

"What? That she lives far away? That she may be with Hannah? Damn, I was standing there and saw the look on her face when she came up behind you at the Christmas party. There's no denying that look."

"I don't know."

"It's just scary when you don't know whether the feeling's mutual. And something tells me I'm right about how she feels. But you're never going to know if you keep taking yourself out of the game."

"Out of her league. Out of the game. I guess we're both using too many sports analogies." Dawn smiled feebly.

Krissy leaned in to give her a hug. "Go with Brett, Sr. tomorrow. At the very least, you really should see your work in action. You did a fantastic job."

"So did you and the rest of the team, Krissy."

"But you're the lead art director. Go."

CHAPTER EIGHTEEN

The film crew had spent the first week lighting and shooting only Hannah and Peter. Later on in the second week, the rest of the actors, including Ralph Markowitz, who had been cast in the role of the villain, would join Hannah and Peter, and they'd finish shooting the rest of the interior salt mine scenes. The exterior location at the Orlando Airport, which would be doubling for the European airport into which Hannah's character would be flying, was also still to be shot. That scene was scheduled for the first day of the last week in Orlando and only required Hannah.

Ralph Markowitz arrived on the set the beginning of the second week of shooting.

Nathan called Kate on her cell phone. "Ralph's being a pill."

"What's going on?"

"Since he has a smaller part than Hannah and Peter, we assigned him one of the smaller dressing rooms. He's complaining about the 'diminutive size of his actor's quarters' as he put it."

"Did you talk to him personally?"

"Yup. He turned me away at the door demanding that the executive producer, not the producer, come talk to him. He wants you to come talk to him."

"When's his call time?"

"In about two hours."

"Tell him that I'll see him on the set at that time," Kate said calmly. "And if he bitches any more, I'll remind him that he signed a contract that says we're paying for his acting services, not a luxury penthouse."

Nathan giggled and hung up.

❖

"Ralph. Welcome." The actor was standing just off camera, rehearsing his lines, when Kate got to the set. He leaned forward and air-kissed Kate's cheek.

"Kate, good to see you." He sniffed.

"I'm very happy to have you on this picture. Have you seen Amy yet?"

"Yes, she saw me in makeup."

"Did you get a chance to rehearse today?" Kate could tell that he was already working up a good sulk.

"Yes." His words were ever-so-slightly clipped. "I came fully prepared, but we ran lines anyway."

"That's great, Ralph." Kate patted his shoulder and began to move away but paused when Ralph cleared his throat.

"Kate, one thing…"

Kate turned, feigning an expectant look.

"Kate, the dressing room. It's rather drab. And small. I just can't fathom two weeks in that little…hole." He was actually talking through his nose, as if the very utterance of the words tasted terrible.

"They're perfectly fine accommodations. No different than what is always provided."

Growing quickly angered, Ralph puffed. "They're horrible and small."

"They're contractually sufficient, Ralph."

Red in the face, he sniffed before saying haughtily, "Not for someone who is very close to Jeffery."

It was laughable that he was going to use his business dealings with Jeffery Salzenberg as leverage, especially since Jeffery didn't know him all that well. He'd seen a script he liked, and that was his impetus in pacifying Ralph with the role on her film.

Kate sighed, giving Ralph a pained nod, not unlike the kind of nod a mafia hit man gives his mark just before he caps him. "Ralph," she paused, "there was a little issue that I had to clear up with the completion bond company." She paused again and achieved from Ralph the sudden nervous look that she'd hoped to get.

Kate moved closer to avoid causing him any embarrassment in the event that they were within earshot of anyone. "It seems that you have a heart problem, brought on by too much cocaine and alcohol. And it also seems that your doctor is concerned that if you ingest any more eight-balls, my production company might have a dead actor on its hands. We all know that dead actors have to be recast and a lot of money has to be spent to re-shoot their scenes. So, I can tell you that no one wants an actor on set who might suddenly drop to the floor in a fit of convulsions and die of brain seizures."

She then leaned in even closer and said softly in his ear for the most dramatic effect, "It seems that the doctor anticipates erratic behavior or a rapid drop in performance. So I had to plead with the completion bond company to allow you to keep this job because, I have to tell you, Ralph, they wanted to have you shit-canned. Getting upset over a dressing room could be a real hazard to your health, Ralph. Don't let those things get you riled. For the sake of your health."

When she pulled away from him, his eyes were as big as saucers.

She smiled warmly. "I know you'll give us a great performance, Ralph. I'm here if you need me."

She turned to walk away, reminding herself to tell Nathan that Ralph would probably not be causing him any more problems.

CHAPTER NINETEEN

D awn and Brett, Sr. had been greeted by Kimber who escorted them from the guard gate at the entrance of Universal Studios to the soundstages. Film people with clipboards and tools talked on two-way radios and criss-crossed in front of them as Kimber made small talk with Brett, Sr. on their walk.

The first place Kimber took them was to Soundstage Two to see the salt mine entrance and the Maiden of Salt statue.

Dawn stood in the empty, quiet soundstage and was amazed. The maiden had looked great in the shop, but the way that it looked in its resting place on the mine wall made the statue almost come to life. Hanging from the mine entrance, it looked like it had been there for decades. Kimber then took them to Soundstage Four, where the crew was filming that day.

Dawn had seen TV shows on the behind-the-scenes secrets of movie making, though she wasn't prepared for the captivating magic of the genuine thing.

As her eyes adjusted to the darkened interior of the soundstage, lights and sets and people slowly became detailed and solid.

Soundstage Four housed three of the salt mine tunnel sets, long, deep, echoing sets that were scenically painted to portray hundreds of years of mineral deposits and miners' toils. Though each tunnel was, in fact, only one side of a tunnel, the design of which enabled the camera to sit far back enough to have the focal length to shoot the actors, the half-tunnels looked almost real, especially when lit by the film's lighting department. Brown, amber, red, and green colored gels cast both ancient and sinister looks in different parts of the sets. Flames from the torches mounted on the salt mine walls flickered and licked upward, seemingly in search of fleeting fresh air.

The film crew was getting ready for a scene, so Kimber guided Brett, Sr. and Dawn to two director's chairs.

"Please sit here. We're going to be rolling film in a few minutes. You're first going to hear Jennifer, that's the woman standing over there in the red shorts, say 'roll 'em,' which cues the camera to start rolling. Then the sound man, he's sitting over there staring at that sound recorder, he'll say 'speed' which lets everyone know that the sound recorder is up to speed."

Dawn and Brett, Sr. followed her as she pointed to each step. "When that happens, the camera assistant, the guy right over there who's got the clapboard, will hold it up to the camera. See that hinged stick on the top of the clapboard, the one with the black and white diagonal stripes? Well those are called the sticks, and he will clap them together as he reads out the scene number and take number. The clapping will allow the editor, back in LA, to take these separate bits of film," she pointed to the man by the camera, "and sound," she pointed to the man with headphones on, "and synchronize them. Then what happens is the Director, Amy Parsons, that's the woman in the Levi's and faded red shirt, will say 'action,' which will cue the actors, the special effects people, and the rest of the crew, to begin the scene." Kimber finished with a broad smile. "Between the time Jennifer says 'roll 'em' and Amy says 'cut,' which signals the end of that take, no one talks or makes any noise. Be careful shifting around in these director's chairs, as well. They can squeak. Now I have to go for a few minutes. Please enjoy watching and wave at me if you need anything, okay?"

Brett, Sr. and Dawn nodded as Kimber left to go stand beside Jennifer, and then they sat down in the director's chairs. Brett, Sr. turned to Dawn. "I think I got that all, but I'm pretty much gonna shut up starting right now so I don't screw up anything."

Not taking her eyes off the set, Dawn heard him and chuckled.

Back in the production office, Kate was in the middle of solving a number of issues. As was typical, the phones were ringing incessantly and Kate, Jamie, the production manager, and Nathan, along with the production coordinator and two production assistants were climbing around and over each other on treks to the copier, the phones, and the files.

She had Charlie Gunner on the phone. He was teetering on the brink of losing the one exterior scene they had to shoot in Orlando. The location was the Orlando International Airport, of which they planned to use a small portion. The northern-most section of the airport could be easily dressed to double for the European airport. Using the Orlando airport enabled them to spend a lot less money and go through a lot less red tape, given that the European bureaucracy of shooting in a foreign airport had only gotten worse after the attacks of September eleventh.

"What happened, Charlie?" Kate pulled her Long Beach baseball cap further down on her head. For no reason, thoughts of Dawn wandered into her consciousness. Lately, in the middle of unrelated conversations, recollections of Dawn would interrupt her concentration. She'd flash back to their first meeting in the conference room, their discussions together of the props being built in the shop, and especially the time they spent at the FDF Christmas party.

She hadn't quite understood what had happened between them that night in Dawn's studio. As the Christmas party carried on in the shop, Kate was more than happy to escape to Dawn's creative place. And the kiss that almost happened had felt so natural. There had been no thought, no plan. Just feelings. And sensations. And Dawn's eyes.

After Christmas, when Dawn and the FDF team had come out to the Universal Studio soundstages to install the set pieces and props, Kate was still in LA getting ready to move the production across the country. And though she thought to call Dawn at least fifty times, she didn't. She wasn't sure what she would even say. She didn't need an update on the work FDF was doing; she already had that information. She couldn't thank her for a nice time at the Christmas party because Dawn had neither invited her nor taken her, so expressing gratitude would have appeared out of place. What she wanted to tell her was that she'd been thinking a lot about her. She'd often thought about their talks, about watching Dawn sculpt the Maiden of Salt statue and the little angel. She wanted to tell her that no one had ever looked into her eyes like she had. She wanted to tell her that sometimes when she kissed Hannah, she imagined it was Dawn.

And when she had gotten the message that some folks from FDF were coming to the set, she had cursed the conference call that conflicted with their arrival. The call couldn't be changed, so she entrusted Kimber with receiving them.

"The Airport Commissioner has a problem with the permit," Charlie said. "It's been signed for weeks, but now he's saying he doesn't want us to shoot between the hours of eight a.m. and ten a.m., and four p.m. and six p.m."

"That's silly," Kate said as she shuffled through the rest of her phone messages. She wondered what Dawn had done for New Year's Eve.

"He wants to speak with the executive producer. In person."

Kate shook her head. *I'm not about to go run after the airport commissioner.* And as an afterthought, she added, *but I'd sure as hell run after Dawn.* "I'll send Nathan." Maybe she shouldn't be thinking so much about Dawn. Still, the thought made a smile arise.

"Okay."

"Are you doing all right otherwise?"

"Yeah," Charlie replied. "I just about had twins when I got that call, though."

"Make sure you talk to someone at the Executive Airport across town just in case Nathan can't talk the commissioner out of the restriction." The smaller airport needed to be readied as their Plan B, just in case.

"I'm headed over there now."

"Good. And don't worry, Charlie. We'll get the shot, no matter what. Just keep pushing. You're doing great."

Charlie blew out an audible breath. "Thanks, Kate."

Kate hung up and Betsy, the production coordinator, called over to her, "Kate, Carrie's on line three. She's got a question about dailies."

Kate had hired her friend, Carrie Monahan, to edit the film. Carrie stayed in LA receiving each day's film via an overnight service. At the conclusion of each day's shoot, the film was shipped overnight to a film lab in LA. The film was processed, and the original would get delivered to Carrie with digital copies sent to the StormRunner production office in Orlando and Jeffery Salzenberg's office at World Film Studio.

It was standard that Kate and Amy Parsons would view the digital footage each evening after the crew wrapped. The speediness of the digital copy, though much poorer in quality, allowed the production to minimize time lost. If no anomalies were discovered, Carrie would continue editing and the film would continue shooting. Any significant anomalies were communicated to Sandra Batnow and Hal Rosen. If the problem was a technical, camera-related problem, Sandra handled its resolution. If the problem was with the look of the sets, the production designer got involved. Sometimes the decision would be made to re-shoot a shot or a whole scene or add a new shot or scene. And it was always better to find out as soon as possible that something like that was required.

The cast and crew were invited to watch the dailies each night after wrap. Sometimes Amy would talk to one of the actors about a particular scene and apply changes in future scenes. Sometimes the lighting designer, having seen the dailies, would correct small nuances in the scenes to be shot. At times, Carrie would call to discuss with Kate how a scene was coming together in the edit bay.

"I think we need a transition between scene 211 and 212," Carrie told Kate over the phone. "In 211, we see Tracy turn to Kip, but in scene 212, the only footage I have of that part of the scene is as he's already walking away. It doesn't cut together well."

Kate agreed. "Amy and I wondered whether that would be a problem. We talked about a possible solution. We'll shoot a new scene, called 211XX, which will also give us the opportunity to add a line of dialogue that we think was missing as well. We'll shoot Kip walking away from Tracy and he'll be saying, 'Let's try this way.' I'll tell Amy that we talked. She can shoot that scene tomorrow."

"That'll work fine," Carrie said. "How are the rest of things going out there?"

"As well as can be expected. Normal problems, but we're on schedule."

"How's Hannah?" Carrie had always kept up with Kate and Hannah since they first began dating.

Kate sighed. "I don't know, Carrie. It's not easy."

"Is Hannah being difficult?"

"Well, Hannah's being Hannah."

"I'm sorry to hear that. She doesn't much act like you're a couple unless it's for appearances sake, huh?"

"Is it that obvious?"

"Yes, Kate, it is."

"Beth was pretty much telling me the same thing yesterday." She chuckled. "Sometimes I really don't understand why we're still together."

"Well, you're a big girl and you have your reasons."

"I suppose."

"Are you doubting you're choices?"

"Every time the fights get ugly."

"You mean every time she gets ugly?"

"It takes two to fight."

"Kate, I've seen you fight. You're not a dirty player. Hannah is."

"Casting her in this film might not have been such a good idea."

"Well, on a professional level, she's a good actress, Kate. And I challenge you to show me a film shoot where there aren't at least a handful of romances going on."

"There's not a lot of romance with us, lately."

"I'm sorry, sweetie. Would you like me to fly out and visit? I can get there by tomorrow, no problem."

"Thank you, but it's okay. Beth is here to slap me around if I get any stupid ideas, like buying her a ring or something."

"You listen to Beth. She'll watch your back."

"Okay, I will. Thanks."

As soon as she hung up, Betsy called out to her again, "Laney's on hold on line one, she said it's really important, and I'm supposed to remind you that the folks from Florida Design and Fabrication are on the set. They've been here for about an hour."

Kate hoped that one of them was Dawn. Rapid flutters in her stomach felt like June bugs around a porch light. But she was still stuck at the office.

Damn, she said to herself as she picked up the line.

"Kate, Leo Buckley's been calling here wanting to get Carrie's cell phone number. I must say, he's been pretty forceful."

"Did he say why he wanted it?" Kate knew the production executive for the studio was calling about something related to the control of the film. Still, she wanted to know specifics.

"No," Laney said. "He just keeps barking orders. It pissed me off so now I have Frances intercepting the calls."

Kate laughed, picturing Frances, StormRunner's sweet and youthful receptionist, holding him at bay. "I'm sure that's pissing him off. Sorry about the hassle."

"No problem. You know that I've been barked at by much more formidable men than Leo. Shall I put you through?"

"Yes, thanks."

Kate checked her watch. It was two p.m. in Orlando, eleven a.m. in LA. She wondered how long the FDF people would stay on set. If Dawn was there on set, she so badly wanted to see her again.

Laney came back on the line. "Leo's secretary is putting you through."

At the moment that Leo answered, Kate got directly to the point. "What's this about wanting Carrie's number, Leo?"

"It's not me, Kate, you know that, huh?" Leo offered quickly. "It's Jeffrey. He didn't like yesterday's dailies. He just wants to chat with Carrie. It's really a little thing, you know?"

"You tell Jeffery that if he has a problem with the dailies, he needs to call me. He has my cell number. Tell him that I don't appreciate him trying to go around me to get to my editor."

"Kate, come on, he just wants to have a little chat with Carrie, that's all."

"Tell him to have that little chat with me."

Leo changed his tactics and became brusque. "Kate, do I have to remind you that Jeffery runs the studio that finances your movie?"

Kate almost laughed. "Do I have to remind you that my last two movies for your studio grossed over $200 million at the box office?" Kate was getting bored, "Drop the stiff arm, Leo."

"Kate…"

But before Leo could babble on any further, Kate said, "I'm hanging up now. Good-bye, Leo."

The next call she made was to Jeffrey.

"Jeffrey Salzenburg's office."

"Gwen, it's Kate Nyland."

"Hi Kate. Jeffrey's at Keith Oberman's office. I don't expect him to be gone long."

"Would you have him call me on my cell, please?"

"Sure will."

She hung up and then called Carrie to tell her that Jeffery and Leo were trying to get a hold of her. Carrie told her that there was no way she'd take any calls from either of them. With the Jeffery issue temporarily on hold, she finally got away from the phone and the production office and headed over to Soundstage Two.

"Kate," Ralph Markowitz greeted her with grandiose aloofness when she entered the soundstage.

"Hello to you, too." Kate smiled nevertheless. "How are you?"

"Just peachy," he replied.

Per usual, he tilted his head back and sniffed the air a little higher than everyone else, as if attempting to avoid breathing "common man air."

Kate knew that an inquiry of a more personal type would appeal to his ego. "How are your scenes today?"

He brightened immediately. "Going quite smoothly."

Per usual, it worked.

Kate found Kimber at the crafts service table in Soundstage Two. She had just bitten into a carrot when Kate greeted her and asked where the FDF folks were.

"They just left. I started to radio you to let you know that they were about to leave, but they told me not to bother you."

Disappointed, Kate nevertheless nodded quickly. Kimber looked remorseful. "I tried, I'm sorry."

Kate reached up to squeeze her shoulder. "It's fine, really. Thank you for escorting them around."

Kimber beamed. "You're welcome. Any time."

Kyle walked up to Kate. "Hannah just broke the torch prop, and we don't have a backup."

"How'd she break it?"

Kyle looked sheepish, "She was playing croquet with it."

"When do you shoot with it again? And tell me it's not the next shot," Kate said.

Kyle smiled through clenched teeth. "We'll shoot around it for the rest of today, but we'll need it tomorrow."

"Okay." Kate said calmly, "Get on the radio and ask Nathan to call Florida Design and Fabrication and have them make another one. And tell the property master that we're handling it."

Kyle nodded, having gotten his orders and sprung into action so readily that Kate couldn't help but admire his youthful gusto.

"And another thing, Kyle…" Kate sighed audibly. "Tell Kimber that I asked you two to keep an extra eye on Hannah. Let her play with whatever she wants as long as it's not needed on camera." Kyle nodded his understanding. With dismay, Kate realized that to an outsider the conversation could have easily sounded like they were referring to an annoying three-year-old or someone's pesky dog.

Kyle trotted off and as Kate turned to make her way to the set, Kimber called out, "Oh, I forgot…"

As she turned back around, Kimber pulled a box out from the

utility bag she always had strapped to her shoulder. "Dawn said to give this to you."

So Dawn had just been there. Kate's heart sank at the thought of missing her. She took the box, slightly perplexed, and thanked Kimber as she made her way to the set. Her director's chair was always right next to Amy's. Moved from set to set, location to location, director's chairs for the cast and crew were a Hollywood tradition. Her name was embroidered on the back, and saddlebags were fashioned on either side to hold scripts, pens, and bottles of water.

Amy was ready for the next setup, so as Jennifer called for the commencement of the scene, Kate took a seat in her chair. By the time Amy called for "action," Kate had quietly opened the box.

She was glad that the crew was busy shooting a scene, for what she found in the box made her heart jump. She couldn't control the smile that spread widely.

It was the clay angel that Dawn had sculpted weeks ago when they were meeting about the Maiden of Salt statue, the one whose wings reached out, half unfurled as if ready to embrace someone. It had been given more detail and had been fired with a warm amber glaze. Dawn had inscribed the back, For K –from D. She turned it over and over in her hands, feeling what Dawn must have felt as she so lovingly sculpted it. The angel was beautiful and Kate was moved by it.

She reached for her cell phone to call Dawn and thank her but realized that she didn't have Dawn's number. *I could call FDF now, and even though Dawn wouldn't be back yet, I could speak with the receptionist and leave her a message to call me as soon as she…*

"What do you have there?" Hannah's voice came from right in front of Kate. She looked up and realized that Amy must have called "cut" because the crew was again moving in all different directions, getting ready for the next setup. Hannah's hands were resting on the arms of the director's chair and she leaned forward to kiss Kate.

Kate chose to change the subject. "How's the scene going?"

Hannah sat down in Amy's chair. "Okay. Peter's nice enough. I'm glad that Jennifer and Kyle are on the shoot, but honestly, this town sure sucks."

"What sucks about it?" Kate was used to Hannah's adeptness at never being too far from a complaint.

"Jennifer and I went to downtown Orlando last night to check out the scene, and there wasn't one. What a hick town. We ended up going over to Disney's Pleasure Island, for shit sakes. Can you imagine the picture in *Hollywood Live* magazine?" Hannah made quote marks in the air. "'Hannah Corrant boogies with Mickey Mouse.' It would be absolutely embarrassing."

So that's where Hannah had been. Not that Kate and Hannah needed to spend every night together, which had especially not been the case since they'd gotten to Orlando, and had not been the case even more so since they had fought. But Kate thought at the very least Hannah would make an effort to get together at least once.

Admittedly, though, Kate hadn't made much of an effort toward Hannah since the dinner at Emeril's either.

"Maybe Austria will be more fun," Kate said.

"Hopefully. Oh, I asked Jamie to book a flight for me to LA. I need to go after we wrap on Wednesday. I'll be back Friday morning."

"What's the trip for?" Not that Kate was nosey, but her request for a first class ticket meant that StormRunner would be paying for it.

"I'm meeting with Geraldo Sanchez about his next film."

"We have a week and a half here and a week in Austria. Can't it wait until we get back?"

"No, it can't," Hannah snapped back. "Christ, Kate, if we weren't sleeping together I doubt you'd be giving me the third degree."

Kate hadn't been ready for the barb. She took a deep breath and considered correcting Hannah's erroneous conjecture. Not just because Kate had the right to ask questions of anyone who wanted to spend the production's money, but because every actor who signed a StormRunner Productions contract committed to being present for the entire run of the production, especially while they were on distant location. Certainly trips home from location shoots were granted, but with Hannah's short turn around time, any number of monkey wrenches could get thrown into the film's already tight six-day work schedule: a forgotten alarm clock, a missed limo ride to the LA airport, a storm over Texas. Kate just didn't like the particular risk of the request.

Each hour that the crew was on set, ready to shoot but forced to wait for an absent actor, would cost the production thousands of dollars.

But having the ability to manage problems was Kate's strong suit. And keeping the lead actress happy, not because they were sleeping together but because it was good for the film, was still important.

"Let me see what I can do."

"Thanks, doll," Hannah said, suddenly finding her manners. She pecked her on the cheek and got up to leave.

"I can't promise anything." Whether Hannah heard or not, Kate was unsure.

As she watched Hannah walk away, Kate's cell phone pulsated in its holder.

Since the crew was not quite ready yet for the next setup, she took the call.

"Kate," she heard through the receiver. "It's Jeffery. How's the shoot going?"

"Very well, thanks."

"I've seen the dailies, and they look great so far."

"We're pleased with the dailies as well," Kate replied before pausing a moment. "Jeffery, I know that you really care about this film," she began with a softer preamble given that Jeffery had a very large and a very touchy ego. "However, I need to ask you to call me directly rather than calling Carrie." Normally, orders like this would send Jeffery through the roof, and such commands would typically be the last words spoken to him by soon-to-be ex-film industry workers. No one told Hollywood demi-gods like Jeffery what to do. But Jeffery and Kate had a long-standing respect for each other that went back to the days when Jeffery and Kate were both fledgling production executives at Buena Strada Pictures.

When they were in their early twenties, both had been hired at Buena Strada Pictures, the very new, but soon to be the biggest and most dominant film studio in Hollywood. Jeffery had come to the studio via a well known and well established father, who was a film mogul in his own right. Jeffery's father had been the king of animated films and had made a personal request of Buena Strada's studio head to hire his son for the summer. That summer turned into a career, and by the time Jeffery had climbed the ladder at the studio, he was well seasoned to run his own.

Kate had started that same summer, fresh off a string of non-union films that had tested her every step of the way. She'd first worked as a script supervisor, then as an assistant director, and then as a production manager.

Of the four assistant production executives that came aboard that summer, the first year that Buena Strada Pictures was launched, Kate was the only one with actual film experience. Soon, Kate was promoted to production executive, then to senior production executive, and was the first female to do so. Like Jeffery, the others were products of a nepotistic industry, but each had worked hard and acquired actual production experience through difficult trials by fire. And in the early days, Jeffrey had benefited from Kate's helpful advice.

Still, Kate had to be careful with Jeffery. He had struggled in the studio system while Kate eventually left the studio confines for the world of independent production, and Jeffery was now in a power position. He had approved the very lucrative development deal for StormRunner Productions, and World Film ultimately called the shots. And though Jeffery never forgot that Kate had been one of the ones who helped him learn the business, he could still be a bastard when it came to control. He wasn't above breaking the rules or infringing upon a sacred trust to get his way.

"I hear what you're saying," Jeffery said finally. "I just get nervous when my money is away on location. And I wanted to establish a good working relationship with Carrie since she's here in LA."

Kate knew the odor of bullshit when she smelled it. But she didn't yet know just what he was up to, so she wasn't inclined to confront him. If Jeffery had a mind to try to sway Carrie's edit decisions, Kate was convinced that Carrie wouldn't budge. And while he hadn't told her his motive, he had graciously conceded. For the moment.

"Just call me directly if you have any concerns, Jeffery. You know my phone is on twenty-four-seven."

"Will do, Kate. Good luck to you. Keep Leo posted."

Leo would get production reports just like Jeffery and the rest of World Film Studios, but no more than that. Those reports would portray the most accurate state of affairs on *The Glass Cross* set. And the dailies would show everyone the look and the performances that were being captured. The rest, as every independent producer knew, should be left to the expertise of the executive producer and her crew.

Kate called FDF and reached their receptionist who informed her that Dawn wasn't yet back in the shop. Kate left her cell number and asked that it be given to Dawn as soon as possible. A stirring warmth spread through her, knowing that Dawn would soon have her number. A connection had been made that seemed so simple yet so important.

After the cast and crew wrapped, Kate went by to see Hannah in her motor home. Hannah invited her in and turned toward the bathroom.

"Jeffery loves the dailies," Kate said to the back of Hannah's head.

"Really?" Hannah turned around quickly. One of her dreams was to become the "it" girl of World Film Studio. That would mean that Jeffery would personally push her to every producer that made a film at his studio. It would mean that he would handle very high-priced deals for her. It meant that people would have to think more than twice before hassling her about anything.

"You're doing a great job," Kate added.

"He said that?"

"No, I said that."

"Oh."

Kate looked at her watch. "Would you like to have a late dinner with me?"

"I don't think so."

Kate waited for an explanation, not because she felt Hannah needed to supply one, but because Hannah had dragged out the end of the sentence making it sound like the reason would be forthcoming. But all Hannah did was shrug.

Kate left the motor home feeling stung. Hannah hadn't spoken to her for most of the day except when she had asked to be flown to LA. Kate had been waiting for Hannah to make some kind of an effort to make up since their fight at Emeril's, but it hadn't happened. But she realized that she had been just as guilty of stonewalling, so she had attempted to reconcile with Hannah by asking her out. However Hannah had no inclination to have dinner with her, nor did she provide any kind of reason. Even a pretend "I'm really tired" would have felt better than a stare and a shrug.

Kate headed back to the hotel for another night of solo room service.

CHAPTER TWENTY

"Production office to Kate." The radio call came when Kate was on the set working out a dialogue problem with Amy.

"Go for Kate," she said in two-way radio speak that was every crew member's automatic second language. Normally people called Kate on her cell phone, but she'd left it in the office to charge.

"What's your twenty?" It was Betsy, the production coordinator.

"I'm on set with Amy."

"Kurt from Florida Design and Fabrication called."

"Yes?"

"The replacement for the torch prop that broke yesterday is ready, and he wanted you to know that it's finished. And he told me to emphasize the words 'on time.'"

Kate laughed. "Okay, thanks."

"Production, clear."

When Kate got back to the office to retrieve her cell phone, there were five messages on her voice mail.

The first was from Jeffery, so she called him.

"About the dailies," Jeffery began, forgoing any greeting. "More close-ups of Hannah."

Kate almost laughed. It sounded so damn Hollywood. "Any particular nostril you want to concentrate on?"

"Ha ha." Jeffery wasn't laughing.

Kate now had the reason that Jeffery had wanted to talk with Carrie. "Okay, Jeffery. I'll talk to Amy and Carrie."

The next three messages were from LA, and one was from Dawn.

"Kate, it's Dawn." The voice sent a warm surge through her. "I suppose you're on the set and can't talk. After we left the set yesterday, I went straight to another job, and I just got your message from the receptionist. So now I have your number." She chuckled then sighed softly. "Well, I hope to talk with you soon. Good-bye." Kate listened for the gentle click and Dawn's voice was gone.

Kate had to see her.

The Transportation Department had given her a convertible Cadillac to take, and driving with the top down in the Orlando sun was magnificent. Butterflies rose in Kate's stomach as she approached the off ramp that would take her to FDF.

Dawn, she decided, was magnificent. And Kate was fairly sure that Dawn had no idea how astonishing she was. Above her intense beauty, she was amazingly competent, and Kate appreciated her work.

Her sense of self was bold, something that made Kate feel strangely vulnerable and raw. It was as if Dawn could see everything about her, good and bad, explicit and implicit. When Kate closed her eyes at night she often felt as if she were soaring through the night skies, looking down on Dawn who held her in flight, connected to her as a sort of safe anchor, a boundless spirit coaxing her to keep flying because assuredly Dawn would remain steadfast, on the ground, watchful and protective. And when she woke up in the morning, the memories of her night imaginings stayed with her long into the day.

It most certainly was crazy for her to make a run that her production assistant should have made. But it had also been crazy for her to be thinking about Dawn so much. On the way over, it had occurred to her that Dawn might not even be there that day. But even being back in the shop would make her feel good. She knew the memories of working with Dawn as well as of the Christmas party would come right back.

Krissy was outside finishing a cigarette when she recognized Kate. She held her hands high as if either directing her in or requesting a hug. Or both. And they did hug when Kate got out of the car.

"It's great to see you, Kate," Krissy said.

"And it's great to see you."

"What are you doing out here? Aren't you busy with the movie?"

"Well, I am, but I had an opportunity to visit, so I took it."

"The torch prop that we remade?"

Kate nodded.

"Well, we're the lucky ones." Krissy beamed. "Dawn told me all about being on the set yesterday. She really loved it."

"I just wish I could have seen her."

"Yeah, the woman who showed them around said that you couldn't get away from phone calls."

Kate shrugged modestly. "Yeah. Regrettably."

"Would you like to see her?"

"More than you know." Her thoughts had come out without edit.

Krissy regarded her, deadpan. "I doubt it."

Dawn heard Krissy calling her name from across the shop. She had been at the far end, in the corner by the supply cabinet, and as she turned, Krissy had taken a step away, revealing the silhouette of Kate, who was walking toward her.

As sawdust particles floated in the space between them, Dawn took in the woman that she had been unable to rid her mind of. And it made her deeply happy.

Between them, other workers manned machines that turned out shards of metal, grinding steel against more steel, causing metallic moans that screamed for more oil. Planks of wood surged past the edge of her line of sight and she raised her hand to wave.

"Hey," Kate said as she reached Dawn. "How are you?"

"What are you doing here?"

"I snuck away to come get the torch prop."

"You snuck away?"

"Yeah. I played rock-paper-scissors with the production assistant and finally beat him two out of three." She smiled squarely at Dawn. "I used it as an excuse to see you."

"You did?" *Had she really said that?*

"Yes." Then she took in a deep breath and blew it out. "I wanted to apologize for not being able to see you yesterday. I can't tell you how disappointed I was."

"So was I." Dawn smiled. "But I really liked being there. It was really exciting."

"It can be," Kate said. "But more importantly, I wanted to see you personally to thank you for the angel. It's magnificent."

"I'm glad you liked it."

"I more than liked it…" And for the first time since she'd walked up, Kate dropped her eyes from Dawn's, which wasn't the best idea.

The ultra thin material of Dawn's T-shirt strained evocatively at her breasts. Kate couldn't help but notice, and her glance was totally automatic. And though the double take was not intentional, Kate didn't look away the second time. Through the thin cotton T-shirt, it was evident that Dawn's left nipple was hard, its tip generous and firm, pushing against the fabric. Her right nipple did the same but there was something different about it.

"Kate?"

At once embarrassed, Kate chuckled. "I'm sorry." She blinked, realizing her stare was impolite and shook her head before confessing, "I'm sorry, I was…it was…ah…"

Dawn lowered her voice, "My nipple ring?"

Kate's breath caught in her throat, forcing the immediate task of trying to settle the gulp of air lodged there. With words escaping her, she just nodded.

You're acting like a goofball, Kate thought. She'd seen nipple rings before. Living in LA made it almost commonplace to see piercings through practically every body part imaginable. Nothing was really new to her in that respect. Admittedly, she'd never actually been with a woman who had a pierced nipple, and it hadn't been on her things-to-do-before-I-die list. Pierced nipples had just never been significant one way or the other.

Not until that day.

"Your nipple ring," Kate managed to repeat.

When Dawn gazed at her, a slight Mona Lisa smile forming, Kate fumbled to clarify. "Ah, I just hadn't noticed it until now. Did it hurt?"

"When I had it done. Not now."

"Does it…enhance…things?" *Oh, shit,* Kate immediately caught herself. "Oh, hell. I'm sorry. That's personal…"

"It's okay." Dawn's slow southern accent sounded so sultry. "And yes, it's supposed to."

Kate saw Dawn's expression change and turned to see Kurt approaching. She reluctantly dropped the subject, and they fell into superfluous conversation.

CHAPTER TWENTY-ONE

H ow are you?" On her walk between the soundstages and her motor home, Kate had called Dawn at FDF. The thought of Dawn's nipple ring had dominated her thoughts so completely that she couldn't banish it from her brain. It was amazing to Kate that she had become fixated on such a simple image. And it had driven her to imagine foolish notions.

"I'm great. And very happy you came by yesterday."

"I was lucky that I caught you in the shop." Kate had imagined what the nipple ring might feel like against her breast if they held each other closely.

"I have a very demanding client that needs a lot of work done. I'm basically stuck there."

"Your client must be horrible." She had imagined Dawn slowly lifting her shirt off and how shiny the ring would look against her dark nipple and tanned breast.

"Terrible."

"Persistent and overbearing, I suppose." And she'd imagined her mouth wrapped around it.

"Persistent, I hope. Overbearing, hardly."

"Well, after I saw you yesterday, I realized that I completely forgot to ask you something."

"I wonder why?" Dawn ribbed.

"You're teasing a woman in a self-admitted moment of weakness."

"All right, I'll be good."

"I wanted to invite you out to the set again. This time, I'll be available. Will you come?"

"When?"

"Whenever it's convenient for you. As long as it's soon." As soon as she said it, Kate wasn't sure if her last comment was flirtatious or just polite.

"How about tomorrow?"

"Wonderful. I'll have Kimber come get you again at the security gate. What time?"

"How about eleven?"

"That'd be great. And please stay for lunch. Our caterer is fantastic."

"I'll see you then."

Should I be doing this? Kate wondered. *Yes, because Dawn helps me find that balance. And I just want to see her. What was wrong with that?* She was far superior in character to most people Kate knew. Being around her made her feel appreciated and valued.

❖

Kimber brought Dawn back to the set. They were shooting a scene toward the end of the movie where Hannah's character slips and falls into a deeper cavern, and Roger's character, who is blind, must try to save her.

"Here." Kimber offered Dawn a director's chair. It had Kate's name on it and sat just off camera range at the line where the salt mine set began.

"Kate said she'd be here really soon, and this time she promised that she wouldn't be kept away with some problem."

"Who's sitting in the big chief's chair?" Beth walked up to Kimber and put her arm around her.

Kimber smiled widely, "This is Dawn and she's a guest of Kate's."

Beth reached her hand out. "I'm Beth, Kate's best friend. And on this set, I'm also the motor home wrangler."

Dawn took Beth's hand in hers. "A pleasure to meet you."

Kimber pardoned herself saying she had to get back to the set, and Dawn thanked her again for getting her. Beth took a seat. "Kate was telling me about you. You did some work for the film?"

"I work for the Orlando company that built some of the sets and props."

"Have you ever been on a set before?"

"Just the other day, but that was the first time, yes."

"Well, welcome," Beth said

"I know this might sound silly," Dawn turned, saying to Beth, "but it seems that there are a lot of people crowded in this small area around the set, and a lot of them seem to be just standing around."

Beth chuckled. "I know it must look bizarre and it is. Having a job in the film industry isn't like having a normal job. Everyone you see that's not running around or doing something is in kind of a ready mode. There are a lot of things that have to happen between each setup. And all the different tasks have to finish right about at the same time, so that the camera can roll as often as possible. And that's because it costs an arm and a leg for every minute we sit here not shooting." Beth paused to make sure Dawn was keeping up with her. "So then the camera stops and everyone knows what they have to do next and they go do it. When they get done, they stand close by waiting for the next shot. Some people might not have a lot to do at a particular time, but every single one has to be ready to spring into action. It takes a lot of concentration and awareness to stand by because the work comes in bursts of very rapid action. In the industry, we call it 'hurry up and wait.'"

Beth then pointed to the people most directly on set who were standing underneath very large overhead lights, looking directly up into them. "See those people? They're in the lighting department. They're adjusting the lights for the next setup of the scene we're shooting right now. While they're doing that, the first assistant director, that woman in the beige shorts over there, is talking to the script supervisor. She's making sure that the script supervisor's continuity notes reflect what's happening on the set."

As Beth was explaining the process, Kate walked onto the set from out of the darkened shadows just behind the klieg lights. Beth nudged Dawn. "There's Kate. The woman she's talking to is Amy Parsons, the film's director. They're strategizing about something or another: the creative look of the film, the actors' performances, or something more mundane like the schedule or budget. It's hard to tell whether the topic is good or bad because they both keep their cool so well."

Dawn nodded. "I've seen Kate in action before. She's amazing." And it was something that Dawn was able to witness with much pleasure.

To have seen her argue with, or better yet, completely command, Kurt at FDF was remarkable, but to see her on her own turf was even more exciting. She looked incredible. Radiant, strong, and confident. Kate, standing in a close huddle with Amy, looked completely self-assured and wore her grace and authority capably. Dawn only wished she could listen in on the conversation. It was obviously an important topic, the way they nodded and murmured.

"I have to agree," Beth said. "Kate's something else."

"She sure is," Dawn's reply was a low rumble that came from her chest, and she realized too late that there had been much more feeling in that simple response than she should have revealed. She stole a glance at Beth to see if she had caught it. Beth stared back, a crooked smile on her lips.

Dawn smiled self-consciously and turned back in time to see Kimber interrupt the twosome and whisper in Kate's ear. Kate nodded, and though she couldn't hear what they were saying, Kate's lips formed the word, "where?"

Kimber said something else and Kate smiled and mouthed "thank you."

Presently, Kate wrapped up with Amy.

Walking over to her director's chair, Kate knew she couldn't contain her delight at seeing Dawn and didn't try to. Automatically, Dawn stood when Kate approached and, rather impulsively, she hugged her.

Kate held her before reluctantly pulling away. "I'm so glad you came back."

Dawn grinned back.

Kate said hello to Beth who returned the greeting with a wide-toothed hello of her own.

Getting up out of the director's chair, Beth offered, "I need to get back outside. It was very nice meeting you, Dawn. I hope to see you again before we wrap."

"I'd like that." Dawn waved as Beth strode off toward the soundstage door.

Jennifer called out that they were going for the next setup. Kate sat down in Amy's chair and reached out to squeeze Dawn's forearm. "Finally a short break."

Dawn smiled warmly making Kate flush inside. How could this

woman trigger such intense joy in Kate's heart? She thought of her non-stop. Thought of what she was doing, wondering whether she was at work with her hands massaging red clay or at home lying in bed with a warm night breeze blowing in her window. She wanted this woman. Wanted her close. Wanted to make her smile and sigh. At once she understood how it felt to want to crawl inside someone.

Kate held onto the firmness of Dawn's forearm and took in a deep breath. Just before speaking, she slowly blew it out. "I've been thinking about you."

"You have?" Dawn said,

Just then they were interrupted by Kyle who had a question for Kate.

While they talked, Dawn concentrated on the intense energy she felt from Kate's hand on her forearm. Kate was wearing the acorn bracelet that she'd given her. Her heart warmed seeing it there on Kate's strong arm. When Kyle had gotten his answer, a woman stepped in behind him with some information for Kate. They spoke in a seemingly different language with foreign terms like golden time, B-roll, and aspect ratio peppering the conversation. While they talked, Kate must have been aware of her hand on her forearm because she felt her squeeze, very slowly, two times.

Replaying the last thing Kate had said to her, it hadn't actually seemed real, Kate telling Dawn that she'd been thinking about her. And in the way she'd said it, Dawn was sure it wasn't meant to be a casual remark: "I was thinking about you and wondered if you liked the car you drive." And it sure hadn't felt like a business comment: "Oh, I was thinking about you and wondered if you had finished the work I need." Kate's eyes burned into her, intensely and magnetically. In the same desirous way that Dawn would have said it had she voiced the notion first.

Excitement fluttered in her throat and her fists balled up in sudden stimulation. The motion had rippled up her forearm, connecting with Kate's hand, making Kate's eyes flicker a moment in Dawn's direction before returning to her conversation.

Dawn watched Amy with an actor she recognized but whose name she couldn't recall. A moment later, the man standing behind the camera called him Peter, and she flashed on one of the last movies she saw. She remembered that his name was Peter Carson. And then, from within the shadows off of the set's perimeter, Hannah stepped out and into the klieg lights.

Dawn froze. There she was, one of the biggest stars in Hollywood. And Kate's girlfriend.

The actors discussed the scene with Amy, moving around the set, asking questions about the way to turn and where the camera would be at that point in the scene and what kind of shot it would be, close up or medium close.

Dawn had to admit that it was exciting to see a Hollywood celebrity not more than twenty feet away from her, but what really mattered was that this was the woman who had captured Kate's heart. She imagined how electrifying their lives must be with Hollywood parties and their pictures in national magazines. Hannah, a movie star, and Kate, a ground-breaking film producer, seemed to be an unmatchable pair. And matched, they were. An ache formed in her chest, something she hadn't felt in a long time. She recognized it as the ache of longing. And more agonizingly, it was the ache of longing for something she couldn't have.

Though Amy and the actors were close by, their discussion competed with the noise of crew members getting ready for the next shot, lights being adjusted, cables being pulled, and camera men calling out numbers. Again, snippets of terminology of the strange new language punched through the conversations as crew members talked about rack focus, day-for-night, and MOS.

"I'm sorry about that." Kate broke into Dawn's thoughts.

"I'm just mesmerized with this process," Dawn said.

"Crazy, huh?"

"Exciting. I imagine most people would love to get a close up view like the one I'm getting."

Exciting? Exciting was the thought of Dawn's nipple ring. Kate often found herself actually shaking her head in desire-filled astonishment. Why couldn't she keep that one vision out of her mind? If a lawyer tried to intimidate her into breaking a contract or if an overly arrogant agent snubbed her, she'd drop the thought like the inconsequential fact that it was, but this new awareness that just underneath the shirt of this incredible woman was a nipple ring, there for the sole purpose of sexual satisfaction, was riveted in her brain and completely incapacitating her.

Kate cleared her dry throat. "Probably just as exciting as watching you and your team create all those great props and set pieces." She waved her arm over the salt mine set. "Everything looks great, Dawn."

"Thank you. But for your kicking our asses, they might not have gotten here on time."

"Being a bitch right off the bat is not usually my style," Kate replied a little guiltily.

"Well, at least you got to the root of a problem that I've been frustrated with for a long time."

"Did I?"

Dawn took in a relaxed breath. "Mostly it's things like management promising crazy deliverables that the shop people have to bust butt to complete. In your case, it's management not sending the work to the shop when they should have." She looked into Kate's eyes, feeling their inviting attention. "They hold on to drawings because they forget, and then we get started weeks late. We're behind from the get-go."

"Don't tell me anything that'll make me go kick their ass again." Kate narrowed her gaze.

Dawn laughed warmly. "I've been at FDF since Brett, Sr. started the business. It was just him and me from the beginning. I ran the shop and he ran the office. We grew, of course, and I've always stayed out there. He knows what's wrong with the management. He also knows I'll be the first to tell him."

"Have you ever considered going into management to help effect a change?"

"I have, but I don't think it's a good match."

"Why?"

"First of all, Brett has a boy's club going on in there. He only hires guys to be project managers. Don't get me wrong, as long as I've been here, he's treated me better than anyone, but he just has some hitch in his get-along about women in upper management positions."

"So he's discriminated against you?"

"I suppose. But I've never really pushed the issue. It's kind of like, 'be careful what you ask for.' I'm not sure I want to trade my paint brush for a pile of papers that need to be pushed around a desk."

"True. Do what you do best," Kate said and then added, "Do what you love. I'm glad that he appreciates you and your work."

"Yeah, he'd certainly have a cow if I threatened to leave. He gets into such a panic when I'm not there to run the shop. I think he feels the place would fall apart if I wasn't around."

"From what I observed, it just might."

She's looking at me that way again, Dawn thought. *Like she wants to say something else. And I so much want her to. Just like I want to tell her that my chest starts to swirl every time I am close to her.* "I like being here. With you."

Kate's sincere expression deepened and she let out a sigh. "Me, too."

After the next take, Nathan called Kate away from the set. Kate flashed a smile at Dawn, rolled her eyes, and excused herself, promising to be right back. Dawn was content again to watch the workings of the film shoot.

Amy had just finished talking with Peter and Hannah on the set. Jennifer called for the next take and then a flurry of activity ensued, but only for a few moments. It was as if a thousand birds had flown down to a lake, jostling for position, and within seconds had all settled down at the same time. Suddenly the set was very quiet.

Amy gave last minute directions, "Hannah, cheat your face just slightly to the left."

She nodded to Jennifer who called for the cameraman to roll film, and then waited for the sound man to let the crew know that his equipment was up to speed.

After the sticks were snapped closed, Amy called for action, and Dawn watched as Hannah fell onto a thick mat. Dawn remembered from reading the script that this was the scene where Hannah falls into a deeper part of the mine. A stunt man was lying down, just off camera range, to make sure Hannah landed squarely on the mat.

It was all so interesting and exhilarating to see the inner workings of a film. The camera had been mounted on a dolly, which rolled down a small track following the actors. When Amy called "cut," the entire set sprang into action again. The cameramen pulled the dolly and camera back to their original position, and the actors walked to their original positions as well. A woman darted onto the set and fiddled with Hannah's hair while another woman stepped onto the set and took a Polaroid picture.

Just then a man walked up and sat in the director's chair next to Dawn. He smiled at her and said, "Hi. I'm Ralph." He reached out his hand.

Dawn took it. "I'm Dawn."

"You're new on the crew, right?"

"No, I'm just visiting."

"Oh." He paused and then nodded conceitedly as if what he were about to say was so apparent it shouldn't have even been necessary to verbalize, "I'm one of the main actors." Roguishly, he leaned in toward her.

Dawn nodded. "I see. Nice to meet you." He did look familiar, but what was more familiar was his substandard pick-up manner.

"I play the villain." He raised his eyebrows a few times, his stare lingering long after it was appropriate.

"That's nice."

Jennifer then called out, "Let's get settled, people. Ready for take two." And the crew moved back away from the set, and the process started all over again.

He leaned over and purred, "I know this is an exciting business to you, and probably very complicated, but if you need any assistance, I'll be…" He actually leered at her. "…happy to help you with it."

Luckily, Jennifer was calling for quiet on the set, and Dawn turned her attention toward it. They ran through the scene a third time, and then Jennifer and Amy conferred a moment. Jennifer announced that the crew was to move to the next setup.

Kyle came over and retrieved Ralph, telling him he was to be in the next setup, so Ralph excused himself from Dawn, momentarily squeezing the top of her hand in a sweaty grip, and then luckily he left.

The next setup required the camera to move its position, which caused the lighting guys to change a few lights, but basically, everything else was the same. Ralph was alone in the scene, yelling at someone off-camera as he ran through the salt mine. Before each take, he complained quite a bit about the torch he carried. It was too heavy, the flame was too hot. Each time, Dawn noticed that the crew pretty much ignored him or said, "You're a trooper, Ralph." After three takes of that, Jennifer announced that the crew would be breaking for lunch and everyone was to return to the set in exactly one hour.

As the crew meandered away from the set, some lingering a moment to turn off a light, cover the camera, or readjust a prop, Dawn wondered whether she should follow them or just stay where she was.

Presently, she felt a hand on her shoulder.

"I'm sorry I took so long." Kate smiled down at her.

"It's definitely okay. I could watch this all day."

"Ready for lunch?"

"Sure." Dawn stood and they walked outside into the sunshine. "Is Hannah joining us?"

"No, she isn't. We haven't been doing a lot together lately. It's more just…business."

The film's caterer was set up along the side wall of the soundstage. Smoke rolled out of a large mobile kitchen that faced a tented canopy. Under the canopy, many rows of picnic tables were lined up and covered in red and white checkered tablecloths.

The crew was moving through the caterer's lunch line at a fairly fast pace, and Kate and Dawn joined them. After filling their plates, they picked out a picnic table at the far end of the tent, away from most of the crew.

"If you don't mind my asking, what did you mean about it's mostly business with Hannah?" Dawn said after they'd begun to eat.

"I don't mind. It's something I don't like to admit but it's true. The relationship is on a down swing, I suppose you could say. We've been fighting a lot, and I'm realizing it's not been the kind of relationship I've wanted."

"What are the fights about?"

Kate chuckled. "Pretty much everything. Hannah doesn't like it when she doesn't get her way. And I've been guilty of giving in a lot. But lately, I've been resistant to her whims, and that's the problem."

"Have you tried to talk it out?"

Kate looked glum. "There's really no talking it out with her."

"I'm sorry."

"It's my fault. I should have begun to find my voice a long time ago. At the beginning of the whirlwind, it was easier to shrug and get over it. But I did a major disservice to the relationship by doing so."

"It matters to have a voice."

"It's beginning to matter to me."

Dawn watched Kate's solemn expression. "You've got a lot on your mind."

Kate sighed deeply. "Don't we all?" She smiled at Dawn, changing the subject. "I love to listen to you talk. You've got the most wonderful accent."

Dawn played with her salad. "Thank you. Before moving to Florida, I spent my life in North Carolina."

"Well, it's a beautiful accent."

"I like yours, too."

"Mine?"

"Californian. Yankee," Dawn joked.

"As long as you don't call me a Valley girl."

"Deal."

"So tell me," Kate said, enjoying the time with Dawn immensely, "What instigated the move from North Carolina to Florida?"

Dawn shrugged. "A woman."

"Really?"

"Yes. A woman who's long gone now."

"And has there been anyone since?"

"Just one serious one."

"Care to share?" Kate smiled at her.

"She thought I'd be a pretty good meal ticket." Their eyes locked and they both fell silent. The feeling that swelled up inside her was overwhelming. She wanted to tell Kate that she was all she thought about. She wanted to tell her that she was the most amazing woman she'd ever met.

"So your ex didn't work?"

"Not unless you call golfing and trips to Disney a job."

Kate laughed "No, really."

"Really." Dawn laughed quietly. "She spent the first six months of our relationship claiming she couldn't find a job. She played golf every day, however, and became thoroughly knowledgeable of all the theme parks in the greater Orlando area. While I financed it."

"That sounds like a nightmare for you."

"It wasn't fun. I finally told her I wasn't interested in supporting her play time. She was capable of working, and I was done with giving her a free ride."

"Good for you."

"Yes and no. She finally found a golf pro that wouldn't nag her about her unemployment. I caught them having sex. I don't think I've ever felt pain like that. I was terribly unhappy, and the betrayal was finally too much to bear."

"It's my turn to say I'm sorry."

"The other idiot, as I like to call her, wanted a wife at home, so my ex left me for her."

"The other woman might have been an idiot for being a part of the breaking up of your relationship and for taking in such a manipulator," Kate said, "but you weren't the other idiot."

"Yes, I'd say so. I didn't put my foot down hard enough and she walked all over me."

"You made your decision to support her on good faith. It's not your fault that you were taken advantage of."

"Well, maybe not after a couple of months. But two years was a little long. And I let her just run around until she ran into someone else's arms."

Kate saw the pained look that flickered across Dawn's face. "Her loss."

"That's what Krissy says." Dawn shrugged.

"That's what I say as well." Kate smiled at Dawn. She watched as Dawn looked down at the table, her expression turning sad. "Do you miss her?"

Dawn looked up. "At first I did. Deeply. I was a wreck. Now, I'm just disappointed in myself. It's embarrassing to tell that story."

"We all have an embarrassing story, Dawn."

"What's yours?"

"I guess my embarrassing story isn't about one particular person but about my love life in general."

"Meaning?"

"My picker's broken."

"Your picker?"

"My ability, or lack of, to pick the right person."

"We all have done that, Kate."

"But I especially suck at relationships."

Dawn looked at her with a raised eyebrow.

Kate shook her head, confessing, "I'm a serial monogamist."

A grin spread out on Dawn's face. "You make it sound like you're a murderer or something."

"Might as well be. It should be so simple, but I'm really, really bad at it. I just can't seem to get it right."

Dawn nodded. "So you'd like to settle down but can't find the right person?"

"Something like that."

"That's embarrassing?"

"Well, I suppose when you examine the aggregate of my dating life, my past girlfriends, it's a pretty ugly picture."

"How so?"

Kate inhaled, thinking carefully. "Poor choices. I pick people who generally are not good for me. Or I'm not good for them."

"But that's what dating is all about. I mean how many people do you know who've picked correctly the first time and are still together?"

"You've got a point. It's just that I seem to pick dooseys."

Dawn had finished her lunch and was leaning on her folded arms. "I've had some of those in my life as well."

Kate smiled. "Kindred spirits."

"Kindred spirits that have had foul experiences."

"How is one supposed to know what evil lurks in the hearts of some women?"

Dawn laughed. "I think that that's just an artifact of dating. You're supposed to figure that out somehow before moving to the next level."

"Yes, however, I don't give my dating choices as much careful thought as other things in my life. Like work."

"And you must spend a lot of time working."

"I do. Which probably explains my inability to make good dating choices." Kate raised her glass of iced tea and took a long draw.

"Maybe it's not so much whom you pick, but who picks you."

Kate slowly lowered the glass, deeply considering the words.

They talked about the work that Dawn's company had done for Kate and the work Dawn had done previously. They talked about the film crew, and Kate answered Dawn's questions about who did what and generally how things worked on the set. They were sharing childhood stories when Kate's radio crackled to life. "Jennifer to Kate."

Kate picked up the radio that had been sitting on the table between them. "Go for Kate."

"Hannah's out of make-up and wrapped for the day and transportation's taking her to the airport in about ten minutes. Just wanted to let you know."

"Ten-four, Jennifer, thanks."

The radio crackled again and Hannah, who had obviously been standing by Jennifer, said, "Bye, baby," which was followed by an uproar of laughter.

Kate shook her head. "Bye." And almost as an afterthought, she added, "Jennifer, remind her of her call time on Friday. Kate clear."

Dawn nodded toward Kate's radio, "Do you want to go say good-bye to her? I can leave."

"No, it isn't needed."

Dawn folded her napkin and placed it on the table. "Well, I need to get back to the shop anyway."

"Oh," Kate said, suddenly sad that her time with Dawn was over. "May I walk you back to the studio gate?"

For a brief moment, Dawn reached out and covered Kate's hand with her own. It was a light touch and too fleeting, but Kate's heart pounded ferociously.

"I would like that very much."

On the way across the studio lot, Kate felt incredibly comfortable. "I really enjoyed lunch with you."

"It was great. I got to have a real Hollywood movie set lunch, pomp and circumstance and all." Dawn looked over at Kate and smiled.

"Just a lot of hungry people on a work break, really."

"Yes, but it's still pretty glamorous, at least to us southern folk."

"Well, you southern folk aren't without your pomp and circumstance," Kate kidded. "Your Christmas party was pretty elaborate."

"We do know how to torch up the spirits."

"And the woman you were with that night...you're dating her now?" Kate grimaced at the terrible segue.

"No, not anymore." Dawn chuckled. "Actually, the Christmas party was our first and last date."

"Did it have anything to do with the amount of alcohol imbibed?" Kate had remembered that upon their return from Dawn's studio workshop the evening had come to a quick end. She remembered that her chest hurt watching Dawn and Bridget leave. She'd felt such a strong connection to Dawn, excited beyond reason, and their time in Dawn's studio had almost resulted in a kiss. *God, she is magnificent.*

"Well, I'd say that that was certainly the clincher," Dawn said and then added, "So where'd you go off to that night?"

"Me? I believe you left before me."

"I did. I dropped Bridget off at home. Her roommate was there and said she'd take care of her, so I came back hoping that you were still there."

Suddenly it felt right to take Dawn's hand. "You did?"

Dawn clutched back. "Yes."

Stopping to turn toward her, Kate said, "I should have stayed." It was simple, but Kate felt the words connect them.

Dawn smiled. "I wish I hadn't left."

Kate's lungs felt full of fresh air, and a rush of excitement sizzled in her nerve endings. She felt like a school girl experiencing her first crush.

And Kate remembered that she couldn't have pursued anything anyway. Sure, her relationship with Hannah was over. They were virtual strangers lately, but there was Hannah and there had been the woman who had been with Dawn. Those two facts had governed their actions, yet had also seemed so unimportant that night. Just as it did at that moment. "It's funny how things go."

They reached the front gate and security checkpoint at the entrance of the studio.

"Thank you so much for coming." Kate lightly placed her hand on Dawn's shoulder.

"I had a wonderful time, Kate Nyland."

"So did I." She reached out for her and brought her close. Her arms felt full and alive holding Dawn. For a moment, Kate relaxed into her and Dawn held fast, her arms embracing Kate with certainty and assurance. And Kate couldn't remember, in all the arms that ever held her, feeling so right and so complete.

They held each other a long time, not saying a word. When Kate finally pulled away, Dawn looked sleepily at her. Kate wanted to kiss her but hesitated just long enough to watch Dawn turn and walk through the gate.

After Dawn departed, Kate walked back toward the production office, moving at a luxuriously slow pace. The mugginess of the Orlando air had lifted a little, and in that carefree moment, she took deep breaths full of happiness. With the fingers of her right hand, she played with the acorn bracelet she wore on her left wrist, the one that Dawn had given her at the Christmas party. An image of the nipple ring flashed into her mind again and she smiled.

Just as she reached the edge of the first soundstage, she heard a horn honk. Beth pulled up alongside her in a Lincoln Town Car, which carried Hannah and her assistant. It slowed to a stop and Hannah and Beth both rolled down their windows.

"See you Friday," Hannah said. "And I do know what time my call is."

"Be back soon, boss." Beth shrugged apologetically and pulled away.

Kate had agreed to let Hannah go to LA for the day and had arranged for a private jet. Jets were standard practice for a famous celebrity, orchestrated for the purpose of avoiding detainment due to the star's notoriety, but equally prudent for a producer who wanted to avoid any problems that might crop up with an airline carrier, like a canceled flight or delayed departure. Kate had also approved the trip to keep Hannah from raging, something that could affect the crew and the rest of the cast. And Kate knew she could always use the trip as leverage in case Hannah asked for something else. Well, not if, but when she asked for something else.

Kate had pulled Paula, one of the movie's production assistants, from set work to travel with Hannah. Knowing Hannah's tendency to do whatever she wanted, regardless of what she was asked, Kate made it very clear to the assistant to make sure that Hannah made it to the Burbank Executive airport late Thursday night so that the private jet could take her back on time.

CHAPTER TWENTY-TWO

K ate had arrived on set ready for the first day of the last week of shooting in Orlando. The Orlando airport would be standing in for the Austrian airport.

Four days before, Nathan had met with the airport commissioner who had suddenly announced a problem with the permit. Citing possible loss of business due to the film crew being in the way of incoming and outgoing traffic, he had said that he wanted to limit the access for StormRunner Productions to shoot only between the hours of ten a.m. and four p.m.

Many demands came in for all different reasons during the attainment of locations, and this normally would have been a standard setback, if it had only taken place back when the permit was originally filed with the city of Orlando. Then Charlie Gunner could have had more time to secure another location, if needed. When the call finally came in to the production offices that the commissioner had threatened to call the Mayor of Orlando to have the permit rescinded, they were four days away from needing that location. The permit had actually been signed for weeks, and this new tangle could have cost StormRunner big time.

But Kate had been glad that Nathan had convinced the airport commissioner that they would do everything in their power to reduce the loss of business, a promise which was fairly easy to keep since the part of the airport that StormRunner required was largely under construction by the airport. Business couldn't really be that much more hindered by the film crew, and when Nathan reminded the commissioner that he already had a hefty check in his airport coffer in the form of the location fee, the commissioner had sounded off a few more minutes before leaving in a huff.

The sun hitting the end terminal of the Orlando International Airport glowed radiantly. The rain cover provided by the roof structure allowed the lighting department to get the full benefit of the indirect rays of the sun without coping with the robust Florida glare. The director of photography filtered the sun to the extent that it took on the look of Europe's unique latitude and weather, and the result produced a picturesque, tawny glow of brilliant amber.

After a day off, the crew looked rested and happy. Hannah was due back that morning from her day trip to Los Angeles. Much earlier that morning, at four a.m., Kate's cell phone rang. It was a call she'd been anticipating.

"Kate?" a timid voice said. "She's in the bathroom. This is the first chance I had to call."

"Paula, how did it go?" It was the production assistant, and Kate could tell by the background noise that she was on the jet that Kate had arranged.

"Not great at first, but it worked perfectly."

"So you needed the silver bullet, huh?"

"Yeah," she said. Kate knew Paula would have an impossible time making Hannah do anything Hannah didn't want to do, so she had armed the assistant with a way to do it. "About an hour before we had to leave for the airport, she was partying and having a blast. Well, I told her that the jet was scheduled to leave at midnight in order to make it to Orlando by seven thirty a.m. eastern time. She pitched a fit. She told me that she was going to get the jet to take her in the morning, instead of midnight."

Kate listened, knowing beforehand practically every word Paula was going to say.

"Then," Paula continued, "I told her that the pilot of the jet would be leaving at midnight, with or without her."

Kate couldn't help but grimace a little as she pictured Hannah reacting to the comment.

"Anyway, she really went ballistic, and then I told her the other part of what you told me to tell her."

Even though it was four in the morning, Kate decided that this was definitely worth getting woken up for.

"I told her that she could absolutely take a morning flight, and that she could take Delta or American Airlines, and that the first class seats were always full because the LA to Orlando route was such a busy business route, but that there could easily be a *coach* seat available."

"And how did that go over?"

"She asked me how I knew that the pilot was leaving with or without her."

"And ...?"

"And I told her just what you told me to say, that you had arranged for the pilot and jet, personally, and had given him explicit instructions because you were paying, not Hannah."

"Then did you duck?" Kate asked.

"What?"

"Just kidding. So she's with you, I take it."

"Really pissed, but here."

"Thank you, Paula. You did a fabulous job."

Hannah and Paula had been picked up at the airport and had gotten to the set with plenty of time for Hannah to get through hair and makeup before her call time. Still, Hannah remained in her motor home for half an hour longer while the crew sat around waiting.

Both Jennifer and Kimber made trips out to her motor home. She'd refused both of their requests to get to the set by yelling through the door for them to get lost. But Hannah had it timed perfectly. Just before Kate upped the ante and made the trip herself, Hannah appeared on set.

And she was a complete bitch.

She harangued anyone who came near her, she spat her lines during rehearsal, she shoved Peter when he tripped over a cable and accidentally fell into her arm.

She berated the crafts service guy, the second assistant cameraman and even the first-aid guy who had run over to hand her aspirin and water when she'd barked at him to do so.

By lunch, which Hannah took in her motor home, the crew was glad for the reprieve.

Kate, who had been on the phone most of the morning but had heard about the incidents from more than one person, had asked Kyle to radio her when they wrapped for lunch. Kate needed to confront Hannah about her inappropriate behavior but would wait for the right time. Each time she had to deal with a lead actor, she always first chose to do so in private. If they refused to take heed, the second time would be an embarrassing lecture in front of the cast and crew.

"A word with you," Kate said, rather than asked, as she entered the motor home.

"Here are two words. How about fuck you?"

"This is going to stop. Now." Kate stood just inside the door to create an air of proclamation rather than discussion.

"You treated me like a goddamn child telling that fucking pilot he could only take orders from you," she yelled. "I'm a fucking celebrity."

"If you think you were treated like a child, it's because you're being one."

"You're a sadistic asshole," Hannah said and then repeated loudly, "My girlfriend is a sadistic asshole."

Kate realized it was easier to handle Hannah while in producer mode than girlfriend mode. "Let me get this straight, you ask to leave the set and get flown to LA, I pay for the flight on the promise that you'll get back here in time, then you screw that promise and you're mad at *me*?" Kate glowered at her. "You'd better think about your words before they spew out of your mouth, Hannah."

"I got back here on time," she seethed.

"But you wouldn't have if you'd gotten your way. You were going to blow the flight schedule and get to the set late and cause this production to lose thousands of dollars by waiting for you. So instead, you hole up in this motor home for a half an hour, just to make a point, and still cost the production money."

"I was getting ready." She sniffed.

"And then you were a raging bitch to the crew members who don't have any part in this."

Hannah got quiet, just staring at Kate, who reached for the doorknob to leave.

"In case you weren't aware, this film schedule is thirty-four days long, which makes this production cost just shy of 1.65 million dollars a day. Divide that into fourteen-hour days, and it costs us fifty-nine thousand dollars for every half hour that you're late to the set. So the next time you decide to meander onto the set whenever you feel like it, and I don't care what the reason is, I'm going to take the cost out of your pay. Check your contract. You signed up for that penalty." And Kate walked out the door.

Just past four, the crew was busy lighting for the next scene, and Kate was sitting side-by-side with Amy in their director's chairs. They were going over the next scene and how it would match the scene that occurred just prior in the script. They'd shot the previous scene two days earlier and had viewed it in dailies the night before.

From behind, Kate felt a hand on her shoulder. She looked up to see Hannah, who then came around to the front of Kate's chair.

"I'm glad you're both here," Hannah began. "I'm sorry for being late to the set this morning. And I apologize for my shitty mood."

Kate blinked.

Amy nodded. "Apology accepted, Hannah."

Hannah bent down and kissed Kate lightly on the cheek. "I'm sorry, Kate."

"Okay," Kate said. Hannah reached out and hugged Kate before excusing herself and walking away.

For the rest of the afternoon, Hannah was gracious and professional. She breezed through her scenes, and Kate even saw her apologize to Peter and a number of crew people. Perplexed, Kate thought, *was she really trying to make amends and be nice?*

Kate watched Hannah for a long time.

She was undeniably fascinating, and those sporadic moments of righting wrongs were one of the reasons Kate was attracted to her. Kate watched the way Hannah moved, her long legs strong and stunning, and her movements deliberate. She seemed to captivate anyone within her perimeter and she liked doing so.

The crew quickly got past the rough morning and was back in a groove. Hannah had realized that she caused problems and then had gone about making a change to put things right again. It was just as she had done with the fantasy auction for the trip to New York.

❖

Just past midnight, Beth found Kate in the production office.

She let herself in and sat down across from Kate, who was sitting at a small desk by the fax machine.

"Another day, another dollar." Beth groaned as she stretched her arm muscles and adjusted her back.

"And a dollar and a half after eight," Kate teased.

"Mama's gotta bring home the over-time bacon."

"Yes, she does." Kate laughed. "So how is Sarah?"

"She's great. I sent her off to the hotel with the posse about an hour ago." Beth watched her for a moment. "Almost finished, yourself?"

"Yes." Kate straightened the stack of papers she was working on. "Some of this can wait until tomorrow, I suppose."

"Why aren't you with Hannah? You could be having a nice, albeit late, dinner somewhere."

"Ahh, I'm pretty busy."

Beth reached the toe of her boot out and nudged Kate's leg. "You know, my friend, that's bullshit."

Kate raised her eyebrow. "What? I'm buried here."

"No more than you ever are."

Kate fell silent, unable to come up with another retort, so Beth filled in the gap. "Things not going so well with Hannah?"

Kate looked down at the paperwork she was no longer interested in. "Well, if I said yes, that would indicate that at one time things *were* going well. I guess I'd have to say they're worse than usual."

"So why are you settling?"

"I'm not settling."

"Okay. Then what are you running from?"

"I'm not running from anything. I have my career and it takes away from our relationship."

"Do you believe that?" Beth prodded.

"Shouldn't I?"

"You can have a love life and a career, Kate."

"I have a love life and a career."

"What you have is this...this dating thing with Hannah, but I hate to tell you, Kate, you're mostly just attached to her arm, you know?"

Kate stared again at the paperwork, no longer seeing the words or scribbles written on it.

"Are you in love with her?"

"No," Kate said slowly. "But we've only been dating..." Beth waited while Kate calculated, "...for about a year."

"Long enough to know."

"Sometimes love takes a while."

"Bullshit, Kate."

Kate looked back up at her.

Beth went on. "Answer me this, when you have a date with Hannah, but she's about an hour late and doesn't call, what's your first thought?"

"That she got caught up with some fans or…whatever."

"What about when you finally see her, what is your first thought?"

"I usually don't have a first thought because she always rushes through the door saying we're late for a party or wanting to make sure she doesn't miss the paparazzi."

"Okay, so after that, what's your first thought?"

Kate sighed. "I usually think, 'well, that's typical,' then I bite my tongue from saying something sarcastic like, 'Hello to you, too.'"

"And then, what's the feeling that goes with that thought?"

"I'm hurt, I suppose." Kate nodded with a sigh. "Yeah, it's pretty much all about her."

"So when she's an hour late, what ever happened to the feeling of dread that something might be wrong? Like, 'Oh my God, she could have had an accident.'"

"I guess I should feel that, but I always know the reason she's late is because of some kind of Hannah drama."

"And what about that crazy feeling of excitement you feel when she does finally walk in the door? The feeling that you are so excited to see her that you can't contain your smile?"

Kate thought of Dawn and knew she had a true answer to the question. She inhaled deeply, blowing out the sigh that meant the real response wasn't an option at that moment. "Seems like there's no time for that because Hannah's in a mood or too focused and business-like. It feels like a whirling dervish has just come through the door. And I get sucked up in the spinning."

"And what about the feeling of sheer satisfaction and warmth when your lover walks in the door and actually notices you and is giddy and happy to see you?"

"With Hannah? Doesn't happen."

"I've been debating telling you this, Kate," Beth finally said.

Kate looked up at her expectantly.

"The time you had to stay in Orlando, the night of the AIDS fund-raiser, the table you bought?"

Beth paused until Kate nodded in acknowledgment.

"Hannah wasn't behaving very well."

"The flirting…" Kate shrugged. "Well, everyone knows she does it."

"But it was more than flirting," Beth replied gently. "She got the phone number of a woman who was all over her. And I mean arms and legs."

"How do you know that?" Kate hadn't been completely surprised by this, but it still hurt. She'd never really trusted Hannah's self-serving behavior.

"I saw Hannah ask her for it. And I'm telling you, the request didn't stem from a business pursuit."

"What else?" Kate knew there had to be more, not just because of the hesitant look on Beth's face but because, with Hannah, there was always more.

Beth bit her cheek, growing more angry than uneasy. "She kissed her. Macked right in front of Sarah and me. At the end of the night, while waiting for the valet. My car came first so I have no idea what she did after that."

"What did you say to her?"

"How did you know I said something?"

Kate laughed sadly. "I know you, Beth. You don't back down from an injustice."

"You're right." Beth looked her square in the eyes. "I just walked up to her and when she turned and saw it was me, I went nose to nose with her and told her she was skating on thin ice."

Through her dejection, Kate chuckled. "Thanks for telling me."

"You always hope people will snap out of it, you know? Confront them, let them know you're on to them, and then they straighten themselves out."

"There's nothing straight about Hannah."

"You said a mouthful, sister."

She took in a deep breath and blew it out. "It's so hard with her most of the time."

"Are you happy?"

Falling silent, Kate stared off in the general direction of the refrigerator, not really focusing on anything, not saying anything.

Beth waited a few minutes and then got up. As she quietly made her way past Kate, she kissed her on the cheek and reached for the motor home door.

"No," Kate finally said. "I'm not happy." She looked over at Beth. "Do you think that it's possible that maybe it's not so much who you pick, but who picks you?"

"Who said that?"

"Dawn."

"I'd listen to her more." Opening the door, she nodded once. "It *is* possible to be with someone who gives you that wonderful feeling of so much joy that you can't even contain your smile.

"You think so?"

"Yeah. I saw that look on your face once."

"In college when that cheerleader sat on my lap?" Kate joked.

"No," Beth replied frankly. "Just the other day. When you saw Dawn." Kate stared at her for a long moment. A smile widened on Beth's face. "You heard me."

Kate looked away. She didn't want to admit Beth was right, that she had been caught in a truth. Her best friend knew her through and through and there was no fooling her. She looked back at her. "Dawn's just so different."

"I'm sure she is."

"I feel so comfortable around her. She…makes sense."

"And I bet she treats you well."

"Better than that."

"In this crazy world, that's vital."

Kate suddenly blinked, looking out the production office window. "But who am I kidding? She's all the way across the United States. And I'm with Hannah. She's my *girlfriend*, for crissakes. And I'm leaving here in a few days. It's crazy…" Kate's voice trailed off.

And when she realized that no response had come from Beth, she glanced back at her. Head cocked toward the door, Beth said, "You're tired, Kate. Come on. I'll drive you back to the hotel."

CHAPTER TWENTY-THREE

With five days left in Orlando, the crew was making good time. They were on schedule, and despite Jeffery's attempt at controlling the dailies, everything was looking very good.

Ralph, Hannah, Peter, and three day-players, including Kiley Warner, had a long scene which would take the whole day. The production crew was entrenched on Soundstage Two. They would be spending a long fifteen-hour day in order to nail the scene. It was their longest day of the shoot. And since most everyone was required on set, the streets around the soundstages were deserted and quiet.

Inside the soundstage, the crew was getting ready to shoot part of the next scene. Amy and Jennifer were in the thick of things in the middle of the set while Kate stood by the cameramen and occasionally looked through the camera's viewfinder.

Kate watched as Jennifer dismissed Hannah and the other actors. As they all filtered away, Hannah intentionally snubbed Kiley Warner, the one who'd supposedly spread detrimental rumors about her, by cutting her off as they walked off the set.

Hannah then made a beeline to Kate and put her arms around her, pulling her into a serious squeeze.

"Stop it, Hannah."

"Stop what?"

"I don't know who you're creating the show for, but I don't want to be part of it."

"What the hell are you talking about?" Hannah's nostrils flared.

"Our relationship sucks privately and looks great publicly. It's ridiculous."

Hannah raised her voice. "Our relationship is ridiculous?"

"You've got to get back to the set in a minute. I want to talk about this later."

"Fuck you, Kate."

Kate chuckled incredulously. "Oh, that's real good."

❖

Under Amy and Jennifer's control, the set was running very smoothly. Knowing that they were still ahead of schedule, Kate and the crew had begun to make bets with each other on how many takes each setup would require. Currently, Jennifer was leading and was just a few more scenes away from a free dinner.

Kate sat off-set a ways, as she always did when she wanted to concentrate on some paperwork but still keep close to what was happening on the set. She looked up to watch Hannah and Peter who had grown comfortable working together. Peter had been very accommodating to Hannah, anticipating her temper and imparting well-timed compliments that would stave off some of Hannah's mood swings.

However, it wasn't to last.

Just after lunch, as Hannah and Peter were rehearsing the next setup, Kate was interrupted from her work by a commotion.

Jean, the script supervisor, had gone to talk with Amy about Hannah's position in the scene. Continuity from scene to scene was her main responsibility. She took concise notes to enable the editor to cut all the many different pieces of the film together so that everything made sense and flowed well.

Just before the crew was to roll film on the next setup, Jean told Amy, "I need you to look at the Polaroids of Hannah's last position in scene 118."

Jean showed her the photographs and they studied them as Jennifer walked over. "When we shot the first part of this scene a few days ago, Hannah was bent at an angle like this." Jean pointed to the photo. "Facing the south wall of the salt mine. For the shot you're about to do, she's positioned wrong and it won't match."

Jennifer nodded. "You're right. I'm glad you caught that before we shot it."

Hannah then walked over and joined the group. "I heard my name. What's up?"

Jean showed her one of the photographs. "You need to be in this position to match the last shot."

"Why didn't you tell me that before we rehearsed it just now?" she barked at Jean.

Kate started to get out of her chair but paused to see what would happen.

Jean immediately cowered mumbling, "I…I…"

Amy interceded. "She's doing her job, Hannah."

"Well not fucking fast enough," Hannah snapped and then launched one last shot at Jean before walking off. "Get your shit together and quit wasting my time."

Jennifer momentarily froze, looking at Amy whose stern look signaled that she'd handle it.

In disgust, Kate shook her head as Amy walked over to where Hannah had gone. Jennifer patted a very shaky Jean who looked as if she would burst into tears right there.

That night, sitting in her production office, Kate fumed.

She was unhappy. Miserable, actually. And the relationship with Hannah was ridiculous. Though Kate had always taken Hannah's verbal abuse and inconsiderate treatment, it wasn't until she saw Hannah abuse the script supervisor that something finally snapped inside her. How dare she act like a raging bitch and treat people like shit. It angered Kate that she'd let herself be associated with such a malevolent human being.

Kate needed to break up with Hannah. She also considered firing her from the film for her behavior.

Sitting in her office in the production motor home, she was bent over the desk with her head in her hands. Her office was the back room of the motor home and as such, she had an interior door, which was now closed.

She had a massive headache, but most thoughts were coming in fairly clearly. The impulse to break up with Hannah was the right one, firing her from the film was not. Certainly both options seemed reasonable, at least emotionally, but she needed to separate her personal life from the business.

To see Hannah treat the crew like they were dogs was the last straw. Kate could no longer be a part of a horrible relationship, one she was certainly not happy in. But at the same time, the significance of the last on set flare-up rang with heavenly arranged intervention. She supposed she had just needed one clear-cut incident to tip her over the edge, and fate had just presented that to her. Not that innumerable rude comments, despicably bad behavior, and boorish self-centeredness weren't all scale tippers in and of themselves, but they all added up to the end.

That was it, she thought sadly. She was through with Hannah. And as the night went on, she got angrier and angrier. She'd gone through hell with her at times, putting up with the tantrums and the nasty attitude. Kate had been second to Hannah's needs. *Hannah always had to be served first, whether it was a party she needed to be seen at, the dinner she needed to attend, or a film she needed to do press for. And it had all been under the guise of "the importance of a star's life," when in actuality it has been all about the world of a narcissistic spoiled brat.*

But Kate was madder at herself than at Hannah. It was her own fault for putting up with a relationship that rendered her virtually invisible to her girlfriend. She had let that happen.

And what exactly had she seen in Hannah? The sex was great, but that made her feel cheap.

It was more than that. Was it the glitz and glamour? She'd been involved in the Hollywood scene her whole career but never in a limelight quite as brilliant as Hannah drew. It was exciting, but that made her feel shallow.

The deeper truth was that she wasn't good at making sound personal decisions. She never scrupulously considered exactly who she was dating or what kind of person they really were, before making it more serious. She had picked Hannah too quickly. And that made her feel foolish.

She knew Hannah had cheated on her in the past. She knew Hannah wasn't to be trusted at all. Kate had herself to blame for looking the other way, knowing that women were always available to Hannah. But she didn't blame herself for Hannah's constant need for attention, praise, and control.

And those three things would lead Hannah into someone's bed. Kate thought of all the 'next mornings' when Hannah's stories wouldn't add up. And she had seen it in the eyes of some of their mutual acquaintances who must have known more than she did about particular nights when Kate was either working or out of town.

She'd confronted her a few times, but Hannah had just raged and screamed, and it usually wore Kate out before anything was resolved.

She shuffled aimlessly through paperwork for a while, got angry, pitched a few things off her desk, and then sat completely motionless, trying to understand how she got from there to here.

But the trip was a short, easy one. She had known that the relationship needed to end. Hannah was Hannah. She'd been arrogant and self-centered from the beginning. Her sense of entitlement filled every space she walked into. Hannah was smarmy when she wanted something, cruel when she didn't get it, unappreciative when she got it, and callous when she got bored of it. And she had gotten bored with Kate long ago.

And Kate had allowed it all. *For what? Because Hannah was exquisite? For the sex?* Kate sat in silence, staring at her hands. And then slowly, the sad truth surfaced.

Kate had allowed it because she hadn't imagined she could have better.

The relationship was over. Absolutely, positively over. And Kate sighed a profound, bottomless sigh. She was hurt and angry, but she was actually relieved.

She opened the door to her office, numbly fielded a few questions from Betsy and Jamie and then headed out to the set. She waited for Hannah to finish a take and walked up to her just as she was walking off the set.

"We need to talk." Kate tried to conceal any look on her face that would reveal the topic.

"What about, babe?" Hannah cooed.

Kate cocked her head toward the set, indicating all the crew people swarming about. "Back at your motor home."

"Sure," was all Hannah got out before Toochee, the hair stylist, came over to fuss with Hannah's blond locks.

Kate went back to the office and filled the rest of the day with the business of the film. Her heart felt beyond heavy and her head and eyes ached. It angered her that she had become nothing more than a nice attachment to Hannah's arm.

She spent over an hour fuming, angry with herself, berating her stupid choices. Then sometime around eleven thirty p.m., and just as the crew was setting up for their last shot back on the soundstage, Kate felt a clearing of the anger. She also felt a strangely tranquil acceptance of the termination of her relationship with Hannah. She realized that she'd known for a while that this day was destined to arrive. And it was here. She needed to move on.

She took a deep breath, the first it seemed in a long time.

Nathan called for a wrap just after midnight. Kate waited about ten minutes then headed out the production office door.

❖

Knocking on Hannah's door, Kate entered to find her poking around rather contemptuously at a tray of celery.

Hannah barely looked up at her, "You look like shit."

Kate took a deep breath and felt a sharp ache in her chest. "That's it, Hannah. It's over between us."

"What are you talking about now? Geez, what's gotten into you?"

"I can't do this anymore."

"Do what?"

"This relationship."

Hannah straightened up in her chair. "You want to break up with me?"

"Yes."

"And your *reason*?" Hannah sounded as if she thought nothing could ever make someone want to break up with her.

"I'm not happy. I haven't been for a long time."

"So get happy. That's not my responsibility."

"You're right, it's not. Here are some other reasons. You're rude, you aren't an equal partner, and I know you've cheated on me. I just don't know exactly how many times."

"Oh, come on, Kate," Hannah protested. "This doesn't mean we have to break up."

"So I'm right about your fucking around?" Before, Kate had assumed. Now she knew for sure.

"Well…" Hannah paused before suddenly yelling, "I got sick of waiting for you to finish at the office or get back from your fucking trips."

"And that's my fault?"

Hannah looked away and flipped her off.

Kate pointed a finger at her, realizing that the infidelities hurt her more than she'd realized. "You've fucked around on me."

"All right," Hannah looked back with a dramatic sigh. "I won't ever do that again. okay?"

"You can do it all you want now." Kate bristled at Hannah's nonchalance.

"Why are you being such a bitch?"

At once, Kate's anger raged. "*You* fuck around and you're calling *me* a bitch? Explain that to me." Kate suppressed the urge to clench her fists.

"Shit happens," Hannah said indifferently. "Haven't you ever had an indiscretion?"

Kate almost turned to walk out, but she wasn't done. Through clenched teeth her answer was resolute. "No."

"It wasn't anything, Kate. Believe me." Hannah almost sounded sincere and it sickened Kate. She realized that Hannah was acting innocent and, worse than that, refusing any culpability, something which didn't surprise her but hurt nevertheless.

"It's over, Hannah."

Hannah changed tactic again, her face growing concerned. "We can't be over, Kate, it's too good."

"You mean it *looks* too good. In magazine pictures."

Hannah's pause was almost imperceptible. "We're really good together."

"We're really good for *you*, Hannah."

"What the fuck does that mean?"

Then Kate's anger receded. The air blew right out of her storm. And there before her was the painful end of a miserable relationship. "It's all about you," Kate said. "Your schedule, your parties, your needs. You know nothing about my needs."

Hannah dismissed the comment with a snort.

Kate paused before lowering her voice. "You know nothing about me."

"That's absurd." Hannah sniffed. "You're being ridiculous."

"When's my birthday, Hannah?"

"Your birthday?" Hannah shrugged, confused.

"Yes. And what's my middle name?"

Hannah stalled, laughing nervously. "Your middle name?"

Kate waited for a response. *Please,* Kate thought, *say either "Your birthday is January 11," or "Your middle name is Joy." Just one correct answer,* she bargained with herself, *and I might not be so pissed off at myself for picking such a shitty girlfriend.*

Hannah opened her mouth to speak, her jaw dropped open like an out-of-water trout. "What the hell is this about?"

With a concentrated sadness welling up to the point of pain, Kate replied, "I've been asking myself the same question." She turned to leave.

"Baby, don't go," Hannah called out.

❖

"Wow. You did it." Beth was with Kate behind Soundstage Two. Kate had found her after leaving Hannah's motor home and had taken her there to talk privately.

"Yeah. Not a good time, being in the middle of this shoot. But there was no good time, really, and I couldn't wait until we were done shooting this whole film. I couldn't bear that many days."

"I agree. I couldn't wait either."

"I think I'm most disappointed in myself. I should have done this a lot sooner."

"This is not your fault, Kate."

A half laugh escaped Kate "It's my fault for staying and putting up with her shit."

"She's a fucking moron." Beth grew angry again. "I could rip her a new asshole."

"She wouldn't feel it." Kate took a deep breath. She leaned and hugged Beth. "For being my best friend."

"That's easy. And for forever."

Kate turned to walk away.

"Maybe we should hang out for a while, until you're feeling okay."

"No, it's okay. I need to clear my head. I love you," Kate said and wandered off.

"I love you, too."

❖

That night in her hotel suite, Kate soaked in the tub, a snifter of brandy perched on the edge. For hours she'd ached about her breakup. She had run through the gamut of feelings: sadness, anger, relief, incredulousness, and back through them all again. And now, completely wrung out, her thoughts turned to the film and what might happen now.

Certainly, the film would go on, but she worried that a shift in the dynamics on the set might come across negatively on film. Hannah's work, up to that point, had been exemplary. Would Hannah sabotage the rest of the film to get back at Kate for dumping her? A series of scenarios raced through her mind. She pictured Hannah disrupting the flow of the acting by changing her approach. She pictured Hannah deliberately fudging her lines. She pictured Hannah cutting her hair short, which would shut the set down for a few days while the hair department scrambled for a wig. She began to get anxious about the impact of breaking up with Hannah.

And then Kate got a hold of herself. *Fuck the movie. Don't put your career in front of your feelings.* And just as that thought had occurred to her, another thought emerged. Hannah was an actress. She was always acting. She doubted a break up would stop Hannah, or her ego, from delivering a great performance on screen. If Hannah was nothing else, she was all about performance. Hannah was for anything that would further Hannah.

CHAPTER TWENTY-FOUR

There was a knock on the door of Kate's hotel suite. It was a few minutes before six in the morning and Kate had just gathered her things to make her way to the set.

Beth stood in the hallway, bright-eyed and smiling. "Good morning, buddy."

"Morning. What brings you here?"

"I'm taking you to the set today. The transportation captain lent me the limo."

Kate chuckled, pulling the door closed behind her and joining Beth in the hall.

"Has something happened overnight to require this escort?"

"No. No catastrophes that I'm aware of." Beth walked with her to the elevator. "I just thought we could ride in together. We sure haven't gotten to spend that much time hanging out on this shoot."

But Kate knew the real reason why Beth had shown up that morning. Just as Beth had called her three times the night before to lovingly offer encouraging words, she was again looking out for her. She didn't want Kate to walk on the set alone with Hannah planning lord knows what. Beth's presence was meant to provide a solid front, a strong back up for Kate. Beth knew the true meaning of the word posse.

On the way over, Beth asked, "You okay?"

Kate sighed. "Yes. And no. Mostly no. It's shitty what happened, and I'm hurt and angry. But I've seen the real Hannah for a long time. I just wouldn't allow myself to do anything about it."

"It's hard when you're involved, when you're smack dab in the middle of it."

"Isn't that the truth?"

The film crew had just finished their third setup when Kate walked onto the set.

Amy needed Kate to be by her side to work through a particularly difficult sequence of shots, one that had plagued them from the beginning of preproduction and still needed to be perfected. Kate focused on her work and felt a sense of relief. She had no desire to go lament in her office.

And though Hannah played it up pretty well by ignoring her, Kate felt truly okay.

It wasn't until lunch that Kate could excuse herself from Amy and head for her office. Beth brought her lunch from the catering truck and Sarah joined them.

"I heard about the break up." Sarah squeezed Kate as she greeted her. "How are you feeling?"

"Would it be mean to say relieved?"

"Not if it's the truth."

They spent the rest of their meal talking about the movie and reminiscing about times on other movie sets. It relaxed Kate to be with friends and talking about other things, and it was a surprise when Sarah changed the topic.

"Who's this Dawn person I've been hearing about?" Sarah smiled mischievously.

Kate shot a glance at Beth who managed a wide smile smeared at the edges with barbeque sauce from a large side of ribs.

Kate tried to answer as indifferently as she could. "Dawn works for the company that built the sets and props for the salt mine."

Beth wiped the barbeque sauce from her mouth. "She likes you."

"What makes you say that?" Kate asked.

Beth shrugged. "It's obvious."

Sarah leaned forward and touched Kate's knee. "It's okay, you know."

"Okay, what?"

"That she likes you."

Kate looked at Sarah and then to Beth. "The bruises from hitting the ground haven't even shown up on my ass yet."

Beth's chuckle sounded like the low roar of an incoming plane. "The falling-off-a-horse analogy…I get it."

"We're not rushing you, Kate…" Sarah began to say, but when Kate shot her a sideways glance, she added, "Okay, maybe a little. But hey, Dawn's here, you're here, and she sounds really wonderful."

"You noticed," Kate replied.

Then Sarah leaned toward Kate and said, "Fuck Hannah."

Kate blinked, not used to hearing curse words from Sarah. Kate and Beth burst into guffaws. "And from Sarah," Beth said, "that's saying something."

Kate shook her head in amazement. "I suppose so."

"I'm so sorry Hannah hurt you, buddy. But good riddance to her now."

Kate sighed from some deep place within her. "I just wish this shoot was over so I could get away from her."

Sarah leaned forward again and hugged Kate. "We'll do what we can to keep you distracted."

"Yeah, like remind you about Dawn."

And as much as Beth and Sarah kept checking up on her the rest of the day, Kate still had to be on the set at least half of the time. The crew, who had figured out pretty quickly what had transpired, virtually tiptoed around the set, trying their best to respect the recent news. Amy pulled Kate aside during a break in shooting to ask her if she was okay.

"I admire your courage and strength to get through the rest of this, Kate," she said, "I will do whatever you need me to do to help you."

And quite a few other crew members came to her with the same message. Peter found her sitting in her director's chair at one moment that afternoon and put his arm around her. "I know Hannah's gonna make this picture great, but I just can't believe how horrible she's being to you. And what a bitch she's being to the crew. It's unprofessional, but most of all, it's cruel." He gave her a gentle kiss on the top of her head before walking back under the klieg lights.

Later that night, as the crew was shooting a close up of Peter, one which didn't require any other actors in the shot, Kate's phone vibrated. Her caller ID showed that it was Jeffery's office, which was strange since he rarely called. She turned to race off as quietly as she could to take the call. She reasoned that ducking behind the row of extra set walls that were stacked at the far end of the studio would provide a good place to take the call and not disturb the audio that was being recorded.

As she turned the corner, she clicked the receive button on her cell phone but never lifted it to her ear. There, pushed against the back of the set walls were Hannah and Jennifer. All she registered was

Jennifer's head thrown back, Hannah's hand down Jennifer's pants, and the faint voice of Jeffery's secretary saying, "Jeffery Salzenberg's office...hello...hello?"

❖

"Whoa! Whoa! Where are you going?" Beth grabbed Kate's arm as she sailed past her just outside the soundstage.

"I've gotta get out of here." Kate placed her hand over the one that was holding her arm, trying to peel it away.

"What happened?" Beth's grip stayed sure, and Kate slowed down.

"Hannah and Jennifer."

"What?"

"Hannah's suddenly decided to take up with Jennifer."

"On the freakin' set?"

"More like behind the set," Kate said.

"Fuck," Beth said under her breath. "This should drive home that your decision to break up with her was a good one."

Kate shook her head. "Hannah will never change."

"What can I do?"

"Nothing. I'm just disgusted, that's all. Please tell Amy that I needed to run an errand and to call me on my cell if she needs me."

Beth checked her watch. "I'll tell her. And hey, it's almost nine p.m. I'm thinking we'll be wrapping within an hour or two. Just go and get some fresh air."

Kate nodded.

"Are you okay to drive?"

Kate nodded again. "Yeah. I just need to get out of here."

Beth reached in her pocket and handed her a set of keys. "The green Range Rover is parked next to the production office."

Kate hugged her before taking off. "Thank you."

"I love you. Be careful."

"I love you, too."

Kate hoped she could get back to the production office and get into the Range Rover without anyone else seeing her to get a signature or ask a question.

The Range Rover was not more than fifty feet away, and just as she passed the production office, the door swung open. Kate kept her head down, hoping that whoever was exiting would read her mannerisms as being that of a person in a hurry and not to be bothered.

No such luck.

"Kate," Kimber's voice called. "We were just about to come see you on the set."

Reluctantly, Kate slowed down and looked up. Following Kimber out of the production office was Dawn. Kate gasped in surprise. Dawn wore a snug pair of jeans with a pale blue button-down shirt, and Kate watched closely as Dawn walked toward her. She was magnificent.

"Dawn stopped by and wanted to surprise you," Kimber said. "Betsy called me to come get her and take her to the set."

"Well, I'm certainly surprised." Kate smiled as they approached.

Dawn and Kate stood face to face, smiling.

"Hi," Dawn said, her eyes twinkling in the relative darkness.

"Hi, yourself," Kate replied.

Dawn inhaled contentedly. "I missed you."

Kate exhaled with the same sentiment. "No more than I missed you."

"I'm heading back to the set. Need anything, Kate?"

"No, but thank you, Kimber."

When they were alone, Dawn furrowed her brow. "Something's wrong."

"I'm fine."

"Why don't I believe you?"

Kate's lips tightened slightly. "Because I'm lying."

"Is there a problem with the film?"

Kate shook her head then quietly said, "Hannah."

"Did you have a fight?"

"We broke up."

"You broke…why?"

Kate wasn't sure how to respond. Should she be vague? Should she generalize? Should she be politically correct? *Fuck that.* "It never worked really. We're too different."

"I'm so sorry, Kate." She touched Kate's arm gently. "Can you leave right now?"

Kate held up the car keys. "That was my plan right before I saw you."

"Okay, let's get out of here."

Once in the SUV, Kate turned to Dawn. "Where to?"

"After you leave the studio lot, go left and then take Interstate Four North."

They drove in silence, Dawn's reassuring hand on Kate's shoulder. A mile or so down the freeway, Kate finally spoke, her voice a little shaky. "Every mile I get away from the studio feels better and better."

Dawn smiled, feeling the humid air as it washed in from her open window. "Well, where we're headed is going to feel even farther away." She studied Kate's face, the pain and discontent that had pulled the corners of her mouth down slightly. "I'm sorry about your break up."

"Thanks." Kate reached up and placed her hand over Dawn's. "Not unexpected, though."

"No?" Dawn was puzzled.

"No." Kate smiled at her.

After a short distance, Dawn pointed toward the next off ramp. "Take Kaley Avenue and go east." She paused. "So it's over?"

"Completely"

"You sure?"

Kate looked at her. "No doubts. I guess I've known for a long time that she and I think differently about relationships."

"The things she and you wanted in a relationship?"

"Well, I suppose. She wanted me to be there for whatever she needed whenever she needed it. Oh, and then she also wanted other women."

"That's terrible to hear. She went outside your relationship."

"Yes. I just never wanted to confront it, or the way I let her treat me, which wasn't nice."

"Not everyone is that way," Dawn said.

"I hope not." And Kate certainly did. "It's just that I feel like shit. Like a failure." She rolled her head toward Dawn. "I told you I suck at relationships."

"You don't suck."

"Well, I'm having my own little pity party now."

"It's wholly natural given what you just went through. Give yourself a break."

"I'm just amazed at how I can't seem to pick the right people. Maybe it was just convenient to date someone who was in the same crazy business as I am."

"You're a pretty busy person. Sometimes it's hard to stop and really take a look at where you are from day to day."

"I suppose. But I really feel good inside, too. I mean I'm not too confident in my relationship capabilities, but having Hannah out of my private life feels like a huge relief."

They drove through an old section of Orlando. Its overgrown trees leaned over each side of the road, creating shade from the harsh southern sun. Beautiful houses with manicured lawns stretched on for blocks and blocks.

After a while of silence, Kate said, "Do you know why this drive is so great?"

Dawn glanced at her before turning back to the road.

"You're nothing like Hannah."

"Yeah, my bank account can attest to that."

"No," Kate nudged her shoulder, "I'm really comfortable in your presence."

"I know what you mean. I thought I'd be too nervous to interact with Kate, the big movie producer, but if I hadn't known who you were, I never would have guessed."

Kate smiled.

"Would it help if I told you that I couldn't look you in the eye the day we met?"

The brightness in Kate's voice was palpable. "Yes." Then she added, "Why?"

"I remember it perfectly. Oh, my God…I wasn't expecting such a beautiful creature. You have a way of commanding a room, you know."

Kate shrugged. "I was a woman on a mission."

"Yes, you were. Your eyes were so intense, it was hard to look your way." Dawn's southern accent rolled off her tongue like warm honey from a sun-baked bee hive.

They rolled to a halt at a stop sign and Dawn turned to her.

Kate wanted so much, but didn't dare imagine what 'so much' meant. "You couldn't look me in the eye. And I couldn't keep my eyes off you."

Dawn blew out a breath that turned into a chuckle. "I would say that sums it up pretty well."

Kate finally managed, "Where are we going?"

"Somewhere where we can be alone."

Kate's voice threatened to desert her. "I'm not sure that's safe."

"I'm not either."

"But do you want to?"

Dawn simply nodded.

"Me, too."

"Turn right." And Dawn led her to a small park hidden in the middle of downtown Orlando. When they got to the parking lot, they were the only ones there.

They got out of the SUV, and Kate pointed to a small wooden sign. "Cherokee Park?"

"Coincidence." Dawn shrugged. It's my favorite little hidden treasure. The name just makes it that much more special.

They walked among the trees as a few parking lights lit their way. The long shadows cast by each tree crisscrossed the grass, and in the darkness, their many branches and thick foliage, seemed to be reaching out to each other as if settling in for the night. They walked a while until Dawn touched Kate's arm, causing her to stop. Before them was one of the largest trees that Kate had ever seen.

"The age of this tree is unknown," Dawn said. "I went to the library a long time ago and did some research. I found some sketchy documents about this type of tree that seemed to indicate that she could easily be four hundred years old."

"My God." Kate took in the gigantic circumference of its base and the strength of its lowest branches. "It was probably a thriving little sapling when St. Augustine was established."

Dawn grinned. "You know your Florida history."

"Catholic school. Nuns with menacing, wooden rulers. Lots of memorization." Kate grimaced and then laughed along with Dawn. When they fell silent, Kate turned to her, regarding her dark and exquisite features. "Thank you for bringing me here."

"You needed it." Dawn hesitated. "For your soul."

"Yes." Kate stepped closer to the tree. "It's so regal."

"Do you want to know what else is good for your soul?"

Kate turned around to face Dawn. "Do tell. I'm from LA. I need all the soul helping I can get."

"Give her a hug."

Kate turned back around and leaned into the tree, stretching her arms as far around the trunk as she could. The width of the tree made it feel more as if she were splayed across it, being unable to actually get her arms around it. But she rested her cheek against its crusty bark, and it felt great. She closed her eyes, drinking in the moment, feeling superbly calm.

The recent commotion with Hannah seemed to fall away. Funny, she felt better hugging the tree and felt more in return from the tree than she'd felt most of the time with Hannah. For that moment, she felt centered. She felt the inspirational stillness that true peace imparted.

When Kate finally let go of the tree and turned around, Dawn turned to walk away slowly, letting Kate catch up with her in a few steps.

"How sublime," Kate said, looking back at the tree one more time.

"It's important to push the pause button on your crazy life every once in a while and engage in something wonderfully simple."

They walked back to the SUV and Kate mulled over what Dawn had said, "I know what you mean. A pause button would be a great thing to have every once in a while."

"Oh yeah?" Leaves crunched under their shoes.

"Yeah. Like that day at the shop when you had on that thin T-shirt."

Dawn laughed. "You should have seen the look on your face when I told you about my nipple ring."

Kate grinned. "You caught me off guard."

"I caught you looking,"

Kate's smile warmed considerably, and she shook her head. "I don't know about you."

"What does that mean?"

"When I first saw you, that day I was in the conference room at FDF, you—" And then something inside Kate told her not to say anymore.

"What were you going to say?"

Kate gulped in some air, shaking her head. *I can't tell her she took my breath away. I can't tell her that I feel more for her than I ever felt for Hannah. It's too soon. I hardly know her.* Kate knew she had started a thought that she wasn't sure she should finish. But what was holding her back? Dawn was right there with her, wanting to be there with her. And Kate had never felt so at ease around anyone else. "I thought you were incredible."

Dawn smiled warmly and reached for the passenger door of the Range Rover.

When they climbed back into the SUV, Kate turned to Dawn. "I don't want to leave just yet."

Looking out at the park, Dawn said, "It's nice here."

"No," Kate said, "I don't want to leave you just yet."

"So don't."

"It's late and I know you have to get up early."

"I'm a big girl, Kate."

"Yes, you are." She watched as Dawn scanned the park, the darkness erasing the recent memory of the sun that had completed its descent into the western sky a few hours earlier. Her profile was amazing. The American Indian features of high cheek bones and strong nose struck an amazing profile against the sliver of moon now shining into the Range Rover. Kate looked down at Dawn's neck and then to her shoulders. Kate almost shook her head in disbelief that she was actually alone with her.

And her eyes dropped once again and caught the noticeable contour of Dawn's chest. Suddenly winded, Kate sucked in an unexpected gasp. She turned away in a feeble attempt to rid her memory of the sight of Dawn's breast, a perfect silhouette of her nipple and the piercing.

Her head spun, trying to make sense of this crazy desire, a craving that centered on a simple yet relentless impulse. She wanted her mouth around that ring. She wanted to worship Dawn's breasts, feel the metal and flesh against her tongue. The axis of the universe was right there, and she wanted to meld into her.

When she turned back, there was a look of concern on Dawn's face. "Are you all right?"

Kate reached up and gripped the wheel with both hands, hoping that something solid and real would help center her. She looked out toward the black that enveloped the trees and nodded mutely. *Calm down, Kate. Get a hold of yourself.*

And then the worst happened. Dawn reached for Kate. Kate watched Dawn's fingers lightly grazing her wrist as she touched the acorn bracelet with a satisfied smile. Then Dawn's hand wrapped over Kate's. *No. Don't you know what you're doing, Dawn?*

Kate knew what she wanted to do. *Stop this, Kate. You can't do this. It's crazy.*

"Kate..."

Don't...Don't.

She turned, afraid to see in Dawn what she knew to be in herself. And Dawn moved closer, just a slight shift, but closer. In a low voice, much sexier than Kate could handle, Dawn said tenderly, "Come here."

And Kate did. Their lips met so lightly at first, Kate could hardly tell they were kissing. So tentative and soulful was it that Kate got light-headed. And gradually their kiss intensified, their tongues swirling together in perfect unison.

When they eventually broke the kiss, Kate sat back in her seat looking down into her lap. She quietly savored the taste of Dawn's lips.

Kate broke the silence. "The day we met," she said and Dawn looked up at her, "You furrowed your brow. It was so slight that I wouldn't have noticed if I hadn't have been staring straight into your eyes."

Dawn nodded.

"Why?" Kate asked.

She paused. "Because what was going on in the conference room didn't make sense."

The cryptic nature of her answer made Kate say, "I don't understand."

"There was just a difference between the way the others reacted to you and the way I reacted to you."

When Kate still didn't register Dawn's meaning, she continued, "When I walked in the room, the FDF people were pretty tense and serious, which would have indicated that you were the devil spawn or something. When Brett, Sr. introduced us, I certainly did not get that from you. So it wasn't matching up.

"But then I watched the way you took over and ran the meeting and how you handled FDF, which suggested to me not the devil spawn, but a determined woman who knew exactly what she wanted."

"Are you sure I'm not the devil spawn?"

A smile crept into Dawn's face. "More like kick-ass-and-take-names woman."

Kate laughed. "Thank you for the compliment, but my bitch façade didn't fool you, huh?"

"You're not a bitch," Dawn said, then smiled. "But I'm sure glad I wasn't Kurt that day."

They both laughed easily, with Kate adding, "I don't think Kurt wanted to be Kurt that day either."

Dawn laughed. "Wow, he was pissed."

"The look on his face was priceless."

"You had a look on your face another time that was priceless, as well."

"Yeah, yeah, the nipple ring." Kate dropped her head. "I'm so embarrassed."

"Don't be. I was flattered."

At the same time that Kate murmured, "You can't imagine what was going through my—" Dawn said, "Just that day I had been thinking of removing it—"

Suddenly Kate blurted out, "No, no. Don't," and was so shocked she laughed out loud, and then Dawn did as well.

The laughter helped release the tension, but Kate's laugh finished in more of a growl of frustration. She bent her head to rest it on the steering wheel.

"I can't stand it," she said.

"Can't stand it?"

Kate leaned back again. "Ever since you told me about your piercing. I don't know what it was. I keep thinking about it." Kate had Dawn's full attention. "It was the sexiest image. I don't understand it, but I haven't been able to get it out of my mind..." Kate's last words caught in her throat and trickled out scarcely loud enough to hear, "… and I want to see it."

Dawn gazed at her, the way she had already done many times. The silence seemed less a pause to consider the response and more a desire to be in the moment.

Kate held her breath, not knowing what would happen next. And then Dawn reached down and began unbuttoning her shirt.

"And I want to show you," Dawn said. As she unbuttoned her blouse, Kate suddenly felt lightheaded. Her heart pounded such a strong cadence that she was sure Dawn could hear it. She also noticed that Dawn's hands shook so much that she might never get to the last button.

At first, Kate was unsure whether or not she should move Dawn's hands aside and take over, but she found her answer in Dawn's resolute smile. She wanted to do this for Kate.

And when Dawn let the sides of her shirt fall away, the contrast of the silky auburn bra against her bronze skin stole Kate's breath.

Dawn shifted forward in her seat to reach behind and unclasp the bra which fell away as effortlessly as the shirt. Tanned like the rest of her chest, Dawn's breasts looked radiant in the darkness of the car. A single ring of gold ran through her left nipple, a ruby red ball of glass connecting the ends of the ring.

Words would not come to her mouth. Fifteen or twenty seconds passed before Kate realized she'd been staring. And when she finally did realize it, that was the impetus to lean down toward Dawn's nipple, and she felt the warmth of Dawn's hand on the back of her head as she gently guided her.

Kate's mind whirled. Just as her mouth found Dawn's nipple, she closed her eyes letting her tongue softly taste its incredible essence. Her lips tenderly encircled her nipple, and Dawn moaned. The moan came low and deep from her throat, as Kate drew her ringed nipple deeper into her mouth, slowly, and then rolling it back toward the tip of her tongue.

Kate played with the ring, flicking it over her tongue and teeth, dazed at the intensity of her feelings and the tightness between her own legs. To Kate nothing else existed, just her mouth and Dawn's breast. And it was the most mind-blowing feeling. Softly sucking, the sensation of the ring's steel against Dawn's firm nipple seemed a jarring contrast at first, but then the purpose of the nipple ring became evident as the sensitivity Dawn must have been feeling from the tugging hardened her nipple, causing the ring to react to the constriction. The more the nipple hardened, the more the ring became erect as well, slowly rising, until it was standing up against Kate's tongue.

She was keenly aware of the subtle sound of her teeth clinking against the metal of the ring.

Again Dawn moaned, but louder this time. Kate resisted the urge to squirm in her seat, rebuffing her own sexual arousal so she could drink in every second of Dawn's pleasure.

Dawn's head was back, her chest arched toward Kate, offering her breast. Kate could hear the ragged cadence of Dawn's breathing, but she didn't dare change any part of what she was doing for fear that any extraneous movement might interrupt Dawn and end the incredible dream from which she did not want to awaken. Kate felt dizzy, feeling Dawn's hands in her hair tugging in response to her sucking, and it almost caused her to miss the shallow gasps that began to come from Dawn.

Gripping Kate's hair, she moaned, "Harder, Kate." The words came urgently. "*Suck...harder...*" And Kate did.

Dawn began to shake, her whole body trembled, and more moans escaped.

She hung on to Kate but then, frantically, she reached back to clutch the back of the head rest with her left hand while her right hand groped futilely at the window and then dropped to grasp the door handle.

Blindly, Kate reached up with a free hand to travel the length of Dawn's shoulders, neck, and farther up until she found Dawn's face tilted back in ecstasy. Having that connection, cupping Dawn's lovely face in her hand, increased the sensory overload that was already exploding inside Kate's head. She could feel Dawn's mouth open with every moan, the heat from her face searing her hand.

"God, I feel that on my clit, too," Dawn's voice sounding winded. "Don't stop...ahhhh...mmmm, don't stop, Kate."

And then Kate felt Dawn's body tighten momentarily. Her breathing, sucking in and out, came in large gasps. She shook and then she came in a surprising torrent. Dawn's orgasm ripped through the both of them, cascading like two robust leaves tumbling together, over and over down a white-water river, and then at last over a waterfall. Kate held Dawn down against the car seat when it seemed as if she would catapult out of it, bucking against Kate's mouth as she cried out each wave of her contractions. Kate held steadfast, until Dawn's moans slowed, each breath coming in raspy gulps.

And whether it had been two minutes or two hours, Kate was reluctant to comply when she felt Dawn's hands reach down to her face and pull her upward. But when she did, she was enormously satisfied to be held, her face buried in Dawn's neck and hair.

CHAPTER TWENTY-FIVE

Krissy and Dawn had been at the shop since five a.m. A professional basketball team had ordered four extremely large hoops to theme their stadium entrances, and the two women were putting the final touches on the scenic paint.

They had been painting side-by-side chatting about work, mostly, when Krissy left to go to the soda machine.

"Want a Diet Coke?" she called back to Dawn.

"Sounds good, thanks."

As Krissy walked back to the hoops, she tossed Dawn's can to her, but had thrown it before Dawn turned to see what she was doing. Dawn tried to compensate and catch the incoming can, which she did, but not before it hit her chest.

Dawn doubled over with a groan.

"Oh shit, I'm sorry, Dawn." Krissy quickly covered the last few feet to hold Dawn's shoulder as she bent over.

"It's okay." Dawn moaned as she straightened up.

"I didn't think I threw it that hard."

"You didn't."

"So what's the matter? Are you sore?"

Dawn nodded sheepishly.

"What happened?" Krissy asked. Dawn's hesitation confused her. "Spit it out, woman."

"My…ring." Dawn pointed toward her breast.

"What about it?"

"Kate."

"Kate?"

Dawn nodded again.

Krissy's eyes widened suddenly, and her words came in a staccato beat, "What? Kate? No. What? Damn." She reached out to grasp Dawn's arm. "When?"

"Last night."

"So she…" Krissy tilted her head to the side, studying Dawn's expression, trying to understand exactly what happened. "Wait a minute…like she was…"

Slightly embarrassed, Dawn smiled.

"She had her mouth…" Krissy made a small circular motion with a finger.

Dawn nodded.

"Mercy." Krissy clutched at her heart as if it might stop. "I don't believe it."

Dawn's nod turned into a slow head shake not believing it herself.

"Was it…*fantastic?*"

"Beyond." Dawn marveled. She remembered the night in a way that seemed like she'd just watched a movie of someone else, not Kate and herself.

"Beyond?"

Dawn nodded again. "I came."

Krissy's hand shot up like a cop commanding someone to halt. "Wait a second. Didn't you just jump over a whole lot of details?"

Dawn pulled away to look at her. "Like what?"

"Like she threw you into bed, tore your clothes off, jumped on top of you."

"No, she only did…that." Dawn tilted her head down, indicated her breast.

Astonished, Krissy lowered her voice. "You mean you came with just her mouth on your…?"

Dawn drew in another breath. "Yes."

"No." Krissy sat down hard on the shop stool. Her mouth agape, she tried to think of something to add but could only manage another, "*No.*"

When words did finally come, Krissy looked up. "Is that…easy for you normally?"

"No."

"Oh, lord." Krissy was dumbfounded. "I'm speechless."

As was Dawn.

❖

The sun was just beginning its ascent in the east, casting the view out Kate's hotel suite window in a deep yellow glow. The grounds of the hotel were beginning to awaken. Sprinklers spritzed diagonals across the grass, maintenance workers clipped that and fixed this, and various species of birds snatched the last of the nighttime bugs for their morning breakfast.

After tossing and turning in bed since just after four, she'd ordered coffee to be delivered. Unable to sleep, she'd tried to read the paper but couldn't focus on the articles. She'd then showered and gotten dressed for work, which only burned about twenty more minutes.

Was it too early to call Dawn? That had been the central thought that had consistently occupied her brain. That, and the memory of her tongue wrapped around Dawn's nipple ring.

A fervent yearning broiled inside Kate to see Dawn, to talk to her again. No matter what it meant, how smart or dumb a thing it was to do so, and no matter what impact their being together the night before or seeing her again would make.

❖

"I was right. I thought I heard the front reception phone ring." Krissy walked up to Dawn in the shop. She grinned widely. "It's Kate."

"Kate." Dawn failed to wait for the answer and raced out of the shop. "Kate?" she puffed into the phone.

"Good morning. I took a chance that you were in early."

"That's usually a good chance to take," she replied gulping a little more air. "There's no one in front to answer the phone until eight. Krissy just happened to be in the copy room."

"Then I was very lucky. And very remiss for not asking for your cell number."

"I'll give it to you before we hang up." Dawn put her hand to her chest to slow down her heart beat.

"I've been thinking about you all night."

"So have I. And all morning as well."

"Dawn," Kate began after a moment of silence, "I could tell you that things happened too fast last night."

Dawn held her breath, afraid where the conversation might go. She would just die if Kate said it had been a mistake.

"That I'm barely out of a relationship."

Dawn's heart dropped.

"But that would be complete bullshit."

She waited for Kate to continue.

"Dawn, last night was…oh my God. I have been trying to come up with words to describe how I felt. If I could have stopped time, we'd still be in the SUV together."

In the SUV that night they had held each other for a long time. The intensity of what had happened stayed thick in the air, so they'd talked about their feelings, moving no further than gently holding hands. As the night grew late, Kate returned Dawn to her car in the studio parking lot. Neither spoke of taking it any further that night. What had already happened had been intense enough. And it had felt natural to tenderly kiss good-bye and leave that perfect moment just that. Perfect.

Dawn was glad Kate felt the same as she did. "I didn't want to leave either."

"I want to see you again. Soon."

Dawn felt a magnificent warmth course through her. "I do, too, Kate."

"Is this crazy?"

"Yes. Incredibly crazy."

"Well, I'm okay with being crazy."

"It's fine by me," Dawn said.

"Tonight after wrap?"

"I'll tell you where…"

❖

With three days left of shooting in Orlando, the crew was still on schedule. It had begun to rain just after ten in the morning, but since the crew was on the soundstage, the weather had no bearing on their work. Even the thunder outside was muffled sufficiently to avoid detection on the sensitive recording machinery on set.

And as wonderful an evening as she had had with Dawn the night before, and as much as she began to realize that the relationship with

Hannah had been a bad idea, it still gave Kate a stomachache to watch Hannah and Jennifer carry on.

Kyle Penny walked away from the script supervisor with a Polaroid in his hand. On set, Hannah and Peter were getting ready for the next setup, and Kyle showed Hannah the picture. "Hannah, you're going to be holding the torch in your right hand for the next shot so it will match the scene we shot yesterday."

"So get me the fucking *torch*, Kyle," Hannah shot back.

Peter watched Kyle walk away before turning to his costar. "Be nice, Hannah. Christ, he's just doing his job."

Hannah scowled at him. "Since when did you become the fucking polite police?"

"Hannah, chill out." Peter tried to quell the nastiness.

"Don't tell me to chill out, asshole. Who do you think you're talking to?"

Kate was about to jump out of her chair and deal with the fracas occurring on the set, when Amy, who had been standing just a few feet away, interceded.

"This is going to stop now," Amy said, pointing mostly to Hannah. "We've got work to do."

Peter apologized to Amy and turned away from Hannah.

From behind Kate's chair, Sandy Batnow said under her breath, "Let's hope Hannah's crap doesn't escalate all the way to Austria."

Kate nodded. "Let's just hope we get through Orlando."

Sandy squeezed Kate's shoulder. "I'm sorry about what happened between you two. I can't say that I'm sad that you split, given the way Hannah can be, but I know it still hurts."

"Thanks, Sandy." She placed her hand over Sandy's and squeezed back.

❖

The Roadhouse Grill was easy to find, and Kate pulled into the parking lot at eight thirty p.m. She'd left the set early, which had been easy to do given that the last few shots were simple reaction shots of Peter. Hannah and the rest of the cast had been dismissed around seven thirty. Hannah had kept her distance from the crew, as she had for the remainder of the day after Amy had scolded her. As soon as they wrapped, she demanded a private car to take her to the hotel.

Before leaving the set she'd told—not asked—Kate to call her later in her suite. Kate had refused, simply telling Hannah no. Strangely, rather than spew obscenities, Hannah took the rejection by storming off.

So Amy had gently pushed Kate off the set telling her to enjoy what was left of her evening. And as Kate walked toward the entrance of the Roadhouse Grill restaurant, inhaling the heady scent of barbequed ribs and burning oak, she knew that she would.

She followed the hostess across a floor that was covered in peanut shells that snapped and crackled with each step. There was a darkened, romantic, honky-tonk feel to the restaurant. Bathed in convivial neon light supplied by the bar, as well as small red lamps at each table, a happy Friday night feel pervaded the place. Each table was occupied by wide-grinned patrons taking great pleasure in each other's company. Whether a table was filled with blue-collar or white-collar people, everyone was enjoying ribs, chicken wings, and big, juicy hamburgers. Certainly the day was winding down, but the evening, for many of these patrons, was just cranking up.

After Kate sat down, Dawn reached across the booth's table, taking Kate's hand in hers. "I suppose I got lucky that you were able to leave early two days in a row."

"We both did. I was so happy to get out of there and come see you."

"It was a long day for me, waiting until now."

Kate smiled. "Very."

When the server approached, Dawn and Kate reluctantly unclasped their hands. They ordered dinner and when the server left, Kate said to Dawn, "I wasn't sure whether it was okay for the server to see us holding hands."

"Granted Orlando's not Hollywood, so it's hard to know when it's cool and when it's not."

"What about now?"

"I think it's okay." Dawn reached out again.

Taking her hand, Kate marveled at the fact that she couldn't keep the smile from her face. "I still can't stop thinking about you…in the SUV."

Dawn let out a quiet whoosh of breath, and Kate watched her chest lift slightly as she inhaled.

"Being with you…," Kate started to say, "it was the most amazing…"And found no appropriate words.

Dawn sighed. "Yes, it was."

"Are you okay with it?"

"I was wondering the same thing. With Hannah and everything."

"Hannah is over. Should have been over a long time ago. But more than that, there's something about you, the way I feel when I'm around you. That's all that's coursing through me."

Dawn couldn't believe what she was hearing just as much as what she was feeling. "Tell me more. About Hannah."

"Well there's a lot to tell and not so much. What I could tell you about what didn't work between Hannah and me falls pretty much into the same general category."

"How she treated you?"

"That and how I treated myself. It takes two to screw up a relationship. I was the one that didn't speak up at the beginning when I knew there were many things I didn't like. The relationship never really formed into a real one."

Dawn's voice was soft. "What does that mean?"

"It means that we just…just got together. We were a couple immediately, and I never questioned much else. At least at the beginning. And then I just gave in to the business of our relationship. It was very public, and it was easy to go through the motions." Kate took a sip of her water. "God, I sound hideous."

Dawn shrugged. "I don't think finding yourself in a relationship that goes nowhere is a rare thing."

"I suppose. But I knew from the start that she didn't have any of the personable qualities I really wanted. It was a bad relationship that I was too slothful to get out of."

"Until now."

"Until I realized what I really could have."

"Which is?"

"It's simple, really. A wonderful, kind, loving woman who sees me for me. Something I am not good at finding."

A moment passed between them. Kate then squeezed Dawn's hand. "What attracts me to you, other than the fact that you're beautiful, is how amazing it is to talk to you. I can't remember talking so deeply to anyone I've ever been with."

"I really like being with you."

Kate smiled. "That warms me inside."

When the server returned with their meals, they began to talk about Dawn's work, the film, and a million other things. It wasn't until Kate noticed that it was strangely quiet around them that she realized they were the last ones in the restaurant. The employees were trying to close down and had cleaned up everything around them.

Kate and Dawn sheepishly took the bill to the front register, leaving a very generous tip for dominating the table.

Out in the parking lot, Dawn walked Kate back to her car.

"Oh, no," Dawn said.

Kate caught the tease. "I know…it's the Range Rover again."

Dawn nodded in obvious mock-seriousness. "This car tends to get people into trouble."

"So you think we got in trouble last night?" Kate asked.

"Yes," Dawn replied earnestly. "And in trouble is a great place to be with you."

Kate sidled up closer to Dawn, taking her hand and turning her toward her. They stopped face-to-face in the middle of the parking lot. "Care to go there again?"

A smile curled up the right side of Dawn's mouth. "Unlock the door."

CHAPTER TWENTY-SIX

Two days left of principal photography in Orlando, was Kate's first thought when she had awoken that morning. And then she thought of what it meant to her. She was grateful that, so far, the shoot was going very well. They were on budget and on schedule. If she got through the Orlando shoot unscathed, all she had to do was get the crew to Austria for some fairly straight-forward filming, and then back to Los Angeles where the filming might be unpredictable, but easily managed, since they were on their home turf.

She lay in bed thinking about her impending departure. In order to make sure everything would be ready for the crew's arrival in Austria, Kate and Nathan were to leave for Salzburg in three days, ahead of the crew. A small production office was already being set up over there, and a few Austrian locals were already getting the office in order and double-checking the Austrian locations.

And while she was grateful that they were almost finished shooting in Orlando, it occurred to her that if she were lying here on her first morning in Orlando, there would have been no plausible way that she would have had this next thought. *I don't want to leave.* She hadn't anticipated that thought at all. And she certainly hadn't anticipated the last two nights with Dawn.

Dawn then filled her mind again with wonderful, stirring thoughts. She was deeply moved by Dawn's depth and compassion. Being near her made Kate feel whole. Dawn listened to her, really heard her. The conversations were not only shared, they were meaningful and full of incredible feeling. There was a profound connection between them, and it was more extraordinary than Kate could ever have imagined.

She'd fallen pretty hard, and leaving Dawn would be the most difficult part of the last weeks.

As Kate was walking past the soundstages on her way to the production office, she flipped open her cell phone and dialed. Presently, Dawn answered.

Dawn had barely uttered hello when Kate said, "You're still on my mind…"

Kate could hear Dawn suck in a breath. "So are you." They had spent some time during the previous evening in Kate's SUV in the parking lot of the Roadhouse Grill. Thankfully, no one bothered them. Though they hadn't gone as far as the first night, they talked about wanting to. After the initial rush of desire the night before, it seemed right to take it easy with each other. And as they held each other, they kissed until their lips felt like mush and they laughed until their bellies hurt. It had felt strange leaving Dawn that night and driving back to the hotel alone, but it had also felt right.

"Can I see you later?"

"When?"

"In five minutes?"

Dawn laughed. "How about after wrap?"

"I'll call you when we're about a half an hour from breaking. Is that okay?"

"It's more than okay."

❖

"Do tell." Beth caught up with Kate as she was opening the door to the production office.

"Tell what?"

"Where've you been, little lady?"

"Been?"

"Oh, stop being coy with me. It doesn't work. You've been absent from your typical late night work sessions in the production office. And you've got a silly smile on your face right now."

Kate noticed with surprise that Beth was right. "I've been with Dawn."

"Oh, wow. Good for you."

"Well, yes and no. We're all packing up and leaving in two days."

"So?"

"Beth, we're leaving. Gone from here."

"That's what planes are for."

Kate pondered the comment as Beth poked her in the shoulder. "Is she marvelous to be around?"

"Beyond marvelous."

Beth reached out and hugged her. "That's awesome. Just enjoy it."

Kate's heart had already started to fill with a sense of foreboding. "For only two more days."

"Or more, if you want it."

Kate looked dubiously at Beth, shaking her head.

"You'll figure something out. But either way, I'm very happy for you, Kate."

Kate waved good-bye and entered the production office. "Good morning, Betsy,"

"Hello. Ready for the onslaught?"

"Onslaught?"

"Today's the day the *Hollywood on Hollywood* crew will be here to shoot a segment for tomorrow's broadcast."

"Oh shit, I forgot." It had slipped Kate's mind that she had okayed the nightly entertainment show from LA to shoot the goings-on on the set. *Hollywood on Hollywood* was a magazine format prime time TV show that featured Hollywood celebrities and followed them around for the day. Today they were coming to film Kate.

"When are they arriving?" Kate picked up the mail and production paperwork that spilled out of her inbox.

"At eight. In one hour."

"And remind me when they'd said they'd be wrapping their shoot?"

"Probably around eight tonight."

This was the last thing Kate needed. Sure, she was appreciative of the coverage and the fact that they were interested in her. It would certainly give the film publicity even though the release date would not be until the following summer. But right now, with the breakup with Hannah, having a film crew follow her around all day was not a very good plan.

But somehow she'd navigate through the next twelve hours. And as long as Hannah wasn't acting up, the camera crew just might end their day with a small fizzle and sputter.

❖

"I'm Derek," said the director of the *Hollywood on Hollywood* film crew making introductions to Kate. "This is Stan on camera, and that's Barry with the sound equipment." They were outside the production office and, as if on queue, Stan did a perfect clean and jerk of the camera up and onto his shoulder as Barry began clipping a wireless microphone to the waistband on the back of Kate's pants.

"Very pleased to meet you," Kate said as Barry expertly ran the microphone cord up and over her shoulder and clipped the tiny microphone to the collar of her shirt.

Derek didn't waste any time getting to the instructions, "So, we'll be following you around. We'll record all your conversations, and I'll be asking you questions throughout. In a little while, we'll also have you sitting on the set, and we'll do an interview with the set in the background."

"Sounds good to me," Kate said, though Derek's brain was running so far ahead, she doubted he'd even heard her. Moreover, she was convinced that he wouldn't have even noticed if, instead, she'd answered with "my ass is on fire."

Kate had been interviewed many times before, but this was the first time she was to be wired and followed. She sighed and said, "Let's get going then." And the *Hollywood on Hollywood* crew started their day.

If the exclamations of "Wow!" from Derek were any indication, the *Hollywood on Hollywood* crew was getting a lot of good footage. Having them follow her throughout the day, Kate had surmised that the one word shouts were his way of saying "cut," because after each yell, Derek would shake Kate's hand and comment on what just happened. "Wow! That was fabulous when you decided to cut that scene from the script."…"Wow! The way you handled the radio, cell phone, and three crew people at the same time was…Wow!"

Each time, Kate would just smile and pray for eight p.m.

Hannah did become quite bitchy a few times during the day, but Kate simply left the set each time, leading Derek's crew away from recording any evidence that there was foolish behavior on the set. Kyle had been sharp enough to pick up on what Kate was having to deal with and would covertly radio her with some bogus question which would indicate that the coast was clear for her to return.

At a little after six, her cell phone vibrated. Kyle was on the other end, and since he had chosen not to use the radio, Kate knew something was not going well. "Kate, Hannah just stormed off the set and went to her motor home."

With Derek staring at her, smarmy anticipation washing across his face, Kate managed, in her most bored voice, "Why?"

"She's been yelling that you haven't been on the set most of the day."

"And that would be a problem?"

"Apparently."

"Okay, I'll take care of it," Kate said as she made her way toward Hannah's motor home.

When she arrived at the door, Kate unclipped her microphone unit from her belt. "Listen, I need to have a few private moments."

Derek held up his hand. "But we're capturing everything. Every problem, every conversation."

"Not this conversation." Kate handed the microphone unit to Barry before disappearing behind Hannah's door.

She found Hannah sitting on the couch, her feet up on the coffee table, her arms folded defiantly across her chest. Kate took a few steps inside. They looked at each other in silence for a moment before Kate sighed. "What's going on?"

"You were supposed to call me last night."

Kate shook her head. "I told you yesterday that I wasn't going to call you."

"I just thought that's because you were mad."

"I was, Hannah. And I still am."

"I miss you, Kate."

"Uh, huh," Kate said cynically.

"I want you back."

"Well, isn't that just perfect?"

"What?"

"You don't get it, do you?"

Hannah ignored the comment. "You know, with Jennifer, it was just a stupid thing."

"Well, stupid or not, it's yours to own now."

"That's just it, Kate. It's not anything now. She's out of my life."

"I'm sorry for you, then."

"Sorry for me? What does that mean?"

Kate felt a bile-flavored anger rise in her throat. "It means, Hannah, that you decided to fuck me over and lost me, and then you fucked Jennifer for a few days and then decided to dump her. So you find yourself without either of us. And now you're thinking I might come back?" She took a breath before adding, "That makes me feel very sorry for you."

Hannah grew angry, snapping, "I don't need your sympathy."

"It's not sympathy, my dear," Kate bit out the words, "Watching a train wreck doesn't make me sympathetic. It just makes me sad."

Kate grabbed the doorknob to leave. "And if marching off the set in the middle of a scene was your way of getting me to talk to you, I suggest that you seriously consider that to be the last time you pull that stunt. The next time it *will* cost you fifty-nine thousand dollars. I've had enough of your spoiled behavior. Get back on set."

Derek and the *Hollywood on Hollywood* crew followed Kate for the next two hours, not picking up much that Kate thought would make for a compelling story. Nevertheless, Derek gushed forth a few wow's anyway.

On set with the rest of the crew, just before eight p.m., Kate began to relax knowing that it would be a very short time before Derek and company would pack up and leave. Hannah, Peter, and Ralph Markowitz were rehearsing a moderately difficult scene that required them to run the length of one section of the salt mine. From where she was sitting in her director's chair, Kate noticed that from the span of the first to the fourth run-through, Ralph had slowed down significantly and now, as he stood off to the side while Amy discussed some story intricacies with Hannah and Peter, Ralph was dripping with sweat.

Kate slowly stood up and was about to walk over to ask whether he was okay when he suddenly slumped to the floor. In five paces Kate covered the distance between them and was kneeling at his side.

"Call 911 and then get the medic here." Kate yelled to no one in particular, but since everyone had a radio and cell phone, multiple calls went out that instant. The film's medic was on hand every day of the shoot, just in case, and in the back of her brain, Kate registered a couple of voices yelling into the radio to locate him.

Ralph appeared to be unconscious, so Kate called out to him, "Ralph."

He did not respond. She repeated herself, even louder, and gently shook his shoulders. When there was still no response, the ABC's of CPR came quickly to her, airway, breathing, circulation. Kate first rolled Ralph onto his side to clear his airway. She was aware of many people crowding around and wondered where the hell the set medic was. Suddenly someone was kneeling next to her.

Jennifer said quickly, "I know CPR as well, if we need to do it together."

"Okay, good." Kate pushed her fingers into his jugular in an attempt to register a pulse.

Before Kate could finish saying, "He's not breathing and there's no pulse," Jennifer moved around so that she was at the side of Ralph's head. "I'll do the breathing."

They rolled Ralph onto his back, and Kate unbuttoned his shirt to release the collar that appeared to be tight. He lay there, still motionless, without even as much as a gasp.

Jennifer breathed for Ralph as Kate pumped his chest in sets of fifteen rapid compressions.

At once, the medic was there kneeling next to them. He quickly assessed that the women were trained and doing well so he said, "Don't stop unless you want me to take over. Keep going but let me know when one of you gets tired." The medic took Ralph's wrist. "I'll let you know if I get a pulse."

After five or six rounds, the medic checked to see whether he needed to step in. Kate shook her head, feeling so shot full of adrenaline, she could have run a marathon.

One of the crew members held open the soundstage door, and the sound of approaching sirens grew louder. And then the paramedics were there, instantly unloading a menagerie of equipment and monitors.

The paramedics were simultaneously preparing a portable hand-activated airway and were getting the defibrillator hooked up and ready to punch Ralph's heart into life, when Ralph suddenly sputtered and gasped.

Kate and Jennifer were quickly replaced by the paramedics. They rose to their feet. Jennifer distractedly placed a hand on Kate's shoulder to steady herself. The rest was a rush of activity as the paramedics stabilized Ralph for transport. The place was fairly quiet as the crew stood there, mouths agape. As the paramedics and a few crew members who'd chosen to accompany Ralph to the hospital began to leave, Kate heard Derek's distinctive voice. "Wow!"

And then there were hands on her. Crying people gripped her. And at that moment, what had actually just happened suddenly hit her. She started shaking as her adrenaline continued to pump, suddenly finding nowhere to go.

She turned to Jennifer and heard her say, "Do you think he'll be okay?"

Kate shook her head. "I don't know."

Then Beth was there. "I'll drive you to the hospital."

"Jennifer," Kate squeezed the hand that was still on her shoulder, "Are you okay?"

Jennifer nodded.

"Okay, then…wrap the crew for tonight. Tell them we'll get word on Ralph's condition back to the hotel just as soon as we know something. Tell Betsy to call me with Ralph's contact number, the one he gave us for emergencies. He's not married so I don't know who it is, but I will call them myself. And ask her to get me Ralph's manager's number. He needs to know. I'll call the studio, too. But all other calls, from the press or anyone else, tell her to tell them 'no comment yet.'" She turned to Kyle and Nathan, who were hovering close by and asked them, "Would you please help Jennifer with what I said?" She rushed with Beth to one of the transportation cars.

Dawn's cell phone rang around nine o'clock, the caller ID had a California area code, but it wasn't Kate's number.

"Dawn?" the voice said.

"Yes?"

"It's Beth."

Dawn was momentarily confused.

"From Kate's movie."

"Oh. Yes, hello."

"There's been an emergency on the set and Kate's tending to it."

Suddenly a jolt went through Dawn's chest. "Is Kate all right?"

"She's fine, though it's been a hell of a night. One of the actors had a heart attack. She's with him at the hospital right now."

"Oh my God," Dawn gasped.

"I know that she was looking forward to seeing you, so I told her I'd call you to let you know that she's not standing you up."

"Okay." Dawn couldn't imagine the stress Kate must be feeling at that moment.

"She will call you later, for sure."

"Thank you." Dawn could hear the gentleness in Beth's voice. "Thank you very much for calling."

Beth paused. "She likes you, you know."

Dawn momentarily lost her words.

"She's my best friend. I should know."

"She's lucky to have you."

"That's what I always tell her."

"Thanks again, Beth."

"You bet. She'll call you, okay?"

"Okay."

❖

In the fluorescent glare of the hospital's emergency room waiting area, Kate sat with Amy, Sandy, Peter, Hannah, and the crew medic. Kyle and Jennifer handled the wrap of the set, and Nathan stayed back at the production office to help Betsy field the calls that would most certainly come in about Ralph's condition. Though a hospitalization on a movie set was always news, no information was to be dispersed until Kate called.

As they sat in the ER's waiting room, no one spoke. Kate was the only one to get out of her chair long enough to make some phone calls.

She called Ralph's sister at the number he'd left on his personal information sheet. The sister mumbled that she knew something like this would happen and then said she would drive to LAX immediately to catch a flight to Florida. Kate reached Jeffery next. He was still at the studio and she quickly told him the news. He said that he would make the call to the completion bond company, the one that Jeffery himself had insisted she utilize to cover Ralph for this very type of incident. She had wanted to confront him about the studio's push to keep Ralph on the picture. But now wasn't the time.

After calling Ralph's manager, who hadn't sounded any more shocked than Ralph's sister, she called the production office to tell Betsy and Nathan that there would be a small production meeting at eight a.m. in order to figure out the next steps. Kyle and Jennifer were to be there as well. Then they would inform the rest of the crew as to the course of action.

The last call was to Derek, the director of the *Hollywood on Hollywood* crew. She told him to keep the news and footage of Ralph's crisis silent until the next day.

"Do I get the exclusive?"

Kate shook her head in abhorrence. "Yes."

"Okay. So anyway, who would I tell? Except for my executive producer."

"No one else," she said, "and not any of your producers. Just let me have twelve hours."

"Wow," Derek had happily agreed.

After an hour, Jennifer appeared in the waiting room and walked over to Kate. One of the only empty chairs was next to her, so Jennifer sat down.

"How's Ralph?" she asked anxiously.

Kate shook her head. "No one's been out to tell us yet. They took him in right away, of course, but there are no updates."

Jennifer nodded apprehensively. "God, I hope he's okay."

"Me, too."

"It was pretty scary, huh?"

Kate thought of Ralph's collapse and the CPR they had given him. "Yes, it was."

They had been sitting in silence awhile when Jennifer offered, "I released the cast and crew. Nathan and Betsy said it's been quiet so far except for one call from a reporter that had been monitoring a police scanner and was asking for details on the ambulance request at the studio. Of course, he got nothing further from us."

Kate nodded. "Every time we're on location the newspaper reporters listen for any dirt that might be caused by our presence. It's only a matter of time before someone connects the dots on this one."

Sandy and Peter were chatting quietly with Amy, and the crew medic had gone off to find a cup of coffee. Hannah sat by herself in a lone chair by the window.

"I feel horrible," Jennifer said.

"You did a great job with the CPR." Kate had been impressed with Jennifer's quick action.

"No, I mean about Hannah. Kimber told me you saw us."

They both automatically looked over at Hannah who was slumped down in the chair, arms folded across her chest, looking bored beyond all comprehension.

Kate pursed her lips. "It's over now."

"But I shouldn't have done that with her so soon after. Especially on the set."

"Yeah, you're right. That was fucked up." Kate was too tired to think of anything else to say.

"I totally deserved that," Jennifer said humbly.

"And I don't mean this with any animosity," Kate added, "but you're not the first, and you won't be the last."

Jennifer nodded soberly. "That still doesn't get me out of being an asshole."

Kate pinched the bridge of her nose. "No, I suppose it doesn't."

"I am so sorry, Kate."

A socially sensitive mother had taught Kate to always redeem someone's apology with "Oh, it's okay," but tonight, she just couldn't. She turned to Jennifer and scarcely nodded.

The medic returned with his coffee, as well as three more cups that he balanced in his hands. As he offered them around, Hannah huffed audibly. "What a dingy place. Who'd want to be sick *here?*" she griped to no one. And that is exactly who paid attention to her comment.

CHAPTER TWENTY-SEVEN

Just after two a.m., Kate heard some people talking down the hospital corridor. She had already sent Amy, Peter, Hannah, and Sandy back to the hotel, promising them she'd let them know what the news was as soon as she heard it. She'd also tried to send Jennifer, but the first A.D. wouldn't budge. So they'd sat for the next few hours, side by side, in a companionable silence that was filled with thoughts of Ralph, of Hannah, and of the logistics of shooting the rest of the motion picture.

A doctor rounded the corner and called Kate's name. Kate and Jennifer jumped to their feet, and the doctor walked over to them.

"I suppose you're the responsible party until Mr. Markowitz's family gets here?"

"My office will get you our insurance paperwork."

"Mr. Markowitz has had a severe heart attack. There was no time to wait for someone to find his family. We had to perform surgery to repair a damaged ventricle, and he's now in the intensive care unit in critical condition."

"He's alive," Kate said with relief.

"Yes, he's very lucky."

"Is he going to make it?"

"Well, the first forty-eight hours will tell. He's being watched very closely. We really won't know any more for a while."

"Can we see him?" Jennifer asked.

"No, he's not going to be conscious until sometime tomorrow."

"His sister will be here in the morning," Kate said.

"That's good. I would check back in the morning, and we might have more for you then. Just make sure the nurse's station has your phone number, and we'll call you if there's any change in his condition."

Kate and Jennifer rode back to the studio in the car that Jennifer had taken from the transportation department. Nathan and Betsy were asleep in the production office but jumped to when the door opened.

Kate told them what the doctor had said. Nathan related that they'd fended off a few more phone calls. They spent a few moments discussing the early morning meeting, and then Kate told them that they all needed to get back to the hotel for some sleep. It was almost three thirty in the morning when Kate and the rest got back to the hotel.

There was a message on Kate's hotel room voicemail. "Kate, it's Dawn. Beth called me to let me know what happened tonight. I hope everyone's okay. I am so sorry this happened. I know it must be really tough for you. I am sending prayers to all of you. Call me anytime. I doubt I'll be sleeping."

Kate lay down on the bed and rubbed her head trying to alleviate a ferocious headache. She just wanted to lay there in complete silence for a few minutes and then she'd call Dawn.

The next thing she knew, a dull orange glow was shining in her room. The sun was coming up over the Orlando horizon and her clock read 5:45 a.m.

She sat up and cringed at what felt like the weight of one hundred hangovers pummeling her head. What she needed to do was lay back down and sleep for another hour. What she had to do was get up and check on Ralph's condition. She wanted to call Dawn. She had to figure out how she was going to get through the last day of principal photography in Orlando without one of her actors. Kate shook off the fog in her head and made her way to the production office to go over the rest of the shooting schedule. When she got there Amy was already knee-deep in script pages. They exchanged a weary smile and got down to work.

At the eight o'clock production meeting, Kate told everyone that the hospital had reported that Ralph's condition remained unchanged. He hadn't awoken but he hadn't gotten worse. Beth called to tell Kate that she'd just picked up Ralph's sister from a red-eye flight and dropped her off at the hospital. Kate asked her to call Betsy to arrange a hotel room for her at the Peabody.

Then the group sat down to discuss the course of action.

Amy spoke first. "We have two scenes left to shoot with Ralph's character, Claus. One is where Claus and his band of bad guys are chasing Tracy and Kip, and he tells his cohorts to go down the south tunnel while he tries the north one. So for that scene, we wrote Ralph's character out and have the one bad guy telling the other that Claus went down the north tunnel so they're to try the south one. That was easy enough since it wasn't a pivotal scene.

"The other scene, however," Amy continued, "is a bit trickier. As you all know, it's the one where Claus waits in the shadows and beans Tracy in the head."

Kate nodded, "That scene is supposed to establish that Claus knows the tunnels better than Tracy and Kip and has taken a shortcut to get ahead of them so he can bash Tracy."

"You're right. Originally, Sandy and I were going to shoot Claus in the shadows and convey the tension through his facial expressions as he waited for Tracy to come running by, then he'd jump out and knock her unconscious. So what I want to do now is set up the shot instead from Tracy's vantage point. She'll be running and running and come around the bend and then we'll flash cut to a close up of her reacting to the surprise. All of a sudden she gets beaned by something off camera and out go her lights."

"Fade to black," Sandy offered.

"Exactly. Kate and I think it will work."

"Because in the next scene," Kate said, "the scene that we shot two days ago, we see Ralph's character, Claus, dragging Tracy farther into the tunnel while Kip, not being able to see what happened since he's blind, is frantically calling for her. So it's after the deed is done that we find out what Tracy saw just before she gets knocked out."

Amy looked around the room. "Is there anything that anyone can think of that we've missed?"

Jennifer asked, "Did you call Carrie Monahan to see whether she could think of any problems with the plan?"

"I did," Amy said. "She was thinking a lot clearer than I was since it was only midnight, LA time when I called. She was okay with the plan and thought it'll cut together nicely. She thinks the change of the 'knocked unconscious' scene will actually work better since it causes more mystery in the last moment of the previous scene. We don't know what's happening, just Tracy's anticipatory reaction when she realizes she's in trouble."

Kate and the others who were at the hospital with her then met with the rest of the cast and crew on Soundstage Two. They brought everyone up to speed on Ralph's condition and explained how they would shoot around him.

Everyone seemed eager to do well, mostly for Ralph's sake. And since it was the last day in Orlando, there seemed to be an added energy, that last push for success.

It wasn't until the cast and crew were entrenched in the first shot of the day that Kate finally retreated to her office and called Dawn. She had a million phone calls to make, not the least of which was to Jeffery about Ralph and the completion bond fiasco, but she first needed to hear Dawn's voice.

"I've been thinking about you so much," Dawn said as soon as she picked up the phone, "Are you okay?"

Kate told her about Ralph and the night at the hospital and how she'd really wanted to call her that morning but passed out instead. "I'm so sorry that I didn't call you. I was supposed to call you after we wrapped."

"Don't worry at all. I knew that you'd call me when you could."

"Please don't think that I wasn't thinking about you."

"I don't...and, Kate?"

"Yes?"

"Everything's going to be all right."

Dawn's response was so calming and so reassuring that tears welled up in Kate's eyes. *Dawn, stay with me. Don't let me go to Austria.* She was beyond tired and had little left. Dawn must have sensed this. "You sound exhausted, Kate. And I'm sure you have a lot to do. I'd love for you to call me later."

"Would that be okay?" Kate felt grateful for the consideration and understanding.

"I'll be right here."

The rest of the morning flew by in a blur of phone calls and jogs out to the set. At lunch she went over to the hospital to check on Ralph. He was partially awake but couldn't talk because of a breathing tube. Kate talked with his sister for a while, told Ralph not to worry about the film but to concentrate on getting better, kissed him on the forehead, and left for the studio.

On her way back, Beth called on her cell phone. "I didn't get to pull you aside at the production meeting this morning. How are you, buddy?"

"Okay."

"Tired?"

"No more than anyone else."

"Tough old ass, aren't you?"

"Well, I'm kicking my tough old ass for not listening to my gut and taking Ralph off the picture."

"Something tells me that your gut was trumped by something else."

"So that gossip got out?"

"Nope. But I know you, and the only times you don't go with your gut are on two occasions. And I'm guessing this occasion is the one where you got bullied by the big boys."

"You've been in Hollywood too long, my friend."

"So, I'm right?"

"Yes."

"Kate, you know the Hollywood game. You have to play it a certain way. It's not about always fighting for what's right. Sometimes, it's about picking your battles."

"But I didn't pick the battle that had to do with Ralph's health."

"Don't you think that Ralph should have been responsible for his own health? You didn't force him to take this role."

"I should have been stronger in that decision." Kate growled in frustration.

"Kate," Beth said firmly, "quit beating yourself up. These things happen. Ralph's in good hands. And you have a movie to finish."

"Shit."

"And another thing," Beth said, "saying 'shit' is another way of saying 'I should have done this, I could have done this.' Forget the things you can't do anything about now. There's too much other stuff out there that you can do something about. Life's too goddamn short."

Kate sighed and then thanked her. "Hey Beth, before we hang up, what is the other occasion where I don't go with my gut?"

Beth laughed. "You don't know?"

She thought a moment. "No."

"In true matters of the heart."

"What? Come on."

"What did your gut say about Hannah?"

"Oh, man," Kate muttered.

"See? What did your gut say about Hannah?"

It was inarguable. That hadn't been a true matter of the heart. "Shit."

"And, here again, 'shit' means 'I should have—'"

"Stayed away from her," Kate finished the sentence.

"Go with your gut."

Kate muttered again. This time it was barely audible, "Life's too goddamn short."

"What?"

"Everything you said. It's sinking in."

The receptionist was holding out the phone receiver when Dawn came out of the shop.

"Did you page me? It was loud out there."

Smiling, the receptionist nodded and handed her the phone.

That certain electronic static clued Dawn in immediately that the call was coming from a cell phone. "Hello?"

"I'm driving to the shop. I need to see you."

"Please come."

"Can you meet me in the parking lot in about five minutes?"

"Sure."

As soon as Kate got out of the car, Dawn was right there. Kate relaxed into her arms.

"Come with me." Dawn led her back to her studio.

Closing the door behind them, they were enveloped in the shadows of her workspace. The lights were off and thin tentacles of sun sliced in from the sides of the window shades. Paint smells and a tinge of turpentine hung in the room. Dawn and Kate slid their arms around each other.

"You feel so good," Kate said in her ear.

"So do you. Has anything else happened?"

"Happened?"

"Well, it's just after one thirty. I would think that'd you'd be on the set right now."

"Everything's fine. Ralph is awake and doing better. The set's running fine. I just needed to see you."

"I'm really glad. I haven't been able to concentrate today. I wanted to drive over to the studio and see you except I knew you'd be busy. But I've thought about nothing else but you."

A sense of urgency drew Kate toward her and they crushed into one another melding in their craving.

Kate had ached for her and groaned when Dawn's hands found her ass and pulled Kate into her. She felt Dawn's legs shaking, and she knew she was growing wet.

Kate drew her mouth to the base of Dawn's throat, licking and sucking as Dawn's pulse beat, pounding furiously against her lips.

Kate's cell phone rang but she ignored it.

"It could...be...important..." Dawn said in between gasps.

"No," Kate mumbled against Dawn's neck.

Dawn moved Kate's arms aside to unzip Kate's pants.

Kate reached down and helped tug her pants and panties down to her ankles as Dawn gently pushed her to lean against the workbench.

Kate felt the coolness of a paint can against her back as she pulled Dawn back into her. Legs now spread, Kate opened herself up to whatever Dawn wanted to do.

Dawn's hand was ardent and certain as she massaged Kate's thighs.

"I'm crazy about you," she said and then dipped down between Kate's legs. Immediately, an explosive current surged through Kate and a loud, "Ahhhhh..." filled the studio.

Dawn's fingers stroked Kate's clit in slow, unbearably soft circles, and the touch was so yielding that she knew she was incredibly wet.

Dawn moaned, "Yesssss," in her ear, and Kate held on tighter to her.

Kate wanted her, wanted Dawn in every way. A jumble of desires ping-ponged in her head. She wanted to be taken by her, to be fucked, to be made love to. She wanted to be conquered, to be vulnerable, to be subservient, exposed, loved, and to be swept away. All of it, all at once. And one at a time.

The first surges of ecstasy began quickly, a swirling throb starting at the base of her spine. Hot surges burned in her pelvis and stars danced under her eyelids. Her breath quickened and Kate moaned, "Dawn... Dawn..."

"I'm right here," she said, kissing Kate's shoulder.

Kate pictured Dawn's fingers on her clit, those incredible fingers that she'd watched sculpting clay so exquisitely. She remembered the feeling of her own mouth on Dawn's nipple ring, tugging, while Dawn came, and suddenly Kate's orgasm was upon her. The sudden rush sent her bucking and crying out as Dawn held her up with the strong arm she had wrapped around her. The workbench lurched against the back wall and cans and tools rattled in rhythm to Kate's contractions.

And just as the spasms subsided, Dawn plunged her fingers inside Kate who gasped and cried out, "Yes. Oh my God!"

Each time Dawn pulled out and then pushed back in, she stroked Kate's G-spot, pushing up and out, in just the right place. Kate went wild, throwing her head back, almost hyperventilating.

She cried out, "Uggghhhh...uggghhhh" to each thrust, inhaling in a raspy gasp every second or third stroke. Nothing existed but the two of them. Her heart swelled and pounded against her chest.

Quickly, Kate stammered out, "I'm going to come again." And as she did, she buried her head in Dawn's neck, holding her even tighter.

Kate could feel her contractions squeezing Dawn's fingers, and Dawn cooed loving encouragement to her. She held fast until Kate's muscles relaxed and they stayed there, motionless, for a long time.

"My God," Dawn murmured in her ear and then kissed her cheek and neck. "I want to stay inside you."

"Oh yes. Please."

Kate didn't know how long they stood there holding each other, but her breathing had returned to normal and she thought she could speak complete sentences again. "I want to touch you," she said. Fingers still inside, Dawn leaned her head back so that she could see Kate's face, "Let's just concentrate on you right now, okay?"

They kissed. "Okay."

Later, when Kate shifted slightly and Dawn said, "Ready?"

Pursing her lip, Kate said, "No."

Dawn laughed and then, ever so slowly, pulled her fingers out.

Kate looked into Dawn's eyes as she did, watching them sparkle with desire.

They kissed again, and held each other, and in that moment Kate realized that sex with Dawn was about connection and consideration. It was about mutuality and togetherness. With Hannah sex had been about power.

"I don't want to know what time it is," Dawn said.

Kate remembered what day it was and felt her gut twist. She hated saying what she had to say, unable to reconcile the logic herself. "Dawn," she started, hating the reality of her situation. "Today's my last day here."

"Austria."

Kate nodded. "Fucking Austria."

Dawn opened her mouth but no words came out at first. "Will I see you after you get back?"

Kate looked squarely at Dawn. "Most definitely."

"Our lives are so different. And so far apart. We live on opposite coasts."

Beth's words came back to Kate. "That's what planes are for."

"Hmmm," Dawn said, "I'd better save my frequent flier miles."

Kate laughed and Dawn gingerly added, "Austria. Why couldn't it be Fort Lauderdale or somewhere a little closer?"

"I have to admit, I was looking forward to that trip. Now…" She brushed a lock of Dawn's hair from her face. "I'm not at all."

They kissed, this time tongues tenderly stroking each other, swirling amid soft, sexy moans.

This is insane, Kate thought. She had flown out to Florida with Hannah, and suddenly not only was Hannah gone, but Dawn was in her life, feeling better than any relationship had ever felt, and she was about to leave it all. She couldn't just walk away from her. But she had to. The motion picture was like a freight train, and Kate was not only on it, she was the conductor.

And the conductor can modify the course as she sees fit.

"When we were talking earlier today…" Kate took a deep breath before continuing, "I kept thinking to myself, you know, that little voice that talks to you? It kept saying, 'Dawn, stay with me.'" Then

Kate stopped. She felt a surge of anxious fright mixed with a sudden rush of dogged determination.

Kate finally resumed voicing her thoughts, "And then I said to myself, and the plea was very strong, 'Don't let me go to Austria.'"

At once, Kate felt calmer. "But then I realized that there was more to the sentence. More that I was really feeling." She reached up to Dawn and stroked her face. "The truth is, what I was feeling was, 'Don't let me go to Austria...without you.'"

Dawn took the words in for a moment. "Are you saying what I think you're saying?"

"I want you to come to Austria and be with me."

"You…"

"I want you to come to Austria and be with me," Kate repeated. "I'll arrange the flight. I'm asking you, so I don't expect you to pay for anything. I just want to be with you. It's only for a week, but it's too long to be away from you."

"I…I don't know what to say."

"I know you hardly know me. The plane ticket would be in your name. It would be yours to hold. I don't want you to feel kept or uncomfortable. Hell, this just came to me, so I haven't really thought it through. All I know is I'm crazy about you, and I'm finding it next to impossible to be without you." Kate smiled nervously. "Will you think about it?"

Dawn reached down to hold Kate's hands. She took two deep breaths. "I don't have to think about it."

Kate held her breath, not trusting what exactly it was that she didn't have to think about. Staying? Or going?

"I have a week's vacation that I need to use before March."

Kate exploded into a beaming smile. "You'll come?"

"As soon as I pick Brett, Sr. up from the floor. He's gonna freak out when I tell him I'll be gone in the middle of two big projects."

They laughed and kissed, and Kate told her she'd make the arrangements and call her as soon as she could.

On her way back to the studio, Kate wanted to just swim in thoughts of Dawn but knew she had to call Jeffery Salzenberg about Ralph.

"Tell me good news," was how Jeffery answered her call.

"He'll be fine."

"That's good to hear."

"But that's not the point of this call."

"I know what the point is, Kate." He sounded bored, "You didn't want him on the film for this very reason. And I did."

"That about sums it up."

"Things like this happen. You say he's fine. And I can see by the production reports that you shot most of his scenes. Are you able to cover what you didn't get?"

"Yes, Jeffery. But damn it, we're running on about the film when Ralph could have died."

"But he didn't. And you're covered with the completion bond, so any additional costs you accrue to shoot around his absence will be covered."

Kate took in a slow breath. Jeffery knew damn well why Kate was so agitated, but he wasn't going to address it. What Kate really wanted to say was, "You wanted Ralph so badly for your other money-making venture that you put him at risk on this picture," but she bit her tongue. The truth was obvious to the both of them. And in Hollywood, the truth was sometimes better left unspoken.

But Kate couldn't resist one last comment that came in a low rumble from the back of her throat. "I don't like this at all, Jeffery."

He paused for a moment, the silence speaking volumes. Then, as if he damn well heard her but would never acknowledge it, he said, "Call me if you need anything."

CHAPTER TWENTY-EIGHT

Krissy and Dawn had gone to Faces after work. They were there less for the beer and more for the big screen TV that sat in the back of the bar. Many of their co-workers, both straight and gay, had converged upon Faces to watch that night's broadcast of *Hollywood on Hollywood.*

The segment on Kate's film was airing that night and word had gotten back to FDF. Though they were eager to see if any of their work would be shown, they knew that all of that would be overshadowed by the news of that actor's heart attack.

As everyone gathered around the big screen, Dawn suddenly wished she were at her home, alone. All the noise and whooping jarred her. She wanted to concentrate on watching Kate without the distraction of excited co-workers who were anxious to see shots of their cave sets and prop work on national television.

She also wanted to be home packing for her trip to Austria. She could barely contain her excitement. *Being anywhere with Kate would be fabulous, but Austria. How exotic.* All she knew of the country was what she remembered seeing in *The Sound of Music.*

Krissy had just about burst when Dawn told her about Austria. Soon after Kate had left FDF, Dawn had gone into the main shop to find her.

"Are you shittin' me?"

"No," Dawn laughed. "I'm going for a week. Kate's leaving tomorrow, and I'll be flying out Sunday."

"And Hannah's gone? Kicked to the curb?" Krissy had shaken her head in astonishment.

Dawn could only nod and think about seeing Kate again.

"I told you," Krissy said and then whooped loudly. "She liked you from the second she saw you."

"I can't believe it."

"Well, start believing it, sugar. She's a smart woman to notice you."

❖

The *Hollywood on Hollywood* host started the segment by setting up the "dramatic footage taken from the set of *The Glass Cross*." A quick shot of the cacophony of activity just after Ralph Markowitz collapsed played, and then the show cut back to the host who said, "Our film crew went to Florida to capture a typical day filming. But it was hardly a typical day…"

Clips from the beginning of the day played with Kate being interviewed and followed around by the film crew. After a few shots of the cast filming the mine scenes, which caused the FDF shop workers to erupt in cheers, the host's voice began to narrate the next clips. "Actor, Ralph Markowitz, seen here with Hannah Corrant and Peter Carson, suddenly falls to the ground, afflicted by a devastating heart attack…" The clip played out as Kate, and then Jennifer, rushed over to Ralph and began CPR.

The voices of the Faces patrons dropped to a hush as they all watched the drama unfold. The narration continued, "Amazingly, Kate Nyland, the film's executive producer, and first assistant director, Jennifer Billington, began CPR on Markowitz, who undoubtedly needed immediate emergency treatment to save his life. The tense moments unfold as they try to keep him alive." The clip went in and out of focus as Derek's cameraman darted left and right trying to get a good shot amid the chaos.

Finally, the clip ended and the host's face came back, filling the screen. "Ralph Markowitz is expected to make a full recovery, and word on the street has it that he's slated on yet another World Film's motion picture…"

Dawn stared at the screen. A steamroller of emotions flattened her. She ached for Kate, wanting to be close to her. She had watched as Kate had courageously saved Ralph's life but had been too humble to speak of it when they'd been together. This Kate, the one she'd just seen on TV, had asked her to go to Austria to be with her. The woman she'd just made love to. The woman she was falling for.

CHAPTER TWENTY-NINE

Monday morning Kate arrived at the airport in Salzburg to pick up Dawn. The day before, the cast and crew had arrived, and Kate had sent two passenger vans to pick them up and drive them through the snowy Bavarian landscape and deliver them to the Hotel Sacher. She had given the instructions that they all had time off to rest or explore the city until their call time on Tuesday morning.

Kate was excited that she and Dawn would have all of Monday to reunite. As a new group of travelers made their way from the gates, she craned her neck looking over and past each person as her exhilaration and anticipation rose.

Kate saw Dawn before Dawn saw her. Dawn was pure magnificence as she walked down the airport corridor in Salzburg toward the crowd of greeters where Kate stood. Through the Plexiglas security panels that separated them, Kate could see that she wore comfortable tan corduroy pants and a forest green sweater. She gripped a carry-on bag that was slung from her shoulder. Her sleepy smile and tussled hair sent a lightning bolt through Kate's stomach.

Dawn searched through the crowd for Kate. The flight had made her head fuzzy, but she was certainly excited to finally arrive. Kate's ear-to-ear grin was the first thing she spotted. She had thrown caution to the wind and taken a flight halfway across the world to see the one woman who'd both thrilled her and petrified her. One last walk through a security checkpoint and they'd be reunited.

Kate waited impatiently while Dawn got through customs and then rushed to her. They hugged and held each other for a few long minutes.

Kate felt Dawn sigh against her shoulder. "Tired?" she asked.

"No, just relieved to be here. With you."

"So am I." Kate picked up Dawn's carry-on bag, placing a gentle arm around her. "Let's go."

The production's driver maneuvered through the streets of Salzburg while Kate and Dawn sat close together in the backseat of the town car. They talked and giggled, excited to be reunited.

Kate shook her head. "I can't believe you're actually here."

"Neither can I." Dawn grinned and took Kate's hand. "How are things going?"

"Good. We're still on schedule. The weather's holding up."

Dawn smiled, but there was another expression that belied her words, and Kate knew that Dawn was merely making small talk while the driver made his way back to the hotel.

Kate leaned toward her. "Tell me what you're feeling."

Dawn nodded and smiled again, this time reaching up briefly to caress Kate's cheek. "I'm a little scared. I'm far away from home."

Kate's heart swelled and she put her arm around Dawn, pulling her closer. "I know it must be scary, but it's okay. Truly."

Once in the room, they held each other again. Kate wanted to remain eternally in the embrace. Dawn must have felt it too, because she held on just as tightly and made no move to break their union.

"You feel so good," Kate said.

Dawn softly moaned her reply.

As much as Kate wanted to gently lay Dawn back across the bed and make love to her, to be close to the woman who was body and soul so incredible, she didn't want to appear aggressive. Plus, she wanted to check in on Dawn's feelings. Her own feelings for Dawn had grown deeper, and what she really wanted to do was protect her and make her feel safe. She held her tightly and listened to her breathing.

As they slowly pulled away from each other, Kate said, "You're a most amazing woman, Dawn. I cherish who you are, so please know that whatever you want, or don't want, just tell me."

Dawn hugged Kate again, speaking into her neck, "I had first considered dragging you into the shower since your body and hot water were the two single things that I'd dreamed about during the long flight. But having finally made it here, the intensity feels almost too overwhelming."

She felt Kate hold on tighter.

"I want to rush and I want to go slow…do you know?"

"I do." Kate said. "There's time, Dawn. And I'm just so happy to see you. So, how about first things first? Did you have breakfast on the plane? Are you hungry?"

"No. They gave us a late dinner so I'm fine."

"Today we get to do whatever we want. I don't have to be on set until tomorrow morning."

"How about some sightseeing? Is it too early for that? I'm not sure what time it is."

"It's ten o'clock. Salzburg is absolutely beautiful in the morning. Hell, it's beautiful all day and night, too. We have all day today to rest or explore the city. Are you sure you'd rather not take a nap and quell some of that jet lag? Maybe a shower to unrumple?"

"You're talking to someone who's never been out of the U.S. I'm too thrilled to sleep. And I freshened up in the lavatory on the plane." Dawn took hold of her arm. "I'll shower and nap later."

"Okay, then," Kate reasoned as she took a step toward the door and then pulled Dawn in for a gentle kiss. Her lips tasted sweet and inviting. The brisk winter air caught them for a moment as they inhaled sharply, turning their heads down into their chests.

"Are you sure you're up for a walk?" Kate remembered how tired she'd felt when first arriving in Salzburg.

"Yes. This is great."

From the hotel, they headed toward the first bridge that crossed the Salzach River.

"Tell me what you know about Salzburg." Dawn walked shoulder to shoulder with Kate, their arms intertwined.

"Well, I don't know much," Kate said, "but I do know that Salzburg was largely built by three bishop-princes in the late-16th and early-17th century. The summer is their high season, with large crowds and high prices. Of course, it's cold as heck in January, but I think more beautiful than ever."

They walked around Salzburg, and Kate showed Dawn some of the locations from *The Sound of Music*. Alone in the St. Peter's cemetery, Kate snuggled up to Dawn who took Kate's face in her hands. "Kiss me." Just then, a fleeting sprinkle of light rain fell, and Dawn pulled Kate under the thick canopy of leaves from some chestnut trees.

"Stay close," Dawn said, wrapping her arms around Kate.

"Thank God for the rain."

As darkness fell upon them, they watched storekeepers close up shop and carriage drivers head their horses home for the night. Most of the tourists ambled into restaurants or back to their hotels, but Kate and Dawn braved the crisp winter night air a little longer.

Subdued city lights sparkled through the darkness. Streetlamps lit their way as they strolled down centuries-old cobblestone roads. When they crossed the bridge over the river, Kate hugged Dawn closer. "Let's cross back over to the right bank. We might want to be a little closer to the hotel in case the weather decides to turn more frigid."

"How can you tell which is the right bank?"

Kate stopped Dawn at the apex of the bridge and turned her toward the river. Standing behind her Kate said, "Well, first you turn, like this, to face the direction that the water current is flowing. See?"

Kate moved closer to take in the fragrance of Dawn's hair. She remembered how wonderful she smelled the first time she was that close to her in the SUV. Dawn watched the water flow away from them, downstream and into the darkness, watery swirls lit occasionally by streetlights and ferryboats.

"Now that you're facing this way," Kate picked up Dawn's right hand and pointed it out away from her side toward the bank, "that's the right bank…" She let Dawn's right hand down as she picked up her left hand, pointing it toward the other bank. It was dark enough that Kate knew it was okay to nuzzle into Dawn, kissing her neck. She mumbled, "And that's the left bank."

For Dawn, it was like a first date. It was as if she were experiencing Kate as never before. She suddenly saw the whole world in a new light. She laughed inwardly. She was in a foreign city, so everything looked new, but in her heart, a renewed sense of love filled her.

Dawn turned around to face Kate. They both smiled, and then, tenderly, they kissed. Dawn felt Kate shaking as much as she was and reached up to hold the hands that gently cradled her face. She felt the acorn bracelet, making her feel less apprehensive about taking such an impulsive flight.

The few streetlights along the bridge cast long shadows that intersected, and Kate steered Dawn into the dark between the spots of light. A motorboat chugged and rumbled dutifully underneath them, and distant voices could be heard from its deck. *Here we are*, Dawn thought, *in Austria, kissing on a bridge in the winter snow. And just a few days ago, I had no idea that I'd be with Kate, let alone standing here in another country with her.*

When they separated, their breath commingled in puffs of icy gray. Kate reached up and touched Dawn's nose. "Let's get you inside somewhere where it's warm."

An Austrian tavern greeted them warmly and loudly. They hung their coats on a tall rack by the front door and found a small table close to the front window. They ordered beer and spatzle, mostly because they didn't understand the rest of the Austrian words on the menu.

"I feel like I've been transported right back to the Baroque era," Dawn said.

"Ah, a time of grandeur."

"You'd look great in all that layered clothing."

"Really?" Kate laughed.

"And, at the risk of getting slapped, you'd also look great out of all that layered clothing."

Kate shook her finger. "You would have been a naughty lesbian back then."

"With you, yes."

"Feeling frisky?"

"Desiring you. Wanting to spend more time with you. Wanting to find out everything there is to know about you."

"Then there are many things we agree on."

"On the plane coming here, I tried to imagine what it would be like, being here with you."

"And?"

"It's better than I pictured."

"It is for me, too. I am truly blessed that I met you. Never could I have thought that I'd travel to Florida and meet you."

"Thank goodness for slipped schedules."

Kate chuckled. "Yes. I was worried that FDF would never make up the lost time, but as soon as I met you, I knew we'd be okay."

"You had that much confidence?"

"In you, yes. I like your work ethic. I think you have amazing talent."

"Thank you. That means a lot to me."

Kate watched Dawn survey the room, taking in the ambiance and the pink-cheeked patrons. *This would be a perfect place to stay forever,* she thought.

"And another thing…" Kate's words made Dawn turn back to her. "I have a horrible crush on you, Dawn."

"Just a crush?"

Kate looked around the room, smiling slyly, as if the next thing she was going to say was top secret and then leaned toward her. "Much deeper than that."

"Really?"

Kate considered her feelings. Her chest was swirling with emotions. She hadn't felt this good about being with someone in years. *Tell her you love her,* Kate suddenly thought and drew in a full breath. *You do love her, don't you?* She asked herself and then countered with, *But you don't even know her that well yet.* As she looked into Dawn's eyes, her thoughts chattered on. *Falling quickly and totally is not something you do, Nyland. But you can't ignore these feelings for her. You can't think about anything without Dawn popping up. You are completely happy with her. You are in love.*

"Really."

Dawn reached over and held Kate's cheek with her hand. "Tell me more."

Kate wanted to tell her more. Since arriving in Austria, things had felt better in her life. Even though she was still on the film shoot, she was away from Hollywood, with all its manic stress, and that had allowed her thoughts to slow down.

She had accepted Hannah and her lifestyle because there hadn't been anything else that forced a comparison. But now that Dawn was in her life, she actually felt embarrassed that she'd let the relationship with Hannah go on as long as it did. Though she seldom cared what other people thought, she could only imagine that there must have been tsking and the shaking of heads at her continued one-dimensional union with the spoiled starlet.

But Dawn made her heart swell. Dawn was real. And sincere. And sexy. And amazing. Kate had never felt this way before and she knew that it was love.

The last few weeks had brought such drastic changes in her life that she felt a clutching sensation in her heart. She'd left California in a well publicized relationship with Hannah, suddenly ended it, and had fallen into Dawn's wonderful arms. When she looked at it from an outsider's perspective, it sounded quite impulsive.

Kate looked into Dawn's eyes. She wanted to tell her that she loved her. She wanted to let Dawn know that her heart was firmly wrapped around hers. Kate felt her throat tighten and was startled to realize she hadn't gotten *that* far away from Hollywood, because she couldn't do it.

"Tell you more," Kate repeated, feeling a little shaky. "I can tell you that this is the most remarkable night, and you are a most incredible woman." *And I'm scared to death. I'm crazy about her, but I feel sucked up in a severe whirlwind. Can I trust my feelings? Can I trust my choices? Hannah had been a terrible choice. I suck at choosing people. Focusing on my work has been the safest thing to do. Before Hannah came along, there was only work. That I can handle.*

"Yes…?"

Say what you feel, Kate. "And that I had a hard time being without you after leaving Orlando." *That's so true but shouldn't I be focusing on this film? Then again, how can I focus when I'm with Dawn?*

"I did, too." Dawn said.

Tell her you love her. Kate tried to smile. *Shouldn't I be concentrating on the film? Tell her you love her.*

"Is everything all right? You look different…are you feeling okay?"

"I…" Kate took a shallow breath. "I'm fine, Dawn." But she could tell that Dawn wasn't completely convinced.

❖

Later that night they walked the cobblestone streets and meandered past a few fountains drawn quiet in the late night hours. Kate held Dawn's hand, wishing the night would last another ten or twelve hours. This is perfect, she thought.

They made it back to the hotel eventually, chilled but happy. The walk through Salzburg had helped them reunite at a slow pace, and it felt exactly right to do that.

"How about I start a shower for you?" Kate said taking off her jacket.

"That sounds even better than the spatzle." Dawn said as she watched Kate walk into the bathroom. She'd been feeling a little unsure since they'd had the talk at the café. She knew that Kate was feeling something that she wasn't sharing, but what was it?

Was Kate beginning to have doubts about them? Their relationship had been quite a whirlwind experience. And Kate had a lot on her mind with the film and her breakup with Hannah.

She didn't want to push Kate for information, but as she sat in their foreign hotel room, thousands of miles from home, Dawn certainly felt vulnerable. Maybe she'd been too available or too eager to fly to Austria.

God, I feel so much for her, Dawn thought. *What if she doesn't feel as much for me? What was Kate feeling? Was it all too much for her?* She couldn't remember feeling so exposed. *Just give her time. I'm tired and making too much of this. Aren't I?*

When Kate came out of the bathroom, Dawn searched her face for any sign of doubt or apprehension.

Kate smiled before saying, "It's all ready."

Dawn took her hands. "Would you join me?"

In a long, steamy shower, they were naked together for the first time. They moved slowly, taking each other in with gentle caresses. Everything Dawn had imagined about Kate's body when she'd made love to her in her studio was right here, next to her and in her arms.

As Kate soaped Dawn's chest and shoulders, a million wet sensations coursed through her. She watched the drops of water fall from Kate's slicked back hair. And the water cascading off Kate's full breasts made Dawn's legs grow suddenly weak. She turned Kate away from her and wrapped her arms around her, pulling Kate in nearer. She held her in a spoon position falling into the feeling of Kate so close. Kate reached her arms back to hold her, pressing herself close.

After a while, Dawn reached for the shampoo and washed Kate's hair, massaging it into a lather, and rinsing with her under the steady stream of water. Dawn took the bar of soap again and reached between Kate's legs.

"I think you already got that spot," Kate gasped.

"Let's make sure," Dawn said, dropping the bar of soap as her fingers massaged Kate.

Wrapping her arms around Dawn's back, Kate hung on, moaning.

"You feel so good," Kate said as her head dropped back onto Dawn's shoulder.

"I've thought about nothing but you," Dawn replied, burying her face in Kate's neck.

When Dawn felt her fingers grow slicker than mere water could make them, she turned Kate around and moved inside her, easily finding her G-spot. An intake of breath racked Kate, and Dawn used her other arm to hold her up. Kate's moans matched Dawn's strokes until Kate murmured in her ear, "Oh, God, I'm going to come."

Dawn's response was an aroused moan, suddenly sending Kate over the edge. The pulsing contractions that gripped Dawn's fingers and the way Kate's arms felt as they clutched her sent shivers through Dawn. Kate's orgasmic cries drowned out the shower sounds, echoing around the tiled enclosure.

Dawn kissed Kate's face and neck and shoulders, then they turned off the water and giggled as they dried off.

"I'm glad you held me up. Again," Kate said as she combed through her wet hair.

Dawn smiled. "Yes, I remember us in my studio."

"My legs buckled almost the minute you began touching me."

"In the studio or just now?"

"Yes."

Dawn chuckled and then stopped drying her legs to take in all of Kate. She was beautiful inside and out. She had never felt this much for someone else. She had developed deep feelings so overwhelmingly for Kate. But swirling among her emotions was a niggling uncertainty.

They fell in between crisp, white sheets that smelled of lavender. They made love many times that night, drinking in each other's body in a rhythm that slowed and quickened along with the cadence of their breathing.

CHAPTER THIRTY

During the early morning hours, as Dawn lay with Kate, she swirled in and out of her jet-lagged state. At times she was not aware of where she was, only of the warmth of Kate's body. At other times, a strange noise outside or a glimpse of their room would jolt her to the consciousness that she had just traveled thousands of miles. She fought the drowsiness to stay awake and drink in the feel of Kate.

Finally, at four a.m., Kate wrapped her arms around Dawn. "You have got to sleep."

"I'm fine." Dawn curled up against her.

"You need sleep." Kate hugged her. "There's lots of time," she said as she stroked Dawn's hair. After a while, Dawn began to relax and soon was asleep in her arms. Kate stayed awake a while longer, holding Dawn tightly. She was so much more a woman than anyone she had ever been with. Dawn was giving and warm. She was confident and certain. She saw Kate for who she was, not what she could get from her.

Dawn's presence gave her joy. And the magnitude of the feelings that expanded inside her scared her as well. Kate had had so much experience with bad relationships, the kind that hadn't called for too much of anything deep, that she wasn't sure what to do with all these emotions.

❖

A bright white light filtered through the lace curtains of the hotel room. Somewhere outside, birds chirped happily and children shouted in the distance.

Dawn awoke slowly and eventually found her watch on the bedside table. It displayed 12:00, but for a few cloudy minutes, she had absolutely no idea which time the watch was representing. Was that

Orlando time or Salzburg time? Her head was fuzzy and her stomach grumbled. And then she remembered that she'd adjusted her watch to Austrian time when the flight attendant announced their impending arrival into the Salzburg airport.

She lay there trying to kick start the rest of her brain. *What time was it back in Orlando? It might be about three in the morning. Yesterday. But who the hell cared anyway? I am in Austria with Kate, and even though my lack of sleep makes it feel like I have a bruiser of a hangover, it's all marvelous.*

She felt the exhaustion in her body and the slight soreness in muscles that had been overworked while making love the night before. Her ringed nipple was slightly tender from Kate's mouth as they both had taken extreme pleasure again in the added sensation of the metal.

A note was waiting for her on the bathroom sink.

> *Dawn,*
> *Good morning. It was virtually impossible to leave you this morning. You were sleeping so soundly, and you looked like an absolute angel.*
> *I briefly considered telling my boss that I was calling in sick, but I remembered that I am the boss, and I would know that I was lying. And then I realized that the sooner I could start the day, the sooner that we could be alone after we wrap.*
> *Please call my cell from the hotel phone, here's my number again. Or, when you're ready, have the concierge call me, and I'll send a driver to bring you to the set. Take your time and enjoy yourself.*
> *Charge breakfast to the room—the pastries are out of this world.*
> *I'm so happy to have you here with me.*
> *Kate*

Dawn smiled broadly. Maybe her uncertainty was for naught. With a sleepy smile, she gently folded the note and packed it in her suitcase.

❖

The first day of shooting in Salzburg started very slowly. All of the shots in Austria were to be exteriors to establish the European look of the film, and the restaurant that the crew had set up to shoot seemed to Kate to take forever to get ready.

The archetypically Bavarian place had lacey curtains adorning dark-wood latticed windows. A thick wooden door as appealingly aged as Salzburg itself sported a brass handle worn shiny from years of use by devoted customers.

Part of the narrow street had been blocked off for the crew. Staid police officers stood at each end explaining in German that a group from Ah-mer-EE-kah was making a movie. In front of the restaurant, director's chairs were lined up along with the camera equipment, various lights, sound equipment, and miles of cable.

Moody gray clouds threatened rain, but Kate was happy that the cast and crew managed to get through the morning shots and remain dry. Something about the crispness of the air, the beauty of the country, and the charm of its history cast a collective spell on everyone, because by noon, they were actually three shots ahead.

One of the Austrian drivers delivered Dawn to the set just as the crew was breaking for lunch. The catering truck had been parked and set up just around the corner, on a side street, and the cast and crew made their way there to eat authentic Austrian fare.

As Kate and Dawn stepped up to the catering truck to stand in line for lunch, Kate inadvertently caught Hannah's stare. There was a moment of confusion on Hannah's face as she attempted to discern the identity of the woman with Kate. And then there was a flash of recognition so evident that her brows fleetingly shot upward in astonishment. Hannah quickly recovered from the surprise and just as suddenly, she closed her eyes into slits, indicating a cold anger brewing. And, as was predictable with Hannah, a sinister grin appeared on her face. Kate understood that patent look. This was when she was most dangerous.

Kate did not want Hannah causing any trouble, so she steered Dawn to the far corner of the canopy. While they ate lunch, Kate asked her about her morning and whether she'd slept well.

"I think I'm feeling jet lag, but I'm not sure it's completely set in yet."

"It may not." Kate shrugged. "But we didn't get to sleep until really early this morning, so it may hit you later."

"How are you feeling?" Dawn asked.

"Me? I'm dragging, but knowing we're only shooting here for a week, I can get through this."

"But did you calculate our nights into the equation?"

Kate rubbed her chin. "No, actually, I didn't. Hmm, I may be in trouble."

Dawn took her hand. "Seems to me we got into some trouble not too long ago in the SUV."

Laughing, Kate squeezed Dawn's hand. "You think we're establishing a wayward pattern?"

"I hope so."

"I want to get you back to the hotel." Kate's gaze turned intense, needful, as she growled. "Now."

Dawn returned the gaze, feeling her chest flash hot. "You don't know how much I want that."

"Want what?" Hannah stood over them.

The look on Kate's face washed away, and she slowly sighed. "It's nothing that would concern you, Hannah."

"Well, you didn't introduce me to your friend, Kate. How rude." Hannah reached her hand out to Dawn and said, "I'm Hannah Corrant."

Dawn waited a beat and then took her hand limply. "Dawn Brock."

"Oh yes," Hannah said. "You're the construction worker from Orlando."

Kate bristled. "She built the sets for the salt mine, Hannah. She's a designer."

"Oh," she said, purposeful indifference registering on her face. "Whatever."

"If you'll excuse us now…" Kate stared defiantly.

Hannah's mouth dropped open slightly in clear disbelief. And for the second time in less than ten minutes, that sinister grin appeared again. This time, the look definitely said "I'll get you back for that."

After watching the shooting for a couple of hours after lunch, Dawn went with Kate to the production office, which was situated in two adjoining suites back at the hotel.

Dawn sat on Kate's lap while she made a few phone calls and went through paperwork. They kissed passionately and deeply in between each task. The Austrian production assistants respectfully stayed in the other half of the suite, leaving them alone. Dawn and Kate then parted as Kate had to return to the set for the rest of the day, and Dawn set off to explore Salzburg.

Just before wrap, Kate rushed back to the hotel. There had not been the need to stay around to view dailies as there hadn't been anything shot the previous day. And it was Jennifer who had come up to Kate, saying, "Look, I can get the rest of this wrapped up tonight. I'll double check the production report and tomorrow's call sheet. I'm sure you have things to do, so get out of here." Since Ralph's heart attack, Jennifer had been respectful to Kate. They hardly spoke, and after the movie wrapped, Kate would certainly never hire her again, but it was clear that Jennifer was remorseful.

Back at the hotel, Kate had hardly closed the door behind her when Dawn rushed into her waiting arms.

Now back in the room, they fell into bed. Slowly peeling off each other's clothes, they fused together, entwining legs and arms. Kate was over Dawn, kissing her lips, then her chin, sucking gently on the flesh. She moved down her neck, and Dawn moaned in submission. Kate ran her tongue just behind Dawn's ear, down to the dip in her neck raising goose bumps as she continued down along her shoulder, over her collarbone and to the lift in her chest.

Kate's mouth circled around, down Dawn's breastbone, covering the warm area underneath her breasts. Dawn was beside herself waiting for Kate to get to her nipples, the racing of her brain reminding her of the first time Kate had tasted them. Kate stayed away from direct contact, circling dangerously close, causing small shudders to ripple through Dawn.

Dawn's breath was coming in slight gasps as she reached down to grab the hair at the nape of Kate's neck, not knowing whether she was going to guide her to get to the point or pull her up because she couldn't take this anymore. Kate moaned as Dawn tugged at her hair, and just when Dawn thought she'd pass out, Kate ran her tongue slowly across her pierced nipple, sending shock waves up her entire body. Kate raised her head and looked at Dawn and then flashed a smile. She took a breath and blew slightly on Dawn's now wet nipple. Dawn shuddered as the cool air hit the moisture from where Kate's tongue had been. As Kate encircled her warm mouth around Dawn's cool nipple, Dawn moaned and laid her head back.

As Kate concentrated on both breasts, moving back and forth, Dawn reached down to her back, slowly massaging Kate. Ever so slowly, her excitement rose and she dug her nails tenuously into Kate's back. Dawn's moans grew louder and then Kate stopped. She lifted, moving back up to her neck, kissing every inch along the way.

"Why did you stop?" Dawn gasped into Kate's hair. "You were starting to drive me crazy."

"There's no rush."

She gently moved on top of Dawn again, resting the lower half of her body between Dawn's now open legs. They kissed for a long time, Dawn pushing her hips slowly up into Kate.

Though the Austrian winter chilled the panes of the hotel window, Dawn could feel small pearls of sweat on the small of Kate's back. Wet with the dampness of their own excitement, the moisture between them heated up their skin as they moved back and forth together. Dawn wrapped her legs around her and kept up the cadence of her hips pushing into Kate. The friction they caused as they drew into each other was working Dawn into a frenzy. The sheets were rumpled, the pillows were cast aside, and suddenly all the rubbing made Dawn begin to shake. *Too soon,* she thought, and broke the kissing, raising her head until they were face to face.

Dawn was trying to catch her breath, her breasts rising and falling. And each time she exhaled, their breasts grazed each other's. Overwhelmed with the sensation, Dawn concentrated on the exquisite feeling of their nipples touching, receding, and touching again making her shudder as they moved together.

"You're beautiful," Kate said.

Feeling the length of Kate's body, she couldn't quite believe they were here together. Dawn slowly opened her eyes. She knew without a doubt that they were, right then, connected in body and in emotion.

Kate began moving her hips into Dawn again.

Dawn's eyes fluttered and closed as she met Kate's slow thrusts with her own. Slowly, their movement increased as Kate and Dawn pressed into each other, rocking together.

Dawn's breath quickened, and she held Kate even harder. Slowly, Kate moved her hand down between them and slipped two fingers inside her.

Suddenly gasping, Dawn cried out, "Yes," and Kate stroked her in time to their rocking hips.

Dawn's head arched back, feeling Kate's fingers and hips, and breasts against her, moaning loudly. "Yes, Kate, ahhhhh, yes."

Dawn felt her wetness against Kate's fingers, the sensation of small gushes drove her to bury her face in Kate's neck, shuddering as she lost herself in the feeling.

And as Kate stroked her, Dawn finally let go as well, a surge of orgasm suddenly exploding against Kate's fingers, surging and pulsating with strong contractions as she cried out Kate's name.

After a while, Dawn rolled Kate onto her back and a vague protest came from Kate. "I'm not done pleasing you."

Now over her, Dawn smiled at Kate, sliding down to kiss and lick all the curves she could find. She knelt between Kate's legs. Kate raised herself up on her elbows, watching.

"You shouldn't have started this nipple ring thing back in Orlando."

"Is this what I get for behaving badly?" Kate laughed.

"No," Dawn said, "*This* is what you get…"

Kate tilted her head back, quivering at Dawn's touch. Dawn gently spread Kate's legs and with her mouth hot and wet, suddenly drew across her clit.

"Uh…oh…yes…" Kate stammered as she reached down to cradle Dawn's head.

Feeling exquisite warmth and pleasure, she was tasting the woman she so very much desired. With Kate's arms over her head and clutching the corner of the bed, Dawn drank her and savored her.

The sensation of Kate lifting her hips up into her felt highly erotic, making Dawn inhale deeply. They rocked slowly together, Kate's breathing growing louder as she began to moan in time to the swirling of Dawn's mouth against her.

Dawn felt Kate's legs begin to twitch, growing more and more uncontrolled in their jerking. She lifted higher against Dawn's mouth.

"Dawn…" she called out as her orgasm exploded in a sudden rush, drowning Dawn in fragrant juices.

Dawn stayed with the bucking against her mouth as Kate screamed out her ecstasy, clawing blindly at Dawn's shoulders. "Oh my God!"

In the quiet that followed, Kate moaned that she felt paralyzed. Dawn lovingly kissed the insides of her thighs. She kissed her stomach and moved up to hug her.

Kate hugged back. "That was incredible."

Dawn lifted up, studying her. "Yes, it was." Then she smiled the warmest, most satisfied smile.

CHAPTER THIRTY-ONE

Wednesday's call time was scheduled for four p.m., as the rest of the scenes to be shot in Salzburg took place at night. For the next four days, the crew would arrive at four and spend a couple of hours getting the equipment ready. By then the cast would have arrived and gone through makeup, hair, and wardrobe. And by the time they'd rehearsed the first setup, the sun would be below the horizon.

Kate and Dawn awoke around eight a.m. and lounged around the room, enjoying a fresh batch of eggs and toast from room service. They discussed taking a shower together, which they finally managed to do after another two hours of lovemaking.

They filled the late morning and early afternoon with more walks around Salzburg. On the way back to the hotel, they ducked into the Café Bazar, which was located on the right bank of the Salzach River. Inside, they ordered coffee, a selection of rolls with marmalade, ham, and cheeses.

Kate checked her watch. They had less than two hours before Kate's call time. "I really hate to leave you."

Dawn allowed herself to picture this moment as if they were further along in a committed relationship. She could imagine them in a long-term relationship with mornings like this, after having woken up together and making love in the first rays of sunrise. "It feels too good to leave, doesn't it?"

"All of this feels almost too good to be true." Kate gently took Dawn's hand.

"Austria?"

Kate laughed. "No. You with me."

"I loved making love to you earlier."

"Mmm, I did, too. You're wonderful to be with."

I think I'm falling in love with her. "And so are you. No one else could ever convince me to travel halfway around the world to see them."

"Then I'm a lucky woman."

"I'm the lucky one."

"Will you come see me on the set tonight?"

"To be near you? Yes."

❖

After a few adventures as a tourist, Dawn returned to the hotel and fell asleep with the pillow over her head. Jet lag finally caught up with her, and she fell asleep immediately.

During dinner break, Kate was eating at the far end of the catering tent. They'd just wrapped a few of the street scenes, and the only hold up had been a half hour wait for a few lights that required repositioning. Kate had called Dawn to ask her to join her for dinner, but hadn't reached her the three times she tried. She left messages each time.

Kate was doing paperwork when Hannah walked over, holding a plate and a drink. "May I join you for dinner?"

"I don't think so, Hannah."

"It's important. I just need to talk to you about the Big Bear house."

"What about it?"

Hannah sat down. "We should talk about selling it, or one of us should buy the other out."

A few months back, Hannah had convinced Kate that the purchase of a vacation home in the ski town of Big Bear, California, was a smart investment opportunity. An actor friend of hers was selling it, and Hannah told Kate that they could have great industry parties there, as well as romantic getaways. Their lawyers had drawn up a contract between them stating that they would own it equally and share in its losses or gains. And with the unremitting rise in value of California property in the past decade, losses would be improbable. They purchased it and as it turned out, the house had increased ten percent in value of its $1,700,000 sales price. Trouble was, they had gone up there exactly twice. Once to direct the move-in of new furniture, only to return to LA that same day due to a movie screening that Hannah just couldn't miss, and once for a romantic getaway that turned into three runs by Kate to the local drug store for cold remedies for Hannah, who'd suddenly gotten achy and feverish.

"We don't need to talk about the Big Bear house today, Hannah."

"I want to buy you out."

"Hannah, I haven't had time to decide anything about the house."

"Well, it was my idea to get it. I think I should keep it."

"I might want to keep it. Have you considered that?"

"I'm not going to budge on this."

"I really don't want to talk about this now."

"Well, I just thought we should."

"Not until we're back in LA."

"Well, we'll work it out, won't we?"

"Yes, we'll work it out."

They both ate in silence for a few minutes and then Hannah laughed out loud. "Isn't this crazy?"

Kate chose not to answer.

"I mean this. Us. Breaking up," Hannah said.

Kate sighed deeply. "Hannah, not this again."

Hannah bit the inside of her cheek. Kate could tell she was thinking of her next move.

"A lot of my clothes are at your house," she at last said to Kate.

"I know. And a lot of mine are at yours."

"And my Rolex is on your bedside table."

"That's my Rolex, Hannah."

"Well, you never wear it, and I always wear it now."

"I suppose you're going to insist on owning that as well."

Hannah shrugged. "I think that makes it mine."

"Not now, Hannah."

"Right. We'll work it out. I really don't want this to get ugly. As far as the house is concerned, I guess we can talk about who buys out whom."

Kate knew Hannah didn't care about the house. With the salaries she was commanding now, the house in Big Bear was a pittance. She could buy a much grander house on the water's edge if she wanted.

What was going on? Was she trying to be civilized? Doubtful. She wasn't going to be convinced of the sudden transformation in Hannah.

But going along with Hannah might be a smart move, for now. She didn't need to be fighting with Hannah over the house or anything else.

"Listen," Hannah added, "If we have nothing other than a great business partnership after this movie is over, that would be good. I mean, the public appearances we have to make for the film are important. Wouldn't you rather have the press talk about that than a nasty divorce?"

She was making sense, Kate thought a little warily. Maybe she should go along with this cooperative mood Hannah was in, for as long as it lasted. To stay on good graces with her would be a welcome relief.

As Kate paused, deep in her thoughts, Hannah went on. "We also bought a lot of playthings. Maybe we can start with that to make talking easier. Can we talk later about the jet skis, the boat, and the other toys we bought together?"

Whatever the motive was that was making Hannah act decently was certainly better than what she'd been experiencing with her lately. She would go with it for now. "Sure. I think that would be good. Let's talk later."

"Well, thanks for having dinner with me." Hannah smiled, got up, and walked away. Kate tapped her pen on the table in suspicion.

Kate's cell phone rang. It was Laney. "Kate, how are things?"

"Going fairly well, thank you." Kate looked at her watch. It was ten p.m., so she did some quick arithmetic. "What are you doing right now? It's one p.m. there, isn't it?"

"Yes. I am finally reorganizing the files in the whole office like I've been saying that I'd do for the past few months. Now that you all are out of the country and out of my hair, I can get some things done around here that aren't crisis-of-the-moment issues."

"You're the best, Laney."

"I know." She laughed. "But what I *don't* know is what's going on with you."

"You know Hannah and I broke up. I called you the night that it happened."

"Yeah, yeah," Laney dismissed quickly. "I mean what's going on with you and Dawn?"

Kate felt herself warm up inside. It was a silly school-girl, all a-twitter thing that made her smile. "Laney, she's so wonderful."

"That's what I hear."

• 266 •

"From whom?"

"Beth. You forget she's back in LA."

"And she wasted no time chatting with you." Kate chuckled.

"Nope. And, hell, I'm mad at you for not telling me yourself."

"I told you that I was seeing Dawn."

"But you didn't tell me that you flew her to Austria."

"Now…how did you know that? I haven't seen Beth to tell her."

"Oh, I didn't get that from Beth. I got that from Betsy in Orlando. She booked her flight, remember?"

"Man, nothing is sacred around here."

"It's not nice to fool Laney."

"I thought the saying was 'It's not nice to fool Mother Nature.'"

"Same thing. Same consequence."

"Yeah, I can hear the thunder now. I'm sorry I didn't tell you personally."

"That's better," Laney said. "But the most important thing is that you're happy. You know, Kate, all the while that Hannah was jerking your chain, you just weren't going to be."

"True."

"So, you really like Dawn?"

"Incredibly so," Kate said. "I'm thinking of asking her to take a prolonged trip to LA with me."

"Do you think she would?"

"Well, if not, meaning if she's too busy at work, then I think I'll just take a prolonged trip to Florida."

"That's what I want to hear. You can do the development work on the next film script from anywhere, actually."

"Exactly," Kate said. "I just hope she wants that too."

"You won't know until you ask."

Just before midnight, Dawn came to the set, which was located in front of a small, unassuming pub that provided a rich background for the scenes that were being shot. She found Kate in her director's chair just down the street.

"Hey." Kate kissed her and pulled a chair over to hers. "What happened to you?"

Dawn sat down. "I crashed pretty hard. When I woke up I had no idea where I was. As soon I could focus, I got dressed and got a ride down here."

"Did you get my messages?"

"No. I'm sorry. I didn't check. I woke up and got dressed as fast as I could and raced over here."

"Well, I'm glad you're here." Kate took her hand and squeezed. Now was as good a time as any, Kate thought. She wanted to ask her to come to California and to tell her if that wasn't feasible, would she mind if Kate spent some time in Orlando. She really wanted to spend more time with Dawn. And in a more thorough way than what had been possible during the whirlwind shooting schedule she'd been on since arriving in Florida and meeting Dawn.

And as much as she was thrilled to have Dawn in Salzburg, she knew that it wasn't the best romantic arrangement given that there were long days of filming. Dawn certainly deserved more attention.

"I wanted to talk with you about something," Kate began. She'd been thinking of her inability on the bridge to voice her feelings for Dawn. *Tell her you love her.*

Dawn smiled warmly, waiting for her to continue.

"I've been thinking a lot about you. And I. Us, I mean—"

Jennifer's voice crackled over the radio, "Okay, everyone pipe down, now. We're rolling."

Kate smiled crookedly and they turned toward the scene as Amy called for action.

Hannah and Peter were running down a side street, and the scene called for them to skid to a stop and decide what to do next. Dawn was still fascinated at the movie-making process. And now, to see it on an exterior set, a real street, made it that much more exciting. Local Austrians watched from the perimeters of the set, just beyond sawhorses set up by the police. The locals stood there, bobbing back and forth and craning their necks, obviously just as fascinated.

After a few takes, Kate touched Dawn's arm lightly. "I need to talk to Amy about this scene. Something's not right." Kate politely excused herself.

As Amy and Kate got into a deep discussion, Jennifer backed up enough to allow them the space to talk privately. Amy was describing something to Kate who, deep in concentration, reached up and held her chin between her thumb and index finger as she listened. A broad smile widened on Dawn's face as she watched Kate, the gesture looking so adorable.

At one point, Amy gestured to Jennifer, who then pressed the transmit button on her radio, sending a message to everyone that they were to take a fifteen minute break. Amy placed her hand on Kate's shoulder and pointed them away from the crew. They began to walk off set, obviously desiring a more private place to discuss the intricacies of the scene.

Dawn walked off set to find the restroom. A grouping of trailers, smaller than the ones in Florida, were lined up on the street, and she found the honey wagon right away. Just as she exited the facilities, she noticed Hannah standing there, seemingly waiting for her.

"Dawn." Hannah touched her arm as Dawn passed her. "Let's talk in my trailer."

"I don't think that's appropriate—" Dawn began to say, but Hannah cut her off and lowered her voice. "We really need to talk." She motioned for Dawn to follow her and walked away.

Though Hannah smiled warmly when she opened the trailer door for her, Dawn entered, stopping at the threshold. Hannah shrugged and walked over to the makeup counter. She turned and leaned against it, facing Dawn.

Hannah took a deep breath and then said, "Kate and I are talking about getting back together."

Dawn's heart stopped, and for a moment her brain jerked, sputtered, and words pinballed inside her skull. *What? Was this true? No, it couldn't be.* An alarm was going off in her head. *Could it?*

"She and I are working things out," Hannah continued, her face doe-eyed and concerned. "It's been rocky, admittedly. And I even told her to date around, if that's what would make her feel better while we worked things out. You see, I'm really *happy* that you and Kate had some…fun. She needed to get it out of her system."

"What?" Dawn shook her head, trying to register the words. She felt her cheeks grow hot and she knew that the color was quickly draining from her face. *This isn't happening. This can't be.* She blinked rapidly, scanning the room around her as if trying to look for something that would rescue her from this sudden onslaught of horror.

"Oh, shit, I hurt you, didn't I? I really didn't want to do that. Dawn… are you okay?" Hannah paused a moment before continuing, "Oh, I know she'll deny it. No one would want to hurt you, me included. And I know this must be really hard to hear. Kate would never tell you this truth. However, I feel that I should tell you. You see, Kate and I belong together. We're cut from the same cloth, Dawn. We're privileged and talented. We are on the covers of national magazines. And that's what Kate wants. Kate and I were just talking about you tonight." Hannah put her hand to her heart. "It's our one-year anniversary. You see, we were having a romantic dinner. We snuck away from the set…I mean it was a brief dinner, but...oh, I'm sorry..." Hannah looked concerned. "I realize that you probably wouldn't have known that."

Dawn blanked out Hannah's last words. She stared down at the carpeting in the trailer trying to control her spinning brain. Hannah went on, "Well, anyway, I told her I was okay with her having…little affairs on the side. She knows I have them. And I told her it was okay with me as long as she kept them out of the press. Like I said, it'd be next to impossible for her to tell you this. Just enjoy your fling with her. And know that I'm okay with it, too."

The shock of Hannah's words spun her in circles. She walked out of Hannah's motor home in silence and retreated to one of the toilets in the honey wagon. She sat down on the commode, utterly frozen.

It couldn't be true, she thought, as she clasped her hands together to steady the shaking. But maybe it was. Was that why Kate seemed so different on the bridge? Was that what she couldn't tell her? That theirs wasn't an exclusive, permanent commitment?

It made sense in a bizarre way. Kate must have wanted a plaything and found Dawn to be available. Maybe that was the Hollywood lesbian lifestyle—picking up women and then discarding them when bored. Or worse, maybe Kate wanted to have her lover and keep a girlfriend on the side. Maybe that was typical of women who lived moneyed lives. She was suddenly frightened, feeling horribly alone.

"Oh, there you are." That was Hannah's voice, Dawn jumped, startled, as she was about to exit the honey wagon's bathroom. She let go of the inside door handle.

She recognized Kate's voice, "Hey, Hannah."

Dawn felt a surge of nervousness race through her. They were standing right outside. She remained still, even holding her breath.

"I'm glad we talked earlier. I feel really good about things between us. I know the bigger issue will be harder to deal with, but can we talk about the toys?" Hannah said.

"Sure." Kate sounded congenial, which alarmed Dawn.

"Well, I want you to have your playthings and I can have mine. It won't change anything with you and me. We'll make sure it doesn't interfere with everything else we're trying to do. Is that okay with you?"

Dawn could hear a pause before Kate spoke, "Yes. That will work with me."

"As long as we agree, we can have our individual playthings, right?"

"We'll work it out, Hannah. Don't worry. For the sake of the press, I understand what you're saying. We don't need to make a big deal about this."

"No," Hannah said, "I agree. As long as we keep the whole thing out of the Hollywood rags, you and I can make the best of this partnership."

Kate said, "Sounds good to me. Thanks for the talk. I've gotta go, now."

Dawn could hear Kate's voice trail off as she departed.

Dawn began to shake when the meaning of the words sunk in. She suddenly felt horribly embarrassed and sick to her stomach. So they were negotiating the women that they would see on the side. How could she have been blind to the charade? Hadn't she thought all along that Kate was in a different world far above Dawn's standing? It had been stupid of her to think that Kate would dump her relationship with Hannah so quickly after just a few trysts with Dawn. Obviously Kate and Hannah were meant to be together, even if they were to be in an open relationship, and any thoughts that Dawn had of being with Kate exclusively were just foolish fantasies.

Could she have so horribly mistaken the feelings that they shared when they made love? She felt, deep in her gut, that Kate genuinely felt something for her. Something unbelievably fervent. But could Kate crave two lovers? Could she just split her feelings that way?

Putrid thoughts roiled in her mind and her stomach and when she was sure Kate and Hannah were both gone, she stumbled out of the honey wagon.

❖

"There you are," Kate said when Dawn returned to the catering tent. "I'm sorry that it took so long with Amy. I came back here and you were gone."

Dawn sat back down next to Kate. Her hands shook and she fought back tears of humiliation and dread. She swallowed hard and then said, "Kate, did you have dinner with Hannah tonight?"

"Yes, if you could call it that." Kate shook her head again, remembering, "And it was brief."

"She said it was."

"You spoke to Hannah?"

Dawn nodded. "She said you two are working things out."

Kate frowned, not understanding, and then sighed in frustrated comprehension. "We are. We have to."

"And you agreed to having your playthings?"

She shook her head trying to fend off the repugnance. "Yes. I mean, we started that whole mess, but neither of us wants to be the one to give those things up." Kate paused wondering why Hannah told Dawn about the investment property in Big Bear. "I'm curious why Hannah thought she had to tell you about that."

"Because she knew you wouldn't."

Kate weighed the topic of conversation and subsequently furrowed her brow. "Well, I can't say that I would have brought it up on my own. I think it'll work out better this way. Believe me, keeping her happy will make my life a lot easier."

"Kate," Amy yelled from the set, "It's urgent."

Kate smiled warmly, reached up for Dawn's shoulder and squeezed. "Shit. I am so sorry. I'll be right back." And ran toward the director.

Dawn sat there frozen, feeling suddenly nauseous. She couldn't believe Kate had actually said those things. A sick feeling of being trapped washed over her and she grabbed onto the armrests of the director's chair for support. She had accepted an invitation to be with Kate in a foreign country only to find that Kate had decided to work things out with Hannah.

Hannah was right. And Dawn felt like a complete idiot. All she'd been to Kate was a fling, as Hannah had put it. She got nauseous.

Suddenly she needed to get back to the hotel.

"What's wrong?" Kate skidded up to a halt in front of Sandy Batnow and Amy, whose cell phone was in her hand, apparently with the speakerphone feature on.

Amy said, "Carrie's calling from LA."

"What's the matter?"

"Hello, Kate," Carrie said over the small cell phone speaker. "Listen, the tail end of yesterday's last reel got overexposed. It's ruined."

"What? How did that happen?"

Sandy spoke up, "It sounds like a major screw up at the film lab."

Amy nodded. "That's what Carrie said. She pushed and pushed the lab and they have finally taken responsibility."

Kate turned to Sandy. "And today's work is safe? It couldn't have been something related to the cameras?"

"Everything here is okay," Sandy said resolutely. "It absolutely wasn't the fault of any of the equipment here."

"So how much did we lose?"

"The last setup. There were seven takes. The first take has some flashes on it, but the last six are completely gone."

"And what do the continuity notes say about the first take?"

"Unusable due to flubbed lines as well as the sound boom being in the shot."

"Crap. We have to re-shoot, then."

"Looks like it. We really can't cut around it," Carrie said.

"Okay," Kate said.

Amy then volunteered, "We'll get the shot today or tomorrow. I'll fit it in."

Kate nodded and spoke into the phone, "Carrie, how confident are you that the lab won't do this again? We could change labs."

"Well, I told them that they did not want to receive a phone call from a pissed off Kate Nyland. I got put on hold for a minute, and then the lab's manager got on the phone and promised me he would personally babysit the rest of the film coming in. As you know, this is a great lab. They just really screwed up. I think we should stay with them, and I'll just happen to make a surprise visit right around film processing time for the next couple of days."

"Thanks, Carrie," Kate said.

"Don't mention it."

When Kate returned to the director's chair, Dawn was gone again. She looked around the set. The only person looking her way was Jennifer. "Dawn said she was tired and went back to the hotel."

"Oh," Kate said, "Thanks." She called the hotel from her cell phone. Dawn didn't answer. As soon as the next scene was set up and rehearsed, she'd call the hotel again.

CHAPTER THIRTY-TWO

Dawn could barely see to pack. She felt intense panic. Tears cascaded down her face and onto the suitcase. *How could Kate invite me all the way out here just to take up again with Hannah?* She went to the bathroom and retrieved her toiletries. Suddenly, a jolt of pain stabbed at her. There on the bathroom counter lay Kate's acorn bracelet. Forgotten. *Dumped. Like me.*

With tearful anger, she realized that it made sense. *Hannah and Kate are in a different league than me. They're rich and powerful and have everything and anything they want. And with Hannah on her arm, why would Kate ever want her?*

She collapsed on the bed and dropped her head in her hands. Racking sobs overcame her.

She had no idea how long she'd been crying when a noise in the hall shook her back. Someone was walking toward the room. She checked her watch. It was midnight. *Could Kate be back that early?* She didn't want to see Kate at all. There was a cough and throat clearing out in the hall, definitely male in origin. Dawn released her breath as he passed, thankful that she would not have to confront Kate.

Hurriedly, she finished packing, washed her face of anguish as best she could, and called the front desk to request a ride to the airport.

As she carried her suitcase to the elevator, all the horribly true thoughts stabbed her, *What the hell was I thinking? I was never worthy of this kind of relationship. I'm just a joke to her.*

❖

"Where's your little girlfriend?" Hannah walked up to Kate as she hung up from trying to reach Dawn at the hotel a second time.

"Why were you talking to Dawn earlier?"

Hannah's eyebrows shot up, "Am I not allowed to talk to her?"

"What did you say to her?"

"We were just chatting, Kate. My, haven't you turned into a paranoid lover."

"Hannah, cut the shit." Kate suddenly clenched inside, her distrust of Hannah suddenly roiling in her stomach. "What did you talk about?"

"Oh, this and that."

Kate balled her hands into fists. Hannah wasn't going to tell her anything. But she knew that whatever had transpired couldn't have been good. She turned and walked away to find a ride back to the hotel. As she did, she heard Hannah call out, "She's really not your type, Kate."

❖

As Kate unlocked the hotel room door and raced in, an air of stillness was the first sensation that hit her. The bed was not only empty, it looked like it hadn't been slept in. She walked into the bathroom.

"Dawn?" Her voice echoed against the tile. She spotted her acorn bracelet. "There it is…" she said to herself as she put it on. The afternoon before, she'd left for the set without it and cursed when she'd realized it wasn't on her wrist. She prayed it was on the bathroom sink where she'd last remembered leaving it. She had found herself subconsciously rubbing her naked wrist throughout the night in hopes that it was there.

She called out to Dawn again but there was no answer.

Confused, she called the production office and asked one of the production assistants whether Dawn had called for a ride to the set.

"Yes. I took her back to the hotel, Ms. Nyland," one of the energetic PAs said in a wonderfully thick Austrian accent.

"When?"

"Almost an hour ago."

As Kate hung up, she noticed a piece of paper on the opposite bedside table. She reached for it.

Kate,
I'm sorry.
Dawn

She stared at it for the longest time. *What did that mean?* She held her breath, willing more words to manifest on the paper, words that would explain what "I'm sorry" meant. *What the hell had Hannah said to her?* She wouldn't listen to anything Hannah said, would she? Was it something Kate had done? Was it something Dawn did? Did Dawn decide she just couldn't be with her? *What the hell did "I'm sorry" mean?*

Filled with confusion and alarm, Kate snatched up the phone again and called the front desk, asking if anyone had talked to Dawn Brock.

"One moment, Ms. Nyland," the front desk manager replied. He came back on the line. "I will transfer you to the concierge, one moment, please."

"Concierge desk," the woman answered, "Ms. Nyland?"

"Yes."

"We arranged transportation for Ms. Brock about one half hour ago."

"Where did you take her?" Kate's mind raced. *Where would Dawn go at one a.m.?* If she had wanted another ride back out to the set, she would have just called the production office. But she hadn't and this confused her. Kate was suddenly frightened.

"Let me see..." the concierge rustled some paper. The pause was excruciating. "The airport."

The fastest ride was a taxi. Kate ran downstairs and startled the sleepy driver by jumping in his car. They sped to the airport, all the while the taxi driver sneaking curious peeks at Kate.

She nearly jumped out of the moving taxi and ran up to the ticket counter, to the same carrier that had originally flown Dawn to Austria. Anxiously, she waited in line, praying that the three people ahead of her were not in the middle of any crisis or desired spending precious time to complain for the sake of complaining.

When she finally got to the ticket agent, she was informed that there was in fact a flight to Orlando, via Munich, that was boarding.

"Can you tell me if Dawn Brock will be on it?" Kate was frantic.

"I'm sorry, ma'am. Federal guidelines do not permit us to divulge passengers' names other than in the event of an emergency."

"This *is* an emergency," Kate pleaded, "I think she's left me."

"The emergency I was referring to," the counter agent said calmly, "was that of an aviation or national sort."

"What gate is the Orlando flight, please?"

"Seventy-two"

If she didn't find her before the security check point, Dawn would be gone. Running past the rest of the airline counters, Kate hurried toward a very long line of people waiting to show their boarding passes to enter the line for the x-ray machines. Anxiously scanning the crowd, she prayed she'd find her. Families mixed with couples and business people shuffled slowly toward the check point. Kate made her way through the line repeating "excuse me" and "*entschuldigen sie mich*" as she pushed through the travelers.

She got all the way up to the ID checkpoint. Dawn was nowhere to be seen. She craned her neck trying to see past the x-ray machines, to the passengers walking toward their gates.

"Shit." She wanted to wail in anguish. Dawn was already gone.

❖

Standing outside the airport, Kate called Dawn's cell phone. "Dawn, it's Kate. You probably won't get this until you land, but we need to talk. Please call me."

Kate's stomach ached. She felt sick, not knowing what just happened.

If Beth had been on the set in Salzburg instead of in LA, Kate would have gone straight to her to pour out her confusion and anxiety. But what would Kate say to her, anyway? *Everything's fucked up, I'm not sure why, and I can't do a damn thing about it right now?* Sure, Beth could comfort her with generic words, *Don't worry, you'll talk to her soon*, but nothing would ease the ache that tore at her chest.

Nothing would help until she could talk to Dawn.

Her phone rang, startling her so much she almost mistakenly hit the end key in alarm. "Hello?" she almost yelled.

"Kate, where are you?" It was Amy.

"What's wrong?"

"The Austrian police have shut us down."

"Why?"

"They're saying the neighbors are complaining about the noise. We showed them our permits, but they aren't honoring them."

"Shit. I'll be right there."

The set was at a complete standstill when Kate's taxi pulled up just after one thirty in the morning. She found Amy and Nathan with the police. She pulled Nathan's arm for him to get close and whispered in his ear, "Get the Salzburg mayor on the phone. The production office has his number. He offered to help us with anything we needed when he welcomed us to town. Tell him he's got to help us now."

"This could die down quickly or it could get much uglier," Amy said.

Kate nodded. "Making up the time we lost and trying to keep the villagers with their torches from shutting us down again would be a major bitch."

While Amy pondered over the schedule, Kate sat in her director's chair watching the crew scramble about.

The film was now in critical mode. They were in jeopardy of not getting all the scenes completed. This could be catastrophic if the political climate became problematic.

But none of that mattered much to her right then. Dawn was gone, and she didn't know why. Had she picked up Kate's trepidation on the bridge? She'd chickened out when Dawn asked how she was feeling. She should have told her she loved her. But would that have helped? She hadn't been the best of company to Dawn with the time she was spending on the set. It hadn't been a very good vacation for Dawn, waiting for her while Kate worked. And even when they were together on the set, they were constantly being interrupted as Kate was pulled away for this and that.

Had she been silly to think that having Dawn come to Austria in the middle of a film shoot would be fun for her? Maybe it would have been easier for Kate to finish the shoot and then give Dawn all her attention.

Kate paused. She was bullshitting herself. She had let the woman she loved walk right out of her arms and onto a plane.

The film would pull through somehow, but her relationship with Dawn wouldn't. In all her years as a producer, she'd gone through the worst of location shoots and dastardly people and had resolved impossible situations to save huge financial investments from catastrophe.

But she'd just lost a woman she'd fallen in love with. And the significance of that loss sat more heavily on her chest than the current trouble with the film. But here she was—on set, tending to her job.

Tending to what she always did. Working. With her head down. Not really taking in her whole life and seeing that there was more than just making movies and having a vapid woman on her arm. She thought of Dawn and how she'd inspired Kate to find balance in her life. It's about balance, she'd told Kate, work with life. Where was the balance in a life with work and no love?

Was that how it was going to be? Was wrapping this shoot successfully really the thing that mattered?

She looked out over the set. Her film was in trouble. There were millions of dollars at stake. And suddenly, she didn't care.

Kate turned to Amy. "I'm flying back to the states."

Amy looked up. "What?"

"I'm leaving. I know this sounds crazy, but I'm leaving."

"What's wrong? Is someone sick? Is someone hurt at home?"

"No. I'll call you in a couple days. Nathan can handle things here. If the mayor wants us to talk to the neighbors, have Nathan do it."

Amy's eyes were wider than Kate had ever seen. "Are you serious?"

"As serious as I've ever been. Dawn's left. Something happened and I am going after her."

Kate could tell that Amy's mind was spinning with all sorts of thoughts. "Amy, listen, this is something you know I've never done, leaving a film in the middle of a crisis. But I've never needed to do something this badly. I know you must think I've lost my mind, but there's something much worse that I've lost." Kate was fearful that what she had with Dawn was over before it began. She gasped and began to struggle for breath.

Amy reached over to steady Kate. "Are you okay?"

"No. Not yet." Fully understanding the magnitude of her decision to leave her film, Kate hurried off to find a driver to take her to the airport.

❖

"There are no more planes out of Salzburg tonight. The airport is closing." The woman at the ticket counter nodded toward the clock on the wall behind her. It was three a.m.

"What's the next flight out to Orlando, please?" Kate asked.

After a few clicks on her keyboard, the woman said, "Ten o'clock in the morning. There's a bit of a layover in Frankfurt with an arrival time into Orlando International Airport Thursday night at ten p.m."

She'd be at least twelve hours behind Dawn. "That's the soonest?"

A few more clicks. "Yes. And I've checked the other airlines for you. That's the soonest."

Kate purchased a ticket and headed through security.

Luckily she had her passport with her, so she went straight from the set to the airport. To hell with packing. She needed to find Dawn, not worry about wrinkled clothes. Now, with the airport deserted, she would wait until morning.

She checked her watch. She guessed that Dawn would be landing in Orlando around eight or nine Thursday morning. With Kate's prolonged layover in Frankfurt, she'd arrive into Orlando Thursday night at nine p.m. If she couldn't get a hold of Dawn before then, she'd be forced to wait until she could go to FDF early Friday morning.

She wandered around the airport and found a coffee vending machine. As she fished around for some Austrian change in her pocket, thoughts of the woman for whom she'd fallen so deeply and relentlessly stabbed at her. Her head throbbed. Her throat tightened on and off so often that the possibility of breaking down and wailing out from the ache that racked her chest was a very real one. She took the vending cup and gulped down the blisteringly hot coffee in an attempt to quell the emptiness she felt inside.

She had about seven hours to wait for the flight. She needed to sleep, if that was at all possible, but she was not going to chance going back to the hotel and risk missing the flight due to traffic on the way back or some other problem. Nothing was going to keep her from getting on that plane.

CHAPTER THIRTY-THREE

Dawn landed just after nine a.m. After an excruciatingly long and agonizing flight, she'd driven straight home, only able to pace around her house, unable to sleep, unable to eat, unable to keep the relentless pictures of Kate and Hannah together from her mind. She had finally given up and gone to work hoping that keeping her hands busy could help turn off her brain.

When she saw Krissy, she suddenly felt like crying again. She turned away, not wanting to acknowledge Krissy's stunned reaction to seeing her. It hurt too much to talk about what had happened. Instead, she busied herself by touching up paint on a large sculpted pirate's head that was getting readied for an installation in Tampa.

"I thought you were in Tampa." Dawn tried to divert any conversation from the obvious topic.

"Yeah, I have been, but I had to come back to the shop to pick up more supplies, as well as that large pirate's head you're working on there."

"It'll be done within the hour."

"Let's be done with this small talk, too."

"I don't want to talk about it."

Krissy followed Dawn over to the paint mixing machine. "Dawn, please talk to me. What happened? Why are you back so early?"

Dawn wouldn't answer. She just continued to work, her jaw set rigidly, stiff in her painting motions.

"Dawn, please…" Krissy said, holding her hand to her chest. "I'm getting freaked out, here."

Dawn couldn't keep a tear from spilling out and falling down her cheek. When Krissy reached out to her, she suddenly fell into her arms sobbing.

"Ah, honey…" Krissy comforted her.

"She's back with Hannah."

"She's what? Oh, I'm so sorry, baby."

Dawn cried even harder and when the sobbing ebbed, Krissy said, "I can't believe she'd do that."

"Let's face it, for a few days I was just a play toy for her."

With her head against Krissy's chest, Dawn could feel Krissy shake her head. "Well, I for sure don't believe *that*. Not the way she looked at you. Not the way she looked when she and I spoke about you. No, ma'am."

Dawn moved away from Krissy's embrace, wiping her tears. "Well then, she fooled the both of us, now didn't she?"

Krissy was adamant. "She may have gone back to Hannah, probably in a moment of weakness or just plain stupidity, but I am not wrong about how she felt about you."

"Hannah said it herself. They're trying it again. They're made for each other…both famous and rich, not like me at all."

Krissy absorbed the words for a moment. "You got this from Hannah?"

Dawn sniffled and took a deep breath before nodding.

"Was Kate there when she said it?"

"No."

"How did it come to pass that you were talking with Hannah?"

"She found me on the set and told me she wanted to talk to me."

"Something just doesn't sound right." Krissy's brow was furrowed. "What did Kate say?"

"That given a choice, she wouldn't have brought it up to me."

"You mean Kate told you that she and Hannah were back together and that she would have kept on with you and not told you?"

"No, she didn't tell me all that, just the part about not telling me. I asked her about her and Hannah working things out, and she acknowledged it. Then I asked her why she didn't tell me, and she said she wouldn't have chosen to."

"She acknowledged it? Plain and simple?"

Dawn nodded.

"Did she at least try to comfort you after the news broke?"

"She didn't get a chance. We were right in the middle of the conversation, and they called her to the set for an emergency, so I just took off. I went back to the hotel, packed, and went straight to the airport. There's too much drama. And I can't believe anything I hear.

Kate and Hannah are still dealing with their relationship, and I'm not even a consideration to them. To Kate." The pain of her last words sliced through her chest, eviscerating her.

Krissy frowned. "That just doesn't sound…" Krissy shook her head again. "It just doesn't sound right."

"Well, all I knew is that I had to get out of there."

Krissy reached out for Dawn and pulled her back in for a big bear hug.

Dawn felt beyond miserable.

How could Kate have played with her affections that way? And to have Hannah tell her was so much worse than horrible. Admittedly, she should have at least said something to Kate before she bolted to the airport, but she had felt so utterly humiliated. It was bad enough hearing the news from Hannah, but to have Kate confirm it had been too unbearable.

And I'm falling for her. Have fallen for her. And all I am is a plaything for her.

And what confused her so much were the unmistakably genuine feelings that she and Kate shared. *When we made love, I knew without a doubt that Kate was as emotionally connected as I was. I know that I may be wide of the mark on a lot of things in life, but the intensity of the sacred, absolute core of a woman's heart was sublime and entirely undeniable. That, I know.*

But none of this makes sense.

She knew that the feelings Kate had for her were real. She couldn't have faked that.

What she couldn't bear was that Kate had given up and retreated to a relationship that…what?…was just easier?

Or one that Kate wanted because of its appearances?

Dawn had listened to Kate's first message. Her heart had pounded when she heard her voice, but she couldn't call her back. When she landed that morning, she turned her phone back on and saw that there were two more messages from Kate. Maybe she was calling to tell Dawn it was all a mistake, that she really didn't want to try again with Hannah, that she couldn't live without Dawn. But the first message hadn't revealed much, just Kate sounding confused. Dawn's head spun again, and as much as she desperately wanted to listen to the messages, she just couldn't. All she could do was turn her phone off.

At eleven o'clock that morning, Dawn helped Krissy load the large pirate's head into the shop truck for Krissy's trip back to Tampa.

"I'm going with you," Dawn said.

Without hesitation, Krissy jerked her head toward the front of the truck. "Let's go. With you helping, we can wrap this up by tomorrow morning."

In an effort to escape the severe ache that racked her every time she thought about Kate, fleeing to Tampa seemed to be the best remedy.

CHAPTER THIRTY-FOUR

After renting a car at the Orlando airport, Kate checked into the Peabody Hotel. Dawn hadn't returned her calls, so she had no option but to wait for FDF to open the next morning. She couldn't stand not being able to get to Dawn. She didn't know where she lived and could only agonizingly wait it out.

She needed to tell Dawn that she loved her. Was in love with her. Beyond that, Kate had no idea what she would say when she saw her. All she knew was that she needed to look into her eyes. She needed to talk to her, even if it was to be told that Dawn didn't want to see her again.

It was more than possible that she would tell Dawn that she loved her, and Dawn would tell her she didn't feel the same way. What had Hannah said to her? And why hadn't Dawn talked to her about it? She thought about the last night in Salzburg.

Dawn had talked to her. Right before Kate had gotten called away, Dawn was asking her about something Hannah had said. *What was it? Working out the details of Big Bear, I think.*

But that couldn't have been what made Dawn leave. It had to be something else. Her mind was so fatigued, she couldn't work out any possibilities.

Growing anxious, she forced her thoughts away from the muddle and went back to their walk on the bridge overlooking the Salzach River. Why couldn't she tell her that she loved her? She should have when she had had the chance. *Goddamn it.* She couldn't tell her the simplest and strongest of feelings that she had for her. And now Dawn was gone.

She felt nauseated. She didn't know if it came from lack of sleep or eating, but she didn't care. She requested a wake up call from the front lobby and lay down on the bed feeling hot, frustrated tears welling up, burning her eyes.

❖

"Something's not right," Krissy said to Dawn as she sipped on a beer at a tavern in Tampa Bay.

"You said that this morning," Dawn replied to Krissy's skepticism. As soon as they had arrived in Tampa earlier that day, Dawn had realized that the distance traveled hadn't helped diminish the pain. She lifted her mug. Maybe the beer would.

"I still think it."

Dawn's mind started to race again. She was sure that Kate felt something when they were together. There was no mistaking the connectedness, the emotion. There had been true sincerity in Kate's face. But then she'd picked back up with Hannah like Dawn didn't even exist. Anguish shot through her with a jolt of pain and her head dropped to her hands.

"…on the horse," Krissy was saying.

"What?"

"You just need to get back on the horse."

"What horse?"

"Kate."

"Kate's not a horse." Dawn snapped, suddenly aggravated, more at herself than at Krissy's persistence.

"For the love of Pete. You need to loosen up, girl. You're liable to crack into a million pieces before we get through this Tampa job."

"And what makes you think I can just start back up with Kate?"

"Because it's not over between you."

"You weren't there, Krissy. It seemed pretty over to me."

Krissy's eyes narrowed to dubious slits. "Something isn't adding up. Has she called you since you left Austria?"

Dawn nodded. "Yes."

"What did she say?"

"The first message didn't say anything. And I haven't listened to the rest."

"And you haven't returned her call, have you?"

"No."

"You should."

"Why?" Dawn grew angrier. "She wants to fuck around. No way. I don't want to talk to her." Dawn took a forceful swig of her beer. "I can't believe I went to Austria. Was I crazy? She probably thinks I was some kind of kid with a school girl crush."

"She doesn't think that. She's regular folk just like us."

"Hardly. She's a big Hollywood producer. Offering the trip to Austria was just a fling to her." The way Dawn felt now, it seemed it all had meant nothing more to Kate Nyland than a polite business gesture, something that held no more significance than a courteous request to send a driver to pick up her dry cleaning. And apparently Kate was attached again. And to a big movie star, no less.

"You know that acorn bracelet I gave her?" Dawn continued, "The night I talked to Hannah, I found it on the bathroom counter just sitting there. My stupid acorn bracelet. She didn't want the bracelet, and she didn't want me. She looked down, shaking her head. "And you know what? Yeah, I'm not in her league. I wouldn't want to be in that league. How could I have ever fallen for that shit?"

"Well, I'm glad you stopped comparing yourself to Hannah," Krissy said. "And to Kate."

"Shit, Kate made a bonehead move by going back with her, so it's her tough luck. Kate doesn't know what she's missing. God I'm so pissed off."

"One more of these will help." Krissy held up her empty bottle.

"Beer me," Dawn called as Krissy got up to go to the bar. Dawn felt miserable. Her nerves felt like frayed telephone cords, disconnected and lifeless.

Krissy returned with more beer and wrapped an arm around Dawn. "What are you thinking about?"

"Nothing."

"That's not the look of nothing. The look of nothing usually has a blank stare attached to it." Krissy squeezed her shoulder. "What I'm seeing is more like the look of…gloom and doom."

Dawn reached up to rub her eyebrows.

"Talk," Krissy said. "Spit it out, woman."

"I've been trying to wipe out that name from my head but I can't. I think of Kate being next to me. I think of watching Kate inspect a prop or how she would be talking about business in the shop but I'd know her smile was just for me. I allowed her in."

"And now you feel embarrassed."

Dawn looked down and nodded.

"I know it was horrible for you, being so far away from home. I mean, I've seen you down before, my friend, but I've never seen you like this."

"Wonderful, isn't it?"

Krissy shrugged, not acknowledging the sarcasm. "Wonderful that you found someone so incredible. Wonderful that you could feel so much for someone. Wonderful that you know the feeling was returned."

Dawn looked up. "Was it? Truly?"

They stared at each other.

"You tell me."

Dawn broke the gaze and focused on her beer bottle, finally slamming it down on the table. "Yes, it was. I know damn well she wasn't faking those feelings. If I don't know anything else, I do know that. And what's even more maddening is that every time I've thought about Hannah lately, all I can see is a spoiled rotten bitch. No amount of…of physical beauty, Hollywood clout, or considerable wealth can erase the fact that Hannah is not the one for Kate. Spending this time away from the whirlwind, I just know that what Kate and I had had been real. I mean, I could feel it, Krissy."

"So what do you think happened?"

"It's clear that I got caught in the middle of a relationship that hadn't quite ended."

"So if Hannah was really out of the picture, things would be different?"

"Yes, I think. Oh, I don't know. I'm just fooling myself. I was a plaything."

"Well you're not going to know for sure until you talk to her."

"Or forget her."

"Is that possible?"

"No."

"So you'll never know if you could have made it work with her."

It suddenly hurt her that she had let this conversation bring her closer to her feelings for Kate, and, given the current situation, it was all a fantasy conversation. "We're talking in a dreamland here, Krissy. She's with Hannah."

"I'm talking about you right now. You as a potential lover. You as girlfriend material."

Dawn considered Krissy's comment. When she was with Kate, there was no Hollywood, no glitz and glamour. It was just two women loving and laughing and feeling. Kate could have been any regular person. She was kind and funny and lovable. And the connection was undeniable. Dawn felt it.

"I *was* in her league."

Krissy smiled. "Now you're talking."

"I was just thinking about the wrong league."

"Okay, stop with the metaphors now, I'm confused."

"The head instead of the heart. Status won over emotion instead of the other way around."

Krissy furrowed her brow. "Maybe the metaphors were better after all."

"What I mean is that I was seeing Hannah and Kate as Hollywood elite when in fact, all they are are people. Kate's just looking for love, too. But with Hannah, she gets the bullshit, too."

"But she doesn't with you."

"Well, certainly not as much."

"You're being modest. You're a catch."

"Well, I am for someone."

"So call her." Krissy was a master at effortless candor.

A picture of Kate with Hannah flashed across Dawn's mind again. "And why the hell would I want to do that?"

"Because, my fine and beautiful best friend, you love her."

"And she loves Hannah."

"Wait a sec. I thought we were talking about Kate and you."

"I was more talking about me. What I mean is, what matters, is that I am okay. I do deserve to be with Kate. Maybe Kate doesn't want to be with me, but that's beside my point. I'm better than that pompous Hollywood crap."

"I see."

"I'm just starting to be okay with me. With Kate, I'd be setting myself up for another nightmare like that last night in Austria. I don't need that. I admit that I've been wondering if I made too rash a decision by leaving Austria without even talking to her. I mean, Kate's always treated with respect. But as much as I've felt less-than, it wasn't Kate that made me feel that way. Hannah had, for sure." Dawn sighed, "And I had myself."

"It is important to treat yourself with respect." Krissy said, patting her on the back.

She took a long pull from her beer. *I know I'm what Kate needs. Not Hannah. Comparing yourself to Hannah was certainly your biggest mistake in a long time. You're better than that. And you're better than Hannah.*

I should call her. I need to tell her these things.

❖

It was only when the wake-up call jarred Kate awake that she realized she'd finally fallen asleep. She showered, put the same clothes back on, brushed her teeth, and combed through her hair.

At eight o'clock, more nervous than she'd been in a long time, she walked into the lobby of FDF.

"Good morning. Is Dawn Brock here, please?"

The receptionist smiled up at her. "She's out on a project."

Kate's racing heart skidded to a halt. "Where?"

"Tampa Bay. We're installing some additional theming on the Buccaneers' new pirate ship."

"The football team?"

"Go Bucs!" The receptionist giggled.

"Is Krissy here?"

"She's with Dawn."

I've got to get to Tampa. "Tampa." Kate said out loud.

"The Bucs stadium."

"Do you know how to get there?"

"It's easy. Interstate 4 West to 275. It's on Dale Mabry highway. Lots of signs for it. Should take you about an hour and a half, two hours."

"Thank you," Kate said and raced out the door.

CHAPTER THIRTY-FIVE

A storm was coming. Clouds as dark as old charcoal rumbled swiftly across the sky. On the Buccaneers' pirate ship, Dawn and Krissy worked quickly to finish the installation before the heavens burst open with an unforgivably wet downpour.

A number of years before, the Buccaneers football franchise had built the enormous pirate ship which sat proudly in the home-side end zone of the stadium. Buccaneer's sponsors, VIPs, and assorted lucky others were invited to watch the games from the deck of the pirate ship. It was the utmost in cool perks, as viewing a game from that vantage point was an unbelievably fantastic experience.

The additional props that FDF had been contracted to build were to cover newly added, contemporary accoutrements that included private wall-mounted phones, a bank of televisions and a small satellite dish. The contemporary trappings were now veiled in high-seas pirate theming that included mounted swords, hung rigging, the pirate's head, and a folded and rolled up sail that looked as if it had seen many sea-faring battles.

The last thing that Dawn and Krissy needed to do before completing the job was to touch up the themed paint on each item. It was inevitable that the installation of props produced small chips that needed to be repaired.

It was ten o'clock in the morning, and Dawn figured that they could wrap up the work in the next few minutes and be on the road back to Orlando before the rain hit. Other than a lone figure at the opposite end of the stadium who appeared to be repairing the turf, the venue was empty.

"Krissy," Dawn hollered down the deck to where her friend sat working on the rolled up sail, "I don't like those clouds. I'm going to get the portable dryer to speed up this paint drying."

"Then bring it here when you're done with the swords. I think it's drying pretty fast, but I may need it," Krissy hollered back.

Rain started to pelt the ship's deck as Dawn fetched the portable dryer. A muggy storm front was blowing across the ship and Dawn squinted as big drops of Florida humidity fell heavily on her. And then, as quickly as it started, the rain stopped. Dawn looked up into the skies. Her years in Florida told her that she might have five or ten minutes of dryness before the really dense and dark cloud, the one that held most of the rain just a few miles away, would be upon them, dumping its wet surplus.

Dawn trotted back to the swords and made quick work of drying them. Krissy had yelled something akin to "Aaarrrrggg!" when the first drops fell and was also now frantically finishing up her work.

A couple minutes later, Dawn gently prodded the swords. They were no longer tacky to the touch.

Footsteps came up behind her. Without looking up, Dawn stepped back, portable dryer in hand, still concentrating on the swords. "I would have brought this to you, Krissy."

"I have one of my own, thanks." The voice was not Krissy's. She swung around to face Kate, her mouth dropping open in shock.

"What are you doing here?" Dawn gasped, unexpectedly confused and winded. All the air left her lungs, and she fought the urge to cry tears of both excitement and anger.

Kate shook her head ever so slightly. "It might sound stupid and, believe me, I thought and thought about what to say to you. There's so much. But, simply, I just needed to see you."

Needed to see me? Because she cared about me? Or because she wanted a little more fun? God how she wanted Kate, but she felt as if her heart was ripping. Suddenly, out of her frantically spiraling mind, she blurted out, "Why? Why did you need to see me?"

The ominous cloud had reached them, and suddenly the rain came down, tropical and vigorous. Within seconds they were drenched, but they both remained right were they stood.

Kate had spent the whole drive to Tampa pouring over a million different things to say to Dawn, trying to come up with the one sentence that summed up why she'd flown across the Atlantic Ocean on this desperate impulse.

And then, as she looked into Dawn's eyes, rain drops falling from her hair, blinking through the downpour, it just came rolling out. "Because all I can think about is you. Because I love you, and I don't care if you don't want me. I mean, I can understand if you don't, but I had to see you again. I know that I must be the last person you want to see right now, and I wouldn't be surprised if you slapped me...or..." Kate tilted her head toward the side of the pirate ship, "Made me walk that plank, but I had to come."

The throbbing anxiety that racked Dawn's body eased slightly. She glanced down the deck and saw Krissy standing there watching them, as frozen as a statue, her mouth dropped open. Turning back to Kate, Dawn studied her face. She so desperately wanted to wrap her arms around her and feel the length of her whole body, warm and firm, against her own. She wanted to fall into her and drink in the taste of her neck and the smell of her hair. But the hurt stopped her. They stayed where they were, facing each other not more than a foot apart.

Dawn took a deep breath, the anger in her voice rising. "Is that what you came here to tell me?"

"Yes. And that I want to be with you. I have since I met you."

"You want a lot, don't you?"

"What?"

"You and me. You and Hannah..." was all Dawn could get out before her throat closed.

"What about me and Hannah? There is no me and Hannah anymore."

So that was the current state of affairs, Dawn thought. More angry tears came and she swallowed hard, finally yelling, "I don't believe you."

Kate blinked hard and jerked backward. They stared at each other. Dawn was stunned and hurt and saw that Kate was frantic and confused. "After Hannah and I broke up, I was never with her again."

"God damn it, Kate. Just stop the bullshit."

"There's no bullshit."

"You said you were getting back with her."

Kate's eyes widened. "No, I didn't."

More tears rolled down her cheeks, mixing with the rain. "You didn't have to say it in those words exactly. Hannah told me about your dinner the last night I was there."

Kate reached up to wipe Dawn's tears but Dawn backed away from her touch. Softly Kate said, "What *about* the dinner? Dawn, I'm confused."

Dawn wiped her own tears. "She said that you two are working things out."

Kate slowly drew out a "Yes…?"

"Remember when I asked you about that dinner? You confirmed that you were working things out. You said it was because you had to. You said that you two had started that whole mess and that it looked like there was no way that either of you were going to give up on it." Dawn coughed in an attempt to choke back more tears.

"Believe me, if I hadn't been so blind, I would have never gotten involved in the Big Bear mess. And…wait a minute, why is Big Bear any big deal? Why would you leave because of the property? Now I'm really confused, Dawn."

"Big Bear?"

"Isn't that what we're talking about?"

"I'm talking about you and Hannah. She said that you two snuck away to the hotel that night and had a romantic dinner and then decided to get back together."

"She what? Fuck." She reached for Dawn, and this time Dawn allowed Kate's hands on her shoulders. "The dinner, which she *interrupted* me during, was on the set in the catering tent. She wanted to hash out the dissolution of a piece of investment property that we bought in Big Bear last year. She and I both didn't want to lose the appreciation on its value. That's what I was referring to when I said that I wasn't going to give up on it. Not the relationship."

"You're not back with Hannah?"

"No." Kate's look was serious. "I never was."

"But I heard you two talking."

Kate held up her hands. "What? When?"

"I overheard you two talking about having other girlfriends." She began to yell, "You agreed to keep your playthings. I'm not a fucking plaything, Kate, I came to Austria thinking we would be together, as lovers. As equals. If I would have known…what you should have told me was all I was going to be was a fun fuck because you can bet your ass I would have never, ever been a part of that."

"Plaything? The only playthings we talked about were the jet skis, the ski boat, and the mountain bikes at the Big Bear place. We weren't talking about you or anyone else. We were talking about things. Water toys." Kate took in a deep breath. "Dawn, I agree that there was something I should have told you. I should have told you that night on the bridge that I have fallen in love with you. I should have told you that I can't picture my life without you. I didn't. I got scared. I wasn't ready for these feelings to happen so soon. And I didn't trust myself to speak the feelings I had.

"I thought I had a little more time in Austria with you to tell you how I felt. That was a big mistake. I lost you before I could get the words out. But they're out now. I love you. I want you in my life. No one else. I want you." Kate's shoulders dropped and her eyes were full of tears.

Dawn could barely process Kate's words. She was so angry and so frightened. Could she trust the woman she'd fallen so hard for? Could she trust that the humiliation she felt had all been a mistake?

She watched Kate's face. Kate was crying and her expression was one of pain. Real pain.

"I'm so confused." Dawn looked down at the deck of the ship, rain and tears rolling off her chin.

Kate blinked through the pouring rain. "I am so sorry you had to go through that. I didn't realize what had happened. What a cluster fuck. I know I didn't give you enough to believe in. I didn't tell you how I felt. I know it's my fault. I wish we could have talked more before you left. I mean I don't blame you for leaving. It was horrible what you thought. Oh my God, I'm so sorry."

"It just all added up to you getting back together with Hannah. I was so hurt and angry. I had to get out of there. And then what Hannah said…that you two were meant to be together, being two of Hollywood's most powerful women. And the way she said it, like I was so…beneath the two of you. I panicked…" Her voice trailed off, muffled and drained.

"Nothing is as you thought. I'm standing here with you right now. You and I were meant to be together. None of what Hannah said was true. None of it. And I am here to tell you that I do love you. I had to come see you even though I knew you might tell me to go to hell. I was scared to death that you would. But I had to find you to tell you that I don't want to live without you." Kate reached up to slowly wipe a few strands of wet hair from Dawn's face.

Suddenly Dawn took hold of Kate's wrist and pulled it down. She was wearing the acorn bracelet.

And then Dawn understood what had happened. Even through all the craziness, with Dawn leaving and refusing to talk to her, Kate had found the strength of character to keep going. Just like the script that they'd talked about.

Dawn pulled Kate to her, clenching her eyes tight. Kate blew out a breath. Though unpleasantly drenched with rain, all Dawn could feel was that Kate meant what she said. Kate loved her. And she loved Kate so very much.

A whoop erupted from the other end of the ship. Suddenly soggy footsteps galloped toward them and with a wet thwack, Krissy threw herself into the hug.

"I was right. She doesn't want Hannah's uppity ass." Krissy stepped back and beamed.

Dawn and Kate laughed for the first time in an eternity.

"I can finish this up, Dawn." Krissy turned to Kate. "Can you give her a lift home to Orlando?"

Dawn spoke up. "She didn't come here to be a taxi driver—"

"I would love to," Kate interrupted.

Kate helped Dawn gather her tools, and they walked to Kate's rental car. When they had loaded the car and were sitting in the front seats, Kate turned to Dawn, "About that ride back to Orlando…"

Dawn looked at her expectantly.

"…do you mind if we delay it until tomorrow?"

Dawn smiled and leaned over to kiss her.

❖

The Grand Hyatt on Tampa Bay had a luxurious suite that was available for early check in. Once inside their room, they embraced and kissed and laughed at the sloshing noises their soaked shoes made.

A phone call to the concierge brought strawberries, champagne, and candles. When it all arrived, they drew a bath in the suite's colossal bathtub. Lavender-scented steam billowed up from the hot, bubbly water. The lights were out, but candles flickered on the counter and edges of the tub. Kate drew Dawn toward the bath, pausing just inside the door.

Kate wanted to say something, anything, to let Dawn know that she'd fantasized about this moment, gone over it in her mind time after time, but no words came. She didn't trust her words, and didn't trust her voice in the midst of her trembling.

The glow from the candles made Dawn's eyes twinkle a hundred glistening chestnut sparkles, and Kate felt drawn in. She was being coaxed toward the expanse of the heavens and all of its lustrous possibilities. Leaning forward, she brushed her lips over Dawn's. Her head swam, and she felt dizzy.

Reaching up, her hands found Dawn's shoulders, strong and confident, and it grounded Kate. They kissed deeply. Dawn's breathing intensified, and all Kate could manage was a soft moan. Dawn's hands moved up to Kate's waist, then her stomach, unbuttoning her way up to Kate's collar. Kate let her shirt fall away, moaning into Dawn as her hands reached around and pulled her closer.

As clothing slid to the floor, Kate and Dawn moved through the haze of lavender steam and into the water. They spooned, Kate laying back into Dawn, wrapping her arms around the arms that held her.

"This feels good," Dawn said.

"This feels right," Kate replied and then sighed. "The first day I met you I didn't know what hit me. I felt struck by some sort of uncontrollable bolt of, I don't know, fate, maybe. Like a lifetime came together in that one meeting." She hesitated, adding, "And then in Salzburg, I was afraid I'd never see you again. I am so sorry for what happened. I should have known Hannah would try something. I should have told you how I felt."

Dawn let out a breath, "I've been wracked thinking I'd never see you again, too. I'm sorry I didn't return your calls."

Kate turned around and Dawn slid down a little so that they were hip to hip, stomach to stomach. As Kate held herself up over Dawn, they kissed softly, gentle tongues dancing delicately. Dawn's hips began to move ever so slowly against Kate. Slow circles that were matched by Kate, became their first dance in days. Dawn's hips surged and Kate pressed back, breaths and sighs increasing in rhythm. And then Dawn's legs opened, wrapping around Kate's hips.

Kate took in a deep breath and slid down, underwater, her tongue swirling around Dawn's stomach and then moving between her spread legs.

Kate tasted Dawn's wetness mixed with the bathwater. Her clitoris hardened in Kate's mouth, and reluctantly Kate had to come up for air. When she replaced her mouth with two fingers, Dawn gasped, suddenly grabbing Kate's shoulders, her mouth biting down as she groaned loudly.

Dawn was able to wrap one of her legs around Kate's back and contort into a position that seemed uncomfortable, but the look on her face told Kate that she was far from that.

Kate's fingers moved in and out, Dawn moving with her, the hot water sloshing around them as Dawn sped to the center of the universe.

Kate was barely aware of anything but the slick wetness of Dawn, so much hotter to the touch than the hottest water the faucet would ever produce. All she could feel was Dawn's muscles inside and the strange tickling sensation of the water as it lapped between them.

Kate wanted to go on like this forever, inside Dawn, joined together.

With each thrust, the steam rose off Dawn's breasts. Kate couldn't believe that they were here, at this moment, so close and so connected. She matched the movement of Dawn's hips, wanting to give her everything. She no longer knew who she was or where she was. All she knew was that, at this moment, she and Dawn were one. And this moment was all that mattered.

Dawn whispered something so quietly that Kate had to ask her to repeat it.

"Don't stop," Dawn murmured again, "Don't stop."

"I won't." Kate felt an unbelievable passion tingling through her. She felt every inch of Dawn's wet body. Reaching up, further inside Dawn, she stroked her, pushing in and pulling out.

Dawn gasped, "Yes."

And suddenly Kate felt her tensing, shaking, and her murmurs turned to moans. Kate held her with one arm wrapped around her, her elbow holding them up in the tub and gripping her as closely as two people could. Dawn's hands moved to Kate's hair, then to her back, and then to her hair again. And in a sudden rush, Dawn cried out, her muscles contracting strongly against Kate's fingers, her climax pulsing in magnificent waves.

They remained there a long time; Dawn's breathing matching the sloshing of the water as it gradually slowed. "Stay inside me," and Kate did, until the water began to grow tepid.

Reluctantly they left the bath, forgoing the opulently thick white cotton robes and climbing into bed, holding each other with bodies still crimson and warm.

"Where do we go from here?" Dawn asked later as they peered out over the rainy Tampa Bay skies. Low rumbles emanated from the rolling clouds, accompanied by flickers of lightning.

"Wherever we want to go."

"Is now a bad time to talk about our bicoastal situation?"

Kate laughed. "No, it's never a bad time to talk about anything. All I know is that I want to be with you. If that means we split coasts, then we'll make that work. That is, if you want that."

"I'm flexible."

"You proved that in the bathtub."

Dawn pinched Kate's side.

"Ow!" Kate chuckled. "I make my schedule. I can rewrite scripts and plan productions from anywhere."

"And I can start taking the vacation days that have accrued for years. As it stands, I have six weeks on the books and another four weeks every year."

"I'd say that's a good start." Kate kissed her. "And then there's the Hollywood premiere of *The Glass Cross*."

"When?" Dawn wanted to make love to her right then.

"We're shooting for a spring release. Would you be my date?"

"Yes." Dawn rolled Kate on to her back. "Definitely a yes."

About the Author

Lisa Girolami has been in the entertainment industry since 1979. She holds a BA in Fine Art and an MS in Psychology. Previous jobs included ten years as a production executive in the motion picture industry and another two decades producing and designing theme parks for Disney and Universal Studios. After six years as the Creative Director for a firm in LA, she is now a Director/Senior Producer at Walt Disney Imagineering. She is also a counselor at a mental health facility in Garden Grove. She currently lives in Long Beach, California.

Her next novel, *Run to Me*, will be available in October 2008.

Read more about Lisa at her website:
http://www.LisaGirolami.com

Books Available From Bold Strokes Books

Hotel Liaison by JLee Meyer. Sparks and wood chips fly as contractor Jocelyn Reynolds and hotel owner Stefanie Beresford struggle not to kill each other—or fall in love. Romance. (978-1-60282-017-3)

Love on Location by Lisa Girolami. Hollywood film producer Kate Nyland and artist Dawn Brock discover that love doesn't always follow the script. Romance. (978-1-60282-016-6)

Edge of Darkness by Jove Belle. Investigator Diana Collins charges at life with an irreverent comment and a right hook, but even those may not protect her heart from a charming villain. Romantic Intrigue. (978-1-60282-015-9)

Thirteen Hours by Meghan O'Brien. Workaholic Dana Watts's life takes a sudden turn when an unexpected interruption arrives in the form of the most beautiful breasts she has ever seen—stripper Laurel Stanley's. Erotic Romance. (978-1-60282-014-2)

In Deep Waters 2 by Radclyffe and Karin Kallmaker. All bets are off when two award winning authors deal the cards of love and passion... and every hand is a winner. Lesbian Erotica. (978-1-60282-013-5)

Pink by Jennifer Harris. An irrepressible heroine frolics, frets, and navigates through the "what if's" of her life: all the unexpected turns of fortune, fame, and karma. General Fiction. (978-1-60282-043-2)

Deal with the Devil by Ali Vali. New Orleans crime boss Cain Casey brings her fury down on the men who threatened her family, and blood and bullets fly. (978-1-60282-012-8)

Naked Heart by Jennifer Fulton. When a sexy ex-CIA agent sets out to seduce and entrap a powerful CEO, there's more to this plan than meets the eye...or the flogger. (978-1-60282-011-1)

Heart of the Matter by KI Thompson. TV newscaster Kate Foster is Professor Ellen Webster's dream girl, but Kate doesn't know Ellen exists...until an accident changes everything. (978-1-60282-010-4)

Heartland by Julie Cannon. When political strategist Rachel Stanton and dude ranch owner Shivley McCoy collide on an empty country road, fate intervenes. (978-1-60282-009-8)

Shadow of the Knife by Jane Fletcher. Militia Rookie Ellen Mittal has no idea of just how complex and dangerous her life is about to become. A Celaeno series adventure romance. (978-1-60282-008-1)

To Protect and Serve by VK Powell. Lieutenant Alex Troy is caught in the paradox of her life—to hold steadfast to her professional oath or to protect the woman she loves. (978-1-60282-007-4)

Deeper by Ronica Black. Former homicide detective Erin McKenzie and her fiancée Elizabeth Adams couldn't be any happier—until the not so distant past comes knocking at the door. (978-1-60282-006-7)

The Lonely Hearts Club by Radclyffe. Take three friends, add two ex-lovers and several new ones, and the result is a recipe for explosive rivalries and incendiary romance. (978-1-60282-005-0)

Venus Besieged by Andrews & Austin. Teague Richfield heads for Sedona and the sensual arms of psychic astrologer Callie Rivers for a much needed romantic reunion. (978-1-60282-004-3)

Branded Ann by Merry Shannon. Pirate Branded Ann raids a merchant vessel to obtain a treasure map and gets more than she bargained for with the widow Violet. (978-1-60282-003-6)

American Goth by JD Glass. Trapped by an unsuspected inheritance and guided only by the guardian who holds the secret to her future, Samantha Cray fights to fulfill her destiny. (978-1-60282-002-9)

Learning Curve by Rachel Spangler. Ashton Clarke is perfectly content with her life until she meets the intriguing Professor Carrie Fletcher, who isn't looking for a relationship with anyone. (978-1-60282-001-2)

Place of Exile by Rose Beecham. Sheriff's detective Jude Devine struggles with ghosts of her past and an ex-lover who still haunts her dreams. (978-1-933110-98-1)

Fully Involved by Erin Dutton. A love that has smoldered for years ignites when two women and one little boy come together in the aftermath of tragedy. (978-1-933110-99-8)

Heart 2 Heart by Julie Cannon. Suffering from a devastating personal loss, Kyle Bain meets Lane Connor, and the chance for happiness suddenly seems possible. (978-1-60282-000-5)

Queens of Tristaine: Tristaine Book Four by Cate Culpepper. When a deadly plague stalks the Amazons of Tristaine, two warrior lovers must return to the place of their nightmares to find a cure. (978-1-933110-97-4)

The Crown of Valencia by Catherine Friend. Ex-lovers can really mess up your life…even, as Kate discovers, if they've traveled back to the 11th century! (978-1-933110-96-7)

Mine by Georgia Beers. What happens when you've already given your heart and love finds you again? Courtney McAllister is about to find out. (978-1-933110-95-0)

House of Clouds by KI Thompson. A sweeping saga of an impassioned romance between a Northern spy and a Southern sympathizer, set amidst the upheaval of a nation under siege. (978-1-933110-94-3)

Winds of Fortune by Radclyffe. Provincetown local Deo Camara agrees to rehab Dr. Nita Burgoyne's historic home, but she never said anything about mending her heart. (978-1-933110-93-6)

Focus of Desire by Kim Baldwin. Isabel Sterling is surprised when she wins a photography contest, but no more than photographer Natasha Kashnikova. Their promo tour becomes a ticket to romance. (978-1-933110-92-9)

Blind Leap by Diane and Jacob Anderson-Minshall. A Golden Gate Bridge suicide becomes suspect when a filmmaker's camera shows a different story. Yoshi Yakamota and the Blind Eye Detective Agency uncover evidence that could be worth killing for. (978-1-933110-91-2)

Wall of Silence, 2nd ed. by Gabrielle Goldsby. Life takes a dangerous turn when jaded police detective Foster Everett meets Riley Medeiros, a woman who isn't afraid to discover the truth no matter the cost. (978-1-933110-90-5)

Mistress of the Runes by Andrews & Austin. Passion ignites between two women with ties to ancient secrets, contemporary mysteries, and a shared quest for the meaning of life. (978-1-933110-89-9)

Sheridan's Fate by Gun Brooke. A dynamic, erotic romance between physical therapist Lark Mitchell and businesswoman Sheridan Ward set in the scorching hot days and humid, steamy nights of San Antonio. (978-1-933110-88-2)

Vulture's Kiss by Justine Saracen. Archeologist Valerie Foret, heir to a terrifying task, returns in a powerful desert adventure set in Egypt and Jerusalem. (978-1-933110-87-5)

Rising Storm by JLee Meyer. The sequel to First Instinct takes our heroines on a dangerous journey instead of the honeymoon they'd planned. (978-1-933110-86-8)

Not Single Enough by Grace Lennox. A funny, sexy modern romance about two lonely women who bond over the unexpected and fall in love along the way. (978-1-933110-85-1)

Second Season by Ali Vali. A romance set in New Orleans amidst betrayal, Hurricane Katrina, and the new beginnings hardship and heartbreak sometimes make possible. (978-1-933110-83-7)

Such a Pretty Face by Gabrielle Goldsby. A sexy, sometimes humorous, sometimes biting contemporary romance that gently exposes the damage to heart and soul when we fail to look beneath the surface for what truly matters. (978-1-933110-84-4)

Hearts Aflame by Ronica Black. A poignant, erotic romance between a hard-driving businesswoman and a solitary vet. Packed with adventure and set in the harsh beauty of the Arizona countryside. (978-1-933110-82-0)

Red Light by JD Glass. Tori forges her path as an EMT in the New York City 911 system while discovering what matters most to herself and the woman she loves. (978-1-933110-81-3)

Honor Under Siege by Radclyffe. Secret Service agent Cameron Roberts struggles to protect her lover while searching for a traitor who just may be another woman with a claim on her heart. (978-1-933110-80-6)

Dark Valentine by Jennifer Fulton. Danger and desire fuel a high stakes cat-and-mouse game when an attorney and an endangered witness team up to thwart a killer. (978-1-933110-79-0)

Sequestered Hearts by Erin Dutton. A popular artist suddenly goes into seclusion; a reluctant reporter wants to know why; and a heart locked away yearns to be set free. (978-1-933110-78-3)

Erotic Interludes 5: *Road Games* eds. Radclyffe and Stacia Seaman. Adventure, "sport," and sex on the road—hot stories of travel adventures and games of seduction. (978-1-933110-77-6)

The Spanish Pearl by Catherine Friend. On a trip to Spain, Kate Vincent is accidentally transported back in time...an epic saga spiced with humor, lust, and danger. (978-1-933110-76-9)

Lady Knight by L-J Baker. Loyalty and honour clash with love and ambition in a medieval world of magic when female knight Riannon meets Lady Eleanor. (978-1-933110-75-2)

Dark Dreamer by Jennifer Fulton. Best-selling horror author, Rowe Devlin falls under the spell of psychic Phoebe Temple. A Dark Vista romance. (978-1-933110-74-5)

Come and Get Me by Julie Cannon. Elliott Foster isn't used to pursuing women, but alluring attorney Lauren Collier makes her change her mind. (978-1-933110-73-8)

Blind Curves by Diane and Jacob Anderson-Minshall. Private eye Yoshi Yakamota comes to the aid of her ex-lover Velvet Erickson in the first Blind Eye mystery. (978-1-933110-72-1)

Dynasty of Rogues by Jane Fletcher. It's hate at first sight for Ranger Riki Sadiq and her new patrol corporal, Tanya Coppelli—except for their undeniable attraction. (978-1-933110-71-4)

Running With the Wind by Nell Stark. Sailing instructor Corrie Marsten has signed off on love until she meets Quinn Davies—one woman she can't ignore. (978-1-933110-70-7)

More than Paradise by Jennifer Fulton. Two women battle danger, risk all, and find in one another an unexpected ally and an unforgettable love. (978-1-933110-69-1)

Flight Risk by Kim Baldwin. For Blayne Keller, being in the wrong place at the wrong time just might turn out to be the best thing that ever happened to her. (978-1-933110-68-4)

Rebel's Quest, Supreme Constellations Book Two by Gun Brooke. On a world torn by war, two women discover a love that defies all boundaries. (978-1-933110-67-7)

Punk and Zen by JD Glass. Angst, sex, love, rock. Trace, Candace, Francesca...Samantha. Losing control—and finding the truth within. BSB Victory Editions. (1-933110-66-X)

Stellium in Scorpio by Andrews & Austin. The passionate reuniting of two powerful women on the glitzy Las Vegas Strip where everything is an illusion and love is a gamble. (1-933110-65-1)

When Dreams Tremble by Radclyffe. Two women whose lives turned out far differently than they'd once imagined discover that sometimes the shape of the future can only be found in the past. (1-933110-64-3)

The Devil Unleashed by Ali Vali. As the heat of violence rises, so does the passion. A Casey Family crime saga. (1-933110-61-9)

Burning Dreams by Susan Smith. The chronicle of the challenges faced by a young drag king and an older woman who share a love "outside the bounds." (1-933110-62-7)

Fresh Tracks by Georgia Beers. Seven women, seven days. A lot can happen when old friends, lovers, and a new girl in town get together in the mountains. (1-933110-63-5)

The Empress and the Acolyte by Jane Fletcher. Jemeryl and Tevi fight to protect the very fabric of their world: time. Lyremouth Chronicles Book Three. (1-933110-60-0)

First Instinct by JLee Meyer. When high-stakes security fraud leads to murder, one woman flees for her life while another risks her heart to protect her. (1-933110-59-7)

Erotic Interludes 4: *Extreme Passions* eds. Radclyffe and Stacia Seaman. Thirty of today's hottest erotica writers set the pages aflame with love, lust, and steamy liaisons. (1-933110-58-9)

Storms of Change by Radclyffe. In the continuing saga of the Provincetown Tales, duty and love are at odds as Reese and Tory face their greatest challenge. (1-933110-57-0)

Unexpected Ties by Gina L. Dartt. With death before dessert, Kate Shannon and Nikki Harris are swept up in another tale of danger and romance. (1-933110-56-2)

Sleep of Reason by Rose Beecham. While Detective Jude Devine searches for a lost boy, her rocky relationship with Dr. Mercy Westmoreland gets a lot harder. (1-933110-53-8)

Passion's Bright Fury by Radclyffe. Passion strikes without warning when a trauma surgeon and a filmmaker become reluctant allies. (1-933110-54-6)

Broken Wings by L-J Baker. When Rye Woods meets beautiful dryad Flora Withe, her libido, as hidden as her wings, reawakens along with her heart. (1-933110-55-4)